VISIONS OF ANNA

THE AFTERLIFE TRILOGY

SHE PLAYS IN DARKNESS
a novel by Fern Chertkow

VISIONS OF ANNA
a novel by Richard Engling

ANNA IN THE AFTERLIFE
a stage play by Richard Engling

VISIONS OF ANNA

by Richard Engling

Polarity Ensemble Theatre Books

This program is partially supported by a grant from the Illinois Arts Council, a state agency. General operating support is being provided by The Richard H. Driehaus Foundation and The John D. and Catherine T. MacArthur Foundation. This project is partially supported by a CityArts Grant from the City of Chicago Department of Cultural Affairs & Special Events.

Cover art: *Soul Carried to Heaven* by William-Adolphe Bouguereau, c. 1878
Cover design: Cathleen Ann

ISBN 978-0-9776610-2-2

Library of Congress Control Number: 2014948665

Manufactured in the United States of America

To the beloved women in my life, Gail Wilcinski and Zoë Engling,
to my friends and fellow artists,
to the collaborators who have assisted this project,
to Robert Bly and my brothers of the Minnesota Men's Conference,
and to my dear departed friend Fern Chertkow.

CONTENTS

PREFACE

THE DEATH OF A loved one always leaves us in mourning. When the death is by suicide, the mixture of emotions we feel can be devastating. On October 3, 1988, Fern Chertkow drove her car up into the canyons near Salt Lake City, ran a hose from her exhaust pipe into the back window of her car, stuffed the rest of the opening with rags, curled up in the back seat, and waited to die. She left behind confused and heartbroken friends and family, and a pile of brilliant unpublished manuscripts.

Through the twelve years I knew her, Fern suffered many bouts of depression. Suicide was a regular topic of conversation for us. And she did seek help. She was going through treatment at the time of her death. Obviously, it wasn't enough, and we lost a talented, driven artist and a woman who was a genius at friendship.

Fern had a gift for making those who loved her feel they were her most intimate of friends. She asked probing questions and listened with full intensity. She wanted to know your deepest secrets, and you felt grateful to be so known, and to know her in return. What a powerful gift of friendship it is: to be asked to reveal yourself and to be known and loved for who you truly are.

To lose someone like that is painful. To lose her to suicide so much more painful. There's a moment in my play, *Anna in the Afterlife*:

AFTERLIFE ANNA: You don't believe in mental illness?
MATTHEW: Mental illness?

AFTERLIFE ANNA: Mental illness. Sometimes it's fatal.
MATTHEW: You killed yourself.
AFTERLIFE ANNA: That's what puts the *fatal* into *fatal* mental illness. Dumb bell.

We have a hard time accepting death from this disease. We hate to lose someone to cancer or heart disease, but we can at least make some sort of sense of it. It fits our view of the world. We are not befuddled in our practice of mourning.

Fern stayed on my mind long after her death. Her suicide left a hole that could not be filled. Fern's parents entrusted her manuscripts to me in hopes that I could find a home for them. During the 1990s I began working on *Visions of Anna* as a tribute to her. In this novel I created a fictional alter ego for Fern and attempted to answer unanswerable questions.

Fern and I had become friends while doing our fiction-writing apprenticeship in graduate school. That was one of the keys to the depth of our friendship: It blossomed as we were defining ourselves as lifelong writers of fiction. We took on that identity together as a sacred vocation. So when it came time to write a tribute to my friend, the only fitting form was fiction.

A few years ago I was inspired to return to *Anna*'s story in an entirely new way, from an older point of view and in the form of a stage play. I wrote *Anna in the Afterlife* and developed the script with the help of my friends at Polarity Ensemble Theatre. In that process we came upon the idea of presenting three works together, including *She Plays in Darkness*, *Visions of Anna*, and *Anna in the Afterlife* under the umbrella of *The Afterlife Trilogy*. I showed the works to our colleagues in the Chicago community, and the project stirred considerable excitement. The three works, although each written to stand alone, illuminate and enlarge the others when taken as a group.

This book remains set in the 1990s. I have not updated it for the march of technology or for progress in medical practice. Likewise, Fern's *She Plays in Darkness* remains set in the 1980s.

It's a great pleasure to bring *Visions of Anna* and the other works of *The Afterlife Trilogy* to you.

—*Richard Engling, August 28, 2014*

CHAPTER 1

TWO SUNBURNED PEOPLE

MATTHEW LOOKED OUT AT the mountains and the desert as he drove north toward Salt Lake, the former home of his dear lost friend, Anna Toyevsky. The harsh scenery reminded him of the magic she had written about so much in her later work.

She believed she'd come to know the spirits that inhabited these arid lands. Was it delusion? Mental illness? Or had she actually *known* something about what awaited her on the other side of death? With Matthew's own death now breathing down his neck, that was the most important question of all.

But Anna was a champion of life, too. He smiled as he remembered what she'd done to Natalie and him. It'd been seven years ago, the first time he and Natalie met. It was at Anna's, of course: an intimate dinner for three, with Anna at her vicarious best. She could not possibly have been more manipulative.

"I'm cooking, you're paying," Anna had told him. She drove him around town, gathering the ingredients she'd special-ordered a week in advance: two pounds of tiny clams, no bigger around than fifty-cent pieces, and two dozen fresh oysters, all flown in by a specialty seafood distributor that served the best restaurants in landlocked Salt Lake. Then on to other shops for enoki mushrooms with long pale stems and tiny caps, imported triple cream Camembert, and fresh pasta, bread, horseradish, herbs, and other ingredients. And then to a liquor store for three bottles of vintage champagne, white Bordeaux, and a fine cognac.

"This is the first time a dinner at a friend's ever cost me five hundred bucks," Matthew said as they brought back the groceries.

"You'll be kissing my feet by the time it's over," Anna said. "Anyway, what's the point of all that big Hollywood money you make if I can't spend it?"

"Hard to argue with that," Matthew muttered.

She spread a large platter with crushed ice and handed Matthew the new oyster knife. "Besides, you're going to be so grateful that I made you buy the right tools."

"I thought the deal was: I pay, you cook."

"Well, there's one other part of that," Anna admitted, handing him the first bottle of champagne and one of the oysters. "You pay, you open, I cook."

When Natalie arrived, the kitchen was already transformed. Anna's well-worn table was adorned with cut flowers, flickering candles, and the first treats of the evening: A dozen oysters lay glistening on the half shell atop the ice chips on the platter. There was a basket of thin-sliced, crusty bread, a dish of tart salty olives from Italy, and the triple cream Camembert. Steam from Anna's pasta pot warmed the air. Matthew turned from the sink with an oyster in one hand and the knife in the other as Anna ushered Natalie into the room. A smug little smile curled the corners of Anna's lips.

He'd heard Anna's descriptions, of course, but Matthew was still surprised at her loveliness. Natalie's black hair swept back from her face, accentuating deep brown eyes and high cheekbones.

Natalie was descended from Spanish gypsies. She had their exotic beauty and grace, but the gypsy flamboyance was subdued, except in her wit, which could be caustic. She expressed her art in painting rather than flamenco dance. Her voice was rich in emotion and, occasionally, in sarcasm. But her movements were all about grace. Her whole life had taken on the deliberate slowness of the brushstrokes she used to apply oil to canvas. Her very walk, her gestures, had that elegance. She was like an El Greco figure. Everything about her was long and graceful: her arms, her legs, and especially her neck.

Anna began plying them with champagne at once, pouring the wine and proposing toast after preposterous toast. The three were laughing and talking like old friends in short order. And it took no time at all for Matthew and Natalie to realize that Anna had assembled foods based on their qualities as aphrodisiacs. With each firm, salty, sea-fresh oyster, they willingly swallowed her spell. It coated their insides with the rich creamy Camembert on the tiny slices of aromatic bread. It flowed down their throats with the cold, dizzying wine from Champagne. Anna moved from one to the other of them, petting them, praising them to one another, laughing, talking, drinking, and weaving her witchcraft ever more tightly.

By the time they'd finished the hors d'oeuvres, two bottles of champagne were gone. Anna was at the stove, simmering the wine, butter, garlic, and herb sauce for the pasta. She threw a pound of angel-hair capellini into the boiling pasta pot.

"Come, come," she called to the two of them, "this is cuisine as an *acte de théâtre*. This side, this side," she said as she herded them together into the tight space between the wall and herself. Forced into their first physical contact, Matthew and Natalie smiled at one another and watched Anna at work, glancing back at one another almost shyly now that they were so close together. But then the champagne and the oysters and the wonderful aroma rising from Anna's skillet overwhelmed their shyness. Matthew put his arm around Natalie, and she leaned into him happily.

"Watch now. Watch," Anna said. She took a cup of chicken broth and poured it into the sauce, turning up the fire to bring it back to a simmer. Once the liquid was bubbling, she picked up a handful of chopped parsley and sprinkled it over. Then she poured in the bowl of tiny clams and settled them into the hot liquid. "Watch how they open," Anna breathed. And as the clams slowly opened their shells, revealing their pearly, fleshy, most feminine insides, Natalie caught her breath and laughed and leaned harder against Matthew, mesmerized by the sight of the opening shells. Matthew, too, was aroused by the sight of these opening clams in Anna's bubbling pot. But when Anna poured in the bowl of enoki mushrooms, with their long white stems and compact caps, they were so preposterously like long, slender penises, they all three began to laugh.

Anna grabbed a good handful of freshly grated Parmesan and sprinkled it over the top.

"Sit, sit," she called, and she began to ladle pasta onto plates and scoop over the sauce.

Anna set plates before them and poured them each a glass of the white Bordeaux. She set everything on the table with a flourish, enjoying the sensual spectacle she'd created. She moved from one to the other, grinding pepper and grating cheese to enhance their dishes, and then she sat.

Anna had positioned Matthew and Natalie across the table from one another so they could look into one another's eyes, and she put herself at the head of the table, between them, to enjoy them both.

"I've been trying to get Matthew back to the true art of novel writing," Anna said to Natalie. "But he's working on yet another screenplay."

"I'm not sure I care if I ever write another novel," he said.

"Jesus Christ of the Hollywood whores!" Anna exclaimed. "You're ruined. Ruined by money and attention."

"Jesus Christ of the Hollywood whores?" Matthew said. "You know, Christian blasphemy doesn't really count coming from a Jewess."

"Jewess! Nobody says *Jewess* anymore."

"And I like doing movies," Matthew continued. "I was never going to change the shape of the novel. That's for you and Joyce and Robbe-Grillet. Movies are a wonderful way to tell stories."

"Where do you get them?" Natalie asked. "Your stories?"

"You have to see Natalie's work," Anna interrupted. "Her paintings are like little stories in themselves. Interrupted scenes. There's something amazingly voyeuristic in her work."

Natalie laughed. "Especially since there are often voyeurs pictured in my work."

"You paint what you see," Matthew suggested.

"Whereas everyone in a Matthew Harken story is an alter ego," Anna teased. "His characters are all variations on him."

"That's right. It's an exercise in multiple personality disorder," he said. He dipped a piece of the crusty bread into the aromatic sauce and popped it in his mouth.

Anna laughed. "*The Three Faces of Matthew.*"

"I've seen *Better Strangers*," Natalie said. "You could not possibly be both Jillian and Dennis."

"Thank you." Matthew raised his glass to her. "I'm intrigued by what Anna said about your work. Scenes from life interrupted."

"People assume that I get my ideas from what I see. But that's not true."

"Where do you get them then?" he asked her.

"Through physical sensation," she said. She looked up at the ceiling with her wineglass held between her palms, rolling it between them like a piece of clay. "While working on a figure in a painting I might feel a tingling in my legs. That could cause me to envision the stance of the subject in a way that had not occurred to me. I don't *think* about how I want the subject's legs to look. I feel it in my legs and then paint it—almost without it coming to the conscious level. I just do it. From physical sensation to movement of the brush."

"Wow," Matthew said. "When I'm lost in a story I'm writing, I lose my body altogether. Sometimes I'll finish and discover my foot is painfully twisted. I won't even recognize that my foot has been cramping up until I stop. Then I have to get up and start hobbling around." He laughed. "Once I put an egg on to boil, started working on a scene, and by the time I remembered it again, the water had boiled out of the pan and this incredibly bad-smelling smoke was billowing out of the kitchen!"

"Really, I'm not always aware of the world, either. I zoom in and out," Natalie said. As she talked, she used the tip of her knife to slide clams and mushrooms onto her fork in patterns like hieroglyphics, then slid them in her mouth to eat them between sentences. She winked at Anna to let her know how wonderful it all tasted. "I love to paint outdoors because of that—even when I'm not painting an outdoor scene. I can look at a rock formation or some desert brush and see something in it that tells me how to paint a vase on a table. When I'm working well, anything can talk to me."

"Ah, the voices," Matthew said.

"The voices?" Natalie said.

"Remember Kolelo?" he asked Anna.

"How could I forget Kolelo? I was the one who said we should get jobs and support him."

"We knew Kolelo in Paris," Matthew said to Natalie. "A wonderful African novelist and poet. He taught me about listening to the voices."

"And these voices can come from anything?" Natalie said.

"Yes, but for me they often speak through dreams."

"Yes!" Natalie said. "Some of my favorite paintings have come from dreams. I keep a drawing pad next to my bed."

"The central plot idea for *Better Strangers* came from a dream," Matthew said.

"Natalie and I talked about collaborating," Anna said. "I found her dream sketches really enchanting."

"They're very rough," Natalie interjected. "As you can imagine. I do them half-asleep."

"And that's what makes them so enchanting," Anna insisted. "They're not manipulated. They come straight from the subconscious." She lifted her glass. "To Kolelo, eh?"

The three clicked their glasses together and drank. Matthew refilled them from the white Bordeaux. He was getting drunk, and he loved it. Drunk on the champagne and Bordeaux. Drunk on Anna's seductive dinner. Drunk on the beauty and fascination of Natalie. Drunk on his long-time friendship with Anna. And on the conversation.

"I was over at Natalie's one afternoon, drinking tea, and Natalie showed me the sketches," Anna continued. "We went through them, and she told me about the dreams that had originated them. And I thought what a fantastic book this would make: I would write text, inspired by Natalie's original dreams to go with the images."

As he listened, Matthew watched Natalie with the luxurious hunger that Anna's foods incited in him. All those sensual delights made his lips feel warm and swollen in longing to brush against Natalie's lips. The feel of the tiny succulent clams on his tongue made him long to lick her flesh, her nipples, her sex. And when he looked into her eyes, he saw her shift in her seat as though she could feel an intimation of his tongue on her.

"So what do you think?" Anna said. They each looked down in momentary confusion at their plates, having no idea what Anna had been saying.

"Great," Matthew offered, looking back at Anna, hoping his response somehow answered her question.

"Yes, great," Natalie said, looking uncertainly from Anna to Matthew and nodding her head.

Anna watched the two of them with a slight smirk as she licked and sucked the juice and meat from one of her clams. She made a sound somewhere between a moan and a hum as she sucked it in and swallowed it.

"This really is delicious," she said, still looking back and forth between the two of them.

After the meal, they moved into the living room to enjoy coffee and chocolates and the wonderfully smooth cognac.

"You know I read something," Natalie said. "It was a psychological profile on artists. It offered a happiness/misery quotient depending on the artist's media. Visual artists are supposed to be the happiest. And it said writers have the greatest capacity for misery. Do you agree with that?"

"I believe it," Anna said. "What could be more miserable that having to make your art out of nothing? You visual artists can sit in front of a model or a landscape and away you go. You've got something there to paint."

"Oh, right," Natalie laughed. "As though writers make everything up. You never use a story from your life, or somebody else's life, or adapt something you read."

"Well..." Anna said.

"And being a writer is cheap!" Natalie exclaimed. "All you need is a pencil and paper. Do you know how much we spend on brushes and paints and canvases? And frames and mattes? And then you have a show and people walk by saying, 'Oh, I could have done that.'"

"Well, everybody thinks they can write," Anna countered. "They think since they can talk, they can write. I don't know how many times I've been at a party that some idiot who admits he doesn't even read has told me he's got a great idea for a novel."

"I'd think it would be fun working with materials," Matthew said. "The brushes and paints."

"It is fun, actually," Natalie said. "I just bought a wonderful new set of brushes yesterday. Lovely instruments made with Chinese hog bristle."

"What's wrong with good old-fashioned *American* hog bristle?" Anna demanded.

Natalie shook her head with distaste. "American hogs live too posh a life. They eat scientific diets and are protected from the weather. Chinese hogs still live the old peasant life. They eat slops and live outside in the cold. So their bristle grows in thick and tough."

"What *is* bristle?" Matthew asked. "Is that the pig's whiskers?"

"No," Natalie laughed. "It's the hair on the hog's back."

"So that's what makes a great brush? Good bristle?" Anna asked.

"A great brush." Natalie leaned back in her chair and looked up at the ceiling, picturing her brushes in her mind's eye. She smiled. "A great brush is a work of art in itself," she said. She leaned in toward them with intensity. "Imagine the hair on the back of a hog," she said. Matthew and Anna leaned in with her, drawn in by her passion for the subject.

"The hairs sprout from the hide and have a natural curve back toward the skin. Like our own hair." She took Matthew's hand. "May I?" she said.

"Please," he said.

She held Matthew's hand in her left hand and pointed to the hairs on his wrist with her right. "See how the hairs curve back toward your skin?" They nodded. "Bristle is a thousand times stiffer and the curve more regular. A master brush maker arranges it so each individual bristle curves in toward the center so that the brush comes to a natural point for a round brush or a natural knife's edge for a flat brush. He has to arrange it this way without trimming away the flagging—that's like the split ends at the end of the bristle. You don't want to lose that."

"And you can tell a great brush just by looking at it?" Matthew said.

"I look at it. I feel it. I test the balance of the handle, and then I run the tip of the bristle over this very sensitive skin," she said, rubbing her finger over the skin above her upper lip and beneath her nose. Matthew's eyes followed the slow movement of her finger over this pretty flesh. She paused in her story, her finger at the corner of her lovely lips. A silence settled over the room, and then they were all suddenly back to the pervasiveness of desire.

"I'm sorry. I'm so sleepy all of a sudden," Anna said mercifully. "Matthew, would you mind giving Natalie a ride home?"

And so they did their huggings and good nights, and Matthew drove Natalie home.

When they stood at her door, Matthew saw the mixture of desire and apprehension in her eyes. His own heart was racing.

"Come in?" she asked.

"Yes," he said.

In her living room they spoke not a word. They were already so aroused; they came into one another's arms pulled by the magnetism of their over-sensitized flesh. Their first kiss they approached with caution, like two sunburned people who long to embrace in spite of the pain. Their every nerve ending sang out as they pressed their bodies together as their lips sought one another out.

After the kissing, Natalie led him into her bedroom. She began lighting candles. Matthew felt as though he'd entered a luxurious, private harem. Soft fabrics, scarves, hats, discarded clothes lay in heaps and hung from drawers and from hooks and rings on the walls. Natalie's bed, a soft futon, lay on the floor covered in a tangle of blankets and scattered pillows. Wonderful scents came to his nose: incense and perfume and body creams and the irresistible pheromones of this wonderful young woman. The walls were hung with Natalie's most erotic paintings.

When Natalie had finished lighting the candles and incense, she knelt on the futon in front of Matthew, and he, in turn, knelt in front of her. They looked into one another's eyes, hearing the sounds of their uneven breathing, revealing their longing.

Natalie raised her long, slender fingers to the button at the neck of her blouse and slowly undid it. For Matthew, it was like the grace of God descending upon him. He felt as though his whole body were shining with the great white light of hope, and he raised his own fingers to the topmost of his shirt buttons and slowly undid it as well.

And so they continued, slowly undressing themselves before one another's eyes, offering each other this great gift, this opening of their bodies to one another.

How beautiful they were! Matthew remembered that night like a holy revelation. He could have wept at the thought of their glorious healthy bodies that night. How they made love for hours, licking, tasting, caressing, teasing the delicious curves and nubs and expanses of each other's bodies. The first slippery penetrations. The long, wracking orgasms. How Natalie wept onto his chest after the first time, and then he, too, wept, so overwrought the two of them had become by the long evening of it. And then, after the weeping, how they began once again, charged with desire. They could have eaten one another alive and gladly given themselves up to be devoured.

♦ ♦ ♦

What a time that was. He would have given his fortune to experience that night again—or even just to sit and talk with Anna, the two of them over a bottle of wine or coffee: one of their old, all-night talks.

Matthew looked in the rearview mirror and saw the dark highway stretch behind him. No other cars followed. It was just he on this road, driving through the night toward Salt Lake, the scene of Anna's death.

Tomorrow Matthew would meet with Colin, Anna's lover. On the phone, Colin had told Matthew about the final entry in Anna's journal. She'd written it while waiting to die. In it, she regretted not writing a book about the nightmare that had occupied her last months. She'd hoped that the journals might stand as that work. Was there something there that ought to be published?

Matthew cared so little about that now. What did writing matter, really, when you were facing death? Did your work buy you immortality? Did Shakespeare give a shit about his plays anymore? Did Anna care about her journals now? Her unpublished novels?

Mostly he just wanted to feel Anna again. To look into her face. To share their stories. But since he couldn't do that, he wanted to submerge himself in her journals. To see her life in her own handwriting. To recall all the bits of history that they had shared together. To go back to their days in school, their days in Paris. The long correspondence they'd shared. The love and the passion. All those joys of the immediacy of youth when they were becoming their adult selves and embracing the careers they'd follow until they died.

The rain fell on the desert as he drove. Dirt roads slid off the interstate into the desert sage with a surprising informality. These unmarked roads called to him to pull off. He wanted to find the mystical spots that Anna and Colin had found, but it was as cold and rainy here as the November Chicago he'd left behind, and he kept to the interstate.

Anna knew the secret of death. She'd always shared her secrets with him in life. He wanted to her to share this last one, too.

Chapter 2

THE FREE-LANCE DEAD

Matthew walked down into the arroyo, the ground crumbling under his feet as he crossed over the edge of the gully. He didn't know what he was looking for, and he feared he wouldn't be able to find his way back. The eroded gully took a turn to the left, and he followed it. A tumbleweed blew over the ridge above his head. He went down deeper. There still wasn't any water, just the deep gully left by erosion. A channel cut in from the left after the bend. Anna was standing in the center of that channel. Her face looked dull. Pale. No trace of the ever-present roses in the cheeks.

"Nobody knows anything," she said.

Matthew awoke disoriented, feeling the stiffness of terror. Then he realized the stiffness was the same stiffness of pain he felt every morning. He lay on his back, staring at the ceiling, wishing he could return to the oblivion of sleep.

Useless.

Once he was awake with the pain, it wouldn't let him go back to sleep. He couldn't lie peacefully. He couldn't get up easily. Or turn over in bed.

Where the hell was he? He turned his stiff neck and used one arm to help prop up his head a little.

Salt Lake City. He was at the Inn at Temple Square.

"God, kill me now," he said aloud. He waited for the off chance that a lightning bolt might crash through the window and jolt him into the next world, but when that didn't happen, he wrestled himself onto his side and slithered clumsily to the edge of the bed. "I love being an octogenarian," he said, shuffling into the bathroom.

Matthew turned on the hot water tap full and tore open the instant coffee packet he'd put there the night before. As steam began to rise from the bowl, he looked at his image in the mirror. No, he didn't look eighty yet. He was starting to look a little gaunt, a little extra dark around the eyes, for a man who was still in his early forties.

What would Anna think of him now? Mr. Espresso-Hollywood making tap water instant coffee and washing down painkillers the first thing out of bed. He turned on the shower. Coffee, heavy analgesics, and a twenty-minute pummeling of his back with water hot enough to turn it bright pink were his entrée into the new day. Without this ritual, there was no chance of feeling human.

Matthew crouched painfully to slip off his pajama pants, and something in the movement reminded him of his foot sliding into the crumbling dirt of the arroyo.

"Nobody knows anything," she'd said.

He remembered suddenly his sensations in the dream. He remembered the heat he'd felt radiating from the image of Anna. He suddenly felt certain that her real living spirit had come to visit him in the dream. The thought of it made his heart race.

Then he felt foolish. How could he know it was really her spirit? It was just a dream, after all.

But then again, Matthew Harken knew about dreams. Dreams had made him a wealthy man. A dream had given him the central plot elements in his screenplay for *Better Strangers*, the film that made him famous. Two more dreams helped him through the writing of *Fertility Rites*, the movie that made him rich.

But was this the secret she had for him? *Nobody knows anything?* He wasn't ready to accept that.

He opened the sliding glass door to the bathtub and steam billowed out. The nonslip-textured floor of the bathtub warmed the soles of his feet as he stepped in. He stuck his head under the water and stood with his two hands on the wall, leaning into the water stream, letting it soak through his hair. Then he leaned back his head, opened his mouth to let the water flow in, and spit the water back at the showerhead.

A shower-massage, Matthew observed. *God bless the Inn at Temple Square.* He adjusted the showerhead to a fast pulse and turned around to let the hot water beat on his back.

Over the years he studied dreams with Jungian analysts and New Age gurus. These studies led to other pathways to the inner mind and to altered states of consciousness. But he'd lost touch with most of that years ago.

Now he wanted that contact back. His work with dreams had given him a sense of the *other side*, the invisible world of spirits that surrounded us, to which for most of our lives we remain oblivious. Now that he was facing premature ejection from the world of the living, he wanted a feel for what awaited him. He'd lost his religion over twenty years ago, but he'd never lost the habit of believing one had to prepare for death. The afterlife, he suspected, was a whole new world. And he didn't want to enter it as a complete naïf. He'd had that experience often enough, every time he'd passed into a new stage of school, career, or life.

He feared being lost in the world of the dead, like those confused souls who haunted the places of their deaths, uncertain whether they were dead or alive. He suspected that those who stuck with their religions had a leg up. They'd kept open their lines of communication with their own spirit factions. He imagined all sorts of in-groups on the other side. The Jesus fan clubs. The Buddha-ettes. The ecstatic Sufis, singing and dancing through the netherworld, scooping up their new dead like a traveling amusement park hurricane.

But what happened to the throngs of the free-lance dead? All those, like him, who hadn't kept up with one of the powerful noncorporeal political action committees? Those who'd dropped off the Wonderful Wicca Wagon? Or the Great-Spirit-Father-in-the-Sky Society? Or the Mohammedan Mob? Even devout atheists probably pulled together on the other side. He imagined the atheists walking in a huge group, looking slightly embarrassed, and whenever a new one of their number died, they took him or her in hand to say, "Hey, listen, there's something we gotta tell you..."

But who in heaven would show all of the loners the ropes? Matthew had been a devout Catholic as a child. But by the time he reached twenty-one, he'd become disenchanted. Aside from the odd wedding and funeral, he hadn't set foot in a church in decades. Matthew had lost his old-boy network of the beyond, and it scared the shit out of him.

His dream of Anna worried him, too. *"Nobody knows anything,"* she'd said. Is that where she was? Lost in the ozone without her guardian angel? Without her magic homing device tracked on the celestial House of Russian Jewry? It was five years since she died.

Matthew turned the water up yet hotter and faster and let it pummel his back. He felt his heart go out to this image of the long lost Anna Toyevsky. A wandering spirit. A suicide.

Why had she done it? That was the first question he wanted answered.

CHAPTER 3

GLOSSOLALIA

"I KILLED HER," COLIN said. "That's what some people will tell you." He shook his head and looked down, speaking almost to himself. "Maybe it's true. Maybe Owl Creek Canyon was the last straw." Colin ran his fingers through the ringlets of his tightly curled, bright red-orange hair as he stretched. He felt tired. His face was gaunt from being ill, and his skin was pale in a way that made his multitude of freckles look like some strange kind of spattered discoloration on his skin.

Colin picked up some pasta with his fork and turned the tip of the fork slowly against the inside of his spoon, wrapping the pasta around the tines. He put it in his mouth and chewed thoughtfully. He took a sip of red wine. "So maybe I killed her," he said. He picked up the bottle of wine, a Chianti Classico, and refilled Matthew's and his goblets. They were drinking the wine with a thirst, and Colin was starting to feel the effects. On the restaurant sound system, a female vocalist began crooning "Goin' Out of My Head." Colin noticed and pointed his fork in the general direction of the overhead speakers. "There you go," he said with a dry, half-smile. The smile faded.

"We argued. Two days later, she was dead," he said.

It annoyed Matthew that Colin was being so flippant about this, but he didn't want to pick a fight. He wanted to get the whole story.

"Owl Creek Canyon," Matthew said. "Is that the place Anna told me about—where you two were thinking of building?"

"That's right."

"From what Anna told me about the place, I could never understand what you saw in it."

Colin gave him a look of startled surprise. "Why?" he said.

"Anna told me as you walked in, there were the remains of abandoned building sites. Like a place of incredibly bad luck." Colin nodded in recognition. Matthew continued: "A place where she sensed strong malevolent spirits."

"All true," Colin admitted. "But that's the lower canyon. Our intent was to build in the upper canyon. You have to pass through the lower canyon to get to the upper canyon, but we were trying to figure out some other way of access."

"This was to be a place to live?" Matthew said.

"As much time as possible," Colin said. "It's not like there were jobs available out there. It's pretty remote."

"Anna told me about some traumatic experience she had."

Colin nodded. "The first time we went. A friend of mine who works for the Department of Natural Resources told me about the place. He noticed some stone chips that suggested prehistoric tool making. He said the place felt haunted. When I told Anna about it, she was fascinated. Anna of the spirits." Colin raised his glass again, and a silly, slightly drunken smirk crossed his face.

"She wasn't like that before she came out here," Matthew said. "In graduate school or Paris."

"Well, this is the place," Colin said. He gestured toward the large picture windows at the front of the restaurant and to the canyon walls and desert outside. "The whole state is haunted."

"So she was really interested."

"Absolutely. She was interested in the site archeologically. She was interested because it was maybe haunted. But most of all, she was interested in it as a possible source of power."

"How would you get power out of a place drenched in bad luck?"

"That's just the lower canyon," Colin said. "Anna and I believed that you often had to pass through the negative to get to the positive."

"What happened to her there?"

"The 'traumatic experience'? You have such patience, Matthew." Colin smiled in teasing admiration. "Anna's other old friends just wanted to hear about Anna's final days. After that, they didn't really want to talk anymore. It was clear they'd had enough of me." Colin smiled, and Matthew suddenly suspected that he relished his standing as a pariah.

"There may be more than one reason for that," Matthew said. "At her funeral service, I discovered that Anna had a habit of compartmentalizing her friends. Each of them had the feeling that they were Anna's very best friend. And they each had a slightly different vision of who Anna was, because of what she chose to reveal or conceal. Hardly any of her old friends knew of her fascination with spirits."

"Loose lips sink ships. Anyway, we drove out to the canyon for the first time about a year before her death. This quiet, sacred energy of anticipation was glowing from Anna's face. You could sense how eager she was." Colin looked out the window into the desert beyond. A sudden deep sorrow crossed his face. He shook his head, and his face seemed to grow even paler. His freckles looked practically gray beneath the shocking orange-red ringlets of his hair. The grief could come on him so quickly, even after all this time. He took a sip of his wine, and then another. *That's it, Mr. Grace,* he told himself. *Time to self-medicate!* He took a deep breath.

"She took me to places I didn't think I'd ever know," he said. "I'd been married for thirteen years to Susan. We had two kids together. I'd never had an idea of what love meant. And from the way things look, Anna will be the only woman I ever truly love. This lifetime."

Matthew looked down and dutifully cut a piece of his beef. He didn't much feel like eating at the moment. Colin's sorrow had infected him, and he remembered how much he missed Anna, too.

"You're dying, aren't you?" Colin said with a quizzical expression on his face. "I get these funny little flashes of knowledge, now and then. I'm learning not to censor them. It's true, isn't it? I'm HIV-positive, and you're dying. And Anna beat us to the grave without the benefit of a major disease."

"Your 'funny little flash of knowledge' wouldn't have anything to do with the fact that I look like shit, would it?" Matthew asked. He lifted his wine and smiled. "Here's to camaraderie among the doomed." Colin lifted his, and they clinked goblets.

"To the dregs," Colin said.

"To the dregs," Matthew agreed. They drank their goblets to the bottom and set the glasses sharply down on the marble tabletop. A chip cracked off the base of Colin's glass. He flicked the chip to the floor.

"Well," Colin said cheerfully. "I don't often discover another dead man walking, just socially, over lunch. What have you got?"

"Prostate cancer."

"Prostate cancer!" Colin began giggling. It brought some of the color back to his face. Matthew smiled, then began to laugh with him. "Prostate cancer," Colin said again, giggling away. "I love that."

Somehow the words sounded ridiculous now to Matthew, too. "Prostate cancer," Matthew said, laughing harder, falling into Colin's sudden tipsy silliness. If you couldn't laugh about death, what could you laugh about?

"*Cancer*," Colin repeated darkly, giggling more.

"Prostate," Matthew said brightly, enjoying the word immensely. In his belly he felt a strange, giddy hysteria rising.

"We have more in common than I thought," Colin said suddenly, inspired. "We both loved Anna. We're both going to die *way* before our time. And we've both been fucked by our own organs!"

This brought shouts of laughter from both of them, and annoyed looks from around the room. Colin wiped the tears from his eyes with his napkin. "The attack from down under. Oh, I love that."

"Ain't death grand?" Matthew added.

Colin looked around in mock abashment, noticing the looks from the other tables. "Oopsy," he stage-whispered, still giggling. "I think I said the word *fucked* a little loudly."

"Don't worry," Matthew told him. *"Being terminal means never having to say you're sorry."*

This one killed them. Colin laughed so hard, he fell off his chair. Matthew doubled over in hilarity, bumping his head on the tabletop and overturning the half-empty bottle of wine.

As they regained their composure, the waiter came over with a towel and began mopping up the spilled wine. He looked annoyed.

"Thank you very much," Colin said, wiping his eyes with his handkerchief.

"Gentlemen, we have had some complaints..." he said, finishing the cleanup.

"Don't worry," Colin told him. "We'll be good."

"Would you please bring us another bottle of that same wine?" Matthew requested.

The waiter looked from one to the other of them. "I'm not sure that would be a good idea," he said.

"Oh, we're not drunk," Colin assured him.

"No, no, we're not drunk," Matthew said.

"No," Colin continued, sobering up from his laughter. "Really it's just that we're upset. Actually."

His sudden super-serious expression struck Matthew as ridiculous, and he began to laugh again. Colin fought to keep the smile off his own face.

"Please ignore him," Colin said to the waiter, "because it's true. We're both quite upset. We were just reminiscing about a dear friend who committed suicide."

Matthew lost it again, laughing until his eyes ran with tears.

"Shut up," Colin whispered at him, losing the battle of sobriety. He turned back to the waiter, straightening his face as much as possible. "Please don't feel insulted," he said. "I'm not bullshitting you. We just have a strange way of dealing with our grief."

Matthew pulled himself together. "Please, if you wouldn't mind getting us the wine," he said. "We could use a break here."

"That's right," Colin agreed, "because neither one of us is likely to live another year."

At that, Matthew clapped his hands tightly over his mouth and shook with silent laughter. Colin managed to keep a straight face as he looked into the waiter's eyes. Matthew looked from the waiter's face to Colin's face and shook all the harder. Finally, the waiter turned and walked away.

Matthew dried his eyes again and took a deep breath. "Oh! I haven't laughed that hard since they found my tumor," he said. He immediately lost it again. He doubled over and laughed so hard that drool ran out of his mouth.

They wiped their eyes and caught their breaths, calming down from this final attack.

"It's a shame Anna is missing this," Colin said at last. "No one loved morbid humor so much as she."

"That's right," Matthew agreed. "Unless, of course, she got pissed at us for having terminal illnesses," he said.

Colin shrugged. "You never know. She might have been envious."

"Oh hell," Matthew said. "By now, she probably would have had HIV from you."

"Actually, she may have been the one to give it to me. I don't know. She was interested in the principal at the school where she worked. You know Anna. Always shopping. This principal was gay." He shrugged, correcting himself: "*Bisexual.* Married. But there was a rumor he had HIV. I don't know whether it's true or not. I don't know if they ever did anything, either. Or even if he knew Anna was interested."

"Oh, God bless him," Matthew said, nodding toward the waiter. "Look who's coming, and look what he's got."

Colin looked, then looked back at Matthew, surprised. "I didn't think there was a prayer in hell that he was going to bring us another bottle of wine," he said.

The waiter brought the Chianti to the table and uncorked it. The two watched him quietly with repressed smiles as he poured them each a half glass.

"Bless you," Colin said. "Bless you to your bones."

The waiter set the bottle on the table and looked at them each. It made Matthew realize again how sick they both appeared. "So is it true, what you said," the waiter ventured. "You might not live out the year?"

"Hard to say, exactly," Colin said. "Though I'll probably outlive this poor bastard." He indicated Matthew.

Matthew was surprised when that one fell with a thud on his heart. The waiter retreated without another word.

"Sorry about that," Colin said.

"No, no," Matthew insisted. He smiled wanly. "It must have been true. Another of your 'funny flashes'?"

"Just a joke," he said. "Really."

Colin's delayed *really* had the effect of contradicting what he'd said. They sat quietly for a moment and went halfheartedly back to eating.

"You were going to tell me about the first time you took Anna to Owl Creek Canyon," Matthew said.

"Ah, yes," Colin said. He swallowed a small mouthful of pasta and wiped his lips with the corner of his napkin. It tasted and felt better in his mouth now. The salutary effects of laughter, he imagined. "I was really curious about bringing Anna there—what her reaction would be.

You know, I had sensed things there, but I didn't want to set her up too much. I wanted her to have her own reaction, without preparation."

"Why's that?" Matthew said.

Colin took a sip of his wine. "I don't know about you, but sometimes I can have the most uncanny, powerful experience, and then later, because the experience was so strange, and because I have nothing else in my life that it compares with, I start to doubt the whole thing. So I wanted to see Anna's reaction. All on her own. I'd told her I thought it was a powerful place," he interjected. "And I told her about the Indian artifacts we'd seen there. But I didn't get any more specific than that." Colin spun some more pasta onto his fork.

"To get into the canyon," he said, talking and chewing at the same time, "you have to park out at a fence and hike through private property, unless you want to climb down a steep canyon wall. I'd met the two property owners that have cabins out there, but they tend to be on the paranoid side. A lot of these people do, who live out in the middle of nowhere. I think that's why they choose to live out in those areas, because they don't like people in the first place. So you always feel a little nervous as you walk past the fronts of their cabins. They all have firearms. Big, mean dogs sometimes. So we went by the two cabins where people still live. Next, you walk by this abandoned ranch. It used to be a residential mental health-care facility in the sixties. That closed up under a big scandal. This charismatic psychiatrist ran the place. He was one of the early proponents of LSD, back before it was outlawed. Apparently he was handing it out like candy." Colin chuckled. "To aid in the transference process, or some such nonsense, the therapists would drop acid with the patients. Essentially, the nuts and the shrinks were just having acid parties together. Tripping out. Playing music. And—this is what really put the nail in the coffin—they were screwing like crazy. Everybody was screwing everybody else. Nuts and shrinks alike."

Colin scooped up some more pasta and ate it with relish. "Inevitably, some of the nuts got their brains fried. You know, when you drop off your neurotic teenage daughter at the nuthouse for a little mental health vacation, and you get back some drooling, psychotic wreckage who babbles obsessively about the chief shrink's pecker, you want some answers. I don't know if the guy did jail time, or if he just lost his license, or what happened, but the place got closed down. I hear the guy is practicing again. Not as a psychiatrist, but as some kind of New Age counselor. All that LSD gave him the ability to channel psychological advice from Mars." He gave Matthew a look. "That might be rumor."

Colin chuckled and stuffed some more pasta in his mouth. "My doctor is going to be so glad you and I got together," he said, talking with his mouth full. "Laughing and eating. That's what she tells me I have to do. I've lost fifty pounds, you know," he confided.

"You've doubled me," Matthew told him. "I've lost twenty-five." Matthew dutifully sliced another piece of his beef. He still didn't have much of an appetite.

"So, Anna and I walked past the abandoned former nuthouse–slash–former ranch," he said. "Then we walked into the lower canyon proper, past the last remnants of modern man, and I showed Anna where we'd seen evidence of an ancient Native encampment. Anna found a round stone that looked like it might have been used as a grinding stone. We found more chips left from fashioning stone tools. The most exciting thing was that we found some petroglyphs on the rock wall that I had never seen before. I was ready to go on into the upper canyon, but Anna wanted to meditate. You know about Anna and her meditation."

"Anywhere she happens to be."

"Right. So, I hadn't wanted to tell her too much of my impressions of the canyons. But I told her I thought it would be better to meditate in the upper canyon. She said she could feel the power in the lower canyon, and that was where she wanted to meditate. Well, I had to agree with her, there was definitely power in the lower canyon. But the upper canyon had power, too, I told her, and it would be a better place to meditate. Well, Anna dug in her heels, and nothing I was going to say would change her mind. She was going to meditate in the lower canyon, right where she had found the grinding stone. She was going to sit with the grinding stone in her hands and meditate, and I should take a walk. So that was that. I took a walk." Colin stuffed more pasta in his mouth and continued the story without hesitation.

"So I was walking up around the canyon walls in the lower canyon, getting close to the rise where there's a little waterfall. You have to climb up some rocks to get to the upper canyon. And I start hearing this noise. At first, I'm not sure I'm hearing anything. It's more like I think I'm sensing some disembodied wail. Like a moan of deep sorrow that is echoing from some other time. Not like anything that a living human being could make. And I think, Christ, we shouldn't be here. We're disturbing something. We should find some other way to get into the upper canyon. And the sound gets louder, sadder, more disturbing. But I still don't think it's a sound. Because it doesn't seem to be coming from anywhere physical. It sounds completely disembodied. And so terribly sad. It was horrifying, actually.

"The sound continued to get louder. And then I realized it was a sound coming out of a living human throat. And that frightened me. That any human being could be making a sound like that. And then I realized it was Anna. That really freaked me out. I realized it, and it made me so frightened that for a moment, I couldn't move. I had this impulse to run away. I mean, that's how horrible this made me feel. Then another of her wails, louder, broke me out of it.

"I ran back to where she had been sitting. I ran hard, and I was spooked, so that might have affected my vision, because when I got back, I couldn't see her anywhere. I knew where she had been sitting. I looked around to see where she might have gone. I looked back again and saw something on the ground where she had been seated, after all. It looked like just her collapsed skin and clothes. Like she'd only been inflated with air, all along, and now the air was let out. And then, the next moment, I saw her as her full self, sitting on the canyon floor as she had been, but collapsed forward on the ground under the weight of whatever impossible grief she'd been feeling.

"I picked her up off the ground in my arms. She's making all these sounds. Half of it's like she's a miserable little kid. Half of it is like— not human. She's saying 'No, no, no,' over and over. And words I couldn't understand. Not just mumbled, but speaking in tongues."

"Glossolalia."

"What?"

"*Glossolalia.* That's the word for speaking in tongues."

"Glossolalia. Thank you very much." He lifted his glass in a cock-eyed toast.

"I'm sorry," Matthew said. "You were carrying her, and she's speaking in tongues..."

"She's absolutely babbling," Colin continued. "I'm telling you, it was frightening. Because it started with that sound that I didn't even think was a sound. And now here I have her in my arms, and it's like she is totally out of her mind. What am I going to do with her? I didn't like the idea of carrying her out of the lower canyon, past all the failed construction, all the way back to the car though all those bad vibes—and then what? Three hours back to the city? So I think: the upper canyon. And I'm praying to God that my perception is right—that the power I've felt there is the kind that can make her get better. I've never seen her like this, and I'm scared shitless.

"So I start moving toward the upper canyon. The grinding stone falls out of her lap, and she makes this low, agonized moan. So I'm going to stoop down and get the stone, but then this voice comes up in my mind with great authority, and says, 'No.' So I leave it there. As I walk away, she's stretching back to that spot, reaching for it, and moaning; she wants it so much. But I keep going.

"I get her to that little waterfall, and I know I can't carry her up those rocks. I set her on the ground and scoop up some water. It's not a lot of water there, but it's fresh. And I throw it into her face. That doesn't bring her around, but it does stop her babbling. She's sitting there, eyes out of focus, quiet. I take her by the arm and guide her up the rocks. She's like a fucking zombie.

"I get her up into the upper canyon to a place where the sun is shining. I'm totally at a loss. So I walk away for a moment. I feel something pulling at me. I walk. And I feel the attraction stronger. I walk a little more. And then I'm standing in a spot where it feels hotter. Like I'm under a huge magnifying glass that's focusing the energy of the sun. But it's not just heat. Zoom, I can feel it surge in from all around. I run back to Anna and carry her to that spot. I sit down and wrap my arms around her. I hold her for a long time. Then I start singing to her. I don't even know what the song is. It's more like a chant. Maybe something Native American. Something that is coming right into me from the rock around us. Some old sacred song. I sing this chant for a long time. And after a long time, Anna starts to cry. But now she's crying like Anna. I think: okay. She's going to be okay now. She's back. She's Anna again."

Matthew and Colin sat quiet for a time, thinking, the sounds of the other diners, the clinking of silverware and china washing over them.

"So what did she have to say about all that?" Matthew asked, breaking the silence.

"She didn't say a hell of a lot. Once she was really back to normal, I asked her if she wanted to go home. We'd come there planning to camp in the upper canyon. But she said no. She didn't want to leave. I went and carried up our camping gear that we'd left in the lower canyon. And I set up camp on my own. Built a fire. She sat there for a long time. Then she got up and walked around. Really slowly."

Colin stopped, his eyes focused on the far horizon. "She found things," he said in a voice that recalled his surprise. "She had this uncanny ability that day to walk right up to things. She found some more petroglyphs in the canyon wall. Some tools and arrowheads. But she hardly talked the rest of that day. Which is unusual for Anna."

"What *did* she say about it, though?" Matthew asked. "Finally?"

"When she did finally talk about it, I had the impression she was holding something back. But she did talk about it the next day. The next night, actually. As we sat by the fire. She said when she was meditating, spirit people started coming up and talking to her. She tried to ignore them, because she sensed they were dangerous. She sensed this incredible neediness. But they were insistent. Pushy. Pretty soon they were pushing right into her, and she was feeling these awful pains. Awful emotions. But it didn't seem to last long to her. Either she blanked out a lot of what happened, or she was lying to me. Maybe she decided it was private.

"She didn't remember anything of me carrying her, for instance. She had no recollection of talking or making any sounds, intelligible or otherwise. She didn't remember me splashing water into her face and that causing any change in her. None of that."

"And you think there were ghosts or some kind of needy spirits, like she said, in the lower canyon?" Matthew asked.

"There is something, or really, a whole lot of somethings, that are incredibly parasitic in the lower canyon. The life gets sucked out of everything in the lower canyon. For every couple that was screwing in the nuthouse, I have no doubt that there were two or three spirits climbing on to suck up some of the energy in that lust. So yeah, I think there is something powerful going on down there."

"And yet you wanted to build a home there," Matthew said. "Doesn't that strike you as self-destructive?"

"We wanted to build in the *upper* canyon," Colin said. "That's a whole other story. It amazes me that these things are in such close proximity to each other. Maybe it shouldn't: the yin and the yang. Opposites attract. My guess is that all those low spirits in the lower canyon would love to bathe in the power that's in the upper canyon, but they can't get in there."

"Yes, but you had to pass through the lower canyon to get to the upper. Didn't you consider the risk of having to pass through the lower canyon all the time? I mean—especially after Anna collapsed like that."

Colin sighed deeply. "There's risk in everything," he said. "And it wasn't just me calling the shots, you know. I wasn't *forcing* Anna to do anything. You have to understand, the upper canyon was like a classic sacred space. It has that kind of feeling. I don't know if you've ever been to Stonehenge or Machu Picchu?"

"Stonehenge," Matthew said.

"When I'm in a place like that, I get this feeling of reverence. It's more than just the rocks. I think there is some kind of live spirit there. Do you know what I mean? Have you experienced that?"

"Sure," Matthew said. "I always felt that in the old cathedrals of Europe."

"Well, that makes sense," Colin said, "because many of them are built atop earlier pre-Christian sacred sites. Steal from the rich and give to the Church. It's an old tradition. St. Patrick drove the snakes out of Ireland. But who the hell asked him? My ancestors needed those snakes. They were sacred. Which, of course, is the whole point. Drive them out and replace them with Jesus and His Holy Mother. Demote the divine goddess Brigit to a saint. Well, that's what our holy mother whore the Church did all over the world. Why should Ireland be any different?"

"It was different here," Matthew said.

"What do you mean?" Colin said.

"As far as I know, there are no American cathedrals built on Native sacred sites."

"There are in Mexico," Colin said. "Central America. South America."

"That's the difference, isn't it?" Matthew said. "The Spanish conquered, exploited, and converted. But as brutal as that was, remnants of the culture survived. New culture was born. The intermarried Spaniard and Native created the modern Mexican. The English and the Dutch, however, came to North America with the ideal of religious freedom. And since they were not interested in converting the Indian, that left genocide. The only two postures of the colonizing force: either convert them or kill them."

"I hadn't thought of it that way," Colin said. "My God, you've painted a gloomy picture." He laughed. "No wonder Anna was so fond of you. Remember when you and I got together for a drink in Chicago?"

"I think that was a few months after the premiere of *Fertility Rites*. We had the premiere in Chicago, at this beautiful old movie palace, the Granada. Anna came in for the premiere. And the idiot projectionist never managed to get the film in proper focus."

"Anna told me about that," Colin said. He laughed. "Anna said that it was the tiniest bit out of focus and Matthew almost lost his mind."

"Tiniest bit!" Matthew said.

"But yeah. I think it was that year," Colon agreed. "Anna had a campaign going. 'You've got to meet Matthew,' she'd tell me. 'It's important that you meet Matthew.' And then I called her from Chicago. 'Have you met Matthew yet?' And when I told her I hadn't, she went into a flurry of long distance calls to make sure it happened."

Matthew remembered being slightly reluctant about meeting Colin. Despite Anna's enthusiasm about him, there was something in the way she described him that made Matthew distrust him.

"That trip to Chicago was the only time we met before the funeral, wasn't it?" Matthew said.

"I think so," Colin said. "But it feels like there was more."

Matthew nodded. "That's Anna. She talks so much about her friends. When I flew in for the funeral, I don't know how many people came up to me and said: 'Oh, you're Matthew, aren't you?' They somehow knew what I would look like from what she'd said about me."

"Well, you are something of a celebrity, too," Colin said.

"It's not like I'm an actor," Matthew said. "My face hasn't been on the screen."

"A few tabloids," Colin said, remembering the pain Matthew's pictures had caused Natalie.

"Well . . ." He shrugged. "Still, the people who know of me that way always say, 'Oh, you're Matthew Harken, aren't you?' You see? The last name is always part of it when it's a celebrity thing."

"I see," Colin said. "It's like a brand name."

"Exactly. A trademark." Matthew refilled their glasses. Half of his meal was still on his plate, but he was finished. Colin had finished eating nearly his whole meal.

"Have you called Natalie since you've been in town?" Colin asked.

"Not yet," Matthew said. He looked down at his plate. "I'm going to," he said. "But I haven't yet."

"She's doing well," Colin said. He looked at Matthew's face, trying to see what the other man was feeling.

"Good." Matthew wiped his lips with his napkin. "I was interested in what you said about that hot spot in the upper canyon," he said.

"Yes," Colin said, smiling and letting it go. "I was struck by that, too. I worked with this guru for a while. He said that in any room, in any space, there will be a spot in which a person will feel the most power. This was one of his earliest lessons. He was saying: You don't have to know how this works. You don't have to have faith. You just have to do it, and this is what happens. Cause and effect. In that way, it's kind of scientific. The effects are mystical. But you don't have to be mystical about it. You don't have to praise Jesus, or anything else.

"When I started into the upper canyon, despite my worry about Anna's condition, I noticed that fluctuation. In some places, I felt more powerful. And so I walked in the direction I felt it increasing, until I found the strongest spot I could find. I bet you could walk in there today and find that same spot."

"What causes it?" Matthew said.

"Does it matter?" Colin said. "All I know is when I put Anna there, it helped her get better."

"I had a dream about Anna last night," Matthew said. "It made me suspect her soul was lost. Helpless. *I* don't want to be like that. I don't want *her* to be like that."

Colin opened his mouth to speak, then closed it again. "Let's get out of here," he said at last. "I'll take you to my house."

CHAPTER 4

ANOTHER ADVENTURE

"I SEE WHEN ST. Patrick drove the snakes out of Ireland, this is where they came," Matthew said.

"I hadn't thought of that before," Colin said, following him into the room. "I guess maybe I have been reclaiming the heritage."

All around, hanging on Colin's walls, hanging from Colin's ceiling on strings, resting on Colin's furniture, were iconic snakes crafted from wood. There were straight snakes built from saplings. Twisted snakes made from branches of thorn trees. Fantastic snakes sporting two heads and two tails. Their tongues, eyes, teeth, and fangs were sometimes painted but more often were crafted of quartz, turquoise, jade, silver, copper, and other precious and semiprecious stones and metals.

Matthew noticed in the corner of the small living room, resting on a pedestal made from a sliced-off log, an alligator fashioned from a heavier branch. Colin's furniture looked old, probably purchased secondhand after his divorce. Matthew walked into the next room where a large work bench was covered with wood-working tools, trays filled with stones, wires and beads, small pots of paints, brushes, knives, strips of leather, and other paraphernalia. Finished and partially finished animals adorned the room.

"This is one of the things I do now," Colin said. "Being with Anna those two years really opened me up. You know, having HIV really doesn't bother me."

"How's that?" Matthew asked.

Colin thought for a moment, then turned through the other door of the workroom into the kitchen and put the kettle on the stove. The kitchen was another small room in Colin's small house, but it was brightly decorated. He'd painted the cabinets, walls, and ceilings in the bright pastels of Mexico. Brightly painted wood and clay lizards looked down from atop the cabinets. He'd spattered and drizzled many of the surfaces with a rainbow of paint colors. The appliances and fixtures were so old as to have aged beyond passé to a state of kitschy charm: the big old doublebasin porcelain sink with an ancient faucet thrust through its backsplash board; the round-shouldered old refrigerator; the old stove with its oven beside rather than beneath the black, cast-iron range. Hanging from hooks in the ceiling along the sides of the cabinet were bundles of dry herbs. Beneath the window, a large stone bowl full of sand sported an arrangement of small animal skulls, bones, and feathers.

"I like your kitchen," Matthew said.

Colin made a "spooky" movement with his arms and fingers. "It's the place of alchemy," he whispered. "I'm lucky to have found this place." He gestured around. "Everything here that was built in a factory has been here so long as to have completely forgotten that disadvantage. That's allowed everything here to reclaim the spirit of its own ancestry."

"Uh huh," Matthew said, noncommittally.

"You think I'm overstating it?" Colin asked. "Come here. Put your hands on the stove."

Matthew did as he was told. He felt the smooth porcelain of the oven under his right hand. He felt the cold, slightly rough cast iron of the range under his left.

"Now," Colin said. "Let's say you were going to cook some herbs that you'd gathered out in the desert. Let's say you'd been instructed to gather these particular herbs by an Indian medicine man—or maybe you'd seen these herbs in a dream. And now you were ready to cook them to make a tea that would invoke a healing spirit to enter your system. Now, what do you think is going to work better—steeping your herbs in a Teflon pan atop your shiny, new JennAir range—or steeping them in an ancient cast-iron kettle atop this venerable old stove? Which is more likely to coax that healing spirit out of the ether and into the tea?"

"No contest," Matthew said.

"All right," Colin said.

"You were saying something about not regretting HIV?"

"I don't. I'm not afraid of dying. I'm not that wild about feeling pain and being sick, of course," he said with a shrug. "But death does not frighten me. I'm convinced I'll have the time to finish whatever it is I came here to do." He raised a finger and gathered his thoughts.

"One of the nice things about having HIV," Colin said, giving him a look as if to say *Can you believe I'm saying this,* "is that I'm getting complete disability. A few years back, I took a state job that I didn't really want to take. I worked for two years, and now I'm taken care of. I get two thousand dollars a month plus medical coverage. I can do whatever I want. Nothing too extravagant, of course. But. It's like the Universe is taking care of me." Colin twisted the handles on the big old porcelain sink to stop the faucet from dripping.

"And you aren't worried about death," Matthew said.

"To me, death is like: *off we go, another adventure.* One of the things that Anna's death taught me is that all death is suicide. You pick your death. I hope you don't feel insulted by that. But that's what I believe. Whether it's disease, or accident, or a bullet through the head, you pick your own death. In some cases it's conscious. In most cases, it's unconscious. Anna made hers a very conscious choice. The little bitch," he said, with irritated affection. "But she has not stopped doing things here. I know there are a couple of really important things that she set up for me here since she died. And there is the process— whatever it might be—that she started. Or that she was a main agent of. And that process is still continuing. And maybe it will still continue after I'm dead. And after you're dead. I don't even know what it is. It might be connected with her journals. Maybe my job is to get them to you. And you will get them published. Or filmed. Or it might be something totally other."

"You say Anna was interested in publishing the journals?" Matthew said.

"She mentions a regret in her last journal entry. While she was waiting to die. She regretted that she didn't write one more book. And then she writes that she hopes the journals can stand as that book. But her writing was always really difficult for me to read."

"Because it was experimental?"

"Anna's writing scared the hell out of me because of who it said she was."

"What do you mean?"

"I don't know how to explain this. We should talk more about it after you've seen the journals."

Colin led him back into the workroom and pulled a carton out from under the worktable. Inside was a stack of twenty-six journals. Matthew pulled one out at random. It was a plain exercise book with sturdy, hard covers and 120 lined pages inside. Matthew flipped through at random. It gave him a certain thrill of heartsick recognition to see such an expanse of that familiar handwriting. He sat down on the floor next to the carton, pulled out a few more journals, and simply sat with his hands atop them, feeling the texture of the notebook covers under his fingers.

"Take your time reading them. If you want to talk, I'm available," Colin said. "If you want to drive out to Owl Creek Canyon, I'm with you. If you want to see where she killed herself, I'm your guide."

Matthew nodded and sat quietly for a moment longer, holding the small stack of journals. He felt the grief spreading through his body. To be holding this intimate artifact of his darling friend. Her private thoughts. First drafts of her stories and novels. The key, perhaps, to the inner psyche of this friend he'd loved so dearly.

Anna!

How he wished he could talk to her!

"How long are you staying in town?" Colin asked him.

"I don't know," Matthew said. "Whatever is required." He thought for a moment, then corrected himself. "Whatever is allowed."

Colin nodded.

Matthew put the handful of journals back in the carton with the rest. He got up and set the carton on Colin's worktable. "I think first I'd like to take these back to my room. To read. And walk. And tomorrow you could show me where she died."

CHAPTER 5

SOME KIND OF VOODOO

ALL TWENTY-SIX OF THE journals lay spread out in a sunburst pattern on the carpet in front of him. Matthew sat on a pillow on the floor. Then he brought over the other pillow. That didn't do the job, either. He'd sat too long at the restaurant with Colin. He sighed, got the heating pad out of his suitcase, and tucked it under his shirt and into the waistband of his pants. Sitting at the end of a plugged-in electric cord always felt weird to him, but the heat did help alleviate the pain in his back.

All this due to his prostate. For most of his life, the little walnut-shaped organ had managed to exist in its place, hidden away in the center of his groin, without his really being aware of its presence. Now his very existence was threatened.

The pain was from the metastatic lesions on his spine—the result of the cancer spreading from his prostate. He'd spent useless dozens of hours on chiropractic benches and massage tables, in whirlpool baths trying to alleviate his back pain before he finally got the right diagnosis. And then . . .

Colin's seeming peace of mind amazed him. Colin really didn't seem to mind having HIV. He didn't seem at all plagued by the self-doubts that tortured Matthew.

He wondered if Colin's equipoise would be shaken once HIV accelerated into AIDS.

He found once again that he liked Colin, although he didn't fully trust him. He remembered the first conversation that had alarmed him. Anna and he were on the phone, and she told him about discovering something weird in her apartment.

"Colin and I went away for a weekend," she told him. "Two days after we were back, I had the sense of something hovering near the ceiling in the dining room."

"Yeah?" Matthew said.

"I didn't know if it was my imagination, or what. But after a few days, I didn't like walking underneath it, so I was doing this odd thing of slinking around the edges of my dining room to avoid walking straight underneath it—and feeling very stupid about doing that, at the same time."

"So what was it?" Matthew asked.

"Well, listen. After about a week of walking around that spot, looking up at it like I might see something different in the air, feeling sheepish about my behavior, after a week of that, I'm sitting reading in the living room, with my attention fully on the book, when I get this sudden startled feeling that someone is walking toward me in my house. I look up, see nothing, and then this thing is sitting on top of me. It's like a ton of—what?—air. I don't know. It's like this huge weight, suddenly on me, but it has no form. Like instant depression. That really heavy feeling you have when you're really depressed. But without the emotion. And it has some kind of primitive intelligence. I couldn't move for the longest time."

"What do you mean by 'primitive intelligence'?" Matthew asked.

"I had this sense that it was aware. That it had deliberately come over and sat on me. It felt stupid to me. And it was male. Of course. What else would be big and dumb and sit on you?"

"Hey!" Matthew said.

"Well?" Anna insisted.

"A female gorilla."

"I've never been sat on by a female gorilla."

"So how long were you stuck there?" Matthew said.

"I'm not sure. I remember it more as a progression of emotions: Startled by its coming. Shocked as it sat on me. Realization that it was this same thing that I'd been avoiding in my dining room. Then that weight, that feeling that was like depression, without the sorrow. Fear. And as I struggled, panic. Then misery. Like a little, trapped child. I cried like that. Like a child. Miserable. And then the thing moved off.

Like the whole thing was an experiment. 'Let's sit on Anna and see what happens. Oh, she cries. Let's go back to the dining room ceiling.'"

"So it went right back where it was?"

"And stayed there. I told Colin about it. He's listening like he does. That intense expression. He has me describe my impressions of it. Twice. Then he says, 'Yeah, that's Craug. I brought him over to your place.'"

"Craug?"

Anna laughed. "I don't know where he came up with that name."

"He brought it over to your place?"

"He thought it would be good for me. Or something."

"Is it still there?"

"Yeah. Sometimes it goes away. Then it comes back."

"Where did it come from?"

"Colin said it had been following him around for some time. I don't know if it came from one of the canyons, or what."

"And he thought he'd just dump it on you?"

"Well, it's not like that, Matthew."

"I don't think this guy is good for you, Anna. I mean, you both believe there's a big dumb spirit in your apartment, and he says he put it there."

Anna sighed. "I can never get you to understand what we are doing," she said. "I'm not going to give it up."

Matthew remembered another conversation on the phone, earlier in Anna's relationship with Colin. She told him of putting a plant in her garden that Colin had given her.

"As I patted it into the ground, I thought, There: now I am his."

Her statement made alarm bells go off in Matthew's head.

"You know, that sounds like he's doing some kind of voodoo on you," he said. "Or you're doing it on yourself."

"Don't be ridiculous, Matthew. This is something that I want."

But that didn't reassure him. Above all, he feared that in Colin, Anna had fallen in love with her own death.

And what about him? What drove him to spend this time with Anna's journals—with trading stories with Colin? Was he falling in love with death, too?

Well, what should he be doing instead? Allow Dr. Young to rearrange his anatomy willy-nilly? Or perhaps he should work. But on what? A novel? Or no. Something to reach the maximum audience. A movie of the week. No! A miniseries! Nothing could match the aesthetic richness, the complexity of substance achieved by the contemporary television miniseries! He'd begin today. He could visualize the script already in his mind:

```
                The Story of My Disease

                    by Matthew Harken

FADE IN:

INTERIOR. A DOCTOR'S OFFICE. DAY.

Matthew is lying on his back on a
gynecologist's examination table. His legs
are up, and his feet are in the stirrups.
[Special Effects:] The doctor has his arm
shoved up Matthew's ass all the way to his
elbow. He pulls his arm out and strips off a
biceps-length latex glove and tosses it into
a garbage pail labeled "Infectious Waste."
The doctor wears thick glasses that distort
the look of his eyes.

                    DOCTOR
                (in a thick Viennese
                accent)
            It is vorse than I expected, I
            am afraid. I detect lesions on
            your spinal column all the way
            up to your clorox. The lavoris
            is highly enlarged. Your strudel
            shows a deep myopia of the clear-
            asil. And you have the genitalia
            of a man half your age. Unfortu-
            nately, they will have to go.

                    MATTHEW
            They have to go? What do you mean
            they have to go?
```

                    DOCTOR
We must perform an orchiectomy.
Your testes, or orchids, as they
were known to the ancient Greeks,
must be removed. Unfortunately
for you, testosterone is a poison. Ha! So you see, the women
were right all along!
          (He shakes his head in
          bemused glee.)

                    MATTHEW
What the hell are you talking
about?

                    DOCTOR
          (Shaking himself to sobriety)
Well, testosterone advances the
cancer of the prostate. If we
want to slow the cancer growth,
we have to halt testosterone production. We'll give you some
drugs, too, because your pituitary system will immediately
start taking up the slack for
your absent testes. And we'd better take out the prostate while
we're at it, since the cancer can
metastasize and spread from the
prostate.

                    MATTHEW
I thought you said it had already
spread from the prostate.

                    DOCTOR
Oh, it has! How do you think you
got all those lesions up your
spine?

                    MATTHEW
So if it has already spread, what
good is removing my prostate?

                    DOCTOR
Nothing whatsoever! At this
point, all scientific evidence
says you are incurable. But you
don't want to sit there and do
nothing, do you? Don't you want
to fight the disease?

                    MATTHEW
You mean you want me to spend the
rest of my life in the hospital,
undergoing painful and useless
treatments, just so I feel I am
doing something?

Matthew's producer enters the examination
room. He is a large, bald man with a Yiddish
accent and a cigar.

                    PRODUCER
Matty, Matty, whatya doing here,
bubbula? This is not your doctor.

The producer picks up the doctor, who is
now, magically, a full-size cardboard photo
cutout, and sets him to the side.

                    PRODUCER
Correct me if I'm wrong, bubby,
but your doctor only recommended
all that surgery before he found
out you are incurable. Am I
right? Don't answer. I know I'm
right. So why make this cockama-
mie villain out of him? And with
a Sigmund Freud accent, no less.

                    MATTHEW
          (Struggling to get his feet
          out of the stirrups and adjust
          his hospital gown. Defensive.)
I'm dramatizing the material
here, Morty.
                    (MORE)

MATTHEW (CON'T)
This is my first rough draft.
The draft I never even show
you. How did you get in here,
anyway?

PRODUCER
Magical realism! Special effects!
What difference does it make?
I'm here. I'm concerned. Listen.
This is your last project. Am I
right? This is the last thing
you'll ever produce! I want it to
be good for you. I want you to be
honest to your material.

MATTHEW
Wait a minute. Honest to my
material? You're the idiot who
tried to get me to put a car
chase into *Fertility Rites*. You
told me a movie without a car
chase is like a Chinese meal
without rice. And that a Chinese
meal without rice is like a
pretty girl with just one eye.

PRODUCER
        (Genuinely surprised. His
        voice is feminine. He has
        lost his accent.)
I said that?

MATTHEW
You aren't Morty.

PRODUCER
        (Trying to regain his accent
        and composure.)
Bubbula. It's me. Morty.

MATTHEW
You've never called me Bubbula.
What the hell is this?

The Producer gives a sigh of resignation. He reaches under his chin and peels up a perfectly applied latex mask. He shakes out his short blond hair and reveals his real identity as Matthew's ex-wife, Patty.

> PATTY
> All right, so you caught me.

> MATTHEW
> Patty, what are you doing here?

> PATTY
> I just can't stand it. Here you are, and you still haven't learned to face your emotions.

> MATTHEW
> What are you talking about? I'm writing a movie here. And you aren't supposed to be in it.

> PATTY
> You can't possibly spend your last months writing a disease-of-the-week miniseries. The only way this could make sense is if you write something real. Otherwise, spend your time reading your friend's journals. Or meditating. Or anything. You always hated writing junk.

Lighting change. Patty fades away. Doctor Galesberg enters, carrying film of a bone scan. An intelligent man in his early fifties, he looks serious and sympathetic. He sits down across from Matthew and sets the film on the table. He pauses, finding the right words.

> DOCTOR GALESBERG
> Matthew, I've taken you off the surgical schedule.

                    MATTHEW
Why?

                    DOCTOR GALESBERG
The new tests have come in. I'm
afraid surgery won't do you any
good.

                    MATTHEW
What do you mean?

                    DOCTOR GALESBERG
                    (Rises and clips the bone
                    scan into an X-ray display.
                    He indicates areas on the
                    film.)
You see these bright areas. These
are lesions on your spine. The
tumors in your prostate metas-
tasized and spread far from the
original site. There is really
nothing we can do to stop them
any more.

The Doctor steps away from the X-ray.
Matthew continues looking at it a while,
dumbly, and then turns away. He looks at
the doctor.

                    DOCTOR GALESBERG
I'm sorry, Matthew. I think
you should get a second opinion,
for your own peace of mind.
But this does appear very clear
to me. What I can do is pre-
scribe a program of combination
hormonal therapy. This will help
debulk the prostate and slow the
growth. You could have some good
time ahead of you. But we cannot stop it. We can only slow it
down.

CUT TO:

INTERIOR. SMALL HOSPITAL RESTROOM. DAY.

Matthew stands at the toilet in a tiny hospital restroom that contains one toilet, a trash can, a sink, and a shelf. Matthew has a stunned look on his face. He pees into the toilet. The urine stream comes out weakly, in dribs and drabs, due to his swollen prostate. Finishing his pee is a long process that is especially frustrating to him today. He jerks and twists slightly, trying to push all the liquid out. He shakes his penis to get the last drops out, and then stands holding it. Looking down at it. He holds his penis in both hands, and the sorrow comes over him. He drops to his knees and holds his penis. He cradles his penis in his hands as though it were a sick child. He tilts his head to one side in pity for the poor, doomed thing. For his poor, ruined health. He begins to weep for himself. The weeping turns to sobbing, and he curls up on the floor in misery, sobbing like the last abandoned child on earth.

FADE OUT.

CHAPTER 6

LITTLE ANNA

MATTHEW SAT WITH HIS heating pad on the floor. All twenty-six of the journals still lay spread out in a sunburst pattern on the carpet in front of him.

This isn't about me, he thought. *I came here because I wanted to* know.

He picked up the final volume and turned a few pages back from where the paper turned smooth and white and untouched by the hand that would never hold a pen again. *October 1*, it said. A few days before she killed herself.

This was what he had to read first.

October 1 –
It's over. No longer can I pretend Colin will be a man. He is left, and I am left with the canyons. I have the water to talk to me. The light on the rocks. But no one. Beauty and catastrophe. We are over.
October 2 –
All my words are gone, absorbed into the canyon. I talked and talked, and watched my tears drunk in by the rock. My voice, too, is held there. They save my words, like fossils, hidden inside. All the things I said to him. To Mommy and Daddy. And Natalie. The rocks took it all in. They understood. The stream did not care. Kept moving. And when I stepped away from the water, the sound of the quiet frightened me, and I fell on the rocks and sobbed. Abandoned. No one. Only the lizards there, who like to steal things. One lizard stopped to listen.

And so I left. I hitchhiked to Fillmore in three rides. The woman who wanted a new car. The man who built log houses. And after the restaurant, the oil trucker. All of them good people. And so I stayed in Fillmore overnight, and now I have a bus ticket home.

Lilly says I can see now. I'm not the child anymore. I can see danger and so I am not helpless. I can transform fear into protection, and my screams and dreams will subside.

I cannot trust Colin because he lies and admits that he lies. He says he is gay. He meets with gay men. He tells me about it sometimes, for reasons known only to him, and other times he keeps it secret. And he says I am the only one he has ever loved. But he carries me with him everywhere he goes, and this is kidnapping. And the sex he has with others that I do not want is rape. In my imagination, that is the way it feels. And so how can I recover if this is the way he inflicts his love?

I could die. I could so easily die.

And yet the woman in her old Buick was funny. For a moment I actually laughed. And the canyon after my tears, it glowed, so beautiful, so shattered.

You are like a noise inside my head, he said to me. Sometimes you are like a worm, eating my brain.

How could I ever, again?

I hear the rocks speak back to me across the distance. My words flow in their cracks. I feel them through my feet. Live and wait, they tell me. For one is coming. One is coming who knows how to walk the hills, and there we will meet. Hold faith with us, and wait.

October 3 –

Where can this end? Can I end it? I feel the weight come on me like a drug. The misery. I could pull the lower teeth out of my head.

How can I stop this thing? I long to end it. I long to run the hose through my window and breathe deep my death. Gone. Gone from this place. From these betrayals.

But who will I betray? Whose pain will I cause? Will that be the chain? For whom will my death be unbearable?

I can't take anymore. The memories come on me and I cannot live. I cannot sleep. And when I sleep, the dreams are worse. I wake up with them hauling me. I wake up with them tearing my clothes. I wake up with them in me, stabbing with their bodies. Oh please, no more!

Who believes this? Do I believe it? Five men did it. I remember. When I was just a Little Girl. And now my throat swells. Is it from the poison of their semen? Or is it from holding my mouth shut—my mind shut—all those years? Now the veins stand out on my neck. The pressure. Like a balloon, and it rises into my head.

Can I possibly continue? And why? This is not life. Why not wipe the slate clean?

I try to return to a time that was safe. Sitting in Grandpa Vassily's lap. His love was not for his satisfaction. I could stay in his comfortable lap. Live in his comfortable lap. Safe. Not like you, John Jarrett. You stuck your finger in there because you liked the smell of it. And you, Kenny, that my mother loved so much. Such a helpful boy. She did not know of our love. What could it mean to me, four years old, and you, overwhelmed by newly arrived hormones? I just wanted to hug you, Kenny, but what did you do? For you it was a moment. Or moments, stolen moments. For me, the rest of my life.

As for Leon Silver, you took me in the garage. Didn't anyone watch me as I played? Or maybe that was your job. The perpetrator trusted to protect. You showed me the popsicle, and shot your semen in my throat, the throat that would never speak of it for decades, the throat that was swollen shut, because you held me to the garage floor, and I asked, no, no, and pushed you away, and you came again on my legs.

So this is what the trusted men did. The ones my mother could trust. Men and boy.

What about the others? My muscles repeat the actions of what they did to me. Sodomy is a word that claws the back of my throat. I don't even have to say it aloud. Just think and it crushes my windpipe. Lifelong constipation is the guard against letting them back in. How could it have happened? How was I not injured and sent to a hospital? Am I making this up? Who were these strangers?

No peace. No life. Not with this awakening me always, always creeping around the corners.

The voice of the rock rises around me, willing to take me away. Can I let myself go?

I cannot think now why suicide is condemned. It is only me. No one else. And my soul will live on.

I cannot deny people will be hurt. I regret their tears. But I have no children. No husband. No one will starve because I am not there. And my pain is so great. I cannot prevent their pain, and I cannot stand my own.

And so I am resolved. I will drive my car away. I will bring the hose that I have owned for two years. I will shut out the air with rage—with _rags_—I will shut out the air with rags. And I will ask forgiveness, and pray that my pain dies with me, and the slate be wiped clean. I shall become a voice in the wind, whispering, whispering, until the next go-round . . .

Later. 11:35 on my digital car clock:

Did I assume—do people assume—that suicide is a hysterical act. I am calm. Though I do feel annoyed at how everyone will react. Why can't they see it as I now see: an adventure. A journey. It is the right thing.

I do feel bad for my friends. I feel bad that I won't be there to comfort them, that I am not leaving a note for each of them, but there is no time. I realize now I have been planning this act for decades. Who among them has not heard me say the word suicide? And now the time has come, and I am glad. I only hope I am still glad on the other side . . .

What would I say to everyone? How can people really understand? My mother has never understood me, but then she has been dead ever since Esther died, really.

I love you, Daddy. We will meet again. I'm sorry I could not go on like this. I cannot stand the nightmares anymore. _It is not your fault._ I was sexually abused by five men. Or maybe I am making that up. But the nightmares won't stop, and I have been constipated my whole life, and I am afraid of sex.

When I walked out of the canyon, I walked away from my hope. Once we dreamed of a place of healing there. But that was not to be. Instead it was the place of abandoning. That was when I knew. Little girl was crushed, but the other voice was hard. Get on with it. How many times have those words rung in my mind?

Get on with it.

And now I am at peace. How could this be wrong, when I have been planning it for so long?

Natalie, I love you, too. What you said almost kept me from this. I am sorry this will hurt you. Don't forget our conversations and the love that passed between our eyes. I wish I could have stopped this, but I couldn't. I hope you will understand, but I'm afraid you won't. You still have hope, and that is the blinder of the living. I left mine behind, and now I see clearly. It is time to end this.

I worried so about my debts. Now that's all done with. Sorry, Visa, and everyone. I meant to pay you back.

Please spread my ashes in the canyons. Those were the places I loved above all.

When I sat in the canyon where you left me, it was the contrast that shocked me: my tears and misery and all that beauty. How could both those things strike me so at the same time? And that lizard's eye as he talked to me.

Be strong. Especially you with families. I did love you. Do love you. Never doubt.

I took a sleeping pill, and I feel it coming on. I'll sleep soon. My throat hurts. And my eyes burn. Maybe we'll meet again. Some of us. Goodbye. Goodbye.

Matthew closed the journal on his lap. He put his face in his hands and felt he would sob, but the sob didn't quite come, and that made him feel worse. The sorrow invaded his chest like physical pain. Like the dull ache after choking on chlorine water at the swimming pool. Like pain from inhaling caustic fumes. *Carbon monoxide.*

My throat hurts, she wrote. *And my eyes burn.*

Don't do it! he wanted to cry. Don't do it! But he was already years too late.

Five men did it. I remember.

How could that be? It shocked him that Anna had written so much about this idea of sexual abuse. The last time Matthew had talked to Anna, she was troubled by memories of her sister Esther's death. Colin and Natalie had both told him she had recalled memories of abuse in her last months of therapy before she died, but it had never made the impact on him that her journal did. In conversations, it had sounded like one more thing among many.

He hated the thought that Anna's might be a "victim" story. She'd never led her life like a victim. She'd been impatient with people who were weak or unfocused. She'd been the most driven person he'd known.

Victims.

He remembered when he told his ex-wife about his prostate and about the diagnosis. He remembered Patty's face: The blankness first. Then the shock. "You're a cancer victim," she'd said.

"Stop that," he'd said back. The word offended him.

Victims and addicts. Matthew was sick of their stories. America was becoming a nation of whining victims, and the democracy was going to hell because no one would look up out of their own sorry lives long enough to see that the body politic was being plundered and the children were being betrayed.

Please don't let that be Anna's story, he prayed.
He flipped to an earlier page in the journal.

September 9 –
Kenny in my fantasy again. I made us come together, as grown-ups. This is the way to do it. Lovely. What Kenny did didn't stunt my sexual growth. Maybe it helped. I am happy for the sex life I have, and can have. My fantasies. Anna as a gay man. Or straight. Better gay. Nothing but men, both of us.

September 10 –
I could not break myself out of sleep yesterday. Dream after dream, groggy on the couch, and then asleep again and more dreams. It was Little Anna at two years old, with John Jarrett and his fingers in me. And that horrible man, and me holding my sphincter tight, trying to keep him from getting in. This is why I can never shit. Forever holding it against him, keeping him out. It's a miracle I could do it with Colin. What a breakthrough. And what a surprise pleasure. I could never have done that with any other man.

Even though it is impossible for us now, I know I could never have come this far without him. I see the remnants of our magic in the vase of cherry blossoms he gave me. He has turned his back on everything to travel in the world of men. He will not return, and this is best, for to oscillate between men and women would be intolerable for him. He will not return to me or to any other woman. At least that is what I think today.

That's all right. I need a man who does not stir up so much. And now, in any case, Little Anna is my greatest concern. Her fears and memories overwhelm me. She will not leave me in peace until I give her her day. Colin and I both have miles to go. And Little Anna is impatient.

September 12 –
The Lunatics Asylum. Came back here last night. Oddly, it's the sanest place for me right now. Everywhere else is crazy. Here, there is progress. Emma will be leaving soon. Probably by the end of the month. And Christy, too. She still feels the pull of the drugs. But she has been out of lockdown for weeks.

And there is still the question of men. How does it happen, even here, where I have the jigsaw puzzle of my memories? Gorgeous Eric draws me despite his fumbling tongue. He cannot match Colin for conversation. Little Anna wants to crawl into the pillows with him, but why does that make me moist? I could never love him. Just sex. Empty sex. Like Colin, probably, with his men. Sex without all the flows of magnetism and magic that bind us. Sex like what most of the world settles for.

I dreamed of Colin again last night. He is deep in my psyche, but this does not prove anything. I cannot allow him to cause me so much pain. And he cannot see any way to stop. I long to have sex with him, but why? He is an addictive poison.

Little Anna wants to talk but I can't hear her clearly now. When will she stop talking? When will the story be out? Lilly says we must purge what is hidden, but we don't want to linger on it. I wish I knew when this would be done.

Kenny came into my meditation today. He rocked me in the rocking chair. I was so little. Huge pillows filled the room. A fortress of pillows. Warm and soft. And then I was in the pillows. It was nice until I realized he was gone. And then the emptiness...

September 13 –

Hypnotherapy with Lilly. Little Anna screaming. I had to stop her. To speak for her. To tell Lilly what had happened to her. And then, of course, to say I'd made it up. And then, no, it was the truth, my whole body shaking. How can I stand this? Why would I make this up when it's so painful? It's not an illness. It's because of <u>what happened</u>. It could not stay buried forever. And even before—was there ever a time when I didn't know that <u>something</u> was wrong. Impossible.

I cannot have anything less than honesty. For myself. Within myself. With everyone else. That is what makes this moment in the Asylum so important. Words are not spoken to pass the time. Outside, words maintain the distance. They are buffers to keep everyone wrapped in their own sheets of cotton batting. Protected. But alone. I won't accept that anymore. I insist on the honesty.

But then I must have room, too. Privacy. Colin says we could build cabins in the canyons. People flow in to work with us. To heal. To teach. To create. My own cabin. My very own. With a space for therapy? Or is that in another cabin? A communal space. Yes. Better. And a space for Colin and I alone.

This dream does not die. Even when I have rejected the thought of Colin and I, I picture us together again, in our dream of the canyon. How can he be so wrong and so right?

The pains in my chest again. It happens always before more memories emerge. The steam before the volcano. It's that bastard, Leon Silver. He tried to fuck me. He helped freeze that piece of Little Anna, lurking in the shadows of my psyche. And yet I cannot fully believe it happened. No one else would believe. But my fears are so real. Esther's death, I always knew, was not the answer. It didn't happen to me, and no one told me the details. It could not have created this life-long fear of men. Nor could it in any way account for my constipation.

September 14 –

How can I stand this anymore? The trembling. I feel I could vomit my life. The nightmares. The fantasies. Memories? I don't know anymore. I don't know.

I was raped.

I fantasized it.

My parents want me home for a visit. How can I possibly?

How can I pretend to be normal? I would tear the curtains down. I would pee on the floor while they watched. There is no life.

An end to it. That's all I want. Is that what you want? Do you want to be the ones to find the body? I didn't ask you to bring me into this life. Where were you when this all happened? Ah, but you say it didn't happen. It never happened. You never left me unprotected. And I agree. But then suddenly I see, as if through a glass, darkly, and suddenly I know it _did_ happen, and then the glass shatters and there is nothing there. Nothing at all. And how, dear Mamma, can I live with nothing at all?

But this is a question you will never answer. Because you left the room five minutes ago, and I'm talking to myself. Well, that's fitting. That's what crazy people do, right? But then why does it rise through my body? Why do my hips gyrate? Why does my sphincter pucker? Why do I gag and I cannot stop? Why do these things happen that I can't even imitate when the memory is not on me? Why do their faces haunt my dreams?

September 16 –

Colin came yesterday and helped me crawl through hell. I called him. I could feel it coming yesterday. The steam before the volcano. This was the worst eruption of all. I came out of the nightmare screaming, because—it makes me shake all the harder, even to write this—this time they'd got it in me. All the sphincter clutching my little body could do could not prevent them from fucking me up the ass. I am so angry and so horrified and so frightened all at the same time. But I had to do it. I brought it out with Colin listening. I brought out the largest piece of the nightmare. There were *three men, and they tied my hands and feet and covered my mouth with a large piece of tape. Duct tape, I think. That's why I still get a rash around my mouth sometimes. And they did it to me. The pain of it was overwhelming. I could have been split in two. Was I three years old? Four? My shrieks echo in my ears even now.*

Colin believes it. He does not doubt my memory. That's a comfort. I'm so grateful he was there for that.

However, I still feel Little Anna here. Could there possibly be more? The prospect frightens me so. How could this have happened and nobody knew? Did they know? Did <u>she</u> know and cover it up? No. I can't think that. And children do come home with bruises, and who thinks anything of it?

The place where they took me becomes ever more real. It is as though something in me fears they can take me back there again. I would rather die. Much rather.

Much rather.

But I do feel more peaceful, oddly, even after saying that.

Matthew closed the book for a moment. Was he understanding this correctly? Was she recalling these memories on her own, without her psychiatrist?

He turned back a few pages. The entry of September 13. Yes, there she is working with Lilly, apparently. But this last one is with Colin. And if she was doing it with Colin, she must have been doing it on her own, as well. He imagined her daily meditations, crawling with remembered (or imagined) rapists. And then her private, internal analysis, as though she were interpreting *Finnegan's Wake*. No, it would not be like Anna to wait for the protection of the psychiatrist's couch for professional guidance. She would untangle her own psychosis, like it was a home repair project.

September 18 –

Memory creates a groove. These memories, until they are fully out, are like cars in the deep snow. They spin their wheels and move forward a little, then rock back. And then spin their wheels and move a little more. When they come all the way out, then I'll be able to drive on and leave all this pain behind. But for now, my mind keeps replaying what I have recalled. And this means I get raped, over and over. I wake in the morning, and it all rushes back in. The men, their cruel desires, and I am choking and clutching and my body ties up in knots.

I am in the process of drinking a half-gallon of water, hoping it will wash through my intestines and allow me to shit. I will drink another half gallon if I need it. And once it washes through me, I'll actively search the memories again, and tape it so I can listen later. This time maybe I can get out of the snow.

Of course, I am taking sick leave from work. I must purge this. Must.

What I know is that even as I purge it, I will not lose my magic. That is mine to own. That has been sorely paid for. I did not ask for it, but it is mine. I take my power from the rock of the canyon, from the overwhelming cliffs. She came to me in a dream. The witch. Her face frighteningly beautiful. She made me like her. She selected me because of what they had done. It changed the structure of my atoms, so the magic could take hold, could be mine.

I long for the pain to end. Soon I will start the tape recorder. I feel the steam build, so I know it's not over. Little Anna has not yet told her full story.

She is, Matthew thought. *She is hypnotizing herself, tape recording the event, alone, and then reliving it.* He wondered if Lilly had known, had possibly *approved* of Anna's undertaking. Obviously, Colin had known, but he was no psychologist. Was there no one to insert a thread of caution? *And Anna, please,* he thought, *if the witch is as real as the rapists, what does that tell you about all of them?*

September 20 –
I felt good all day. Colin called and told me he loved me. That doesn't change what he told me before. He says all that is still true. He is gay now, that truth is out for him. He would not date another woman, would not be with another woman if it weren't for me. Loving men feels normal to him now. Somehow he sees me as being different from other women. I do, too, I suppose, but I'm not sure. I don't want the normal marriage, based on shopping and owning, and neither does he. We've both had that. It's deadening.

I must not allow myself to become crazy wondering if he is with a man when he is not with me. He, too, is a soul-seeker. Exploring in the world of men satisfies something deep and damaged in him. I understand this.

He says he loves me above all else, and I believe this. I am honored by his choice of me because he chooses with great integrity. He could more easily have suppressed his gay side. We both know that. If I can stay steadfast in my faith in our love and offer him all the latitude for discovery that he allows me, we can rise above everything.

September 22 –

There is a hateful voice that flows through my head. A feminine voice that sounds like my mother. She hates Colin and transforms his every word to lies. She preaches convention. She kills security.

She knows we are not good enough. Not loveable. She swims in the pain in my chest. Swirls in the tension that chokes my throat. She kills me slowly by lack of oxygen. She shuts out the light of the sun.

All night I was awakened by dreams. Rape. Abduction. I awoke, surrounded by spirits. The mother voice sat down with the rapists and joined them.

Colin, too, begins to call up his memories. He amazes me with his bravery. His willingness to face everything. Men frighten him, too. And so now he goes toward his fear? He remembers his beatings. His father gave him bruises on his ass. This is why he dreams of being loved there. Compensation for brutality. And yet the thought frightens and attracts him simultaneously. No wonder. How many men have died horrible deaths from receiving the wrong sperm up the ass?

September 23 –

I hear the voice of the rock, murmuring. I can't hear what it says. But I know it hears everything I think. Everything I say.

Colin is looking into the property. Who owns it. How we might buy it. Can we do this thing? We could help so many, bring so many together. I can see it in my mind: rooms for meditation, therapy, places to create altars, to work magic, to draw pictures based in the psyche. Colin needs to curb his drinking, though. It's not bad now, but it could sap him.

September 24 –

I dreamt of Daddy and woke with a smile. I was little and he played with me. Lifted me high in the air. Tickled me. Rolled me around. His touch is lovely. Not abuse. Not misplaced sex. This is happy touch and it makes me laugh. But the smile fades as I come back to myself. This is not enough anymore. I want him to see who I am today. I want him to comfort me in my pain. Or, at the least, to see that my pain truly does exist.

September 25 –
Another dream. My parents argue about what to make for dinner. It starts with my mother saying, "Anna would like this," and I am happy, thinking she will make something I like. But then I see my father's face. "What?" he says. And I realize it is not something I like, it's something she likes, and she doesn't care if I get something I like or not. And then no one is there, and I'm searching for something to eat, and all I can find are HoHos, and she knows I hate stuff like that. Why did she even bother to have me? I get so angry thinking about this, I lay in bed shaking.

I am in Colin's bed (in reality, not in the dream. In the dream, Colin, too, rejected me). It is good to have him here. He comforts me. But he is not on solid ground, either. He still is out of a job, and can't choose from among what is available. We are both afraid now, and don't know which way to go. I need to go back to sleep. At least I am glad to be in Colin's bed.

September 26 –
I wake up fighting something off. I don't know what. Something from a dream, a memory, or some spirit in the room. This makes me shudder. I can't get comfortable, even now, as I write this. My elbow hurts. I wrenched it in the battle coming out of my sleep.

I want to work on one more memory. The witch. My entry into magic. This one I'll do with Colin, not Lilly. I want to know where she took me. Where is the lair of the witch? If I can find this place, perhaps there is more power...

September 28 –
How is it that I have written so little about being happy? I was remembering having dinner with Bob and his son Tommy. I was at their house, and starving, and Bob offered to make cheese enchiladas. The novelty of being served made me so happy. And Bob enjoyed my pleasure. It smelled so good cooking. I found, too, now that Little Anna is loose in my psyche, even though the memories are so painful, I can relate better and have more fun with children. We went for a walk, all three of us, and created games. Tommy pretended one of the houses we passed had an evil wizard inside, and we had to creep by. He could have a conversation with any tree. We made up songs on the spot, and laughed, and suddenly I could understand what it would be like to have a family.

Still, I know I could not have children. I am not meant for that. But the connection grows. I am happy to be able to be friends with my friends' children.

I will not forget that moment when we were all laughing. A perfect moment. Perfect comfort.

But even this memory does not chase off my anxiety. Colin says he loves me. He will always love me. But also he says he is gay. I cannot reconcile this. Our love is strong. Our conversations have no match. Our lovemaking. Our support of one another. Even the way we fight. And Colin shares his feelings in a way that most men are incapable. This is central to his gayness, even more than his sex preference. Still, I cannot relax.

Later –

I've taken another step, as Lilly would say. I've retrieved another part of myself.

As I meditated, my pelvis began to move. Like demon possession. But no. It was the man, when he'd got me where they were taking me. His hands guided the movement. Don't worry, he said. And this stunned me. But the other one stuck it in my mouth and made me choke, and I shrieked in pain from what the third man did. Did the one come in my mouth? I'd never seen this before. Just the choking, and I didn't know why. But now I see they worked together. And then the one who'd been in my mouth didn't sodomize me. He came again on my legs. The excitement of such a pretty child. Don't worry, he told me. Don't worry. They used such kind voices and I cried and wailed and begged. Don't worry. So kind. Please, don't, I begged.

Matthew felt himself wanting to object. It made him so uncomfortable to read the sessions she did by herself. It was so obsessive. And it struck him as dangerous. Why hadn't she looked for guidance?

But then again, *I've taken another step, as Lilly would say.* Apparently Lilly was encouraging this "memory recall," in her office, at least. The thought of it made Matthew's heart sink.

September 29 –

I am vibrating today, but it's good. Anticipation. Last night I could have done the memory work, but I didn't. Will I do it today, or rest? I suppose there is no rush. I feel like I'm starting my life over, and that feels good, for a change.

The excitement of a new career. A new vocation, really, more than career. I am convinced now I <u>can</u> be a therapist. I have the talent. And I've had a taste of the action, at the Asylum, in group and in individual talk with the others. They show their gratitude for what comes out in our conversations. They encourage me. And I am so grateful for that, I can stand straighter and breathe deeper. I have already been <u>useful</u>. This excites me and gives me strength for my own struggle.

I don't know whether this strength is mine to keep. Will something come in to knock me down again? No one can know these things. Once you have learned what a fragile thing the human mind is, you don't regain your confidence completely. Maybe it just takes time. But I do love how therapy (as a therapist) requires so much that is <u>me</u>. The love of people, of talk, of analysis, of empathy. This is all me, and I will be able to expand those talents.

I will have to work out my issues. There is so much more to do. I have so much anger that I have not yet expressed. I try to look at my anger, its causes, but it blurs. I wonder what is blocking my focus, and I think of my mother.

I remember photographs of when she was young and beautiful. Before she had children. Before there was me and Esther. I loved looking at those pictures. Is it strange to say I found my mother arousing? Her dark eyes made you yearn. They inspired love. Her skin so smooth. Her eyes like velvet, dark and wide. Feline eyes. Like an animal, a doe. But I cannot think of her long without also feeling hate. She resisted my love. She refused to recover from Esther's death. She gave all her love to Esther, who was no better than me. But my hate is only a mask to my pain. What I desire is to share the love that a daughter and mother deserve. But Esther stands between us.

Lilly says love tangles us like cords of steel. It can give us strength or choke us to death. The cords cannot be removed. If we arrange them where they need to be, they can help carry us through life. How do I love my mother without strangling myself to death?

October 1 –

It's over. No longer can I pretend Colin will be a man. He is left, and I am left with the canyons. I have the water to talk to me. The light on the rocks. But no one. Beauty and catastrophe. We are over.

Matthew was startled by the entry. He hadn't realized he was so close to the end already. October first. He reread a little more:

October 2 –

All my words are gone, absorbed into the canyon. I talked and talked, and watched my tears drunk in by the rock...

He skipped down, with that horrible sinking feeling again. But he couldn't stop reading.

October 3 –
Where can this end? Can I end it? I feel the weight come on me like a drug. . . .

His eye skipped down the page, catching a paragraph and skipping on:

Who believes this? Do I believe it? Five men did it. I remember. . .
I shall become a voice in the wind, whispering, whispering, until the next go-round. . . .
And now the time has come, and I am glad. I only hope I am still glad on the other side. . . .
My throat hurts. And my eyes burn. Maybe we'll meet again. Some of us. Goodbye. Goodbye.

"Shit," Matthew said aloud. He closed the book. His insides felt as dry as the rock in the desert. He longed to hold her in his arms, to bring her back, impossibly, to life. He stood up, walked a few steps, confused, and then lay face down on the hotel bed and wept for the loss of his old friend.

CHAPTER 7

APPARENT JOY

Anna and Matthew met in a fiction-writing program in graduate school. There they studied literary structures and prayed at the shrines of the ancestors: Homer, Sophocles, Shakespeare, Tolstoy, Dostoyevsky, and their beloved Hemingway and Fitzgerald, who came to Paris in the twenties and thirties.

Anna's drive and discipline were staggering. Each day she exercised, meditated, and wrote, without fail. She would allow no interruption of her routines, and would be rude to anyone who called on her at home without warning.

Matthew's passion for the work was no less intense but was certainly more chaotic. He could be in turns lazy and driven. He could write with incredible concentration one day and daydream through the next. But when he wrote, he wrote very fast. And nothing mattered to him more.

This difference between the two was more pronounced in how they prepared for Europe. In studying French in graduate school, Anna had taken the most intensive courses. In the summer between graduate school and Paris, she went to a French "total immersion" program, where they were not allowed to speak or read English for the entire eight weeks.

Matthew, on the other hand, spent the summer before Paris painting houses during the day and tending bar at night, to earn as much money as he could. His goal was to spend a year in Europe, working on his first novel. But it was not just work that he had in mind. He wanted enough money so that he could go to clubs and restaurants to enjoy the music, fine foods, and wines.

When Matthew arrived in Paris, Anna already had a parttime job that included a room as part of the pay. She spent two mornings per week shopping, doing light cleaning, and providing companionship to an elderly lady in one of the suburbs just outside the Paris city limits. Matthew had nowhere to live and no command of the language, but he had Anna.

How sweet that reunion thousands of miles from home! Graduate school had made them the most intimate of friends, sharing their passions, dreams, and nightmares—even a brief love affair.

Anna had to sneak him past the concierge of her building to get him up to her room.

She was so happy then. Or perhaps happiness was not the right word, for it was not a giddy joy that Matthew associated with that time. It was intensity. Discovery. Paris, in some ways, was a puzzle to be solved.

Anna had done the advance work on that, having arrived a month earlier than Matthew, and she was delighted to share her discoveries. Her room in the building of Madame Duck (the affectionate nickname for her old lady employer, Madame Canarde) was on the top floor. A *chambre de bonne*—a maid's room. All the old Parisian buildings were topped with a floor of these *chambres de bonnes*. They were the simplest of rooms. Some equipped with a cold water sink, others not. The shared toilet was down the hall. No hot water anywhere. No bath or shower. Usually no heat.

Anna's room had a single bed, a small table and chair, an electric heater, and a double window that opened in. Outside was the mountain range of tiled roofs, spired with chimneys. Matthew stood at the window and appreciated the view.

"This is wonderful," he said.

"And it's all mine," she said, with apparent joy. "We have to find you a room like this. Look." She squeezed past him, turned a brass knob at the center of the windows, and swung them open. The chilly air of autumn swirled into the room. "The Parisian refrigerator," she said, with pleasure. She indicated a vegetable crate she'd attached to the railing at the window ledge. She lifted the lid of the crate, hinged to the box by two wires. The inside was lined with aluminum foil. It contained a few pieces of fruit, a small glass jar of yogurt, some cheese and butter, and two eggs.

"There are markets everywhere here," she said. "Wonderful markets. I have to show you. And you just buy what you want for the day. What needs refrigeration, you put in the crate. As you see, crates are the basic element of furnishing here." She closed the window and gestured to her room. An arrangement of crates stood stacked on their sides with the openings out, along the wall under the window. The bottom crates had flaps of material covering the openings. Anna lifted the flaps to show her neatly stacked clothing. "The walk-in closet," she said. She gestured to the next row up, holding her small collection of books, notebooks, and magazines. "The library." She indicated the crates containing such items as a small skillet and sauce pan, can opener, spatula, a few cleaned-out yogurt jars for glassware. "The kitchen," she said. "Once you have a room, you have to get one of *these*." She pulled out a little blue camp stove.

"You can use this indoors?" he asked, taking it from her. It had a small cone-shaped burner at the top, bordered by four metal arms that made a platform on which to set the cooking pan. Beneath the burner was a bracket that held a half-liter canister of cooking gas.

"Yes. I think the gas is propane. It's something that burns cleanly. And you can get the canisters everywhere because so many people use them. I'm thinking of getting a second one, so I have two burners."

"Luxury," Matthew said. "The call of the bourgeois."

"Dinner parties," Anna said simply.

There was a pleasure in the inconvenience. In the simplicity and austerity. There was a monkishness to their time in Paris that they frankly adored. Hemingway's *A Moveable Feast*, and even more so, Orwell's *Down and Out in Paris and London*, were books they read and traded amongst themselves like basic operating manuals to the life they were living: the daily struggle with language. The inconvenience of having to heat water for bathing. The daily shopping for food. The taking of temporary jobs, he laboring with a remodeling contractor, she typing, to earn those extra francs to extend their time. All of this slowed life to its basics and focused them on the essentials.

Was that the source of happiness?

CHAPTER 8

THE TWINS

"I've been trying to think about my sister Esther," Anna said. "But every time I think about her, I realize that I hate her. And then I can't do anything."

Matthew and Anna sat in a café across the river from Notre Dame, near the Shakespeare and Company bookstore, in Paris. It was late at night, and the two were talking over glasses of red Bordeaux.

"Isn't Esther dead?" Matthew said.

"She died when we were four." Anna looked out the window into the night. Her normally rosy cheeks were flushed a deep red. She'd pulled her wavy black hair into a tight ponytail at her neck, from which it coiled and plunged down to the middle of her back. She felt abstracted and annoyed.

"I'd thought about writing her story before." She looked back at Matthew. "Her story... my story. Whatever," she said, shrugging and bobbing her head from side to side. "But I've never been able to do it."

Matthew finished his wine and poured another.

"When I was back in Chicago visiting my parents before I flew over here, I talked to my great uncle. He's in an old people's home," Anna said. "I found out they'd lied to me."

"Who?"

"My parents. Of course, I can understand why they did at first. I didn't need to know, when I was five years old, that my twin had been raped before she was killed. My grandfather saw it happen. It's part of what drove him mad."

"No. You wouldn't have needed to know that at five."

Anna stared fixedly out the window into the Paris night. The lights on the facade of Notre Dame shone from across the river. She felt deeply annoyed—and that surprised her. Her annoyance overshadowed any other emotion. Sometimes she could not figure where her own emotions were coming from. It was as though she felt that her sister's rape and murder had been, above all, an inconvenience to her.

"I told my mother last year that I was trying to write a story about Esther, and that I was having trouble. I asked her to tell me things. About Esther and me before she died. About what happened afterwards. She would never tell me anything. 'I can't think about it,' she'd say. 'I put it out of my mind.' She always made comments like it was a bad idea for me to write about Esther. 'People don't want to read about things like that. Why don't you write a love story, like *The Thorn Birds*?'"

Matthew laughed, and Anna laughed in spite of herself. "I think you *should* write *The Thorn Birds*," he said. "Forget this avant-garde nonsense you write. Set your sights higher! Imagine: *A Return to the Valley of the Thorn Birds* by Anna Toyevsky."

"*A la Recherche du Thorn Birds Perdu*," Anna countered.

"*For Whom the Thorn Birds Toll*," Matthew said.

"*Across the River and into the Thorn Birds*," she said, beginning to laugh.

"*The Old Man and the Thorn Birds*." Matthew slapped the table.

"*Go Down, Thorn Birds*."

"*The Sound and the Thorn Birds*!"

"*The Naked and the Thorn Birds*!" Anna shouted. "*Tender are the Thorn Birds*."

"*The Taming of the Thorn Birds*," Matthew stuttered.

"*The Thorn Birds Karamozov*."

"*Thorn Birds from the Underground*," Matthew shouted.

Anna hesitated, laughing.

"Aarrr!" Matthew made the sound of a buzzer. "We're sorry, Ms. Toyevsky, but you've gone over the three-second limit. You win a copy of our *Thorn Birds* home game. And better luck next time."

Anna laughed with him and took a sip of her wine. She swirled the wine in her mouth and tasted its richness. It was wonderful. The bottle of Bordeaux was one of Matthew's calculated splurges. She'd helped him find a place to live rent-free so he could spend his money on the great foods and wines of France.

"*Merde alors*, you are such a shit," she complained, still laughing. "I was still one *Thorn Bird* ahead of you!"

Matthew raised his glass and winked at a French couple who'd looked over to see what the laughter was about. The couple looked away. Matthew chuckled again.

"But that's the thing about my mother," Anna continued, the annoyance returning as soon as the laugher subsided. "She always withholds. She sees me struggling, but she won't tell me anything."

"It's probably still painful for her."

"Matthew, it's twenty years ago, for God's sake. We aren't talking about a fresh wound. She could talk about this. It might actually bring a little closeness to our relationship. God forbid. She wouldn't want that. After Esther died, she would never risk being close to me. I remember her when I was little. She was a real mother. You know? A mother who would hug and kiss you. Never again."

Anna looked back out the window into the night. Outside, a young man rode his moped up onto the sidewalk and turned off the little engine. He walked in, and Anna smelled faint ribbons of gasoline fumes.

She loved how this young Frenchman looked, his cigarette screwed into the corner of his mouth. He had a cruel-looking mouth. That was a necessity for her. A man had to look like he had the capability of cruelty. He could never act on it, of course, but he had to have that look. And she loved the way French men smoked, how they held their cigarettes, how they exhaled in that haughty way, even though she hated smoking.

She looked back at Matthew, whom she loved. He did not have the cruel mouth. He was beautiful in his way, but not in the way that attracted her. They had been lovers for only a very short time before they realized it was not for them. He was more like a brother. A dear friend. A confidant. She loved his stillness. His ability to listen. His ability to appreciate. And she loved him for his talent, too.

"When she died, it could just as easily have been me," Anna continued. "Esther and I looked exactly alike. People could not tell us apart." She looked intently into Matthew's eyes. "I knew it when she was dead," she said. "Because we were twins. We had that link. We had a made-up language together before we learned to speak English, and we knew what each other was saying. So when she died, I knew it before anyone else. I knew she'd been suffering. I felt it the moment she died, but I didn't know what it meant. I mean, I knew *something* had happened. Something enormous had changed. But I didn't know what it was.

"I went to my parents, and I asked them what had happened. They were still the same. Worried. Calling the police. They didn't know. They kept calming me, as much as they could, saying we had to trust the police. They would get Esther back. Sometimes they would argue between themselves about hiring a detective. About increasing the reward they'd offered.

"Then they got the phone call. What had changed outside, that I had felt when Esther died, changed inside the house, too. They got quiet and disturbed. It was a sickening feeling. I asked what happened. They wouldn't talk to me. My aunt and uncle were at the apartment. Or they came to the apartment. I can't remember." She shook her head, then stopped, feeling startled. "No! I *do* remember. My parents had to leave the apartment, and my aunt and uncle came over to take care of me." She paused, and a look of baffled discovery overtook her face. "My parents must have had to go identify the body. I never realized that before. That's where they went. And I asked my aunt and uncle. What is going on? They wouldn't tell me anything, either. They just looked at me with that expression like dead fish have, lying on the ice chips at the market. I didn't find out until I heard the word *funeral*. My parents came back, and they were all talking in whispers. When I'd come in the room they'd shut up and send me back to watch TV, until finally I heard my father say the word funeral. I screamed out: "*Whose funeral?*" I screamed it at them. My father took me into my bedroom— into Esther-and-my bedroom—and finally told me Esther was dead."

Anna looked back out the window into the night. It felt like a dream to her, what she was remembering, like a distant dream coming back to her in unexpected fragments. She continued talking, into the darkness: "That's the thing I hate them for. That they wouldn't tell me. And my mother still won't tell me what I want to know."

"Did you ask your dad? When you wanted to write the story, did you ask your dad about what happened?"

"No. I love my dad. But. I don't know. He's so hopeless. I just don't want to ask him." Anna looked into Matthew's eyes. "When he told me Esther was dead, he was so pitiful. He apologized for not telling me. He said he thought Mommy had told me. He said Esther was dead. He said they had to arrange a funeral for her. And that she would never be coming home to us. He started crying. The only thing I really understood was that Esther would never be coming home. And I hated it that my daddy was crying and was so miserable. I took his hand and I told him, 'It's all right, daddy. I'll be Esther now. Nobody will tell the difference.' But that just made him cry harder.

Anna sat looking toward Notre Dame. She did not see the great cathedral, bathed in its nighttime spotlights. She saw her family's living room as it looked when she was a child. She saw the adults moving around like zombies. She felt the crush of her loneliness, like long bandages wrapped tightly around her ribs. She smelled the stale odor of her father's cigars and whiskey.

"After that, hardly anyone talked. My mother came to help me get ready for the wake. I don't know. A few days later I guess. And when she said we had to get dressed for Esther's wake, I said no. I told her it's Anna's wake. I'm going to be Esther from now on. Daddy and I decided.

"She got so angry. She yelled at me that I couldn't replace Esther." Anna felt a childish panic clench at her stomach, and she gulped the air she breathed. "That was a stupid idea, she told me. That's when I realized she thought Esther had been better than me—which surprised me, because I always thought Esther and I were the same. I thought I could replace Esther easily. I was just as smart as Esther. Just as pretty. Just as fast a runner. Just as good a bicycle rider. There was nothing better about Esther. That's when I started to be mad at Esther."

"You think she really thought that?"

"I've always suspected that she liked Esther better. I don't know why. But that's what it felt like."

"Right," Matthew said. He reached across the table and cupped his hand on Anna's cheek tenderly. She leaned into it gratefully, the way a cat embraces a human touch. "So what happened then?" he said.

"At the wake, I told my cousin about the plan: Daddy and I had decided to pretend it was Anna who was dead and I would be Esther from then on, but my mother had said no. My cousin said he thought it would have easily worked. He was my cousin, and he'd never been able to tell us apart. He'd known us our whole lives."

"I think you should write *that* story," Matthew suggested. "That story fits your style better than the abduction story anyway, I think. It's not like you're a true crime writer."

"The story doesn't have to be written like true crime," Anna said. "Any story can be written in any style. She was my twin and she had so little life. The least I can do is to give her a little more."

"Well, you don't have to give her your own," he said, feeling uneasy about Anna doing this project.

"Don't be an idiot, Matthew. I'm talking about writing a story. I'm talking about how my parents stonewalled me from the day Esther was abducted. I don't have to live Esther's life for her. But I do need to write her story. But how can I do that when the main witnesses won't speak?"

CHAPTER 9

THE VOICES

ANNA REMAINED STALLED ON her story about Esther, but she worked steadily at her first novel, *The Labyrinth of Stone*, and read the chapters at open mic readings at the two English-language bookstores in Paris. Matthew did not get down to work until after he'd lost his first place to live. The room had been a *chambre de bonne*—a maid's room—that Rebecca had found for him just off the *Champs de Mars*, the park dominated by the Eiffel Tower. Rebecca was another of their friends from graduate school who had traveled to Europe at the same time. She was staying with an American family that lived in an apartment on the third floor of the building. The maid's room belonged to them. Rebecca took Matthew to meet the mother of the family and plead his case.

The mother wore her short, dyed-black hair tight to her head, like a helmet. When forced to think, she batted her mascara-coated eyelashes at ever-increasing velocity.

"I am reluctant to have anyone stay up there," she said through a blur of flashing lids. "We got complaints about my children going up there to smoke marijuana. So I confiscated the keys, and I vowed that the room would remain locked."

She was no match for Rebecca, who persuaded her in spontaneous iambic pentameter to have mercy on young Matthew. When Rebecca locked her in her owl-like gaze, the woman's eyelids fluttered like wounded butterflies and she relented, telling Matthew he could use the *chambre de bonne* for a few days until he found something else.

Matthew loved the room. It was small, a six-by-nine–foot rectangle, but it had one of the finest views in Paris. Matthew's window was in a tiny dormer that thrust itself from the building's ornate roof. He could look down onto the street, seven floors below, and see the sparse traffic on this residential avenue. Looking over the building across the street, he could see a dazzling collection of the city's monuments. The Eiffel Tower, just two blocks away, dominated the view. To the right was the *École Militaire*, anchoring the south end of the *Champs de Mars*. To the left was the *Palais de Chaillot*, just across the river. Beyond he could see the *Arc de Triomphe*, the *Panthéon* in front of him, and, if the day was exceptionally clear, the domes of *Sacré Coeur* atop Montmartre in far distance.

The room itself had only a table the size of a student desk, a chair, and a small mattress on the floor for furnishings. There was no heat, and the sink and toilet were down the hall, to be shared with everyone else who lived in the *chambres de bonnes*, though many of the rooms were empty or used for storage closets. However, his room had a working fireplace, and it felt to Matthew like the most romantic place he'd ever stayed.

Rebecca and Anna helped him shop for the necessities: a basin for washing both dishes and himself. A butane *Camping Gaz* stove for cooking, yogurt in six-ounce glass containers that could be reused as drinking glasses. A skillet and an all-purpose sauce pan.

They taught him the essential words he needed for buying groceries in the market. It was easy to shop the Parisian markets because they were accustomed to selling in the small quantities that a single person without a refrigerator would want.

He'd arrived in Paris in mid-October, so it was already cool there. Each day part of his time at the markets was spent gathering discarded crates. He smashed all but one under foot and stuffed the shattered wood into the solid one to carry back to his room.

In the mornings he would heat water for bathing and then build a fire in the fireplace. He had to leave the window slightly ajar, or the room would fill with smoke. Then, while the fire was blazing, he stripped off his clothes, quickly washed himself down, dried, and got into clean clothes. He had to be fast because crate wood burned up quickly, and with the window open, the room cooled off again in a hurry. By the time the last smoke rose from the ashes and he was able to close the window again, the room was thoroughly chilled. But Matthew was also thoroughly awake, clean, and ready for a new day. To have a fast, warm sponge bath by the fireside was a wonderful ritual for beginning the day, and he loved it.

Matthew's immersion in Parisian expatriate literary society did not begin until he was ejected from his idyllic retreat. After he'd had four weeks of learning Paris as a live-in tourist, Matthew's benefactress was aghast to discover he was still occupying the *chambre* and, eyes all aflutter, insisted he move out immediately. And so he presented himself to George Whitman, the owner of Shakespeare and Company bookstore.

George grudgingly allowed Matthew to take up residence in return for an hour of labor per day, doing tasks such as cleaning, setting up the outdoor display of used books, and later, when George discovered Matthew was adept with tools, doing repairs, fixing electrical wiring, and building shelves.

George Whitman was an ill-tempered, unacknowledged saint of literature. His wild, gray hair stuck out at several angles. His skin was heavily lined, his eyes were lively, and it was almost impossible to guess what age he might be. His face looked old, but his body was limber. His mustache and goatee made him look something like a mountain goat. His voice was a reedier version of Lionel Barrymore.

The reigning deity of George Whitman's pantheon was Silvia Beach, the proprietress of the original Shakespeare and Company bookstore, which had been located some blocks away from George's store. Silvia had been the friend of many of the great writers of the first half of the century. When no one else would do so, she published Joyce's *Ulysses*, and thus transcended all other booksellers in the history of the world.

George's great disappointment and the reason for his ill temper arose from the fact that he was offering the opportunity of a lifetime, and the right people were not coming to partake. It was a paradise! A young writer could live beneath George's roof indefinitely (or until George threw him out), rent-free. Free access to the upstairs library, a huge collection of books that were not for sale, which George called the *Free University of Paris*. Life in the heart of the city, directly across the river from Notre Dame cathedral. Books! Conversation! Time to write! The company of St. George of the *Quartier Latin*!

But who came? Young adventurers seeking to string out their travel money for as long as possible. Buskers who played their guitars and sang on the street for tossed coins. And the occasional aspiring writer who did everything necessary for a great career in letters except actually sit down to put words to paper.

Ah, and it ate at George! Sometimes he contemplated throwing them all out and hiring someone to do the work his guests did. God knows they were incompetent. Some even had the incredible bad taste to shoplift his books.

So when he heard the tapping of the portable typewriter coming from the back room of the upstairs library, and he looked in to see Matthew there, Matthew with his eyes looking up from the keyboard like a startled deer, George felt no great surge of hope. Probably Matthew was writing a letter home to his mother.

And George had been right. As beautiful as it was, Paris was a frustration to Matthew in the beginning.

He had never planned on staying long in France. His first stop in Europe had been England, where he'd visited a friend and bought himself a vintage Triumph Spitfire for five hundred dollars. Its ragtop looked as though it had been eaten away by giant moths and repaired haphazardly with clear plastic and duct tape. But with the top down, it was a handsome, though unreliable, little sports car. Anna promised to travel with him to Spain, but as the weeks went by, it became clear she was in no hurry to go. Matthew loved zooming around Paris, gleefully honking his horn and getting lost. Driving in the city was impossible, of course. The streets were mostly one-way, and they wound in every direction, so whenever he headed for one place, he ended up somewhere quite other. He'd pull over several times to examine his maps, and when he finally gave up on getting where he intended to go, he'd stop into some chance-found bistro for a bite to eat. He had some of his happiest meals in this way.

The rest of the time, the car sat in a parking spot near Shakespeare and Company with some of his things stored in the trunk. Rather than his escape vehicle to Spain, it was more of a joy ride and mobile closet.

And then his real life in Paris began!

On this particular night, there'd been an open reading at Shakespeare and Company. Now a resident, Matthew felt a little proprietary about the readings, although he had not yet started to read at them himself. He made sure the main room of the upstairs library, where the readings were held, was ready. This did not amount to much, since even the main room was not very large, and only two or three chairs could be dragged in to set along the bookshelf-lined walls. Then it was just a matter of straightening the green velvet bedspread on the bed that doubled as a couch. And make sure there was nothing embarrassing in the tiny water closet off the main room.

George had heard enough bad poetry at open readings over the years that he no longer attended them, but this night Mbella Kolelo came in to read, and George stuck his head in long enough to hear a few of Kolelo's pieces.

Kolelo did not read. He *recited*. His eyes focused on the middle distance, off in the air, and he spoke his poetry from his memory and his heart.

His poetry spoke of his loves and his life and passions. It spoke from the soul of a man separated from his homeland, who loved and left his native people and nation, and loved and struggled with his adopted country and its people.

Kolelo was from Cameroon, and he spoke with a beautiful African accent. He was a short, stocky man with a very dark complexion. His hair hung in dreadlocks to his shoulders. And although he was only five foot eight, he was a man of stature, for he carried himself with great masculine self-assuredness and dignity. One could see that this was a man who knew himself—who he was and what his mission on this earth had to be. His eyes were forthright and powerful and generous. When he looked into someone else's eyes, he expected to find the soul of that person shining forth as did his own. And that confidence emboldened the people who surrounded him.

It was good to be seen by Kolelo.

Matthew and Anna and Rebecca sat crowded together on the wide shelf at the sill of the room's single window. Behind them, across the river, spotlights illuminated Notre Dame in the Parisian night. Inside, Kolelo spoke his words to rapt listeners all around. People were pressed together, sitting on the bed. They sat on the chairs and on the floor, and they stood along the walls. They stood in the galley kitchen outside the main room, and they smoked, and they listened.

As the reading ended and people began crowding out of the little library, Anna squeezed Matthew's knee. "We should get jobs and support him, don't you think?" she said. "He deserves that. I would make him my guru."

Matthew smiled, and they followed the group out as the room cleared and the people headed outside.

"You know what he does to make money?" Anna said. "He cuts silhouettes of tourists. That's his living. Cutting paper images, and selling them to tourists. Does that seem to you what a genius ought to be doing? And you should see his room," she continued. "I visited him last week. He made me some tea. He's got an electric burner, a couple of kitchen things, and then everything else is books and papers. He owns nothing else. But so many books! His room is so small that he has to stack them on his bed, and he sleeps on the floor!"

About a dozen people from the reading, friends and acquaintances, gathered in a café a few doors away. As always, Kolelo had a large zippered satchel that he carried with its strap across his forehead, the satchel resting against his back. He stashed it beneath the table where they sat. He wore a heavy sweater of a dense weave. In each of its two front pockets, he'd stuffed four or five paperback books.

"Why do you always carry so much stuff?" Matthew asked him as they sat down.

Kolelo leaned in toward Matthew. "My visa ran out two years ago," he said quietly. "If the French police caught me, they would not give me time to go to my room. I would be deported immediately. It has happened to friends that I have known. So anything that is of value to me, I must carry always. My manuscripts. Letters. Important books." He shrugged his acceptance. "For me, this is the price of living in Paris."

"So are you carrying the manuscripts from your novels?" Matthew asked.

"No," Kolelo said largely, leaning back into his chair. "I sold those to a University. This is something you must remember, Matthew. Always save the manuscripts. And make them nice and messy. Plenty of changes and corrections. They love this mess. I received more money for the manuscripts than I made from selling the books."

The waiter came and took their order: various glasses of wine, a sandwich for someone. Matthew ordered his usual beer, and Kolelo his small black coffee. He didn't actually like coffee. He would only occasionally sniff it for the aroma, which he did enjoy. He ordered it because a *café noir* could be had for a couple of francs, the cheapest thing on the menu, and as long as the coffee remained, he could stay in the restaurant, conversing, writing, and staying warm. He never drank it.

"If you do a book set in Paris, Matthew," Kolelo said, "here is something I learned from my editor. People want to feel something like tourists." He smiled and shrugged his shoulders at the logic of this. "So you must put in the scenery, even if it does not seem essential. Work it in to the story. Even things like the Metro stations the characters use. This is what they like."

Then someone interrupted Kolelo with a question in French, and he responded in a torrent of words that were utterly incomprehensible to Matthew.

The crowd at the café included long-time Paris residents as well as the English-speaking crowd from Shakespeare and Company. And that meant that the conversation careened back and forth between French and English, giving Matthew only intermittent understanding of what was going on.

Later in the evening, Kolelo caught Matthew looking distractedly into the night out the café window.

"What is it, Matthew?" he asked. "Something is troubling you."

Matthew was surprised by the question. He looked into Kolelo's serious, dark eyes and saw the genuine concern there. It was as though Kolelo had been reading his thoughts.

"I feel as though I am in limbo here," Matthew said. Kolelo shifted his chair to face Matthew directly, as the conversation at the rest of the table continued on without them. "I hadn't been planning on staying this long in Paris," Matthew continued. "Anna and I were going on to Spain, but she isn't ready. I want to settle in somewhere and get back to work on my novel. I'm having fun, but I feel like I'm wasting my time. It bothers me."

"Yes," Kolelo said. "I felt this from you all night. You are ill at ease. It is because you are not listening. It is the time for you."

"What do you mean?" he said.

"There are certain times that your voices will speak to you," Kolelo said. "And when they do, it is your job to listen. This is why you are a writer. If you do not do this, then you are failing your responsibility."

Kolelo raised his coffee cup to his nose for a moment and then set it back down, watching Matthew's face all the while.

"You take it seriously, I think, your intention to be a writer?"

"I do," Matthew said.

"I believe you," Kolelo said. "But this *listening* is something you have not learned yet, and of all things, this is the most important thing to learn. Your voices are a gift. They do not belong to you. They are a gift to you. And if you do not listen when they speak, you disgrace them. You disgrace yourself. If you continue to ignore them when they speak, they will discontinue speaking to you, and then you will be the most worthless thing of all: a writer without voices. For then you will have nothing of worth to say.

"There have been times when I heard my voices begin to speak and I did not have a place to live," he continued. "I did not even wait to find a roof to cover my head. I sat down in an alley and began to write. And that is where I worked and slept for many days. *That* is what is required of us. That most of all, before anything else. Because if we do not listen and work when our voices speak, nothing else we do matters, because we have betrayed our most primary responsibility."

"How do you know when your voices are speaking to you?" Matthew asked.

Kolelo threw back his head and laughed. He smiled and pointed his finger at Matthew. Matthew started to smile even before he knew what the joke was.

"You cannot get away by pretending to be a blockhead, Matthew. You have been miserable! You know you need to write. This is your voices making the demand. It is simple. But don't wait to the point of misery. There is only so much patience your voices will afford."

Matthew felt the absolute rightness of every word Kolelo said. He thanked Kolelo and, for the first time in his life, he left a café without finishing his beer. He loved the conversation and the drink and the night, and he was always in the last group to go. But this night he left while the whole crowd was still there.

Matthew went back to the upstairs library and got George's portable typewriter out of the closet. As he walked to the back room of the library, he felt a wave of appreciation for the place wash over him. He stopped in the main room of the library where the evening's reading had been, and he looked around. He felt nurtured by the rich colors of the worn hardcover spines on the shelves covering every available inch of wall, the aged green velvet spread that covered the bed, the threadbare Persian carpet that covered the ancient ceramic tile floor. He remembered the sound of Kolelo's voice in the crowded room and the look in Kolelo's poetry-possessed eyes.

It all buoyed him up, and he felt charged with energy.

Matthew took the typewriter and set it up on the desk in the back room. This room was dominated by the desk, which sat in the center, beneath a dusty glass chandelier hanging from the ceiling. There were two small beds in this room that slid partially beneath the bookshelves on the walls. They had to be pulled out right to the edge of the desk to sleep in them.

Matthew set to work immediately, to get something done before those beds' occupants would return and want to go to sleep. He looked over where he had left off when he'd last worked on his book, checked over the notes of how he planned to continue the chapter he was on, and plunged in.

It was exhilarating! Matthew had never worked so quickly! He banged on the keys with force, as though he were whipping a horse to make it gallop. His concentration was intense, and he immersed himself totally in the story, typing at the limits of his ability, barely able to keep up with the speed of his thoughts.

As he wrote, he did not notice his fellow Shakespeareans looking into the backroom door occasionally. He did not notice George wandering past the doorway and watching him, George with his incessant mutterings and throat-clearings that signaled the Shakespeareans from afar of his approach—and made most of them nervous. He did not even notice the stray tourist who wandered his way into the library by mistake, who took Matthew's photo from the door, as though he were a Shakespeare and Company exhibit: *The Expatriate Writer at Work*.

And then Matthew stopped. He stacked his typed pages.

As always, he made sure not to write himself all the way out. That was an old Hemingway trick. Leave something to write for the next day. Something to help you get your pace and get moving.

He looked over what he had done.

Ten pages! It was more than he had ever done before in a single sitting. Ten typed pages! He was euphoric! He was *hearing the voices*, as Kolelo put it, more clearly than he had ever heard them before, and he felt confident that he would continue the next day and the next.

He felt suddenly at home. He was finally doing what he'd come to Europe to do.

The next morning Matthew walked to the spot where he'd left his car. He wanted to get his camera out of the trunk.

He looked up and down the street.

No car.

He looked again until he was absolutely certain.

The car was gone.

Matthew began to laugh. He shook his head. He thought over the events of the last twenty-four hours. If this had happened earlier, he would have been devastated. He'd wanted so much to leave, to go to Spain, to find a place and get on with the writing of his book. But as it was, the loss of his car put the exclamation point on the events of the night before. He laughed again and felt delighted with the trick that had been played upon him.

There was nothing he *really* needed in that car. He could get the traveler's checks replaced. He'd get the insurance money for the vehicle. And now he knew he was meant to stay here, in Paris, and work. His voices had been telling him. Kolelo had told him. And the car thieves had told him. They'd all gotten together to teach him this wonderful lesson.

In the following days and weeks, the energy Matthew found was everywhere. It descended with force on the writers of Matthew's circle. Anna, Matthew, and Rebecca began writing and then reading their new work at one or the other of the bookstore readings every week. Anna and Matthew read chapters of their novels in serial. Rebecca worked through a series of strong new poems. And there were others, the friends they had made there—and the travelers who came through, surprised to find this enthusiasm and energy, having stumbled upon one of the readings by accident. These travelers would read a piece of their own, and then come along to share in the conversation and drink at the cafés and to wish that they, too, could stay on in Paris to live in this energy and camaraderie. It had become for these friends precisely the Paris of which young American writers dream. Exciting. Productive. A love affair of words and place and companions. A fantasy fulfilled.

Matthew wrote a good portion of his first novel in Paris. He published it a year later. His friends loved it, as did one or two of the critics, but it sold poorly and made him very little money. He wrote a screenplay next, and set himself onto a lucrative career.

CHAPTER 10

ANGELS ON HER SHOULDER

AFTER THE CREDITS ROLLED, Matthew hit the remote control, and the mural rolled back down, covering the large screen in his living room wall so that one would never have guessed it was there.

"You do have the best gadgets," Anna said.

Matthew smiled. He opened the patio doors to let in the night sea air and the sound of the surf. It was eight years since they had been together in Paris.

"That *felt* so different from the version of *Angels on Her Shoulder* that played in the theatres," Anna said.

"You just saw the 'director's cut,'" Matthew said. "That's what I gave the producers when I finished the editing. Some wine?"

"Please," Anna said. She followed him through the Spanish arch to the counter that divided the dining room from the kitchen. The dining room was old-style California Spanish, and the kitchen (really one big room together) was high-tech stainless steel and copper. But somehow they went together well.

Matthew loved his kitchen. He enjoyed cooking for his friends. He liked to see them gathered at the counter, drinking his wine, as he made the finishing touches on a meal.

"I have a little treat for us," he said, taking a package of fine Gorgonzola cheese from the refrigerator and putting it on the counter with crackers. "Just the thing to go with this," he said, pulling an aged Italian Barolo from his wine rack.

"They bought your script. They hired you to direct it. Why would they then change the movie after you'd finished making it?" Anna said. "The version you gave them is so much richer."

Matthew shrugged, uncorked the Barolo, and took down two goblets from the rack over the counter. "You know. They thought it was too long, so they cut twenty minutes. And they took out most of the narrative voice-over." It had been over a year since *Angels on Her Shoulder* had been released. But this was the first time Anna had seen Matthew's original version. He poured the wine and handed her one of the goblets.

"Thanks," she said. "I still don't understand how you could stand that. If someone messed around with my work, I'd kill them."

"I *wanted* to kill one of them. One of them in particular. I could picture his fat face turning red as I choked him to death. But I didn't. And the good thing about that is that I'm not in jail and he's still alive and he still controls a lot of money and he's going to hire me again."

"And then he'll mess up your movie again."

Matthew came around the counter and sat at one of the stools next to her.

"When I published my first novel, that was great. I got along well with my editor. I traveled around the country giving readings. I knew people had to be reading it, but you are always at this huge distance from your audience. You don't get to see them actually reading your book.

"Then *Better Strangers* was made. All sorts of people were telling me what to do, and that was annoying. But this whole army of actors, tech people, cameramen, set designers, carpenters—everything—all jumped into action. And none of that would have happened if I hadn't written the script. It was really fun. *I* had put all that in motion. And the film did well. Some parts of it pissed me off. But because it did well, I got a better deal on *Fertility Rites*. I got a piece of the *gross*. And *Fertility Rites* did well, and I got to direct *Angels*. And now I can afford all this," he said, gesturing to the room around him. "Even better than that," he said, pointing at her, "I get to make more films. And I'll get to work with better people, better actors, and better cinematographers."

"But Matthew," Anna protested. "*Angels on Her Shoulder* didn't turn out the way you wanted, either. I think this is aging you. Your eyes look older, and you didn't have all that gray back when we were in Paris. If you never get to do your work the way you want it—when does the frustration stop?"

"The released version of *Angels* wasn't bad," he said. "Life is always going to be frustrating." He laughed. "But then again, so what?"

Chapter 11

SHE'D BEEN RAPED

FRUSTRATING, Anna thought. *No one understands this.*

She looked up at the ceiling. The fluorescent lights were humming overhead. She hated fluorescent lights. All bad things were discussed and examined under fluorescent lights. She glanced at the faces around the circle, six other patients and Lilly, her psychiatrist. Five women and two men, plus Anna, all pasty under the fluorescent lights. Some slouching in their molded plastic chairs. Some listening. Others just waiting their turn. It was yet another group therapy session in the Lunatic Asylum. While Matthew's career continued to flourish, Anna's mental health declined.

"She came in to my office complaining of a stomachache," Anna said, resuming her story. She stopped and looked down at the linoleum tiles at her feet. Lilly took advantage of her pause.

"Does everyone know Anna has worked as a school nurse for many years?"

Anna looked up. She looked around at the others in the circle.

Does everyone know that Anna studied nursing in a sick homage to her family of doctors? she said in her mind.

Does everyone know Anna's father is a doctor? That Anna's grandfather was a doctor?

Does everyone realize what a waste of my time it has been to be a school nurse?

"Go ahead, Anna," Lilly said.

The child. Remember the child. "She was a fifth grader," Anna continued. "A pretty girl." Anna shook her head sadly. *Such a pretty little girl.* "I could see something dark, high up on her arms. She sat down on the cot in my office, and she looked nervous. She'd come in complaining of a stomachache. She had a short-sleeve blouse on. That's how I could see high up on her arms."

She remembered how the girl looked, nervous under the fluorescent lights. *Such a pretty little girl.*

"Children get stomachaches like adults get headaches," Anna volunteered. "It's the same thing. I could see she was uneasy. 'What's that on your arms?' I asked her. She pulled at the ends of her blouse sleeves like she was tugging down the hem of a too-short skirt. She told me it was nothing. But I could see it made her nervous. 'Let me see,' I said. And I gently lifted her hand away from one arm, then the other. Her sleeves just barely hid fresh purple bruises that encircled her upper arms. 'Who did this?' I asked her. 'Nobody *did* it,' she said. 'I just fell down, or something.' It was such a pathetic little lie, with that tag on it. '*or something.*'

"I closed the door to give us some privacy, and I spoke to her gently. 'I know you didn't fall down to get bruised like this,' I told her. 'I fell down the stairs,' she said. 'I fell and I rolled and I hit both arms tumbling down the stairs.' 'Did you get hurt anywhere else?' I asked her.

"She got this really sad, lost expression on her face, looking up at me. She nodded her head slowly.

"'Where?' I asked her. She just kept looking me right in the eyes with that lost expression. Slowly she began to lower her hand down and rested it at the base of her abdomen. Tears began to roll out of her eyes, and her breathing speeded up a little, but she didn't sob. It was an uncanny sight, this sad but nearly calm girl, with the tears flowing down from her eyes, one after the other.

"'May I take a look at it?' I asked her. She didn't say yes. She didn't say no. She just kept looking at me with that forlorn expression, hoping, probably, that I wouldn't hurt her, too. But I was going to hurt her; I knew that. I had no choice. As a school nurse, I was required to report evidence of abuse, and that was going to bring her a whole new kind of pain, though it would also bring some kind of relief. One would hope.

"I took her shoulders and gently helped her lay back on the cot. She acquiesced in a kind of horrible anticipation.

"And this is the very worst thing: As I lifted up her little plaid skirt, and even more as I edged down the elastic of her panties, I was hoping that I would discover more evidence. I was hoping that I would see that she'd been raped. As though if she'd been raped, that would lift my burden. For a moment, my heart actually rose when I saw the bruise next to her vagina. The elation passed instantly, and I felt disgusted with myself and angry at whoever had done this to her."

Anna settled into her chair and looked down at her lap. After it seemed clear she'd finished speaking, Lilly said: "You reported what you'd seen?"

"Oh, yes, we went through all that," Anna said.

"So you carried through, and you did what you could to stop the abuse. That's a good thing."

"Yes. But her father ended up going to prison. And that was not a good thing."

"People who abuse their children deserve to go to prison," Lilly said, with a trace of heat.

"I never said he abused the girl. Why do people jump to that assumption? The father loved his daughter," Anna said, her voice rising. "But he was divorced. It was the mother's boyfriend who'd done it. That's who she was afraid of. The father went to prison because he killed the boyfriend."

Anna sat looking at her hands clutched together in her lap. Another of the women in the circle began to hum, then stopped.

"Is there something more you wanted to say about the father, Anna?" Lilly asked.

Anna looked straight at Lilly. She cocked her head slightly, like a little bird would do. "If my father had killed somebody," she said. "I would have brought him things to eat in prison. I would have brought him very good things to eat."

CHAPTER 12

BE THERE

O N THE PHONE, ANNA sounded like she'd awakened from a deep sleep. When she began weeping, Matthew realized he was hearing the fatigue of deep sorrow.

"What's the matter, sweetheart?" he asked.

"Nothing," she said.

"Come on," he said. "Tell me what's the problem."

"It's stupid," she said. "I don't even know what it is." Anna wept harder. "Hang on," she said.

At the other end of the line, Anna set down the phone and walked over to the living room couch, where she'd left the tissue box. Used tissues littered the floor where she'd dropped them. She blew her nose twice and wiped her eyes. How was she supposed to talk to Matthew like this?

She felt the things in the room around her, moving in. She hated that feeling. Why wouldn't they leave her alone?

She took the tiny rake and raked the sand in her Zen garden atop the old bureau that stood against the living room wall. The garden stood in a terra-cotta basin about the size of a large dinner plate or serving platter. Anna had filled the basin with sand and placed rocks in it in a configuration that pleased her. Sometimes she would gaze on it as she meditated. It calmed her.

She gazed on it now, her field of vision narrowing to include nothing more than the Zen garden itself. But still she felt the others closing in on her. She shook off the feeling and grabbed the phone again.

"You still there?" she said.

"Still here," Matthew replied. "So just tell me."

"Right," Anna said.

"You can't keep it bottled up."

"You sound like some nitwit therapist."

"That'll be my new career," Matthew said.

Anna half-groaned, half-roared in self-exasperation. She took a deep breath.

"I've started doing hypnosis with my psychiatrist, Lilly," she said. "It's making me think of Esther again."

"Imagining what happened to her?" Matthew asked.

"No. To me! What happened to me!"

"So tell me," he said. He walked from the kitchen to the hutch built into the wall of the dining room in his big, old Chicago apartment, passing through zones that made his cordless phone crackle. He poured himself two fingers of scotch and lit a cigarette.

Anna dropped her tiny rake and sat back down on the living room sofa. She put the phone in her lap and waited. After a time, she could hear Matthew's tiny voice calling to her. That could not bring her back to the phone now, because she could feel it getting closer. It was Craug, up near the ceiling of the room. She wanted to get out, but she felt so heavy. Then she heard Matthew shout her name through the phone. She brought it back to her ear.

"Yes?" she said.

"Where were you?"

"Someone's come to the door, Matthew," she lied. "I've got to go."

"Wait," he said. "Listen. I've got to fly out to LA tomorrow for re-writes. In a week or two I should be able to break free and come to see you in Salt Lake. Will you be there?"

"Yeah," she said vaguely.

"Call me later, okay? I don't care how late."

"Okay," she said. She hung up the phone and then it was on her. And she couldn't move from the sofa until Colin let himself in at noon the next day.

✦ ✦ ✦

Nine weeks later, the phone was ringing as Matthew came into his house on the beach at Malibu. He dearly loved the little house, and the sound of the surf, and the sand down to the water. He loved how an ocean swim made the hair on his arms and legs stick together with congealed salt. He loved the extreme privilege that was his because of the movies he had written. But this particular night, his rage made him certain that the cost was not worth it.

It was three a.m. Poor Judy Hamilton or Alexander, or whatever her name was had been trying to reach him since eight p.m. mountain time. She'd tried calling his apartment in Chicago, and again, calling his empty house in Malibu until he got in. It wasn't the sort of thing that you could leave in a message.

Matthew walked in. He'd spent the last four hours with an insomniac director, arguing about the changes that he, two idiot producers, and one harebrained movie star wanted in Matthew's script.

He hated when this happened. Sometimes projects were like heaven: working with a director who appreciated the script, everyone bringing out the best in each other. And then there were projects that ground down the soul, in which Matthew's collaborators engaged in the steady chipping away at the original conception. Once everybody had had a chance to deform to poor bastard screenplay, and then film it, the abortion would hit the screen.

So when he walked into his beloved beach house and heard the phone ringing, he could only imagine it was his insomniac director coming up with one more contradictory, plot-breaking, character-violating suggestion. He picked up the phone and yelled: "What?"

He heard a sharp intake of breath, followed by a moment's silence. "Matthew Harken?"

"Yes," he said, lowing his voice immediately. He heard the sorrow behind the poor woman's surprise.

"I'm sorry to call so late," she said. "You are a friend of Anna Toyevsky's, aren't you?"

"Is something wrong?" Matthew said.

Anna was dead.

Whatever he could have done to help her, he'd missed. He'd spent nine weeks turning a mediocre script into a true piece of shit. For that, he missed the last chance he'd have to help his friend.

Anna was dead.

Chapter 13

ARTIST'S RECONSTRUCTION

"THIS IS PROBABLY SIMILAR to the path she took *that night*," Colin said. "Turn right up here." He sat partly turned toward Matthew, his back against the corner formed by the back of the seat and the door. He had adjusted his seat back as far as possible and crossed his legs loosely, ankle over thigh. He looked slouched and befuddled, as though he'd fallen into the car seat from a great height and had not bothered to rearrange himself.

Matthew negotiated the turn and accelerated up the hill. He felt the anticipation and dread of going to the place of his friend's death. He noticed the long rising slope to his left, covered with short cropped grass, like a gigantic front lawn. They were nearly out of town. The houses had become more sparse, and the mountainous terrain of the high canyons closer.

"She stopped off at my house," Colin continued. "She must have been on her way up to the canyon." He sighed. "In general, the suicidal are very particular," he pronounced. "And Anna was no exception. You'd think it would be: Hey, screw it, I'm going to be dead in a couple of hours. Let somebody else clean up this mess. But no. She got everything in order at work so that her replacement at the school would have an easy time finding everything. She cleaned up her apartment to within an inch of its life—which, as I imagine you know, was not like Anna at all. In the process she gathered up a box of stuff that she did not want mingled with her own personal belongings, including all the gifts I'd ever given her and stuff I'd left or kept at her place—just to make it perfectly clear, before she killed herself, that she'd thoroughly rejected me."

Colin looked out the window. There'd been so much promise for Anna and him. They did so many things. There was so much more they could have done. But she'd ended it all. Sometimes he hated her for that. But he couldn't eradicate the suspicion that he was to blame.

They drove on in silence for a minute or two, then he spoke again. "Here's a nice detail: She'd hitchhiked up to Price after our final trip, and from Price she took a bus to Salt Lake City. In the box with all my rejected belongings she put the credit card receipt for her bus ticket." He laughed sourly.

"You left her there: your debt," Matthew said.

"That's right." Colin sighed. "But it's funny. She hadn't put the box right on the steps. It was over to the side, so I didn't see it until the next morning. It's one of those things you wonder: If I had seen this in time, is there any way I could have stopped her? I started to worry the next morning when I saw the box. And then, shortly after, probably about ten thirty, Natalie called me."

Natalie's lovely face came into Matthew's mind's eye. Sad Natalie at Anna's funeral. He hadn't been able to talk to her then. He had to talk to her soon.

Colin pointed to a long, inclined driveway to the left. "Turn in here," he said. "I want to show you the clinic."

Matthew turned up the neat blacktop driveway to the left. The drive was lined on both sides with neat hedges all the way to the top of the hill where it entered a parking lot next to an institutional brick building.

From the outside, all seemed quiet. Cars were parked. No one was going in or out. The building looked as though it could have been an office block as easily as a mental institution. "This is the place where she signed herself in?" Matthew asked.

"Tidy, isn't it?" Colin remarked.

Matthew pulled into a spot, and they got out. At the far end of the parking lot, a low, black wrought iron fence surrounded a graveyard. The fence and graveyard looked as though they predated the clinic by at least a hundred years. Colin and Matthew began walking toward the building.

"She'd put herself in here just a few months before she died. Her psychiatrist, Lilly, is attached to this clinic."

They stopped and looked off down the hill. Below them lay the whole city and the Great Salt Lake fading into the gray beyond. Colin smiled suddenly. "One of the things she loved here: there's a gravestone back in there with the name Anna S. Book. As you probably know, Anna felt like she was completely blocked, working on a novel that she was convinced would have been her masterpiece. When she saw that gravestone, she started screaming and then laughing. She said, 'No wonder I can't write! It's buried: Anna's Book. Let's dig it up!' But the grave made me uneasy. It was one of several omens I should have put together."

"Like what?" Matthew said. He started walking toward the graveyard. Colin turned with him, and they walked together.

"When Anna showed me that gravestone . . . you know I'm just about as morbid as Anna was. That was one of the reasons we got along so well together."

"When Anna and I were in Paris, we used to like to eat lunch in the *Père Lachaise* graveyard," Matthew said. "Dining with the dead." He looked around and did not see a gate into the graveyard, so he raised his leg gingerly over the top of the wrought iron fence. He pulled the other leg over and held onto the top of the low fence for a moment. Spasms of pain ran up and down his spine. A light sweat broke out on his forehead, and he swore under his breath. Colin stepped over, oblivious to Matthew's condition.

"Right," Colin said. "So you know what I mean. This is not like I was easily spooked. But when I saw that gravestone, even though Anna was laughing, I got an extraordinary chill, as if the gravestone read 'Anna Toyevsky' instead of 'Anna S. Book.'"

Colin led him down the rows of the old, worn gravestones. "Another thing," he said. "In the last weeks Anna was here, when I visited her, I saw this crippled magpie going through the bushes. Its wing was damaged. And I remember thinking that that magpie was not long for this world. There's a lot of feral cats here that would find it. I came back again a few days later. I saw the same damn magpie. It was still crippled, and it walked right near me. Unusually close, I thought. And then a third time, probably a week later, I parked over on the other side of the building, and God damned if that magpie wasn't still hobbling around. It seemed so impossible that it could have survived that long. The magpie began to look less like an animal and more like a vision. Now, you remember that Natalie and some of her other friends called

Anna 'Bird' as a nickname. So it's like something was trying to warn me about her death: the crippled bird that wasn't long for this world. Anna's gravestone. But I couldn't pull it together."

"You expected yourself to predict her suicide from that?"

Colin shrugged and started walking again. Ten yards later, he gestured at something ahead of them. Matthew saw a small gray gravestone with the legend, *Anna S. Book, 1875–1887*. Matthew stopped and looked at it. "Twelve years old," he said. "Anna Book was just a child." He felt no sudden chill, as Colin had done. Just a sadness. But to him, too, it somehow felt like Anna's grave.

"I don't know what I'm supposed to predict," Colin said. He sat atop Anna Book's slim gravestone, an action that mildly offended Matthew. "When I left Anna in the canyon, my thought was that things had gone so far bad that the magic down in the canyon was the only thing that might save us. I thought that if things didn't change, one or the other of us would soon be dead. Now maybe I was getting some other message, and I wasn't paying good enough attention. Maybe the message was going: Okay, you know all those things we've been telling you about the danger of Anna's death? Well, here we go. Just leave her here in the canyon, and they'll all come true."

"What happened that day?" Matthew said, struggling to keep his voice from revealing his suppressed anger. "How is it that you *did* leave her there?"

Colin took a deep breath and let it out. "Well, that's a longer story. Why don't we get back in the car, and I'll tell you while we're driving?"

◆　◆　◆

It took Matthew a few moments to cross the fence again, so Colin was already slouched in his seat in that collapsed-from-the-sky posture as Matthew pulled his car door open, feeling the spasms of pain down his back. He wished he'd brought his pain pills with him, though he had already taken his full dose for the morning, and to take any more would make driving dangerous. His hand bumped into the sole of Colin's shoe as he attempted to shift into reverse. Colin sighed and unfolded his legs.

"I don't know how much of the journals you've read," Colin said. "I never read them while Anna was alive. I did quite a bit of reading after she died." He sighed again. Matthew backed the car out of the space and headed back down the drive. "Make a left at the bottom and that road will take us out to Hyrum Canyon," Colin said, pointing. "You read in those journals—she really runs hot and cold on me. At one moment I'm this magical perfect mate for her, at another I'm destroying her life. You know, there were so many things wrong with me: I was not yet divorced. How could I be trustworthy if I'd made this vow to my wife and I wasn't being faithful? What about my kids? During those times when I couldn't be with Anna, she would obsess: Where was I? What was I doing? Why was she wasting her time thinking about me? Nothing would ever work out for us. But then the crowning disaster came when she started worrying about AIDS.

"The infuriating thing is that she was the one who insisted that I explore my gay side. She and I were incredibly open to delving our sexualities. I'm still amazed at the level of that. We played out everything. And when this aspect of my sexuality came out, she really zeroed in on it."

"I'm not surprised," Matthew said. "She always said she wished she'd been born a male homosexual."

"So she really glommed onto this possible gayness with me. She wanted me to explore it. She wanted me to actually *do* something about it—which I probably would not have done on my own—and she wanted to hear every detail."

"Her chance at vicarious male homosexuality."

"Maybe that was it. She'd be fascinated to hear everything, but later, as she thought about it, she'd get upset. Even though she encouraged me to do this—practically insisted that I do this—once I did do it, then I was being *unfaithful* to her. And then she started adding more wrinkles to her jealousy. If I was gay, how could I possibly love her, a woman? That really blew my mind. Here I was exploring this facet of my sexual personality at her behest, and suddenly I'm a dedicated gay man who couldn't possibly love her because she's a woman. And from there, she developed a paranoia that I was going to give her AIDS. The chance of this was all but nil. I didn't have any contacts that were likely to expose me to that. And I'd been tested. At her request, I got tested again. That's how I met Natalie. She was working at the AIDS clinic."

"Right," Matthew said. Of course he remembered that. How many times had he tried to convince Natalie to leave that place?

"But listen how this started: In June, she called me at home one day, and she said, 'I want you to call this number right away.' I said what is it? She said it's the Gay Help Line. I'd never heard of it. 'What do you mean?' I said. Well she'd called there to ask about some lesbian group she'd heard of and she ended up talking to this gay man, and she tells me: 'You really have to call him *right now* and tell him that you think you might be gay.'" Colin shrugged. "So I called him, and he says: 'Are you doing anything?' And I said no, so he invites me down to the office, and we talked for an hour. Now I had never been to any of the gay bars in town. I didn't even know where they were. But he looked at the way I dressed in Levi's and cowboy boots and leather jacket, something like that, he said, 'You know, I think you'd be comfortable in the Deer Hunter.' He called it a leather/flannel bar. You walk into it, and you'd think you were in a country and western bar except there were no women. I really did like it once I got used to it. The first few times were traumatic." He laughed. "But Anna wanted to hear everything. When I'd say I was thinking of not going there any more, she'd object.

"Still, this attraction/repulsion thing she was doing with me kept building: 'He's the archangel Gabriel. No. He's Charles Manson.' This was just adding more fuel to that fire. 'He's the homosexual man I always wanted to be! No. He's a lying faggot that never loved me.'" He pointed through the windshield. "Okay, we'll be going into the East Canyon."

The road had taken them over a high, soft ridge of grass and trees. Now it curved down into rugged terrain. The canyon walls looked like mountains, with steep slopes and exposed rock.

"Here's what I mean," Colin said. "We were driving down to Owl Creek Canyon. It's like a six-hour drive. This is the last weekend of her life, and we're having this conversation. I was telling her about being down at the Deer Hunter and running into someone from work, and she went into this really deep, dejected funk. It's hard for you, probably, to understand what this was like, because you don't know how close we'd become. She and I were so close, her feelings just flowed over onto me. I could feel her going into this sudden funk, and I got really angry. I pulled off the side of the road and walked away. We were about two-thirds of the way down to the canyon. And then I came back and said: 'What are you doing?' It was maddening—to be pushed to explore this, to play on my sexuality as part of *our* sexual mix, and then to turn it around on me so that I was hurting her. Hurting her deeply."

Colin pointed ahead to a wide point in the shoulder of the road. "Pull in here," he said. "This is it."

Matthew pulled in.

They got out of the car, and Matthew followed Colin back toward a turnout they'd passed.

"This was just one of a myriad of ways in which she had cast herself as the victim and me as the victimizer," he continued. "We had started our relationship on a level that transcended all the usual bullshit and went straight to the most intense spiritual connection that I've ever experienced. And now this was like a perverse, almost deliberate destruction of what we had created." He stopped and clutched Matthew's arm for emphasis.

"For God's sake, she'd put herself in the lock-down unit at the clinic. The section where they keep the patients on suicide watch. Natalie and I were flabbergasted. Why was she doing this? It didn't seem like she was at that point. Clearly, we were wrong, but at the time, we figured she was doing it as research. She did a lot of things like that. For the experience. So she could write."

He shook his head and began walking again.

"Maybe she was unaware what she was doing. But I often suspected she just needed the drama. That edge of impending disaster. But by the time of our trip to the canyon, it had gotten out of hand. She and I were tied so tightly at the psychic level that I knew we could not go on. I literally believed that one or the other of us was going to die if something did not change. And I told her: 'I am not going to spend the weekend with you in the canyon.'"

The wind picked up and blew some leaves around their ankles as they walked. Matthew felt the conflict between the beauty of the bright day and the grief in what he was hearing from Colin. He looked up into the branches of a swaying tree and felt comfort from its shape and movement.

"We'd camped at the top Friday night," Colin said. "I hadn't slept at all well, I was so irritated with her. We'd planned to go down in the morning. She said she was going down anyway, even if I didn't. You know how incredibly stubborn she could be. So I thought, 'Fine.' At that point, she was so far gone, the only thing I could imagine saving us was the magic in that canyon. So I left. I put a tape on in the truck and turned it up as loud as I could so I wouldn't think about what I was doing. And I left. That was Saturday morning, the last time I saw her alive. The night she died, Monday night/Tuesday morning, I was at the Deer Hunter. About midnight I felt nauseous, and I left."

They stopped walking at the turnout. A simple packed-dirt lane turned away from the road, pushed a hundred yards or so into the trees and stopped. To the right of the lane, a stream emerged from a culvert under the road and wound down the center of the canyon. Ahead of them, the high canyon wall rose to a clear blue sky. Wispy clouds brushed at the tops of the ridge trees above.

"This spot here is where her car was found?" Matthew said.

"Right here," Colin said. "The investigating officer, it turned out, was someone I knew. I know a lot of cops, having spent most of my career in forensics. So after they decided it was indeed a suicide, he gave me her final journal that was in the car."

"I didn't know you were in forensics," Matthew said.

"Oh, yes. Until I went on disability. I analyzed a lot of gruesome stuff. But I don't want to get into that here, where Anna died."

"No," Matthew agreed.

They walked down the lane. Matthew took a deep breath. The air was good. Crisp. It was a clear autumn day, and it felt good to be outside. His back didn't hurt him quite so much as before. But here he was, walking in this place where she died. She'd been alive here, and then dead. And if he could have just somehow dropped back in time to that night, he would have been able to stop her.

"Her car was parked right here. The glass was spread all round in here," Colin said, pointing to the left side of the lane and around in the surrounding dusty, gravely ground. "They bashed in the window on this side." He looked up toward the road. "I found out there's a highway patrol that makes a run down here every night about one o'clock. It seems unbelievable to me that they wouldn't have seen the car parked here and at least turned a spotlight on it and seen the hose, but they didn't. She wasn't discovered until the next morning. It was a week before the hunting season opens, and there was a deer hunter scouting the area. He found her about six in the morning."

"A deer hunter?"

"Yeah."

"And that's the name of the bar you were in, too, right?"

Colin chuckled to himself. "I hadn't thought of that." He took out a cigarette and offered one to Matthew. They lit them and stood smoking a moment as Colin mused.

"The Deer Hunter," he said. "You know, I told you that I started feeling nauseous around midnight the night Anna killed herself. There was another thing. When I started my truck to go home, I turned on the radio. The first thing I heard was my name. This deep male voice saying: 'Colin Grace?' It was like the voice of God. Bang. It just pushed me back in my seat."

"What was it?"

"They were reading a list of names of people who had contributed to the public radio station. A coincidence, right? But what were the chances that I would turn on the radio at the exact moment for the very first words to be 'Colin Grace.' And now you pointed out this other coincidence: The Deer Hunter bar and the deer hunter who found Anna. And then there's the nausea. I think Anna dated her last journal entry at eleven thirty that night. I'm nauseous around midnight. Then at two a.m. I woke up startled from my sleep. Natalie did, too. The sensation was so startling that we both got up and noticed the time. I sat down and had a large brandy before I went back to sleep."

"So it's like the magpie," he said. "Any piece of this all by itself is just a bit of coincidence. But when you start to put it together with the intuitions you feel, you realize that if you just dismiss all this, you are being aggressively rational. Don't you think?"

"Actually, I've been thinking about that a lot since I read Anna's final journal," Matthew said. "Where do these inexplicable thoughts come from? For instance, I find her 'recovered memories' troubling. That she was abused in exactly the way she remembers strikes me as unlikely."

"I was there when she did some of that work," Colin said. "She was in the clinic for four or five weeks, I think. And then she had to leave because her insurance ran out. I remember going over there, and she hadn't showered in two, three days. Hadn't washed her hair. That was really not like her."

"I got the impression from her journal that she would go into meditation and then these memories would start coming through," Matthew said.

"Right. You know, it's kind of a joke in the medical community around here, but that clinic has sort of a 'multiple personalities' outlook. Like as not, if you have some deep problems, and you go to that clinic, you are going to come away thinking you are a multiple personality."

"And you think Anna fell into that?"

"Well, I feel a little guilty that I didn't look into this until after her death, what with my background in forensics. They were giving her a drug called Halcion. In some users it induces what they call 'Halcion amnesia.' It helps you sleep. You get up in the morning. You function fine. But later on, you can't remember what happened. Well, you start with all this multiple personalities talk in the air at the clinic. Then she starts having these memories of herself as a little girl being abused. She feels the emotions of this little girl intensely. Then she starts having these blackouts. This strikes her as proof that she's a multiple. The reason she can't remember these periods is that the other personality is in full swing. So she starts to believe that sometimes she's Anna and sometimes she's Little Girl, and sometimes she can remember being Little Girl and sometimes she can't."

"I didn't realize she thought she had multiple personalities. *And* suppressed memories. But the whole thing is built on delusion."

"I wouldn't say that," Colin said. "It was very intense when she accessed those memories. And that was pretty much all she was doing for a period of time. Staying in her apartment. Not bathing. Not seeing anyone. Recalling these memories. I'm telling you, Matthew, she was in a lot of pain. This was no game she was playing. You could see she probably wasn't getting all the details right. But she was remembering something real that had happened to her."

"So you believe the memories?"

"*Something* happened to her. Christ, the woman killed herself."

The two fell into a silence. They walked up the stream that ran along the dirt lane. It wound into a meadow further away from the road. Colin plucked a tall wildflower and spun the blossom between his fingers.

"You know, for a couple years after she died, I started recalling memories," he said. "But not from this lifetime."

"Past life recall?"

"Weird, right? This wasn't something I was looking for. It started with these images as I was falling asleep at night. I'd see an image, like a snapshot of a place. It'd be familiar, somehow. And slowly, over a period of weeks, I'd start imagining a story of things that had happened there. People. Events. And it would seem to me that some of the people in these stories were people I know now—though they wouldn't look the way they do now. They might not even be the same sex that they are now.

"The reason I tell you this is that sometimes you discover these memories are real. The first one of these I had was at a site that turned out to be in Chaco Canyon, New Mexico. Probably about 1000 AD. What happened that allowed me to see that I wasn't just whipping this up in my imagination was that a few months later, I was reading *National Geographic* and I saw a picture of the ruins on that site. Alongside it they had an artist's reconstruction—how the site might have looked in its heyday. This site had a great view of the surrounding lands. The archeologists had decided it had been used as a lookout post. The village was farther down below. As I read that, I said: 'No.' I had this solid conviction that the site had been an observatory used by a priestly caste of astronomers.

"Later I went to the actual site. Everybody was following this path that rose over a short hill into the site. And I thought, *No, that's not the way in here.* I followed the edge of the hill around a bend and walked farther on and found the ancient portals of the site."

"So that convinced you that you had lived there around 1000 AD."

"It convinced me that there was more going on than idle imagination. It seems to me that what we are as individual humans is part of some larger soul. There is so much we don't understand that comes before and after life in these bodies. The closest analogy I can think of is that the soul is like an Indian carpet with brilliant colors and complicated designs. That is who we are outside of time and incarnation. And who we are in this incarnate human body—it's like we are a tiny insect trying to learn something about this thing that is us. We're an insect that is creeping along one thread of the carpet. We creep along at sort of a constant rate, and so things come at us at a constant rate. The thread color changes, the texture changes, and that gives us the illusion of time. We see this passage of impressions as we move along. It's a by-product of what we are doing in the overall reality that is too large for our little insect perceptions to see.

"Now maybe what enlightenment is all about is that somehow we come out of that little bug consciousness for a moment and start to see the carpet as a whole. Ordinary reality is the bug crawling along through time. In a broader reality there is no such thing as time, and you can't draw a line between past life and this life, because the whole is the whole. Every life through all time is actually happening simultaneously. There's a whole pattern there that we can try to unfold for ourselves. We keep getting these little hints, seeing these cross-references. And we keep seeing the same people, life after life. Maybe this carpet is not one individual. Maybe the carpet is all of us together, or an interconnected group.

"Is this too weird for you?" he suddenly asked. "There's not many people that when I say stuff like this, they want to keep listening. Anna would, of course. And Natalie."

"The thing that is really weird to me..." Matthew said. "Here you are, questioning past lives, and omens from magpies—but what the hell were you thinking when you left her in that canyon, in the middle of nowhere, all alone? She'd just gotten out of the mental hospital weeks before, and you abandon her in a place where she'd already had some kind of breakdown? It doesn't take a psychic to see that's not going to work out well."

"I did have a bad feeling when I was driving out of there," Colin said. "Like I told you, I turned up the tape really loud so I *wouldn't* think."

"But why? Why would you do that? Why would you leave her there, knowing that she's fragile."

"She never struck me as fragile, Matthew. *She* frightened *me* sometimes. I told you I felt something bad *was* going to happen. And that's why I left her. I honestly felt the magic in the canyon might save her."

Matthew stood and shook his head. He looked away back toward where Anna's car had been found.

"Look," Colin said quietly. "If you came here to find someone or something to blame, I'm your man. I obviously am if you just look at the surface of things. But that's not how we lived our lives. We were living on magical levels. And if you discount that, then nothing makes sense."

Matthew looked up into the sky and then back into Colin's eyes. The matter of responsibility was all blood under the bridge now. "I didn't come here looking for someone to blame," Matthew admitted. "I came because I'm dying. And I'm scared of dying. And I want to understand."

"Well, we'll get to know everything in between the acts," Colin said.

"What does that mean?"

"You know, after this lifetime. Before the next."

"So you believe that after we die, we'll be sent down into another body and keep doing that until we get it right?"

Colin laughed. "I think you want to be talking to the Dalai Lama or something. I don't have the key to the cosmology, but I know something is going on. I also have some very specific memories of Anna and I in our last life." Colin flipped his cigarette butt into the little stream that ran through the culvert under the road. At the same time, as though part of the same movement, a little bird flew down and landed on the ground not more than fifteen feet from the two men. It twittered brightly and turned its head to the side, watching them carefully.

"You see now," Matthew said, gesturing to the bird. "She's here to make sure you aren't passing off any bullshit."

"I wonder what Anna would have thought," Colin mused. "I wish I'd had these memories before she died. Anyway, again I had this experience of being almost asleep and suddenly these visions came to me like snapshots. It was around the turn of the century in France, in Marseilles. It was a large port city on the Mediterranean. Anna was a man. Another friend of mine, Lou Sheridan, was there.

"Anna was the leader. We were mainly petty thieves, drug dealers, drug users, prostitutes, sort of live-by-your-wits in Marseilles in the 1890s. Lou Sheridan got convicted for a murder that he didn't commit. I was there when they hung him. It's so clear to me that I could paint you a picture of the cell that we were in and describe what happened.

"Actually, I will give you some cosmology. Do you want to hear this?'

"Sure," Matthew said. He looked up into the branches of the tree. He felt hollow, like the emptiness after weeping.

"I believe that we come down as a circle," Colin said. "Probably made up of anything from two to two dozen people, and we travel together, and each of us may also have other circles that interconnect. In my circle I would identify Natalie, Anna, a guy named David Mead, Lou Sheridan, and then there are some other people that I have some question about. Anna would be a member of this circle but also a member of an interconnecting circle that maybe involves you and some of your friends who were in Paris. Others. In some sense the people in a circle agree to be incarnated together. There's certain agreed upon things that you're going to try to help each other do. Of course, the help may be in the form of tormenting each other." He laughed. "You can never tell. But we travel in these groups, and we always have. I've had Anna in two past lives that I can remember, maybe three.

"I remember Lou Sheridan and I got arrested. There wasn't much due process in those days. You're caught. Charges are brought. You may find yourself in court that day with the witnesses against you, and a magistrate rules, and you're executed within a couple of days. The magistrate at that trial is a fellow I know now. And I knew him then because I made my living as a male prostitute, and he was a client of mine. He sent me to jail, but he sentenced Lou Sheridan to be hung. I remember the next morning sitting there for his execution. The cell was in the ground. You walk up a set of steps and you're in a small courtyard with high brick walls all around, not a big space, but big enough to fit a gallows that did a lot of business. There were just the two of us in the cell. Lou was a young kid, a farmer's son, who came from northern France. He was sort of a country bumpkin. When he was led up the stairs, I distinctly remember him shitting down his pants.

"Anna had the most charisma, and to the degree that we were a gang, she was the leader. It was very loose knit. These images had been coming to me for some time. Then one night I was thinking about all this. I was feeling really disturbed. I had an intimation that there was something odd about the way I'd died in that life. Suddenly I got up and went over to her journals and just randomly pulled one out. I started reading, and she was describing a dream that she'd had about murdering a man. It seemed to be in France. She woke up from the dream and sat bolt upright in bed and looked over at me sleeping next to her. She was confused as to whether she was still dreaming or not. She thought maybe I was lying next to her, dead. I put down the journal and thought about that for a long time."

"So you think she killed you in Marseilles?"

"That's the way it struck me."

"And what did Anna think?"

"I didn't start having these memories until after she was dead. But I could imagine her immediately glomming onto that and accusing me of trying to get revenge on her."

"In what way?"

"AIDS. She pulled out the AIDS card like I was trying to get us both killed. Of course, the irony is that she might have been the one to give it to me. But never mind that. She was the one who pushed me to explore my gay side. And then for her to turn it into something that was *hurting* her... like I would deliberately risk getting myself infected and then infect her... She was the only person in the world that I had ever been in love with, that I probably ever will be in love with... I got so furious with her. I didn't strike her or anything. I mean, if I were a different sort of person I could have gone into a homicidal rage." He laughed. "But fortunately I'm not. She probably would have preferred that. But since I didn't kill her, she decided, well what the hell... might as well kill herself. She probably would have preferred that I'd murdered her and hidden her body in the canyon."

CHAPTER 14

A SMALL PLATE OF COOKIES

*A*SHES.

Matthew saw ashes floating to the ground outside. It had been burning for a long time.

Anna was talking about her sister, how close they had been all these years. She wanted Matthew to know that Esther loved Colin, even if none of her old friends trusted him. Esther understood the attraction. It was Esther who first let Colin sodomize her. She showed Anna it would be all right. Anna watched the two of them doing it.

Esther bent over Anna's desk. She lay her nude torso atop Anna's scattered manuscript pages and cradled her head on her folded arms. Anna liked the look of her twin's breast pressed against the flatness of her desk. She liked her sister's smile, so very much like her own. Watching her and Colin together was like watching a live psychodrama of her own life. A porno holographic movie starring herself and her lover.

But no, not pornographic, because they had such wholesome smiles. Colin and Esther kept looking over at Anna, like vacationers smiling for souvenir snapshots. And Anna sat in her desk chair not five feet away, watching them in happy suspense, like a child watching Lassie on television.

Esther opened her mouth in a lovely, smiling O, and Anna felt her mouth spontaneously make the same shape. Esther's mouth looked so pretty making that shape. The sight delighted Anna, who ran her fingertip over her own lips, knowing that her mouth must look just as pretty, and she felt thankful to Colin and Esther for showing this to her.

They showed her the pleasure that was in it. They showed her that it would be all right for her, too. Anna wanted it to be all right. Even before she remembered the childhood sodomy, it was important to her to do this thing. It was to be part of her sexual magic with Colin: another of the many unusual things they did together that allowed them to direct the flows of their energies.

This was what she wanted Matthew to understand now: the energies.

How to describe the sensation of sexual magic? It wasn't just for pleasure. Colin and she used the most intense sexual ecstasy in order to feel the contours of their own souls. They used their bodies in order to sense beyond their physical beings. By teasing, by prolonging, by exciting the body well beyond the normal bounds, by touching and withholding touch, they could feel beyond their nerve ends. They could feel the eternal parts of themselves that existed independently of the body, that would live on without the body, that could leave the body and return. They could feel the essences that existed beyond their individual personalities in this incarnation.

Matthew noticed the ashes again, drifting gently in the air outside.

"Quiet," Anna whispered in his ear. "Pay attention."

But wait, *Matthew thought.* This couldn't have happened. Esther's dead.

"We're all dead," Anna said, her voice much clearer now. "It's just a matter of when."

Colin drifted down through the ceiling above and hovered over him. "The soul is like an Indian carpet," he said. "We are like insects creeping along. The thread color and textures change, giving us the illusion of time. The overall reality is too large for our little insect perceptions to see. All time happens simultaneously."

Matthew felt the carpet beneath him. He was lying on it. He looked back up at the specter of Anna's lover.

"Are you dead?" he asked.

"Aren't you?" Colin replied.

With great effort, Matthew rolled to his hands and knees. He felt the dry sandy earth of the desert beneath his palms. He got up and walked down into an arroyo, the ground crumbling under his feet as he crossed over the edge of the gully. He didn't know what he was looking for, and he feared he wouldn't be able to find his way back. The eroded gully took a turn to the left, and he followed it. A tumbleweed blew over the ridge above his head. He went down deeper where there still wasn't any water,

just the deep gully left by erosion. A channel cut in from the left after the
bend. Anna was standing in the center of that channel.

"Nobody knows anything," she said.

"Why do you keep saying that?" he asked.

Matthew felt so tired and sick. A wave of dizziness came over him. It
was so hot in the desert. So intolerably hot. He collapsed back to his hands
and knees. Drops of sweat fell from the tips of his hair.

"Good question," said a male voice. "This is the first step. You must
learn to ask the right questions."

Who was that? Matthew raised his head enough to see Anna's feet. He
saw large snakeskin boots. Dusty black jeans. He looked higher. The stocky
legs were slightly bowed. This was a man, certainly. He saw the man's
sun-darkened hands, the thick hair curling from the backs of the hands,
a large silver and turquoise ring on one of the fingers, a handmade belt
around his waist. A big clump of feathers, like the torn-off wing of a large
bird, hung from a piece of rawhide on his belt. Smoke rose from a bowl
by his foot.

Matthew tried to look higher, to see the man's face, but his neck was
stiff. He tried to push higher, but the effort made his head spin. He was so
hot and sick. He lay down fully on the ground. He felt the abrasive dirt
against his cheek.

♦   ♦   ♦

The first thing Matthew sensed was the wiry wool against his cheek.
It took him a long time, not moving, lying there, to identify what it
was that was so irritating to his face. It was not the multicolored carpet
of time. It was the beige carpet of the Inn at Temple Square.

Why was he lying on the floor? He'd been out. He could feel that.
Some awful version of sleep. Not refreshing, healthful sleep. Some
other kind of unconsciousness. He was so damned hot. There was
some kind of pill he was supposed to take for that. Had he taken it?

His mind became clearer, but he still didn't get up from the floor.
He could see out the window without raising his head. It was snowing.
It was still November, wasn't it? Matthew had lost track. What day it
was. What month. What year. Matthew had lost track of how many
pills he'd taken, too. What was he taking?

Casodex.

He remembered that. He just took one of those per day in the morning. Those were easy to track. He had them laid out in a little blue plastic case with a compartment for each day of the week. The Casodex to quash the testosterone from his adrenal glands. Megace to control the hot flashes brought on by the Casodex. And the first two analgesics of the day to control the pain. That was where he was confused. He had no idea what time it was and how many painkillers he'd downed.

What time was it? What day was it?

It was snowing outside. *Ashes.* It looked like ashes.

He knew he'd taken too many painkillers. He remembered all sorts of things, but they didn't seem like dreams, exactly. He raised his head and put his hand under the cheek that had been lying against the nap of the carpet. It itched and was wet with drool.

Oh, good, he thought. He dragged himself to his knees and crawled into the bathroom where he pulled himself to his feet using the edge of the sink. With exaggerated care, he loaded the tiny coffeemaker with grounds and water. He would have called room service, but he didn't want anyone to see him.

He felt his hot flash getting worse. Megace couldn't control them all. When he first started on the Casodex, he got hot flashes several times per day. Suddenly the room would feel like 120 degrees, and he'd break out in a sweat that soaked him right to the tips of his hair. Like now. He was soaked through. The Megace controlled the number and usually the severity of the hot flashes, but it didn't eliminate them.

Matthew stripped off his pajamas (he'd never gotten dressed that morning) and stepped into the shower. He set the water at a cool luke-warm, sat down in the bottom of the tub, and let it rain down on him.

He was not managing well. He realized that. He couldn't remember how many days it had been since he'd gone to the site of Anna's suicide. He couldn't differentiate among what he'd read in her journals, what he'd dreamed, and what had been real. He was abusing the analgesics. His doctor had never hesitated to approve refills before, but Matthew could imagine it becoming a problem. Besides, was an addiction on top of cancer really such a good idea?

What difference does it make? said the dark voice inside him.

Shut up, he thought. *There were people who lived for years with metastatic prostate cancer.*

The aroma of the brewing coffee began to cut through the cool moisture of the shower. Matthew pulled himself up and sat on the rim of the tub. He reached his watch from the shelf and pushed the button for the day/date readout. It was Friday. He picked up the pill case and opened it. Friday's pills were still there. Thursday's were gone. That was a good sign. He popped the Friday pills into his mouth and sat back in the shower. He opened his mouth under the stream until it filled with shower water, then he swallowed.

Of course, the cancer would eventually kill him, unless something else did first. But that might be off a good long time yet. The drug therapy was supposed to halt the cancer. His doctor had promised that the pain, too, would lessen. *Combination hormonal therapy.* That was the nice name for his treatment. Chemical castration was the more descriptive term. The object was to rid his system of testosterone. Once a month he had to get a shot of Lupron that put his balls in the deep freeze. Then the daily Casodex stopped the testosterone from his adrenal glands. Dr. Galesberg had told him he could forget about the monthly shots if he got an orchiectomy—that is, a physical castration—but Matthew wasn't ready to say good-bye to his balls.

Matthew ran his hand over his chest. A few more chest hairs came off on his palm. Everywhere his hair was getting thinner. His pubic hair was receding toward prepubescence. And despite his weight loss, it appeared to him that he was beginning to grow breasts.

Testosterone is the food of prostate cancer. That was the point of his therapy. The cancer couldn't grow without it. The tumors would, he'd been promised, begin to shrink as they were starved of testosterone. Matthew's Day of Judgment would come when the cancer mutated into cells that could grow without testosterone. Then he could look forward probably to less than a year of life, rapid degeneration, weight loss, spontaneous breaking of bones, and a spectacularly painful death. Unless, of course, medical science got its shit together before Matthew's hit the fan.

It had only been two months since the bone scan that revealed the spread of Matthew's cancer. Then he'd spent weeks of numbed existence in his condo in Chicago. He'd gone to a cancer support group. He found the people there genuine. They were in pain themselves, but they were remarkably willing to help each other. Matthew felt drawn to some of the people, but he couldn't get past the feeling of being under water. He was emotionally disconnected from everything around him. And daily the presence of Anna became more real to him. The unresolved questions of her death. After several weeks, he'd packed his bag and set off for Salt Lake.

Dr. Galesberg was not pleased to have Matthew at such a distance. He needed to monitor Matthew's PSA tests, he needed follow-up bone scans and MRIs to make sure the therapy was working and that the tumors were beginning to shrink. But Matthew refused to be a prisoner in Chicago. Tests could be done anywhere. Bone scans could fly across the Internet to his doctor's PC. Matthew knew one thing more solidly than anything else: He did not have time to waste.

Matthew pulled himself out of the tub and toweled off. He poured himself some coffee, put plenty of milk in it from the mini-fridge in his room, and drank it down. Then he went back to the bathroom and poured some more.

He'd lost all track of time. He knew it was Friday, but that seemed to have no connection with anything. How many days had he been here? He suddenly remembered his doctor had set up an appointment for him with a local pain clinic here in Salt Lake. He didn't want to miss that. Dr. Galesberg held out the hope that he'd be able to get an analgesic patch to put on his back that would dose him more effectively, give better pain control, and not upset his stomach and lower his appetite like the pills did. Since the day Colin and he had visited the site of Anna's death, all he could remember doing was lying around in his hotel room and reading the journals. He was stiff, overmedicated, and steeped in Anna's journal consciousness. And he had such odd, impossible memories.

Dreams. Weird, drugged, vision-dreams.

Clothing, he decided. That was the first step toward a more coherent life. The hot flash had subsided. He picked out some clothes, lay down on the bed to let the last patina of sweat dry from his skin, and then got dressed.

He was deciding whether to order a room service breakfast or to venture down to the hotel café when a knock came at the door. Had he already ordered breakfast? His mind was such a blur; anything was possible.

He opened the door. It was Natalie. Matthew's heart fell.

"You look terrible," she said in that exquisitely rich voice.

"I wasn't ready for this," he said.

"Sorry. You weren't inviting me over, so I thought I'd just drop by before you disappeared."

"Colin told you..."

"Of course."

He stepped away from the door, and she stepped in. They looked at each other for a long moment, and Matthew could see just exactly how terrible he looked from her quizzical expression.

Natalie was still beautiful, of course. She looked a little older. A few stands of gray ran through her straight black hair that was pulled back into a ponytail. The slightest tracings of lines had begun to form above her high cheekbones.

"What happened to your face?" She raised a finger to her cheek.

He put his hand to his face. "I passed out on the rug," he said. "It's red?"

"Yes," she laughed. "And textured."

Matthew gestured to the room service menu on the bed. "Let me pull myself together here. Would you order us some breakfast? Would you mind? Something for a weak stomach for me," he said. "And coffee."

"It's three o'clock in the afternoon, Matthew. Still keeping your Hollywood schedule?"

"Ha, ha," he said. "It's nice you can cut a dying man a little slack."

"I guess you put me in my place," she said lightly, looking around his messy hotel room. "What do you want?"

"I don't know. They do breakfast all day," he said. "Get whatever you like for yourself. I need a moment." Talking with Natalie pulled him out of his dullness and fatigue. But he felt embarrassed. He should have called her when he'd come into town. But he hadn't been able to bring himself to do it.

He poured a half-cup of milk in his coffee mug and took it into the bathroom where he filled it the rest of the way with coffee. That emptied the little carafe. He looked at his face in the mirror. It looked like he had leprosy on one side. He bathed it with cold water and then sat on the toilet, pants up, to sip his coffee and gather his thoughts.

He was not ready for Natalie. He still loved her, but he could hardly bear to be near her like this.

He remembered all the times he'd thought of seeing her before the cancer. Now it was impossible. Even if Natalie and he could recapture their feelings, he was a chemical eunuch. The frustration surprised a sob of grief out of him, and he quickly covered his face with a towel so that she wouldn't hear.

The last time Natalie and he had been together was two years before Anna's death. Seven years ago. When they met, Patty and he had been divorced about six months. He'd come to Salt Lake to visit Anna, and Anna played the yenta, for she loved both Matthew and Natalie and she'd never cared for Patty. Her efforts had worked. Matthew extended his visit. He took a suite at the hotel and settled in Salt Lake for a while to work on the screenplay for *Fertility Rites*.

Matthew remembered the first time he met Natalie. He smiled as he remembered that intimate dinner for three. She had plied them with every aphrodisiac she could imagine. When he drove Natalie home, they were already aroused. Natalie led him into her bedroom.

How beautiful they were! Matthew remembered that night like a holy revelation. He could have wept at the thought of their glorious healthy bodies. They could have eaten one another alive, and gladly given themselves up to be devoured.

Matthew looked at the reflection of his diminished self in the ornate mirror of the Inn at Temple Square. He finished his milky coffee and stepped out of the bathroom. Natalie looked at him from the sofa. She set down his copy of *Variety* that had been on the coffee table.

"Colin says you have prostate cancer," she said.

"Yes." Matthew laughed ruefully and spread his arms to show himself. "Exhibit A."

There was a knock at the door and Matthew let in room service with a rolling tray of food. The waiter set the food on a tiny dining table near the mini-fridge at one end of Matthew's room. He set out juice, oatmeal, a soft-boiled egg, toast, a carafe of coffee and cups, and a small plate of cookies. Matthew tipped the waiter as he left.

"You ordered well," he said, sitting down at the table.

"The cookies are for me," she said. "So hands off."

"I think I'll be okay with the rest of this."

"Colin said you don't have much of an appetite."

"No." He shrugged. "I know one guy who's taking one of the drugs I take, and it caused him to blow up to three hundred pounds."

"Jesus," Natalie said.

"He says when they slide him into the chamber of the MRI, he feels like a cork being stuck into a bottle."

They sat down at the table and Matthew added milk and brown sugar to his oatmeal. Natalie poured coffee for them both. This coffee smelled better, richer, than the coffee he'd made in the little machine in the bathroom. Matthew sliced off the top quarter of the soft-boiled egg with his knife and dipped the corner of his toast into the yolk.

"Thank you for ordering," he said. "I haven't had a soft-boiled egg in a while."

"My years at the AIDS clinic," she replied. "You get to know what the overmedicated stomach can stand."

"Colin told me you left the clinic."

"I'd been thinking about it for a long time." She looked down at her cup for a moment. She looked at him and smiled and looked back down at her coffee. Matthew remembered her pauses. You could miss a lot of what Natalie had to say if you didn't wait through the pauses. She had a beautiful way of speaking. Her body, her lips, her hands gathered themselves around her words and ushered them out like beloved children. She did not rush, but waited for them to be ready, and then released them into the world. If you didn't wait to listen to what she had to say, she'd soon cease to waste her time with you. She was a great believer in quality over quantity. She could be quite happy with just a few good friends. She didn't care much for small talk with acquaintances.

"You and Anna were right," she continued. "It wasn't a healthy place for me. And then when Colin was diagnosed, I knew I could not be there to watch him go through that. Not so soon after Anna's death." She ran her fingertip around the rim of her coffee cup then picked it up and sipped. "When you work at a place like that you become friends with the patients. You see them die."

She turned her eyes upon Matthew suddenly, and he felt her sincerity and her emotion so strongly that it penetrated straight through to his heart. It was almost like when he first fell in love with her, when he felt as though he could drop into the deep brownness of her eyes and never come out.

"Colin and I had been through so much together," she continued, "watching Anna's decline, and then her death. I just couldn't be at the clinic for that with him—and also be there for everyone else."

"Yes," Matthew said quietly.

"And now you," she said.

"Yes."

The two sat for a long time with that thought. Matthew attempted to take a bite of his egg, but he couldn't.

"One of the 'gifts' of cancer," he said at last, "is that you lose the delusion of limitless time." He took a deep breath. She nodded her understanding and waited for him to go on.

"I didn't call you when I got into town..."

"Matthew..."

"Please. I hadn't called you because I wasn't ready yet. But seeing you was one of my most important reasons for coming here. I've thought about you often over these seven years. I always intended to call you, but I always put it off. For a long time after the divorce, I didn't want to see anyone. And then I wasn't sure if you'd want to talk to me."

"You chose Patty, Matthew. You chose her twice. That's enough for me."

"I should never have gone back with Patty."

"But you did."

"Yes. I did. But there's such a contrast between the love you and I shared and any other love of my life."

"Matthew..." she protested.

"I just think of those long conversations we had," he said. "It seemed like there were no limits."

"I don't want to get into this," she said.

"But don't you miss that?" he said. "That's what I miss most of all. And that's what made me hesitate now to call you, when I hesitate about few things that are of any importance to me."

"Because you might die?" she said.

"My cancer is under control for the moment," he said. "But at the same time, my drug regimen often leaves me impotent. And I absolutely hate that this is the way I have to be now, when I am finally able to tell you how I feel."

She breathed a heavy sigh and pushed a few stray hairs back behind her ear. "This isn't what I came here to hear." Natalie slid her chair back from the table and looked toward the window.

"I know it's too soon to be talking about this," Matthew said. "But my physical condition puts that strain on me."

She looked him in the eye again, then leaned back to the table. "Not to put too fine a point on it, Matthew, but you dumped me to go back to your wife. I'm sorry you're sick, but I didn't come here to fulfill your fantasies."

She took her coffee cup and swirled it around as she gathered her thoughts. "When I was still at the AIDS clinic, I knew I had to leave. There I was, in the midst of all those people who desperately needed healing. But I wasn't the healer; I was the office manager, trying to keep order in that chaos. I was like Sisyphus with his rock. I couldn't cure AIDS, and I couldn't bring order. Finally, I realized I could do something about all the psychic pain I'd seen. So I got my degree, and I started up a private psychotherapy practice. But now, the more people I treat, the sicker the world gets."

"So what do you do?" he said.

"I do what I can. And that's going to include helping Colin. And you. Life might have been a lot different if you'd kept your dick in your pants in Hollywood," she said. "But I'll help you nonetheless."

"Thank you," he said.

"You're a pitiful wreck," she laughed. She got up and knelt next to his chair. She pressed her cheek to his and then kissed his forehead, and Matthew felt more comfort than he had felt in years.

"There is someone I want you to meet," she said. "He's a great healer, and I'm hoping he can do something for you."

CHAPTER 15

THE HAPPIEST DAY OF YOUR LIFE

In the beginning, when Matthew and Natalie had first met, being together was a great joy. The endless conversations. The lovemaking. They even enjoyed working in one another's presence, which was something neither of them had ever liked before. Matthew had always written and Natalie had always painted in privacy. But then he began to go out on location with her. She would set up her easel in the canyons and he would bring his notebooks, and they would work in contented silence.

It had been wonderful.

However, it turned out that although Natalie loved writers, she deeply distrusted actors and filmmakers.

When it came time for Matthew's script to go into production, just a few months after Anna introduced them, he begged Natalie to come on location with him. She refused. Matthew and Anna had a campaign going to get her to quit the AIDS clinic where she managed the office, because it constantly overtaxed her. The clinic had the intensity of a war. Perhaps she was addicted to the adrenaline. But in any case, she refused to leave her work or her mountains. She did not want to go onto a film set with the women with their silicone-sculpted breasts and collagen-injected lips.

◆   ◆   ◆

Clive Davisson was directing the picture. He hired the public relations firm of Matthew's ex-wife, Patty, for the picture.

"I would like the two of you to work on some guerilla publicity scenarios," Clive said, giving them a wink as he headed for the table of pâtés, fine cheeses, and Russian caviar on the patio of his Beverly Hills home. He uncorked a vintage champagne and poured for the three of them.

This was the way Clive liked to run his pre-production meetings: in small groups focused on individual tasks, in catered intimacy and opulence.

Clive was a great bon vivant. He was a robust man with thick white hair, a ruddy complexion, and barrel chest. He spoke in a deep-voiced patrician British accent. He threw soirées of heroic proportions and could fascinate a cocktail party audience with stories for hours on end. He'd had drunken adventures with *everyone*. He'd made and lost three fortunes and was hoping to build a fourth.

"Guerilla publicity." Patty smiled her cunning smile. Her blue-gray eyes glinted with the fox in them. "What do you have in mind?"

"I wish to begin to sell this film even as we make it," Clive said. "It is ludicrously crass, but there it is. If this film does not make money—and great, staggering piles of it—I'll be reduced to directing Disney television sitcoms for tweens." He gave an elegant shudder of distaste. "You *must* help me to circumvent that eventuality."

"Don't be silly, Clive," Patty said. "You won an Oscar for directing *Better Strangers*."

He shook his head and waved a caviared slice of toast in the air. "Yes, that allowed the world to love us once again," he said. "*But it made only modest money*. This time, we must impress the studio accountants and devil take the critics. Let us not forget, Matthew and I each have a tiny percentage of the gross, and we cannot allow that opportunity to slip away."

"Can we use the actors?" Matthew asked.

"Yes, of course, dear boy, anything!" Clive said. "We can be very sixties, if we so desire. Whatever you like. You and Patty could create some *happenings*. I will arrange time for them in the production schedule." Clive lowered himself onto a white leather divan.

"My first thoughts were that we could make the production look as though it were totally out of control," Clive said. "Draw all sorts of attention to ourselves. Absolutely panic our investors. And then when the picture is about to be released, the actors will trot out to the chat shows and babble on salaciously, and make it sound so intriguing that absolutely everyone will feel compelled to see the picture." He raised his eyebrows hopefully. "Ideas?"

"I do have an idea," Matthew said. Patty turned her crafty, fox eyes on him with great expectation. He smiled at her enthusiasm. He'd been worried about having to work with his ex-wife, but he remembered how he'd always loved her enthusiasm. This could be fun, he realized.

"Remember *The French Lieutenant's Woman*?" he said.

"Jeremy Irons," Clive said. "Meryl Streep. Playing double roles."

"Exactly," Matthew said. "There was a story within the story. There was the period piece movie they were making called *The French Lieutenant's Woman*, and then there was the modern story of the making of that movie. The audience got to watch the movie, and they watched the movie about making the movie. It cut back and forth between the two stories, which had parallel plots."

"Go on," said Patty.

"We could do the same thing. Only *our* story about making the movie happens in the real world. And our audience will see it over a period of months in the news and entertainment press."

"That's it precisely," Clive exclaimed.

"We can make the production look out of control, like Clive suggests," Matthew said to Patty, "but we'll script our 'happenings' with parallel themes to the picture."

"So you want to create a Hollywood backstage version of *Fertility Rites*," Patty said. "I like it. We'll have Jeremy Reed, the lovable bad-boy actor, and the beautiful, mysterious Lindsay Webber playing themselves out in the real world. The tabloids will eat it up."

"We can have Jeremy and Lindsay to disappear from the set and be spotted with some shaman in Mexico," Matthew said.

"Patty can leak it to the paparazzi," Clive said, slapping his hands. He freshened all their glasses of champagne. "Later, I will explain to Barbara Walters how the actors were driven to do these things by the intensity of their roles." He raised the back of his hand to his forehead in a gesture of comic dismay. Then he pointed suddenly, his whole arm extended, at Matthew. "You!" he shouted. "You will be the voodoo priest."

Patty threw back her head and laughed in complete delight.

"What do you mean me?" Matthew said. "Why not Reg Griffin?"

"No, no, no," Patty insisted. She leaned in toward him from her chair. "I see what Clive is saying. Jeremy and Lindsay are the seekers who become lovers, just like in the script. But who can manipulate them by magic? It can't be another actor. It has to be you, the screenwriter, or Clive, the director."

"And I've got to sell the story to the press, old boy," Clive said. "I've got to tear my hair out as our production goes crashing out of control."

"Absolutely," Patty said. She got up and began pacing the room. "Clive is the spinmeister, using the scenario we will develop. You are the voodoo priest." She stopped for a moment and looked down at her feet, thinking. Then she slapped her hands together. "You and Clive are in a struggle for the hearts and minds of the actors."

"Brilliant! I love that!" Clive shouted. He jumped up and kissed Patty full on the mouth. "A war of the Svengalis."

Matthew laughed and threw up his hands. "Okay," he said. "But you'll have to give me acting lessons, Clive."

"Don't fret, dear boy," Clive said. "Any monkey can act. There's absolutely nothing to it. And you'll have your lovely ex-wife by your side."

✦ ✦ ✦

Playing the role of the manipulative genius-screenwriter, counterpart of the movie's voodoo priest, Matthew turned out to be remarkably photo- and telegenic. His picture appeared everywhere. He was often shown in the presence of his tall, attractive ex-wife Patty.

"She is a stunning woman," Clive said, standing next to Matthew in Clive's office at the studio, watching a segment that had appeared on *Entertainment Tonight* the day before. He turned down the sound on the television. It was late, after the day's shooting. He poured them each a glass of scotch. "One can see how clever she is just by looking at her," he said. "She's a woman who could trick you out of your trousers and make it the happiest day of your life."

"Clive . . ." Matthew said.

"Oh, I admit it. I have something of a lech for your wife. But as you know, I have rather strict rules about that sort of thing."

"Never do anything at which you might be caught." He rubbed his eyes and sat in one of the chairs at the conference table beyond Clive's desk.

"My dear boy, you do me a grave disservice."

Matthew snorted.

"You laugh outright," Clive said indignantly. "Well, I suppose I do have something of a reputation. But you should know that I would never touch a woman who belonged, however tenuously, to one of my friends—or to anyone else really, if I knew about it."

"But if you didn't know about it, that's another matter," Matthew said.

"Well, yes, and I am not particularly nosy," Clive admitted. "A good one-nighter is a pleasure to be savored, like a snifter of fine aged Armagnac."

Matthew laughed again. He leaned back in the chair and put his feet up on the conference table. "I've always wondered what Claudia thinks of your. . . adventures."

"Claudia and I have been married for twenty-two years," Clive said. "I believe part of our success as a couple is her civilized disregard for my extracurricular affairs." He turned off the television and sat on the edge of his desk. "She has, however, set certain limits. As you know, Claudia is quite a fine markswoman. She has an impressive collection of firearms. Even as we speak, Claudia is off hunting caribou on horseback in Montana somewhere." Clive drained his scotch and poured another. "The very first time she realized that I'd had a dalliance with some acquiescent starlet, she promised that if I ever gave her a venereal disease, she would shoot off my genitalia. I have never had the slightest doubt of her sincerity, and so I am scrupulously careful."

"You are a pillar of morality."

"I do my best," Clive said. "And for some reason, I've taken it into my head that it would be a fine, fatherly, benevolent act to bring you and Patty back together." He turned the television back on and replayed the tape. "Look at her," he said. "Stunning. She's a natural blond, isn't she?" He looked at Matthew and immediately waved off the question. "No, never mind," he said. "It's not the sort of question a gentleman asks. But look at her. I love how that short coif shows off the shapeliness of her skull. Her every feature is delectable. And as you are my friend, Matthew, I long to know, or at least to imagine, that you are fucking your ex-wife robustly once again."

Matthew shook his head bemusedly. "A gentleman can't ask if a woman uses Lady Clairol, but he can inquire into whether a divorced couple is fucking robustly?"

"I would never *ask*. Heavens, Matthew, what you must think of me."

Matthew finished his scotch and got up from the conference table. "I've got to go home to bed," he said. "Great footage today."

"Very well, off to bed. Off you go without giving me even a word about this lovely creature," he said, gesturing to the television screen.

"There is someone else," Matthew said.

Clive's interest was immediately rekindled. "Do I know her?"

"She refused to come out here with me. And she sounds more and more distant on the phone every time I call."

Clive looked at the television screen. Matthew and Patty sat on a couch together on a talk show. They were laughing. As they laughed, Patty lay her head affectionately on Matthew's shoulder. "I wonder why," Clive said.

Matthew looked at the screen sadly. Perception was reality. He knew that. And they were creating the reality that was broadcast across the nation.

CHAPTER 16

YOGA POSTURES

FORTY-EIGHT PEOPLE ROSE TO their feet and applauded in the crowded screening room. Clive walked to the front of the room, flush with glory. The applause rebounded and took on more energy as he turned and faced the room. He knew them all. All their names and faces. And at this moment he loved them all beyond measure. He folded his hands as if in prayer and bowed to them. To some who were particularly filled with emotion, he pointed and nodded in empathy. To others he winked. He took a second bow, and the applause began to die down.

"The rough cut does not have the glorious smoothness of the eventual final picture. However, I can tell by your response that you recognize we have captured an extraordinary work of cinema." As he waited for another bout of applause to die down, Clive watched and appreciated the faces: his beautiful actors, his cinematographers, his costumers, his assistants, his set decorators, his lighting designers, and so many more. So many of his staff had been able to come. Many others, of course, were already on to their next jobs. He loved them all.

And now he would trick them again. Only five people in this room knew about the guerrilla publicity plan. And only three more in the rest of the world. *You are such a wonderful liar, Clive Davisson,* he chuckled to himself. *The charade must go on.*

He held out his hands for quiet. "For many of you, this will be our last time together as a company. Now the editing staff, the post-production staff, will take over the project with me. Before we part, however, I feel I must acknowledge what an unusual production this has been." Clive watched as he saw some of the faces turn sober—even worried.

"We have had production delays. We have had angry words. We have even had some questions over the rightful direction of this film." Here he looked directly at Matthew, but then he looked away. A most contagious smirk was curling the corners of Matthew's mouth, and Clive did not intend to lose his composure.

"Whatever delays and expenses we have incurred, I am now convinced they were absolutely worth the pain. Some of you in this extraordinary band of artists did what you felt was necessary to push yourselves to performances beyond what any director could reasonably expect. And for this I humbly thank you. I thank you for the independence you showed in tossing my production schedule into a cocked hat." He gave a comic shrug and acknowledged the first timid laughs. "I thank you for the autonomy you showed in destroying my budget," he said forcefully, garnering more assured laughs. "And I thank you for the self-determination you showed in so thoroughly pissing me off," he boomed, giving rise to hoots and whistles around the room. "For in doing all this," he said triumphantly, turning serious, "we have created one of the extraordinary films of our time. We shall be proud of this work, each and every one of us, for the rest of our days." He waited, pleased and beaming at his friends, for the new wave of applause to wash over him.

"Now let us hear a few words from a man who has been one of the particular thorns in my bum these past weeks and months." He gestured toward Matthew and began a chant of "Author," which the crowd quickly took up.

Matthew got up and received a bear hug from Clive, who then put his arm around Matthew's shoulder and stood with him facing the audience. "This is the man who started it all. Without his conception, none of us would have come together to do this strange project, this *Fertility Rites*." Clive hugged him again and gave him a kiss on the lips, bringing cries and whoops from the crowd. Then Clive ran off to the back of the screening room and their colleagues rose to give Matthew a standing ovation.

Matthew looked from one to the next, seeing the true affection in their faces as they applauded him, and it overwhelmed him with emotion. They clapped all the harder seeing the effect on him. He leaned back against the wall as his vision blurred with tears. He raised his hands to them. "Mercy," he said. "Please. Have mercy." A few laughs came mixed with the applause, which slowly died down, and the people sat. Matthew wiped a tear from his eye.

"I'm not used to this," he said. He looked over at Patty, who grinned and pointed at him and winked. "Although I suppose I *could* get used to it. If I had to." Clive gave a great guffaw from the rear.

"The proudest moment in my professional life came when Clive won Best Director for *Better Strangers*, the first time we worked together. That was a great moment." He waited for scattered applause and for the heads to return after looking back at Clive. "But having seen what you all have done," he said, "every day, all of you and the hundred or so more that have worked on this production—the way you turned my words into reality—and the magnificent result. Truly. I am so grateful . . ." Matthew closed his eyes as he became choked up once again. He opened his eyes and tried to speak but could not. Then he heard a loud pop from the back of the screening room, and Clive came bounding down toward him, pressing a crystal flute of champagne into his hand.

"Get that down yer neck, ye blubbering woosy," he cried in a rough Scots accent.

Matthew gratefully took the champagne and drank it in one slow tilt. Clive took back his glass and smashed it into the corner beyond them, to the vast approval of the crowd. Matthew laughed and hugged Clive and raised his hands for quiet to speak again. "I visited a dear friend before this production got under way," he said to the crowd. "A wonderful novelist. A woman with whom I learned to write. She was trying to convince me to return to novel writing, which is how I began my career." Matthew raised his arms to the audience. "But how could I trade all of *you* for the solitary life of a novelist?" he asked loudly. Some in the crowd called back: "No! No!"

"Little worry of that," Clive said, stepping forward again. "If *Fertility Rites* makes the great piles cash that we fervently pray it does, *I* will produce Matthew's next picture and put him in the director's chair. Then, perhaps, someone will give him as much trouble as he has given me." Clive turned to Matthew. "What do you think of that?"

Matthew was smiling so hard, his face hurt. He nodded, unable to speak at first, choked up at Clive's generosity. Then he found the words that gave him back his voice: "Only if we can hire all of them again," he said, sweeping his arm at their colleagues. This brought the greatest shout of applause yet.

Matthew and Clive embraced, and Matthew returned to his seat where Patty hugged him tight and kissed him. "You deserve it," she said into his ear, as Clive was bringing the stars, Jeremy and Lindsay, up to the front to speak.

"Do you think he's serious?" Matthew asked.

"He told me last week he's been grooming you for the director's chair," she said.

As Lindsay and then Jeremy and others spoke, a half dozen caterers marched into the screening room and passed out and refilled flutes of champagne. The mutual lovefest continued on into the night.

In the morning, Matthew woke up in Patty's bed, for the first time since their divorce. Patty was up in her big, blue, floppy pajamas, stretching her body into yoga postures. She continued her yoga, watching Matthew as he sat up, looked at her, then looked out the window with that faraway expression.

Not good, she thought to herself.

"Hungover?" she asked him, rising up on her tiptoes in the candle pose.

He turned back to her, the faraway expression still on his face. "No headache," he said. "Just a little champagne fog."

She came down from her pose and sat on the end of the bed. "You're thinking of your *petite ame*, aren't you?"

"I was, in fact," he said. He pulled himself up and leaned back against the wall, sitting more fully erect. "But you don't want to talk about that."

"We are old divorced people, Matthew," she said. "We can talk about anything."

Matthew shrugged. "I was thinking about last night," he said. "I was thinking about how fantastic that was. What a great rough cut we'd made. And what a great party afterwards. And I was thinking how Natalie doesn't want to have anything to do with this world. She thinks she wouldn't like the people. And, you know, as weird and affected as some of them can sometimes be, I love these people. This is my life."

"This is our world, Matthew. And most outsiders will never understand what it's like." She sat back on the bed and looked straight into his eyes. "It's *our* world," she said, "and we've got it spinning just the way we want."

"We do, don't we?" he said, starting to smile. I can't believe how much coverage you've got us. The TV; the tabloids; the press. You should write a book about this, when it's all over."

"No, no, no," she said quietly, leaning toward him across the rumpled sheets. "Write a book, and I'd never be able to get away with it again. I like having the power. I don't care about the glory."

She grabbed his ankles and pulled, sliding him down the bed until he was lying on his back. Then she crawled over him, straddling his body until she was face-to-face above him.

"Now, Mr. Harken," she said. "Are you considering going back to Salt Lake City to someone who spurns one of the best parts of your life?"

"No," he said.

She leaned down and kissed him long on the mouth. Then she sat back on his hips and began unbuttoning her pajama top. "You know," she said, "other than the fact that we were off on different projects and so we drifted apart, I can't remember any good reason that we got divorced."

Matthew slid his fingers up her smooth stomach to the base of her pretty breasts.

"Neither can I," he said.

◆　◆　◆

Several months later, however, it came back to him.

CHAPTER 17

SPIRIT OF THE FIRE

"SO WHO IS THIS person you want me to meet?" Matthew said. He was sitting in the passenger seat of Natalie's car, looking at her profile against the sweep of the rugged desert. The speed of the car combined with the effect of his cancer drugs made him feel even more light-headed and slightly nauseous. It felt to him that they were driving *very* fast.

"Tony Cappelli. He's a wonderful healer. He helped me get my act together when I started my practice."

"How is that going for you?"

"I have some clients who are incredibly stubborn about getting better," Natalie said. "Sometimes I just want to slap them and tell them to stop whining and grow up."

Matthew laughed. "You may be on to a whole new therapeutic modality."

"There is a big push toward short-term therapies."

"I could help you make a training film," Matthew said, holding up his hands as though framing the shot. "Fade in on the client, lying on the analyst's couch. 'It's so hard for me to say this,' the client says. 'My mother abandoned me when I was a child.' The analyst gets up. Raises her hand. Smack across the kisser! 'Get over it!' she shouts. The client is in shock. The stunned look. The hand to her cheek. The awed look on her face. And then: 'Thank you, doctor. I needed that!'"

Natalie laughed. "I could become rich taking this to the HMOs."

"Call it the Cagney Technique. You could include pushing a half grapefruit in your clients' faces."

"Forget Cagney. I'm naming it after myself."

"If only your clients could see you," Matthew said. "'Not Natalie! I thought she was so nice!'"

"They think I'm an ever-flowing fountain of breast milk."

"How shocked they'd be to know the truth!"

"Speaking of shock, did I ever tell you about Anna and the women's group?"

"I don't think so."

"Anna and I met in a women's support group. We'd take turns hosting it in our living rooms. One day we were talking about marriage and children. Out of the blue, Anna says, 'I could never have a child.' That's all she said. There was this moment of silence, and then one of the women asks, 'Why not?' Anna looks at her, like reason was obvious. 'I could never have a child,' she says, 'because I'd kill it.'

"All the women looked shocked." Natalie laughed. "I didn't know Anna well yet at this point, but her bluntness and the reactions struck me as funny."

"She could be very funny."

"Yes," Natalie said. "But then you look back at her journals, and you find out what else she was thinking during a time when you were having fun with her."

"Yes." Matthew looked out the window of the car to the west. Beautiful, in its arid way. The sun was getting lower over the desert horizon. It must have been about five p.m.

Despite the scenery, Matthew kept seeing Anna's journals spread across his hotel room floor in his mind's eye. He'd stepped over them so many times, they'd become an intuitive part of his sense of ground. He stepped over them, on them, rolled across the floor to find a volume that he'd marked with a Post-it. He could almost feel her journals in his legs, and he did not like the feeling. Reading her words renewed his love for her, but it also made him impatient. Angry with her. And then it drove him to pity.

He'd been thinking about it too much, and it made him feel claustrophobic. He pushed the image of the journals out of his mind and focused on the scene outside the window.

The sky was a bright, dry blue, with faint streaks of high cirrus clouds. The land here was a flat yellow-gray dotted with sage and scrub and occasionally gullied with dry streambeds. Matthew's nostrils and skin felt dry.

He looked over at Natalie's profile. She was deep in thought.

Despite the conversation, in some way she had felt inaccessible to him all afternoon. Not that he'd expected anything different. He had been avoiding her, after all, until she appeared at his hotel room door.

"The last time we saw each other was Anna's funeral," Matthew said.

"You came with Patty," she said.

"It was terrible at the funeral," Matthew said. "It was already clear that Patty and I had made a mistake, getting back together. I wanted to talk to you, but I was there with her. You were avoiding me. And we were all devastated by Anna's suicide."

"Yes, we were," Natalie agreed.

"I remember this awful moment at the wake," Matthew said. "I was sitting by myself on a sofa at the back of the mortuary chapel, with my eyes closed, feeling the shock and the loss of Anna's death. Then I had this sudden mental image of her. She was floundering. She was lost and frightened, drowning in a swarm of demons. I felt frightened for her, and I remembered reading the *Tibetan Book of the Dead*, years before. I remembered these complex directions for what to do in the spirit world, immediately after death: First you'd see two colors of light. I didn't remember what colors they were, and you had to move toward the correct one. After that, there would be another choice. And another. These choices were supposed to be memorized before death.

"I had that strong mental image of Anna, floundering. There was an open radiance above her. She was reaching down toward me for help.

"'Swim up,' I cried to her in my mind. 'Swim up!'

"The radiance above her opened further. 'Swim up!' I cried again. And then she began to swim up! She pulled out of the swarming demons. They had no power to hold her, only to confuse her."

"The living and the dead can help one another," Natalie said. "I believe that."

"But I felt so depressed after that. And I wondered if what I'd seen had been real."

Natalie slowed the car and began pulling onto the shoulder of the interstate.

"Is something wrong with the car?" Matthew asked.

"No. This is our turnoff up here," she said.

As they slowed further, Matthew saw a dirt road that ran directly off the shoulder of the interstate across the desert. He remembered noticing these unmarked roads on his way into Salt Lake.

Natalie turned abruptly to the right, and they slid down the elevation from the interstate onto the dirt road.

"How did you know how to find this?" Matthew said.

Natalie laughed. "It is out of the blue, isn't it? You have to watch the rock formations to the east. There's a peak that looks something like an upside-down slingshot. When the tip of that peak lines up with another peak that looks like a horse's head, you're almost at the turnoff."

"You're shitting me," Matthew said.

"No. That's it." Natalie laughed again. "A friend brought me out to meet Tony when I was first starting my private practice." She looked over at Matthew and for a moment her eyes showed that openness he remembered. "I felt like a disaster, Matthew. Like my decision to try to heal people was a crime of hubris. Tony helped me to find my way past that."

"What did he do?"

Natalie took a deep breath and blew it out. "Well, I don't want to get into what exactly Tony does. We can talk about that after you meet him. But the result for me was I could begin to use what I'd learned, my intuition, and to trust in the buried strength of my clients. Once I started to do that, I realized that I could be an effective healer. Until then, I felt like an impostor. Worse than that, I felt I was wasting the time of people who needed serious help."

"And Tony did all that?"

"I shouldn't tell you anything. I should just let you meet him."

The dirt road took a sudden turn to the left and then curved right and down a sharp slope. Natalie was driving into a small valley that had been completely hidden until they were practically on top of it. From the interstate, this land had looked flat and dry. One side of the small valley merged with the other, creating an illusion of continuity—yellow-gray desert as far as the eye could see. The little valley, however, was nearly lush by comparison. Several trees dotted the area, and tough grasses patched the ground. A dry riverbed ran through the center. Up ahead, next to the riverbed, Matthew saw a trailer home with an old pickup truck parked next to it. Up the slope from the trailer, a windmill captured the occasional breezes to run a pump for the well.

Natalie wound her car down the long slope and drove through the dry bed of the river and across to the area in front of the trailer. A dog emerged from the shade under the trailer to bark at them. Then he lay down again, stationing himself protectively between their car and the trailer. Two goats and a handful of chickens wandered the nearby land. Matthew hadn't noticed any fences, but there would be no impetus for the animals to leave the little valley.

Matthew reached for the car door handle. "Wait," Natalie said. "Native protocol has us wait for him to come out of the trailer. He knows we're here."

"Anything else I should know?" Matthew said.

"Well, there's a similar thing with conversation. You do it slower. You make sure the other person doesn't have something to add to what they've said before you say your next thing." She smiled at him. "You don't want to be the ugly *wasichu*, after all."

"What's *wasichu*? White man?"

"More or less. But it doesn't refer to color. The word is more about numbers. 'They who come in innumerable throngs.'"

"And give us smallpox, wipe us out, and steal our land."

She laughed. "A word gathers its subtext."

"Well, I'll be careful. I don't want to be an ugly *wasichu*."

"Don't worry too much. Tony is part Italian," she said.

"What else do you know about him?"

"Tony is a shaman," she said. "He speaks four languages. He's something of an historian. His mother was a Paiute. Her tribe was from this area, originally. At some point, Tony made his way to the Amazon rain forests. He was initiated by the local shaman into the local medicine, and lived as a Guaraní medicine man for many years. Then his family and most of his tribe were killed by disease. Or so they thought. It turned out to be cyanide poisoning: toxic runoff from a mining operation. But his tribe had lost faith in him. And so he returned to North America."

"Jesus."

"Yeah. Tony is a remarkably cheerful man, but sometime you can feel the wealth of sorrow he carries. It's part of what gives him his depth of character."

They sat in silence a moment, then Natalie opened her car door. "Come on. Let's get out," she said. "I want to stretch a little."

Natalie went around and unlocked the trunk of the car. Matthew got out as well, stretched, and came back to the trunk. Natalie had brought a half-dozen plastic milk bottles filled with water and a cardboard box with a large can of ground coffee, cigars in foil packages, some cans of meat, two bags of corn meal, some fresh produce, a package of sugar, and a greasy bag of bones.

"What's all this?"

"A few things for Tony."

"More native etiquette?

"More or less."

"You got me covered?"

"I got you covered."

They heard the screen door on the trailer open, and Tony Cappelli emerged. Tony was a heavy-set man with long, curly black hair pulled back in a ponytail. He had thick black eyebrows, but no sign of other facial hair. A pair of wide, short feathers hung from earrings in each ear. He wore a long, buckskin coat that was decorated with fringes on the pockets and sleeves—work that Tony had done himself. He'd embroidered it with thick red and gray cotton thread and inlaid it with porcupine quills and silver. He'd made his boots by hand from the same soft light-colored buckskin as his coat. They laced up to the tops of his calves. A tooled leather belt with a large silver and turquoise buckle cinched his black jeans. Tucked in his belt, showing through his open coat, was a fan of feathers.

He stopped at the bottom of the steps by his trailer door, took a puff from a cigar he carried in his right hand, and blew a semicircle of smoke above his head. He said a few words, as if speaking to something that was in the air there near him, then focused on the two of them and walked to Natalie's car, smiling. The dog got up and walked so closely by his side that his ribs were practically touching Tony's knees. The dog, too, seemed to be sporting a wide smile.

"Natalie," he said, taking her two hands in his, "It is a blessing that our paths come together again. Your radiance breathes from your eyes."

"It is good to see you again, Tony," she said.

He looked at her for a long moment, enjoying her presence. "The spirits told me you were coming," he said confidentially. "I saw you last night in the smoke of the fire. And your friend here. I saw him, too."

"Tony, this is Matthew Harken. He's an old friend who has come back into my life, for better or worse."

"Let's hope it's for better," Tony said. He took both of Matthew's hands as he had done with Natalie's. "Matthew," he said, nodding, looking into Matthew's eyes. "You have been a long time coming. You have been wandering for many years. It is good to see you at last."

As Tony continued to look into his eyes, Matthew suddenly felt as though he already knew him. He had a sudden overwhelming feeling of affection and gratitude toward Tony, which he could not understand. He felt embarrassed as his eyes filled with tears, and he was unable to speak.

Tony turned to Natalie and gestured to Matthew's face. "Look at him," he said admiringly. "He knows he has been lost, but now he understands he can find his way again." Tony shrugged. "Maybe this is true, what I say. Or maybe he just got some desert dust in his eye." Tony gave a hearty laugh, and Matthew sobbed a laugh through the emotions in his throat.

"I saw you coming," Tony said to him. "I recognized you in the smoke of the fire last night. You look familiar to me still."

"Matthew has had his face on magazine covers and TV," Natalie said.

"Oh, so this Matthew is a real famous guy?" Tony said, grinning, continuing to look at Matthew as he spoke. "Well, we won't hold that against him." He took a deep breath and shook his head. "No. I'm talking about some other kind of recognition." He clapped his hands and rubbed them together, sniffing the air and looking up into the sky. "It don't matter anyway. Sometimes I feel like I'm living my whole life for a second time because so many things seem familiar. And then other times, I feel like I'm lost in the strangest strange land and I don't know what the heck is going on!"

"I felt I recognized you, too," Matthew said. He took a deep breath and let it out. "That's what I was feeling when I got all choked up."

Tony shrugged. "Must be something to it." He gave Matthew a pat on the back and then looked into Natalie's trunk and gestured to the things in there. "Hey, you bringing me stuff?" He pulled out one of the plastic bottles. "Bottled water! All right! I can have some coffee that don't taste like salt and sulfur." He pulled out the three-pound can of coffee and the bag of sugar. "Damn! She brought the beans and the sugar, too. And Spam and cigars and all sorts of stuff. And you didn't forget Rasputin, neither." He pulled a greasy bone out of the bag and tossed it to the smiling dog. The dog caught it in the air and trotted off to lie beneath the tree and gnaw.

Tony grabbed the box of groceries and pulled it out of the trunk. Matthew and Natalie grabbed the water bottles and carried them to the trailer.

When Tony came out of the trailer, his expression had changed to one of solemn earnestness. He looked at the position of the sun, which was getting low over the horizon and would be down in less than an hour. He stepped away from the trailer and scanned the entire sky. For a full minute, he watched a raptor circling above the rising slope of the mountains to the east. Then he turned to the west and drew in some air sharply through his nose and pursed lips, as though tasting it for something. He went back to his trailer and, before reentering, he blew clouds of cigar smoke around the entrance. When he came back out, he was carrying a large embroidered cloth shoulder bag and a bundle wrapped in soft hide. He took it up the slope away behind the trailer. Matthew and Natalie followed him.

Matthew was surprised when, after a short distance up the slope, the path dipped down into a gully out of sight of the little valley where Tony's trailer stood. He never would have guessed the gully was here. The slopes up out of the little valley had seemed smooth to him. Matthew was reminded of how invisible Tony's valley had been from the highway. It was as though the space itself was magical and hidden.

Tony laid his large shoulder bag and package near a fire ring in the center of the gully. He gestured for Matthew and Natalie to sit on a log on the other side.

"I was telling Matthew a little bit of your background," Natalie said.

Tony raised his eyebrows and shook his head. "Yeah. I'm a strange, mixed-up conglomeration of this and that." He shrugged and dipped his head to one side. He crouched by the side of the ring of rocks that encircled the smoking remains of a fire. "This land around here is the land of my mother," he said. "She was a Paiute. The other side, my grandfather was Navaho and Italian. He was the first in the family to travel down into Central America. He got to know the shamans down there. Then when he comes back to the Navaho lands, he joins the Native American church—the peyote eaters. My parents thought all that shaman stuff and peyote-eating—that was all the wrong thing. They believe in Jesus Christ, and so when I was born, they named me for my great grandfather, the first Tony Cappelli. Great grandpa Tony was an Italian Catholic missionary who taught on the Navaho reservation. He was a respected priest. Nobody seemed to have any problem with the fact that he lived with a Navaho woman that he never married, and that they had a son—my grandfather.

"But my grandfather, you know, he did the rebellious thing. He didn't take no truck with the Catholic Church. Then, of course, my father did the rebellious thing, in his turn. He wants to go to the Catholic missionary school run by his grandpa. Well, it was the best school around, so my grandpa didn't refuse. So my father grows up a Catholic. He met my mother at the school. They was like a natural match, two outsiders—the Paiute and the half-breed among all them full-blooded Navahos. They fall in love, and get married, and lived probably as more orthodox Catholics than great grandpa Tony, the Italian priest." Tony slapped his leg and laughed.

"But, you know, then I had to rebel against my parents. I joined the Native American Church like my grandpa. And then I traveled south like he did. But I went all the way down to the Amazon rain forests. I got initiated by the shaman into the local medicine and lived as a Guaraní medicine man for many years. I got married, had children. But now most all of them are dead, killed by the poisons that a mining company used. Our tribe was downriver of some minerals they wanted. That's the way it works down there."

"I'm sorry," Matthew said.

"It's a funny world. Lot a pain. Lot a beauty, too. Ah, well." He clapped his palms together and rubbed them. "How about if I take a little look at you?"

"Okay," Matthew said, caught off guard.

Tony crouched by Matthew's side, put his hand on Matthew's shoulder, and looked directly into his eyes—not as though he were looking at Matthew, but as if he were reading something in the center of his brain.

"You have been sick," he said.

"Yes," Matthew said.

Tony nodded somberly. He put his hand on Matthew's chin and moved his head to look at Matthew's face from both sides. Then he returned to the opposite side of the fire ring and unrolled the soft hide bundle. As he worked, he spoke prayers to the spirits, sometimes speaking to the sky, sometimes to the ground, sometimes to the objects he handled, and sometimes in the directions of the stones, fresh wood and burnt wood in the fire ring. As he spoke the prayers, he shifted from language to language depending on who or what he was praying to, speaking in the Uto-Aztecan language of the Paiutes, then Amazonian Guaraní, and an occasional phrase in English and Spanish.

Tony spread the hide over the ground, smoothing out its creases, feeling its well-worn softness. The shaman who had initiated him into the mysteries in Amazonia had instructed him in the ritual way to make this skin for carrying his medicine objects. Tony had stalked, killed, and skinned the animal himself, in the same manner that his shaman/mentor had done years before. He scraped all the fur from the pelt, to conceal its sacred identity. He would tell others only that it was a spirit animal, although it had revealed itself to a few people over time, appearing in their dreams in its living form as a panther.

He spread the objects across the surface of the hide in the order they called to him. This, in fact, was the first stage in his divination. The objects were telling him which of them had the most reaction to the proximity of Matthew. Tony felt heat from the shaft of a bone of a bird he had sacrificed twelve years earlier, and he placed that on the far left. He saw a slight jump from a feather as his hand drifted over it and chose that to position next.

When he'd put all the objects in their places, he prepared kindling in a can that had a length of cord tied to it and several holes in the sides.

"When I build a fire on an occasion like this," he said, pausing in his prayers to return to conversation, "I cannot use matches from a factory. That would insult the spirit of the fire and our rapport would be destroyed. The conversation would begin on a sour note, and the fire might decide to tell me lies. And this, I would not blame it."

He took a small stick and used it to gently shuffle through the ashes against the rocks of the fire circle. "The fire in this circle is always a ritual fire. I first started it with fire sticks, using a bow and a thong to spin the stick into a socket and make friction." He found three coals that were still live and put them in the can atop the tinder.

He stood up and took the cord that was attached to the rope and swung the can around and around his head, until smoke began to stream behind the can. He set the can back down in the fire ring, placed some more tinder and dry shavings in the can atop the hot spot, and blew on it until the shavings caught flame. He carefully added more shavings and then poured the burning mass gently into the center of the fire ring. He added more small kindling and larger kindling to build the fire. When the fire was well established, he sat back on his heels and said a short prayer of thanksgiving.

Natalie took out a pouch of tobacco, took a pinch between her fingers, breathed on it, and placed it into the flames. Then she offered the pouch to Matthew.

"Good," Tony said. He looked at Matthew. "Natalie is giving a little gift to Grandfather Fire. You see, this is what we got to do if we want to sustain all this beauty that is around us. When we see a beautiful sunset, we can't just say, hey, what a beautiful sunset, and take it all in like the world owes that to us. We got to give something back in thanks, because the spirits that keep all this world together are hungry. So maybe we take a little tobacco and put our breath on it to add something of our own spirit to it, and then we offer it to the sunset.

"And that's even more important when we call up a spirit to give us some help. Like the spirit of Grandfather Fire. We call him up to help us. Because Grandfather Fire can maybe tell us a little bit about why you been sick, eh, Matthew? If he got some information for you, something he can reveal to help you be living with a little better health, you'd like to have that information, wouldn't you? That's why you come here, no?"

"Yes," Matthew said. He felt a sudden surge of hope. Matthew had read about and met and been taught by several self-proclaimed shamans and avatars and voodoo priests over the years. He'd seen remarkable things, but he'd also seen a lot of nonsense and some downright fraud. He'd used the best of what he'd seen and learned as material for his work. But he'd never sought out any shamanistic healing for himself.

"So we don't want to leave the spirit of Grandfather Fire exhausted," Tony continued. "We don't take without giving. We got to keep the spirits fed and fat and happy. Otherwise, maybe they lie to us. Or worse. Maybe they start to fuck with us. 'Cause they don't owe us nothing. That's for sure. You know, if we ain't going to feed them, maybe they just as soon have all the diseases eat us for dinner and be done with us. So, in a minute, you take a little tobacco there, and you put your breath on it and your gratefulness for what Grandfather Fire may or may not do for you, and your gratefulness for his warmth and beauty, and drop it in the flames for him. Then his spirit can smoke that tasty tobacco and be happy. But first, you tell me something. You got some kind of cancer going on, no?" Tony said.

"That's right," Matthew said. He looked at Natalie, wondering how much she'd told Tony about him, but Natalie just shrugged. Tony turned back to building the small fire carefully, placing small pieces of wood exactly where he wanted them.

"Yeah, you got that cancer feel around you," he said. "I seen that before. So I don't know, maybe you got some angry issues with tobacco. Lotta people do. But tobacco is a sacred plant. It wouldn't hurt you if you used it in the sacred way. It wasn't never meant to get wrapped up with rice paper and stuck on the end of a filter in some big factory to make a bunch of corporation people filthy rich. That's a defiling of the sacred plant. You smoke twenty, forty of those a day, it ain't no surprise that it decides to kill you. 'Cause the sacred don't like to be trifled with. So I just tell you all that because I don't want you to be offering tobacco to the fire if in your head, you're thinking, 'Oh yeah, this goddamn tobacco, that's what's killing me.' That wouldn't be much of a gift."

"No," Matthew said. "I've never smoked much. I don't think it had anything to do with my problem—though I don't know what caused it, for sure."

"All right," Tony said. "You make your gift."

Matthew dipped his fingers into Natalie's foil pouch. It was an ordinary, cigarette rolling tobacco that could be purchased at any drug store, but when Matthew pulled the heavy wad of curling, dark strands out of the pouch in this fingertips, it suddenly looked like no tobacco he'd ever seen before. This tobacco looked moist and alive. He felt an impulse to push the perception away—as though he were being tricked by Tony's speech. But then he suddenly welcomed the possibility that he might perceive something of the world in which Tony operated. He relaxed and looked at the tobacco more deeply.

Yes, it was alive. And in its life was a profound willingness to experience death.

Experience death? Was *death* the right word?

Maybe not death: it was a transformation by fire. The moment of new life. An activation.

But death, too, because that moment of transformation was possible only once, and then what remained in this world?

Ashes.

Matthew raised the wad of tobacco to his mouth and breathed on it, releasing the gift of his breath onto it, and as he did so, he felt the mingling of his life spirit with the tobacco. He felt the breath go as it left his lips and knew that it was a breath that he would never breathe again. This was one less moment he would have in this body in this lifetime. He had the profound feeling of living in the moment. He had the complete understanding that he was giving this moment to the blessing of this tobacco, to thank the spirit of this fire. It was a simple act—but a rich exchange. He was no longer thinking of the past or the future. He was not thinking of what the spirit of the fire might do for him or reveal to Tony. He was thinking only of the spirit that he saw before him—the flames of the little fire within the ring of rocks. He was not thinking of it in terms of spirit, but in terms of the beauty that he saw, the liveliness of the flames, the warmth, the joy he felt from it that entered through his eyes, through the heat on his skin. And as he breathed on the tobacco, he gave thanks simply for this grace he was experiencing now. He breathed into the tobacco with his grateful spirit and dropped the tobacco into the flames, and watched contentedly as the flames embraced the curls of tobacco.

Meanwhile Tony had taken an abalone shell from the large embroidered shoulder bag and set it next to the fire. He took a few chunks of wood charcoal left from the extinguished coals of earlier fires, held them in the flames to ignite them, then put them in the abalone shell. He took the fan of feathers that was tucked in his belt—it was the full preserved wing tip of a large bird—and used it to gently fan the coals to help them ignite fully. He covered them with dried sage and sweetgrass from another pouch in the big shoulder bag and fanned some more to make the herbs smolder and smoke. Then he used the wing to brush the smoke over his head, shoulders, torso, waist, legs, and feet in purification.

Tony got up and walked a large circle, clockwise, around the outside of the fire ring. He used the wing to distribute smoke around the circle as he walked and prayed. Occasionally he stopped and used the wing to flick at something in the air, as though shooing away an insect.

When he'd completed the circle, Tony crouched down by Natalie and fanned the smoke toward her. Natalie scooped it with her hands and pulled it over her head and shoulders and chest, almost as though it were water and she were splashing it on herself to wash, but in slow motion. Tony brought the shell to Matthew, and Matthew followed suit, pulling the smoke over him.

Something in the air above and behind Matthew caught Tony's attention. He grabbed a handful of ash from inside the fire ring and blew through his hand, hard, sending up a cloud of ash dust.

"Ha! You see that?" he cried.

"What?" Matthew said.

Tony blew up another cloud. "Look into the ashes," he commanded. "Can you see their faces?"

"I don't see anything," Matthew said. "Just dust."

"You been gathering ghosts, boy. They crowding around you like vultures and bloodsuckers."

Matthew wondered if Anna was among them. "What do they look like?" he said.

"I ain't going to tell you what they look like to me, because they might look like something completely different to you. But what I am going to tell you is that we got to get rid of them. Having ghosts around you is about as healthy as keeping a big old chunk of uranium in your pocket. Even if they don't hold you any grudge. Even if you like having them around for some strange reason. Human beings and ghosts don't mix. If you was a shaman, that might be one thing. But these guys you got here don't look like they'd be no use to any shaman, neither. Ghosts and human beings is a toxic mix. Now the only reason I'm telling you all this is because I need to chase these ghosts away before we do anything else, and I want to make sure you ain't going to call the ghosts right back again. Because I find that kind of yo-yo nonsense irritating."

"It is possible that one of the ghosts is somebody I know."

"Uh huh," Tony said.

"It's a friend who committed suicide," Matthew continued. "I've been reading her journals and thinking a lot about her lately."

"Uh huh. Well, I don't suppose anybody ever did a ceremony to free her soul."

Matthew looked at Natalie. "Well, there was a wake . . ."

"Some of her friends on the West Coast had some kind of memorial, too," Natalie said.

"Uh huh. Well. Not meaning any disrespect, but a bunch of white people standing around drinking coffee doesn't do much to free the trapped soul of a suicide," Tony said. "Never mind. So we are gonna have to have some kind of ceremony for your friend, too. 'Cause you been paying her so much attention, she ain't going to want to ever let you alone, unless she can get to where she supposed to go. How long has this woman been dead?"

"Five years," Matthew said.

Tony shook his head. "Five years. Shit. Well, we are gonna have to have a nice big ceremony for this poor confused ghost who been wandering pitiful all this time. Otherwise she is going to be one big pain in the ass to you maybe for the whole rest of your life. Though I'm sure you don't think about her that way 'cause you loved her back when she had a body to walk around in. But you got to realize now, having her ghost around ain't like having a nice, friendly puppy by your side. It's more like taking a long soak in a pond full of leeches. They don't mean you any harm personally. It's just you taste so damned good!"

Tony turned to add a few more chunks of wood to the fire. Behind him, the sun was getting low on the horizon, and the air was beginning to chill.

Matthew felt sad as he thought about Anna's ghost. He felt sad that she'd probably been wandering lost for five years. But he noticed another sorrow at the thought of letting her go. Perhaps he *had* been holding her ghost to him, so that he could feel her presence in his life, if only in this debased way. Would he be able to let his poor, dear Anna go?

Tony pulled another coal from the ring that the fire had ignited and placed it in the abalone shell. He took a ball of resin wrapped in oilpaper from within his big embroidered shoulder bag. He used the bird wing to fan the coal hot, then pinched off a piece of the resin and set it atop the coal.

"This is copal," Tony said. "It's from my days in the Amazon. It's a powerful, sacred resin, gathered from a tree that I'm not going to tell you the name of. Go ahead and breathe in this smoke deeply. Pull it all over yourself."

Tony fanned the coal hotter, and the resin began sending off thick smoke. He held the abalone shell in front of Matthew, who breathed in the smoke and pulled it over his head and all around his body. The smoke had an awake, sinuous, penetrating fecundity to its aroma. It was sweet and green, and dark and secret, like the jungle. Matthew breathed it in, deeply, again. Then Tony took the shell and walked all the way around Matthew, fanning the smoke all over him, and repeated the ritual with Natalie.

Tony set down the shell by the fireside and crouched in front of Matthew, putting his hands on Matthew's shoulders. "You can't hold her no more," he said. "It ain't good for her, and it might be part of what is killing you." He looked over at Natalie. "You, too, I mean. Maybe you got some part in holding this woman. Everybody's got to let her go." He looked back into Matthew's face. "Now you got to trust me, 'cause I can feel that you loved this woman. I'm going to send her to a good place where she can think for a while. She was a woman who liked to think, no?"

Matthew nodded. "She loved to think," he said.

"Well, I'm going to send her to a good place for thinking for a while. You got to let her go there, because that's the best thing for her, and that's the only way I can help you. And then we got to work on you. And that is going to take a bit of time. Not just today. Maybe many days. And then we are going to get back to your friend and help her get to where she's supposed to be. And that's going to be the best thing for you and especially for her.

"Now the reason I'm telling you all this is because I don't want you resisting what I'm doing. We all got to work with the same energy for the same purpose. Otherwise, it's like we're trying to get the groceries home from the store, but we're all pulling in different directions, and suddenly the bag rips and the food is all over the ground. And we don't want that. So, you with me?"

VISIONS OF ANNA • 141

"I am if you promise we can help her, too," Matthew said. "I can't just abandon her. There are a lot of mysteries surrounding her death."

"What do you mean?" Tony said.

"She would wake screaming out of her sleep in the months before she killed herself, coming out of dreams of being sodomized as a child. But she'd only begun remembering the abuse lately. And I'm not so sure they were real memories. She'd had a twin sister who was raped and murdered as a child. For years Anna's mother refused to tell her anything about it. And then, in the past years, she and her lover attracted spirits to themselves. And not necessarily the kind of spirits you'd want to have around. I'm afraid for her soul."

Tony bobbed his head from side to side. "I agree. She need some help bad. But you can't help me help her until I help you. And I can't help you if you got suicide ghosts hanging around. So I can put her in a limbo kind of place where she won't suffer. Where she can think. And we can come back to her. And in the meantime, we can focus on you. Get you strong. And then come back strong for her."

"Okay," Matthew said. "Then I'm with you."

Tony looked at Natalie.

"Yes," she said. "I'm with you, too."

"It is as you say," Tony said. "You are both with me, now. Focus in on the spirit of the fire, and let all other connections be cut."

Tony turned to the fire and spoke words of praise to it in Guaraní. From his large embroidered shoulder bag, he took a frame drum and a beater made from animal bone and gave them to Natalie.

"When you feel the beat, begin to play," he told her. "You don't need to do nothing fancy. Just keep playing, all the time, until I tell you to stop. This is real important, okay?" Natalie nodded. The beater felt suddenly heavy in her hand.

"If the spirits tell you to speed up or slow down, you go ahead and do that," he said. "But otherwise, just hold the beat that I start. Okay?"

She nodded again.

He took a gourd shaker from the bag and began a song, shaking the gourd regularly and dancing in place as he sang. He sang with his eyes closed at first, his knees deeply bent. He rocked forward with each beat, stomping his right foot on the ground as he shook the gourd. After a few moments, Natalie began to beat the drum to Tony's rhythm, gently at first, and then with confidence. As she played, Natalie's heartbeat aligned with the rhythm, for that was what the rhythm was: the rhythm of the human heartbeat at prayer.

After he had sung for a time, Tony bowed his head and faced the west where the last sliver of the sun was setting behind the slope of the hill. He raised his arms and prayed, calling to the guides of the dead. Natalie continued to beat the drum. He prayed for a long time, adding more copal to the abalone shell, making clouds of sweet smoke to attract them to the spot. He blew more dust into the air to locate the ghosts, and bathed them in the copal smoke to calm them and gather them in its spell.

When Tony became aware that the guides had arrived, he spoke to them in Paiute, one of the old languages of the region, the language of his mother. As he spoke, he made large gestures in the air. He created shapes, showed movement, and touched his fingertips to his lips, to his heart, and to his legs.

Then he picked up a machete from among his medicine objects on the animal skin. Matthew was amazed to see the machete. He couldn't imagine where it had come from. It was too big to have been in the shoulder bag. He looked over at Natalie, but she was drumming with her eyes focused on the long distance, hypnotized by the beat.

Tony held the machete laid flat on the open palms of his spread hands and sang a prayer over it. He took it by the handle and purified both sides of the blade in the flames of the fire. He slowly and ceremoniously cut the air all around Matthew and Natalie, severing the ties the ghosts had made to them.

Then he asked the spirit guides to escort the ghosts to one of the caves of the dead, where they would wait in contemplation, away from living humans. He promised to perform a ceremony that would help them find their way on to the land of the dead.

He put a cigar into the fire as a gift in thanks to the guides and promised them a feast to come.

However, when the guides had gone, taking the ghosts with them, one angry, roiling ghost remained behind, swirling hungry and spiteful just beyond Matthew, attempting to cast its luminous cords back around him. Tony warned it in a low voice, speaking still in Paiute, to leave this place, to go with the others, but it would not go. He realized this ghost was not of this place, and he spoke to it again in Guaraní, then Spanish, and finally English, but it either refused to or could not understand.

This creature had to go. Tony had not yet begun his formal divination, so he could not yet know for sure, but it was likely that this being was damaging Matthew's health, if indeed it was not the author of his illness. He hardened his resolve and began singing again, this time to the fire, asking its assistance. He step-danced over to his medicine objects, took a man-shaped bundled of herbs off the hide, and placed it into the flames. He raised his arms and sang in a loud voice, invoking the spirits of the air. The flames surged in the fire ring, urging Tony's song, and sparks appeared in the air all around them. Matthew looked at Natalie, but she did not seem to be noticing anything. She continued to play the drum, the speed of her drumming having increased and intensified.

Tony felt the spirits of the air streaming in, and he called out to them and greeted them in song, one by one, as they arrived. He sensed their hunger, their bloodlust, at the call he had given. The constant anger that had radiated from the ghost who would not leave changed suddenly to panic, but now there was no place for it to go. The spirits of the air surrounded it. Tony's voice grew louder and ruthless, his song erratic now with shouted command, and Natalie rose to her feet, pounding the frame drum as hard as she could. Tony urged on the spirits, who swirled around them, creating suction on the ghost. Then he threw out his arms to the sides, and the spirits flew off, sucking the ghost from all directions, causing it to explode across space.

Matthew clutched his hands to his ears. "God!" he screamed.

Tony bowed his head and sang a song of thanksgiving. He put more tobacco in the fire and more copal in the abalone shell. The pace of Natalie's drumming slowed. When Tony finished his prayer, he told her she could stop, and lit a cigar for himself.

"So Matthew," he said puffing smoke out into the air. "Why did you shout out like that?"

"That horrible sound," Matthew said.

"You heard something, huh?"

"I didn't hear anything," Natalie said. "But I did see something."

"They were there to be seen," Tony agreed.

"It was loud," Matthew continued. "Like a shotgun. But there was something horrible about it."

"There *was* something horrible about it," Tony agreed. "That was the sound of a living creature being torn and scattered to the four winds. That was a life gone, dying for the last time."

Matthew looked suddenly ashen.

"Don't worry," Tony said. "That was not your friend. And don't be pulling her back to you. You got to trust me that we'll take care of her. But right now, it's time to do a little work on you."

CHAPTER 18

A DREAM OF FLIGHT

MATTHEW LAY ON HIS back on the ground. The fire was on his right. Tony was kneeling over him on his left. The moon had risen like a big orange ball over the mountains to the east and then had climbed high in the sky, growing paler, smaller and more brightly intense.

Natalie had begun drumming again when Tony started his divination of Matthew's disease. Matthew hadn't had eye contact with her in at least an hour. When her eyes weren't closed, she was looking up at the moon or the stars or at Tony working, with that mesmerized expression on her face. Long strands of black hair clung to the sweat on her cheeks and forehead. And all the time she kept up the hypnotic beat: a constant slow, deep heartbeat on the drum. Bone beater against animal hide. A beat that transmuted time. Matthew had felt time bend—watching the moon rise, or watching Natalie's face, or Tony working—suddenly he would come back to himself, and feel that he'd been outside time for a while. And while he'd been gone, the moon had leapt higher into the sky.

Tony had entered fully into his world of objects and magic. His eyes no longer focused on anything in the physical world. His breath smelled green, like freshly mown grass. His skin glistened with a light sweat. His every movement seemed otherworldly. First he would select some object from the skin. He'd lay it on one part of Matthew's body. He'd talk to it. Move it to another part of Matthew's body. And listen. Perhaps he'd get up and dance for a time. Circle around the fire. Speak to the flames. Stand and turn his face up to the dark sky. To the moon.

And sing again. Or speak. He'd get down on all fours and keen to the earth below him. And listen again.

Matthew understood none of it. Tony rarely used a word of English.

While the drumming, singing, and dancing, as well as the crackling of the fire, often took him out of himself, some of the time Matthew found himself filled with questions: Why was Tony going to so much trouble? How much had Natalie told him in advance? Did Tony do all this whenever he met a sick person? What was in it for him?

And what was Tony doing? What possible benefit could come from laying a small clay figure on Matthew's abdomen, for instance? When he stopped and listened for those long periods of silence, filled only with the beat of Natalie on the drum, what was he hearing?

When he wondered these things, Matthew remembered the explosion he'd heard that Natalie had not: that horrible crack that Tony said was the obliteration of a being. If Matthew had heard that, what was it possible for someone like Tony to perceive?

Why were ghosts and people a toxic mix? He'd accepted it readily enough when Tony was talking about it, but in retrospect, he began to wonder. Didn't Native Americans welcome messages from the dead in dreams?

Matthew watched Natalie drumming. Her total immersion in the drumming gave her face a spiritual radiance that made her even more beautiful. Did she accept Tony's worldview, including the spirits, ghosts, gods, and all?

But the question that came to his mind most often was: Would all this do him any good?

Suddenly Tony's thumb was pressing something down hard on the center of Matthew's forehead. It came as such a surprise, Matthew nearly shouted. He felt something gooey being squashed onto his skin under the heavy thumb. It pushed the back of his head hard against the rocky ground. Then the thumb pulled away, and the sticky mass clung to his forehead. He smelt the aroma of unburnt copal.

Tony's eyes were looking directly into his, but they seemed focused deep into the center of Matthew's brain. Matthew could see no indication that Tony recognized Matthew was looking back at him.

And then Matthew understood that his questions and his increasing unease were interfering with Tony's work. Matthew's mind was creating static, and Tony wanted it to stop.

Natalie was looking up into the sky with stunned eyes, continuing the beat of the drum. Tony was tracing a fingertip down Matthew's breastbone with his eyes focused somewhere inside Matthew's chest. Each of them was deep in a trance state.

Matthew felt suddenly lonely. He was the only one still operating in "real time."

He closed his eyes.

He felt Tony's finger tracing down his breastbone for a moment, then Matthew's consciousness was drawn away to the spot on his forehead. Whatever Tony had stuck to his skin felt suddenly burning hot. He felt the pressure of it pushing down into his head, boring a hole. All his awareness moved to that spot and flowed into it like sand flowing into the spiral of an hourglass. With his eyes closed, he could see the image of sand flowing as if from above. He could see the interior of the cone it created as it swirled down into the lower chamber of the hourglass—and at the same time he could feel himself flowing down, his mind slowing down, his vision focusing through the point in the center of his forehead. He felt his spirit loose within his body. He felt as though he were moving into a medium like water—that he would no longer have to get up and walk on land to move around, but that he could swim through space.

Then he heard Tony's voice. It was not a voice that vibrated through air currents. It was not his physical voice. It was Tony's soul voice, and it penetrated directly into the center of Matthew's chest.

"Ride the drum," Tony's voice said. "Ride the drum."

Tony's voice came from deeper in the liquid world into which Matthew was descending. It was a world opening for him through the portal Tony had created in the center of his forehead.

Matthew felt the heat from the spot penetrate through his skin into the depths of his mind. It made a shaft of heat into his skull, and its energy drew him down into trance. It was a pillar of fire. It was the tunnel to the underworld. It had become the single gravitational pole of Matthew's transition, and it pulsed with the rhythm of the drum.

Matthew gently pushed away the temptation to thoughts and questions and allowed himself to be pulled into the gravitational field. He felt himself being drawn into the "other world."

Slowly, all sense of his arms and legs—even his torso—faded away. His awareness continued to enter the channel in his forehead taking him out of contact with his surroundings. He lost consciousness of the fire beside him. The smell of the smoke. The feel of the night air on his skin. He felt himself flowing into darkness, surrendering to that flow—and at the same time some part of his awareness was above, seeing it happen, watching a substance like sand flowing into a perfectly round hole in a barren earth, and knowing that when all the sand had flowed in, the transition would be complete.

Matthew noticed again the sound of the drum. He sensed it pulling him into the tunnel. He felt its gravitation and entered into it. He became surrounded by the pulse of it, emerging from within the tunnel. And then he and the pulse were the same. He was sound, pulsing. Then heat. Heat to one side in the darkness. The fire pulsing with the living energy of the drum.

He was beneath the cracked surface of the desert earth.

He stood beside the fire, a fire as tall as he, and saw it for what it was: pure elemental spirit. He saw the portal within it. It was spirit and passageway. And he saw that something had passed down it. A trail of breadcrumbs remained behind: long tendrils of energy to pull someone back through. Bungee cords of the spirit.

Or were the cords to pull someone forward?

Then he heard Tony's voice calling him into the fire.

He touched the cords and suddenly he was everywhere they stretched at once. He sensed everything along their length. This breadth of awareness was so overwhelming, it was more like unconsciousness. He became as liquid as water, diffuse as smoke, embracing all things at once—and losing all particulars.

The understanding, the touching on all things, propelled him into a state of ecstasy, and for a moment he understood that this was one kind of death, to have one's essence scattered into all things, to go back into the indestructible energy of the universe, and to lose forever the life of his individual consciousness.

He could imagine a lovely pleasure in that final letting go.

But he was not dying at this particular moment, and so his consciousness began to reorganize itself around the pulsing energy of the drum. The drumbeats were no longer separate events. They pulsed louder at each beat, but the sound never ended. It moved him through psychic space, like blood moves through the arteries, pulsing harder with each heartbeat, but never ceasing to move.

And then he sensed the spirit within the pulse. First, the numinous spirit of the drum itself, as if it were some pulsing deity brought to life, and then, right along next to it, the personality of his one-time lover, Natalie, the human trigger to this incarnation of the drum.

He sensed all at once the texture of her soul. He saw this texture elaborated by all the images it had fed upon in the course of her lifetime. It was a sculpture, created over time by the cutting away from and agglomeration onto the essential soul with which she'd entered the world. It was a lovely thing, and he saw it more clearly now than he ever had when they were lovers. For what is love at the beginning other than a desire for the lovely surface of the beloved? There are only the vaguest intimations of the soul within. Intuitions, as often based on wishful thinking as perception.

What had stood out for him in the beginning were the eyes. The soulful eyes. When she opened her eyes from the inside and allowed herself to be seen, Natalie's soul shone forth. Then, to the limits of his vision, Matthew was truly able to see her.

And now again, first he saw the eyes. He entered the world of her eyes, driven by the energy of the drum. He began seeing familiar images: A blossom irradiated with electrical energy. Scenes of domestic and intimate life viewed from the outside, through not-quite-fully drawn shades. The beautiful body of a man with the fabric of his muscles showing from beneath translucent skin. Images from within cars, trains, and boats, images from the point of view of a passenger, sometimes showing the back of the head or the side of a forearm of the driver or pilot, but never enough to identify who he might be. He recognized these as images from her paintings, motifs that were grown into her soul and that came out again through her brush.

He sensed how clearly she had become, or had been born to be, a painter. Her work at the AIDS clinic, and now her work as a therapist, was always to the side of her identity. It was what she did. It was not who she was. For even in these things, there was some portion of her that was eternally silent, that saw but did not speak.

The essence of Natalie existed in silence. Matthew had understood some inner part of her as being doggedly elusive. But that was not it. It was simply quiet. It was observant.

And then Matthew's soul did that thing that was so difficult for him and so natural for Natalie: It dropped into silence. What he perceived, he perceived directly, without interpreting into words.

He was in the tunnel now, the tunnel first formed in his forehead by the spot of copal. Then it was the portal in the center of the fire. He was propelled through the narrow space of the tunnel like in a dream of flight: flying like Superman. He saw the long cords of energy once again, the bungee cords of the spirit, stretching beneath him, far down the length of the tunnel, but he did not touch them this time.

Then he was in another space, a larger space, with Natalie flying beside him.

Side by side.

Then face to face.

He saw those eyes again and understood them more profoundly than he ever had before.

He moved in closer, they, each to the other, entering deeply in through the eyes, finding the entry there. The understanding. The memory. Like an irrepressible magnetic attraction. Like a longing to be touched.

And then they were together. Flowing together like twin tributaries moving forward, now conjoined, toward the big river. And as their waters touched, they remembered. My God! How had they ever forgotten this? How had they ever lost this? All their lives alone. Apart. Separated too from all that had come before. The life they'd had. Lives.

No! *Life* was right. Singular. Not plural. For they had been one creature, one consciousness, one *whole* before. And these pitiful things: This Matthew. This Natalie. They were mere slivers of consciousness, struck off alone for a lifetime.

But why? Why did they do this phenomenally lonely thing, without one another? And without the rest? For they sensed now, occupying this single reunited consciousness, that there were more of them than these two pitiful shards, this Matthew and this Natalie. They were not two halves of a whole, but two fragments of some larger being that even together, with their two consciousnesses conjoined, they could not remember, could not fathom, but could only sense in profound and devastated longing, like some forgotten dream of ecstasy, lurking hauntingly just beyond the limits of recall.

Oh, how they clung together in this reunion of soul, weeping in joy and overwhelming nostalgia: this creature that they were together, one thing and still yet two! For they sensed now the necessity of what they did as these lonely shards of soul on earth. They sensed what was still beyond their understanding, even together. They sensed the size of the mind of which they were just a part: Their lives were part of the conversation of this larger being, part of its exploration, part of its intellectual life. They were part of the dinner it was cooking, or eating. Part of the book it was reading. Or writing. Part of the growth of its mind. For the personalities they became and lived and then reunited were the ongoing soul of it. This Matthew and this Natalie bathed in the profound appreciation of each other, of themself together, a pair and a single thing simultaneously, and of the larger soul they would swim into together again one day.

How had they survived being apart all this time? The waste of it! And the necessity of it, too, they recognized. They were living the conversation. The brilliant conversation, filled with beauty as it was. The pain, too, was beauty. And what joy it would be to rejoin the whole and to see the fabric in its entirety, and to talk again to the other large beings—for this too they sensed: Just as they were part of some larger soul, there were other larger souls of which they were not a part, but whom they loved. And what joy it would be to rejoin in the conversation with these . . . these what? These gods?

They continued flying, face to face, Matthew and Natalie, joined in one mind, and then for a moment they exploded into light. Into an immense ecstasy. The tunnel had taken them inside the bright white core of their larger self, with all around them the separate but conjoined souls of the whole, like hundreds of telepathic baby spiders inside the egg. Oh, the love of this thing they were! This thing that was the magnetic field that held them all together and made them one integrated personality! The most wondrous love! Like a gigantic sustaining all-encompassing orgasm. They were the electric-firing cells of this one large brain, separate yet connected, one mind and a host of parts, joyful, joyful paradox!

And then, just as suddenly, Matthew was alone again.

He sensed his body once again, and the fire burning gently beside him.

How had he left the great Self so suddenly? He felt so small and abandoned.

There was no question to him of the truth of what he'd just experienced. The wonder of it dawned upon him, and he felt a profound gratitude for what had been revealed. And a profound love for Natalie, that other part of his larger self that he'd been privileged to find.

And Tony, too. That was why they'd recognized one another when they first met. Tony must have some connection with Anna as well. Tony was a member of this team, and Matthew felt profound gratitude and love toward him as well.

Matthew sensed everything more clearly. It gave him a capacity for patience and acceptance that he'd never experienced before. He had always been in a hurry. That was what drove his dynamic ambition. That was what made him one of the few whose works were seen by the hundreds of thousands—the millions, even.

But now he'd been given a glimpse of where he was really going. And though he couldn't understand it, his joy at the glimpse of its existence was enough. He was living this corporeal life because his larger self wanted him to. He was making some contribution to its, his, existence, in some way that was beyond his fathoming.

At the same time his physical understanding of the here and now was profoundly altered. He could sense the islands of his cancer within him, settled like dark masses on the ocean of his soul. And in this vision, he did not feel invaded as he had before. They were there and he was there, and the cancer was foreign to him, and yet his body and the cancer both were he, and yet none of that physical mass was he. And it was all part of the larger conversation of which he was privileged to be a part—even if he could not hear it now.

Ah, and now he sensed the other thing. From a great height, he saw his physical body far below. On his chest was something familiar. Something he had never seen before. Something known. Something strange. He saw it from the point of view of his own eyes. Lying on his back, his eyes opened and there it was, squatted on his chest: the white spider. Snow white. Spectral white. Large, with spiky white fur on its body, and delicate, long strands of hair on its thighs. It put one dainty leg forward and dipped it into the pool of red, red blood in the center of Matthew's chest. It raised the blood-moistened leg delicately to its mouth and tasted. Matthew awaited the verdict. A fine wine? Had it properly aged? Had the grapes married and melded?

The spider rolled its eyes slowly, comprehending the flavor of the blood, tasting messages from the far-off shores of Matthew's body.

The spider rose up on its legs, higher and yet higher, its body swelling, its decision made.

Then it spat its venom into the pool of Matthew's blood.

Matthew felt the poison seep into his groundwater. He felt his molecules shiver as the venom spread. He felt his whole being tingle and his vision go dark. He shook harder and harder until he was unable to breathe.

And then he knew nothing whatsoever.

Nothing at all.

Chapter 19

WAKE-UP CALL

"DRINK THIS."

The voice came out of the darkness. Matthew opened his eyes. Darkness.

He could hear the fire. He just couldn't see it. He could smell it. He could even feel its heat beside him, where it had been all night.

He looked toward it, straining his eyes.

Ah, yes. There was the slightest glow from the direction of the crackle of the burning wood.

"I can't see," he said. His voice sounded preternaturally loud in his ears.

He felt a hand on his face turning it in the direction away from the fire. He felt another man's breath on his face. It smelled green, like fresh twigs, newly stripped of bark.

"Ah, yes," the breath said. "Wait, I'm going to wash them."

The breath went away, then came back with something that smelled even more profoundly green. Fecundly green. "Keep your eyes wide open," it said. It held a hot, wet cloth up to Matthew's eyes, gently at first, then firmly, pushing the warm liquid that soaked into Matthew's eyes.

His eyes felt suddenly oiled. He realized how stiff they had been in their sockets. He did not want to move them now because the cloth was uncomfortable against the surface of his eyes. It was a torment to try not to blink them. And yet his eyes suddenly felt loosened.

"All right," the breath said, gently pulling the cloth away. "Let's take a look."

Matthew blinked as the cloth came away. He pressed his eyes tightly closed, then opened them wide again. At first opening, the air stung profoundly, as though he'd opened them into thick smoke. But now he saw light and shapes. He blinked his eyes several more times, and the shapes began to coalesce into Tony and Natalie, into the ritual fire beside him, into the now-silent drum, next to Natalie, into streaks of light in the pre-dawn sky, into the tops of the few sparse trees on the ridge at the top of the valley, and into Tony's collection of ritual objects laid out on the hide.

Tony dipped the cloth, a piece of ordinary terry cloth towel, into a steaming smoke-blackened stockpot next to the fire. He handed it to Matthew. "Continue to bathe your eyes. And also begin to drink."

Matthew dabbed the hot cloth to one eye, then the other. "What am I supposed to drink?" he said.

Tony laughed and pointed to the stockpot. "That," he said. "And don't spill too much of that stuff washing your eyes, 'cause you need to drink *all* of it."

Matthew looked into the stockpot. It was half filled with a dark greenish liquid. A pound of twigs, leaves, and flowers floated on top in a variety of reds, greens, and browns.

"*All* of this?" he said.

"Yeah. You need every drop of that. And you may as well get started, 'cause there's over a gallon in there." He handed him a tin cup. "You don't need to eat the stems or leaves or nothing. Unless you need a little extra fiber in your diet."

"What's in here?" Matthew asked.

"Lotta herbs. I got a lotta instructions about you. Took me two hours to cook up all that—after I got all the stuff sorted and chopped. I even had to go out in the desert to get an herb I never used before. Never even *heard of* before." Tony sat back on his heels. "You got some weird ass spirits interested in you. I saw a bunch a spirits I never seen before. Damned bossy ones, too. Put me through the wringer!" he said, laughing.

"So, what did they have you put in here?" Matthew said, dipping in the tin cup and carefully scooping up liquid without the leaves and stems. He brought the cup to his nose and sniffed it. He smelled its fecund, green aroma again. He smelled something burnt underneath, as though charcoal dust had been ground into it.

"Well, this stuff ain't approved by the FDA," Tony said. "You ain't going to find it in the *Physicians' Desk Reference*. And like I said, I don't even know what that last herb is—but I *am* sure it's the one them spirits wanted you to have. I got no doubt about that. And I can tell you just as sure that these spirits ain't trying to kill you with what's in that pot. From what I've seen, any spirit that wanted you dead would just leave you alone at this point. They already done everything they would want to do, and now they would just enjoy the watching and waiting. 'Cause that's the way that kind of spirit likes to work. But these ones I was consulting on you, they ain't like that. Once they was on board to do this thing for you, they was very specific about what they wanted you to drink and how I had to prepare it, and where I was going to find the missing herbs that I don't have in my collection.

"So, I don't know," Tony continued. "Maybe you got some concerns about side effects. That's what all the gringos always worry about with some drug they ain't never taken. And I don't blame you. You already sick enough. You don't want to get any sicker. But frankly, I don't think there's no side effect that could be worse than what you already got," he said emphatically.

"That's true," Matthew said. Tony had been right. He had been worried about drinking this strange stuff. And a gallon of it! How could he fit it in his shrunken stomach?

What the hell? He raised the first cup to his lips and drank it down. It tasted awful. He had to force himself to keep drinking. It felt hot and oily down his throat, and he was afraid he was going to gag. He felt it awaken dormant nerve endings so that he could sense the full inner shape of his stomach. And, surprisingly to him, he soon felt a sense of well-being come over him, as though he'd just finished a tall, cool scotch and soda. He dipped up another cup from the pot and held it in his hands.

He looked into Natalie's eyes, Natalie who had been quietly watching the two of them. He felt a comfort and warmth now, looking into her eyes, that he had not felt since they'd been reunited. The anxiety about her was gone now, and he felt nothing but warmth and comfort and love.

"I saw you," he said simply.

"I saw *you*," she said.

Matthew felt a surge of heat start from his heart and quickly suffuse his whole body. He felt his cheeks blush, but he felt no embarrassment, only happiness. More happiness than he had felt in a long time. He had no doubt but that they were talking about the same thing. And there would be plenty of time to discuss it when they were alone.

"I was unconscious for a long time before I woke up, I think," he said to Tony. Tony nodded agreement.

"Right before I lost consciousness, I saw a white spider on my chest," Matthew said. "It tasted from a pool of blood on my chest, then spat some venom into it, and that's what made me pass out."

Tony looked at him for a long time, then began to chuckle softly to himself. He turned to Natalie. "So he's a real famous guy, huh?"

Natalie shrugged. "He's no Brad Pitt," she said.

"Huh," Tony said. "There's all these bossy spirits who got interested in him. And now he tells me he could see the White Spider. I wasn't expecting that from this pale, sickly gringo." Tony stuck a rough-hewn cigar in his mouth and sucked it alight from a burning stick he pulled from the fire. He blew smoke to the four directions around him.

"So now I'm going to tell you what I was never expecting you would know." Tony puffed his cigar a little more, then arranged the ritual objects on the skin. Matthew had the sense that there was nothing random in the seemingly casual gestures. Tony sat in silence for a time.

"White Spider is my secret Guaraní name," he said at last. "It's my shaman name. There's only a handful of people anywhere in the world who know that. In fact, it would be dangerous for you to reveal it to anyone. Or you, too," he said, turning to Natalie. "The danger would not come from me—although it would be bad for me if you revealed it. I am not the original 'White Spider.' White Spider is the name of a powerful spirit that allows me to ask its help.

"You see, I don't really got power to heal. But I do know them that do. I know how to contact the spirits. In my adopted home village, I was known as the *pajarillo de los espíritus*. The little bird that flies to the spirits. When I walk down the street, and somebody sees me coming, they say, 'Here comes my *pajarillo*.' I fly their story to the spirits. I sing for them. I plead for them. And then it's up to the spirits to heal them or do whatever it is that the person needs.

"White Spider saved my life. He is the spirit that appeared for me in my initiation as a shaman. If no spirit had come to claim me, I would have died. My teacher's other novice failed the initiation. And if you fail, you die. So it's interesting that White Spider let himself be seen by you. He don't *have* to let himself be seen, you understand. That was a choice he made to allow himself to be seen. So I got to ask myself, why is White Spider willing to be seen by this Matthew Harken? What is he to White Spider?"

Tony got up and began to walk around the outside of the circle, looking up into the brightening sky that was beginning to streak with pink in the east.

Matthew drank the second cup of liquid more slowly than the first. When he finished it and was dipping another cup from the pot, he felt a swirling begin in his stomach. The swirling didn't bother him. It just made him curious.

He watched Tony circle them and shared another look with Natalie. It made him feel so peaceful and happy to look into her eyes. It struck him how at ease she seemed here by the fireside. Her eyes had deep circles from having been up all night, and she looked fatigued from the hours of drumming she'd performed. But still, she looked content just to sit and watch and listen.

Matthew slowly drank the new cup and then dipped another one.

"You see, what I think is that the spirits must be expecting something of you," Tony said, looking up at the sky again. "Like there's something you are supposed to do before you die that you ain't done yet. Now, the question is, what could these spirits be wanting you to do?"

"Could it be something to do with saving Anna?"

"Let's keep her out of our thoughts for the moment," Tony said. He pointed a finger at Matthew and then tossed a few more herbs into the fire and spoke quietly to the four directions.

"You see," he continued, "if I'm right, that means this disease has come to you for a reason. It's like—what?—a wake-up call. The spirits want to talk to you, but you just ain't been paying attention. So they got to give you this big whop upside the head. Otherwise, I can't imagine why White Spider would let himself be seen by you."

Tony walked and smoked his cigar some more. Then he crouched and looked into the low fire and continued to talk directly into it.

"See, life is a gift for which we must give gratitude. The spirits don't owe us nothing. Health is not the status quo. So you got to ask yourself: Are you living to your purpose?" Tony held up his hands and looked Matthew in the face. "I don't want to hear your answers. But if my healing is to do you any good, it must come into a body that is at one with the soul. And just maybe, there's this important thing that the spirits want from you, and maybe that's what your whole life is supposed to be about."

Matthew had lifted the cup to his lips and felt Tony's last words go down his throat with the liquid. Suddenly the swirling in his stomach turned vicious. He felt it like a violent spiral starting from the bottom and rising quickly to the top, carrying with it the contents of his stomach. He tilted forward to his hands and knees as though something had kicked him swiftly and forcefully in the ass right through the earth on which he'd been sitting.

Matthew felt the swirling come through the inner surface of his stomach, through his flesh, and harshly knot up the musculature of his torso. Up it came: a rush of the herbal infusion he'd been drinking, vomited on the ground in front of him, and washed up with the greenish liquid, a large globular homunculus of phlegm. Matthew looked at it, straight in front of his face, and felt a horrible shiver of fear rattle his body. A little puff of smoke popped from the top of its head. What the hell was that thing?

Tony pushed him roughly away from it. He grabbed a burning branch from the fire and cut a slice into the top of its head with his knife. A stream of smoke shot from its head and Tony quickly held the branch to it. The smoke burst into a stream of clean blue-white flame and the homunculus deflated into a brown, crusty scab.

Tony looked over at Matthew, sitting on his ass where Tony had pushed him.

"You just full of surprises."

CHAPTER 20

SAVAGERY AND RUTHLESSNESS

"WHAT WAS THAT THING?" Natalie crawled over to look at the dried remains. "It looked like a little man made out of snot. This is all that's left?"

"That is all," Tony said.

Matthew leaned in and looked at the crusty thing. How could something so wet suddenly become so dry? He felt light-headed and very tired. He lay back on the ground.

"He looks pale," Natalie said. She scooted over to Matthew's side. "Are you all right?"

"Tired," he said.

"He's had a lot of action going on inside him," Tony said. "And I'm not just talking about tonight. Some of that action was giving him energy even at the same time it was killing him." Tony filled the tin cup again from the stockpot and brought it over to Matthew. He pulled him back to a sitting position and sat behind him to cradle him upright so he wouldn't sink down again.

"Go ahead and lean on me," Tony said. "And drink. You need to drink more of that infusion."

"Is it going to make me throw up again?" Tears came to Matthew's eyes. He felt like a miserable child. He was so tired.

Tony put his hand flat over Matthew's stomach and held it there a moment, listening.

"I don't think so," he said at last. "But if it does, it won't kill you. And it just might save your life."

Matthew began sipping the liquid again. It tasted different to him now. It tasted like cherries. Like Michigan Bing cherries that he'd loved in his childhood in the Midwest. The taste gave him comfort, and he lost the urge to cry.

"What was that thing?" Natalie asked again.

"Well, that's a hard thing to explain. Mostly because I'm not exactly sure." He looked at Natalie and made an antic face and then shrugged his shoulders. "It's possible Matthew here made himself an enemy someplace along the line. With these famous guys, sometime they can have an enemy without even knowing it. Somebody hate him just for who he is. Maybe *they* want to be Matthew Harken, but shit, there's Matthew Harken in the way being Matthew Harken. And maybe they don't like the way Matthew Harken is being Matthew Harken. If they was Matthew Harken, they could do a hell of a lot better job being Matthew Harken than this fucking Matthew Harken is doing. So maybe the best thing to do is kill this Matthew Harken. You get the logic of all that?"

She nodded. She hated to assent to something so perverse, but she knew it happened.

"So, if this enemy was a living person, it looks to me like they hired a professional. Somebody who knew all about putting a curse on someone. 'Cause this thing was shot right to the belly of Matthew, and it been doing its work."

"What do you mean *if* it was a living person?" Natalie said.

"Well, because I don't know, you see. Frankly, I doubt that it was a living person. More likely it was a dead person. Or maybe Matthew offended one of the gods, and *they* decided: 'The fuck with Matthew Harken. Let's make him waste away.' See, I don't know that. Certain people will even do this thing to themselves. They can't stand life so they swallow up death, little by little."

"But a minute ago you were saying this disease was probably the spirits trying to get Matthew's attention."

"Well, I still say that's true," Tony said. "The way the spirits was willing to help Matthew—the way White Spider was willing to show himself—this shows me the spirits is interested in the future of Matthew Harken. But this thing that come out of Matthew's mouth, that's an evil thing. The same spirits that is helping him didn't do that thing. Both things can be true at the same time, you see?"

"I'm not sure I do," Natalie said.

"Don't worry. We will do another divination. Then we will learn more."

The thing Matthew vomited interested Tony, especially the shape in which it had come out. He'd had experience of these curse bellies before. The difficulty was getting the whole thing out at once. You had to gather it from throughout the victim's body and somehow exorcise the thing, but it was difficult, because a curse belly wasn't like a coherent entity. It was a swirling energy that split off into a million shards, like splintered glass, and lodged in the energy centers of the body. From there it destroyed the body's organs.

Tony had never seen one gathered up in a casing of the body's own goo and vomited up from the throat. He hadn't been expecting it. This was like a leap forward in healing technology. He'd found powerful spirits here in the desert. He was anxious to find one of the local medicine people to discuss the herb the spirits had sent him to find. He wanted to "talk shop."

Of course, he'd have to watch Matthew. He couldn't be sure the herbs had gathered the entire curse belly before encasing it in Matthew's mucous. The portion that had been gathered did remain intact until it was out of his stomach. He'd seen that. He saw it lying on the ground, whole, before the curse essence had begun to leak from the top of it. And he had been able to burn it all, letting none escape.

He'd been amazed to see it burn so hot, concentrated as it was. It absolutely crisped the wet mucous body that had held it. Astonishing.

Tony was excited and grateful to be a part of this. He'd been feeling homesick for his village in the Amazon. But now he could begin to feel there was something here for him to do. And, in a way, this was a returning home. This was the region of his mother's people, the Paiutes.

Matthew finished the cup, and Tony handed it to Natalie. "Get him another, would you please?"

"Sure," she said.

"Can you sit up on your own now?" he asked Matthew.

"I think I can." Matthew leaned forward in his sitting position so he wouldn't fall onto his back. Then he took the tin cup Natalie offered him. Natalie sat beside him and helped support him as Tony rose and began a long prayer of thanksgiving. He thanked each of the spirits for the help they had given. He thanked them for their willingness to meet with him. He thanked them for the new herb they had discovered to him and their instruction on how to prepare the infusion. He thanked them in Guaraní and in Paiute, and apologized for his old and inadequate Paiute, which he loved as the tongue of his mother but with which he had had so little practice for so many years. And finally he promised them a feast.

One of the chickens will have to die tonight, he thought.

♦   ♦   ♦

Matthew slept the day away on Tony's bed in his trailer. Tony and Natalie spent the day talking and drinking coffee and preparing for the ritual of the following night.

They sat out under the tree on the ridge across the yard from Tony's trailer. Tony's dog Rasputin lay on the ground nearby, sleeping mostly, his ear or tail twitching occasionally to dislodge a fly. One inquisitive chicken approached them to watch what they were doing then went off again in search of bugs or grain to eat. Tony and Natalie continued making little piles of tobacco and corn meal on circles of cloth, imbuing them with prayers of thanksgiving, prayers of supplication, and prayers of entreaty, then tying up the circles with a bit of twine. Tony called them prayer bundles. "We need lots of these," Tony said. "We got more spirits helping us here—and more powerful spirits—than I ever expected. We got to feed them all, and treat them real good."

"I want to make some of these for Spider Woman," Natalie said. "She came and talked to me once."

Tony looked at her. "Is that right?" He fanned the coals in the abalone shell and put a little more sweetgrass atop it. He'd started the smoke to consecrate their preparation of the prayer bundles, and now he wanted a little more to accompany the story he sensed was coming. "Tell me about it," he said.

"This was a couple of years ago," Natalie replied. "I'd taken some vacation time for a painting trip in Southern Utah. I wanted to paint the hoodoos—those rock formations in Bryce Canyon. On the way back, I stopped at a place called Freemont Indian State Park. I'd read there were petroglyphs there, and I wanted to see them."

"The ancient rock paintings?" Tony said.

"That's right. It turned out that the park exists because of the construction of Interstate 70, which passes straight through it. When construction of the highway was announced, some local people contacted an archeologist at the University of Utah about the petroglyphs there and about what they thought was an ancient Indian burial ground. The archeologist came down and looked around and agreed there was something interesting there. So he got funding to excavate, but his team had to work quickly. He couldn't get the highway construction delayed. The bulldozers were still coming.

"They started digging, and they discovered the ruins of the largest settlement of Freemont Indians ever found. This Freemont village was atop a star-shaped mesa in a small canyon." Natalie picked up a stick and drew a little diagram of the village in the dirt. "The mesa came together in the center, like this," she said, "and five ridges ran out from this central point. The Freemonts were contemporaries of the Anasazi. Up until this discovery, the Freemonts were thought to have lived only in small settlements of maybe twenty-five people. This Freemont village had been populated by some five hundred people."

"Time to rewrite the history books," Tony said.

"Yeah," Natalie said. She sat up straighter. Telling this story always made her upset. "If you cared anything about American prehistory, this was an incredible find. But stupidly enough, nothing was done to preserve the village."

"Why not?" Tony said.

"The mesa it was on wasn't actually in the path of the highway. It stood right next to it. The road engineers wanted to bulldoze the mesa to use as fill for the highway."

"As fill?"

"To make the bed of the road nice and smooth," Natalie explained with a hint of tremble in her voice. "To level out the hills and valleys."

"My God." Tony laughed and shook his head.

"It only gets worse," Natalie said. "About a half mile from the mesa, a huge boulder, about the size of a semitrailer truck, sat right at the edge of the proposed interstate. Its tip end came up to the path of the highway. Petroglyphs covered it from end-to-end telling an intricate story. So the archeologist contacted the local Indians to find out if this boulder was of particular significance. It was slated for dynamiting.

If a case could be made for the boulder, it might be preserved. Just a slight alteration of the path of the interstate was needed. But the local Indians didn't know what to make of it, so the archeologist couldn't do anything.

"Now, the ancestors of the Hopi were known to have lived in this area long ago. Word of the boulder reached a Hopi shaman who came up from New Mexico or Arizona to view it. The Hopi shaman recognized the story on the boulder at once. This was one of the central myths of his people: the story of Spider Woman creating the world. To him, this was like the discovery of the Dead Sea Scrolls. Or a letter in the handwriting of the Buddha. To allow this to be destroyed would have been a sacrilege."

"And what happened?" Tony said.

"The order for preservation did not move quickly enough through the offices of the state of Utah. Whether through maliciousness, incompetence, or bureaucratic sloth, the boulder was dynamited before it could be marked for preservation."

"Evil flies as fast as the hawk, while good crawls on the back of a turtle."

"But listen to this," Natalie said, her voice rising. "When the Hopi shaman heard what had happened, he was enraged. He put a curse on the entire Utah highway system. From that moment on, the interstate project was plagued. When they poured concrete, instead of it setting up nice and smooth, the way it always does, it dried with spider web cracks all through it."

Tony laughed and shook his head, his eyebrows raised. One of the chickens came over in hopes of getting a taste of the corn meal he was bundling, and he shooed it away.

"They built a bridge over the river that runs through the canyon," Natalie continued. "The bridge has never stopped settling. Its footings have to be pumped up somehow, again and again as it continues to sink into the earth. Problems cropped up on highways all over the state. And whenever these problems were reported in the papers, the Hopi shaman would clip the stories and mail them to the director of the Utah highway system to show him what the Spider Woman was doing in revenge for the desecration of her rock."

"There's the message. You don't want to mess with the Spider Woman." Tony picked up his battered aluminum coffee percolator, felt the side of it, decided it was warm enough, and refilled his and Natalie's mugs.

"Thanks," Natalie said. "I heard this whole story from the park guide in the visitor center. Then I toured the grounds feeling sorrow and awe. I was struck by the beauty and the spirit of the place. But I also felt the regret of all that had been lost.

"I walked under the bridge to get to the other side of the highway so that I could visit the Cave of One Hundred Hands. I stopped beneath the highway and looked, and I could *see* the bridge sinking into the earth," she said in an amazed voice. "I mean, I know it's got to be settling much too slowly to be detected by the human eye, but *I could see* it. Sinking infinitesimally slowly into the earth." She shook her head in wonder.

"You were gifted with a vision," Tony said simply.

Natalie put her hand on Tony's arm and looked him in the eye. "That night, as I lay in my sleeping bag in the tent, a storm blew up. Lightning. Thunder. Wind. It *sounded* ferocious. And *weird*. The sound was echoing down through all the long chain of canyons. Echoing like nothing I'd ever heard before. I got out of my tent. I was thinking of sleeping in the car because I was afraid that a large branch or a tree might be blown down on top of my tent. *But there was no wind.* The wind was passing up high over the top of the canyon. Down in bottom, where I was camped, it was calm. Just a drizzle of rain falling and a little breeze. But from all around, echoing off the walls of the canyon, came the sound of all this wind, and the flashing of lightning, and the weirdly echoing thunder. Everything coming to my eyes and ears told me that I was in the midst of an incredible storm. But against my skin I just felt a little breeze and drizzle. It confused my senses terribly. I crawled back into my tent. Then I started to panic. I imagined one of the other campers in the park might go berserk and come chopping at my tent with an ax. I imagined some mad person tearing open the door flap, and there I'd be, helpless in that little space. What could I use for a weapon? How could I protect myself? And now the panic really dug in. I couldn't stay in that tent. I pulled my sleeping bag out and carried it to the car. They might be able to smash through the car windows, but it wouldn't be as easy as cutting through a nylon tent. So I still needed a weapon. I had a hatchet for cutting firewood, and I had a razor-sharp pallet knife among my art materials." She stopped and more clearly remembered the moment.

"I suddenly knew that if I laid my hands on those weapons," she said slowly, "*I* would be the one to go insane. *I* would be the one to cut through someone's tent with the pallet knife and chop into them with my hatchet.

"I stood out there in all that terrifying noise with the horror of my own violence going through me, but then some sane part of my mind, said: *What's this all about? It doesn't make sense.*

"I thought about the day. I remembered what I'd learned about the Spider Woman and the curse. And then it occurred to me that I had to paint something for the Spider Woman." She clapped her hands once. "As soon as I thought that, my panic vanished. Gone. Just like that."

Tony chuckled and shook his head. "I guess when Spider Woman wants your attention, she don't mess around."

Natalie laughed. "I guess not."

"Did you do the painting?"

"I've done some paintings, but nothing that's satisfied me."

"Maybe you need to paint a boulder the size of a semitrailer truck."

Natalie's eyes widened. "My God, I bet you're right. The archeologist took photos of Spider Woman rock. Maybe I could reproduce it." She thought about that for a moment. "Oh, but they would never let me paint on the rocks in the park. And it ought to be in the park."

"I tell you what," Tony said. "If you go tell that Hopi shaman what Spider Woman has told you to do, and you and him go to the archeologist and the director of that park, and then all of you go to the director of the Utah highways, you just might have a coalition that will not only get you permission, but will find you the funding and everything else you need to replace Spider Woman rock in that park."

Natalie laughed again. "You think so?"

"Especially if the Hopi shaman promises to lift the curse on the Utah highway system." Tony pointed his finger at her. "I mean, you want to present that one in a subtle way. You don't want to make anyone have to admit they actually *believe* in the curse. You know what I'm saying."

"I think I do," Natalie said. "Thanks. This might be fun." She sat and thought to herself for a moment, then spoke again. "You know, ever since Matthew said he'd seen the White Spider, I've been wondering. Do you think White Spider and the Spider Woman are related?"

"I'd be surprised if they weren't," Tony said.

◆　◆　◆

Later in the afternoon they napped under the tree, and the spirits told Tony in a dream which of his chickens they wanted. That night, Tony's approach to entering the other world was different.

After he had built up the ritual fire, which he had been slowing feeding all day, and said the opening prayers and taught Matthew and Natalie a song to sing with him, and after he had sacrificed the chicken and poured its blood in a circle around the fire, he did not simply call the spirits to the fire, he went out in search of them. He took a large round frame drum, a drum that looked like an oversized tambourine without the jingles on the sides, and held it up even with his head, holding it in his right hand and resting the edge of the frame against his shoulder. He took a long, curved beater, carved from a piece of jungle hardwood (he liked to think of it as the jawbone of an ass, one of the many mental remnants of his early training at the Catholic school on the reservation) and began to beat the drum and chant and dance.

He did not play the long, steady beat Natalie had played the night before. This one twisted and sped and ducked through the desert arroyos of the other world as Tony sought out the new spirits that he had only met the night before. This was a courtesy call, traveling to them rather than calling them to him, and it cost him a great expense of energy. He was quickly in a trembling sweat, his eyes rolled back in his head. He chattered frenziedly at the skin of the drum with his jawbone of the ass. The other world here was not populated with underbrush and water snake spirits and jaguars like the other world in which he had learned his craft. This was the desert other world, landscaped with sand and dry earth, eroded gullies, canyons, dry brush, desert snake and lizard, coyote, buzzard and eagle spirits.

He traveled to them to show respect and gratitude, to call them to the feast around his ritual fire (for in addition to the sacrifice of the chicken, he had brought them gifts of tobacco and cornmeal, whiskey and fruit). He was inviting them to the rich feast he had promised, not only in thanksgiving, but to entice them into further relationship with him, courting them with great humility and largesse. Despite the power of the White Spider, who was willing to come all this way to assist him, he needed the local spirits. And he wanted another favor from them. He wanted to know where the curse belly had come from so he could protect Matthew against another one. He wanted to know if all the curse belly had been removed before Matthew left this ritual space. For Tony knew that if he did not get it all now, those pieces that might be left could regenerate their strength. They could mutate to some new form that would be more difficult to remove—and would begin to do new kinds of damage to Matthew in ways impossible to predict.

◆　◆　◆

Natalie watched Tony working. He had been friendly and kind with her the whole day—like the Tony from whom she had learned so much and of whom she had become so fond over the short time she'd known him. They'd made the prayer bundles, sliced fruit, and poured tiny tumblers of whiskey. All this had been casual, enjoyable. But as evening drew on, Tony pulled inside himself. She began to feel out of her depth, like a lost tourist.

She was with him, assisting him, as he went to the side yard where his chickens wandered. She watched as this strange Tony crouched down in the chicken yard and began to sing. She was amazed to see the chickens slowly stop and listen! All the time he sang, the chickens moved slowly, keeping an eye on him. Nervous, but half mesmerized. Then Tony raised the pitch and volume of his singing, and one particular one of the chickens froze and turned toward him. Tony stretched out his hands toward it, and it walked to him. *Like a pet dog*, Natalie thought. This was not what she expected from chickens.

The chosen hen walked to him, and Tony put his hands around its torso and stood, raising it high over his head, chanting loudly. Natalie followed him back to the ritual fire, where they'd spent the whole previous night. The fire was crackling high from the feeding Tony had given it just before he'd gone to the chicken yard.

The chicken panicked and screamed as Tony held it high over his head in front of the fire. Tony's face looked suddenly savage as he chanted, louder yet, and then brought the terrified chicken down, tucked it under his arm, and took from his hide on the ground his ritual knife.

"The bowl," he commanded her.

Natalie picked up a hand-hammered copper bowl from the hide and held it before her.

Tony raised his arms again, holding the long knife in his right hand and the chicken by its feet in his left. He recited another long chant as the chicken flapped its wings in panic, trapped by Tony's grasp. Then Tony knelt swiftly, held the chicken firmly to the ground using his left hand and one knee, and deftly nicked its neck with the razor-sharp knife. Arterial blood spurted from the wound. Tony quickly grasped the chicken in both hands around its torso and held it up, so that the blood squirted into the copper bowl Natalie held.

Tony lowered his voice and recited a quiet prayer as the blood pulsed out. The chicken calmed immediately, as if unaware that it had been mortally injured, and it watched Tony's face as he prayed. Its blood continued to pulse with each beat of its heart, into the bowl. It watched Tony praying until the light went slowly out of its eyes, it shuddered one last time, and its body went limp.

Natalie had not expected to find herself standing in the desert evening with a bowl of chicken blood, trying to reconcile her feelings.

It was one of her analysands that brought Natalie to Tony in the first place. Natalie had been treating this client for over a year, and no matter how much understanding she helped the woman achieve, nothing would alleviate the depth of her depression. The client had found out about Tony and wanted Natalie to accompany her to visit him because she was afraid. Although doubtful, Natalie was glad to accompany her. She was so frustrated with the failure of her own efforts, she was ready to try anything.

To Natalie, Tony had seemed to be primarily a storyteller. He talked to Natalie's client, and burned some incense, and told her one of the long stories from the mythology of the Guaraní people. And when he was done, he gave her herbs for making tea and instructions on how to use it.

And with time, Natalie's client began to feel better.

Tony recognized Natalie's malaise, as well. With his help, she began to find her own true powers as a healer. He helped her to work with her own strengths—her powers of observation—her ability to see connections—her capacity as an interpreter. All the things that made her a fine painter. Once she started to tap into her own silence, her abilities as a therapist began to become clear. She helped her clients find the hidden connections in their own stories that led to the coherence that they lacked.

But now Natalie saw the spirit of iron under Tony's tenderness. A capacity for savagery and ruthlessness that fed his ability to heal.

As disconcerted as it made her feel, Natalie was glad to see this side, for it allowed her to understand how Tony could be so powerful and so tender simultaneously. Her mind still protested at the sight of the chicken's blood, rolling against the sides of the copper bowl. But even as her civilized self rebelled at it, some other part of her recognized that this was a deeper source, a part of something that drove Tony's powerful engines. She was glad she'd brought Matthew to him. She hoped he'd be able to help Anna, as well. She banished the thought as quickly as she had it, not wanting to attract Anna's spirit away from where Tony had left it.

◆　◆　◆

Tony danced around the fire late into the night. He prayed to White Spider and the Spider Woman. He shimmered the wooden jawbone on the skin of the frame drum until his vision changed and everything in the physical world faded to show what was underneath. With great joy he saw the spirits that had helped him the night before. The spirits approached the fire. He greeted them and watched as they bent to the circle of blood around the fire and began to drink, like tiny horses at the trough or like jungle animals at the river's edge.

He danced for them and with them and showed them the banquet he'd laid: the tobacco and whiskey, fruit and sacrificial chicken that he'd plucked and gutted in the evening and spitted over the edge of the ritual fire to roast. He ate the chicken with them, and gave some to Natalie and Matthew to share. He lit a cigar and put the tobacco bundles in the fire for the spirits to smoke. And when they'd all had a smoke together, he put to them his questions.

◆　◆　◆

For Matthew, the day had gone in a blur. He was weak from the night before. So much had gone out of him. He did not doubt that it was a good thing that he'd expelled whatever that was, but it left him feeling debilitated. And afraid.

What was that thing that Tony had made him vomit up? What if that was the little daemon that allowed him to write? Would he spend the rest his miserable life stripped of the thing that had given his work its brilliance?

Bullshit! he thought.

Then he had the sudden suspicion that the thought about his daemon had not been his own thought at all. He suspected it was a thought implanted in his mind by something that had had him in its sway and did not want to let him go.

Oh, Jesus where was he? And what in God's name was happening to him?

Natalie had gotten him out of Tony's bed in the early evening and brought him back out to the ritual fire. They had prepared foods and drinks, some of which was for him and more was for the spirits. They set this out on a rough wood table to the north of the fire. Tony was sitting on the ground, plucking a freshly killed chicken. Matthew sat and ate his late-day breakfast as Tony prepared the creature to cook over the fire. And then he and Natalie took its guts and feathers along with some hot charcoal and incense and copal out to a special spot in the desert to leave as an offering.

Evening changed to night in the flash of an eye for Matthew. He felt memory snatched from him as time dropped into deep invisible crevices in the earth. At one moment he was sharing foods with Natalie and Tony. Then Tony was sticking things into his mouth. Hot bits of roasted chicken. Matthew tasted the adrenaline of the hen's recent death in the cooked flesh. Then Tony was chattering and dancing like a madman. In what order did all this take place? He couldn't keep anything straight. Had he vomited up some portion of his brain?

He saw something moving around the fire. Little shadows. Shadows from the fire? No. Independent somehow. They were spirits. Drinking from the circle of blood Tony had poured. Then he saw Tony's eyes looking at him. Fearsome. And the shadows leapt, straight at Matthew.

My God! His brain was on fire! It was like an electrical storm bursting through his skull. Lightning crashing down and scorching the earth inside his head. All his muscles clenched and throbbed.

◆　◆　◆

When Matthew screamed and fell to the ground, writhing, Natalie jumped to his side, but Tony roughly pulled her back. Where he'd grabbed her, her arm hurt. She tried to pull away from him, trying to get away from the bad hurt in her arm and trying to get to Matthew, whose cries were now strangled in his throat as he shook violently on the ground.

He was having a seizure. Natalie could see that easily enough. Grand mal. Did he have a history of epilepsy?

She twisted hard against Tony's grip.

"You're hurting me," she shouted.

His face was possessed and cruel. She hated him. It hurt terribly where he was squeezing her arm. She hit him and pulled, but nothing could affect him.

Then Matthew fell suddenly still and silent.

He was moaning.

Tony released her arm, and she jerked away from him, rubbing where it hurt. She looked back and forth between Tony and the stilled Matthew, uncertain what to do. She *hated* Tony. But he was clearly unaffected by her emotion. He was watching something invisible moving through the air. He watched it move over the fire and then out into the distance. He bowed to it then laid himself face down on the earth. She heard him muttering something into the earth. Another of his fucking prayers? Her arm hurt so bad!

Then he got up off the ground and looked at her and smiled. His face looked ghoulish in the firelight.

"That curse belly is all gone out of him," Tony said. "And that's a real good thing."

Tony took a handful of fresh leaves from off the hide by the fireside, wet them with fresh water, and lay them over Matthew's forehead. "Lie still," he told him.

Tony took some more of the leaves, wet them, and brought them to Natalie who had to make an effort not to move away from him. He wrapped the wet leaves around her arm where it hurt.

"Let it go into the leaves," he told her.

"What?" she said suspiciously.

"The process of healing is pain," he said. "As you know." He gestured to the darkness around them. "Something here resists healing. Not just here. And not just in the night. I see it many times. And sometimes it uses the friends, the relatives, the lovers of the sick person to carry its resistance. It jumps into the person who fears and misunderstands the pain of healing."

Natalie felt another wave of hate flow through her. *Superior bastard,* she thought. Then she thought she saw something move by the tree up the hill in the darkness. *Let's not start imagining things,* she thought.

Matthew heaved a heavy sigh and put his hand over the leaves on his forehead. His eyes looked clearer now in the moonlight as he gazed up into the sky. He looked like he was doing better already.

Natalie felt ashamed of her thoughts. She felt the coolness of the fresh herbs on her arm. She couldn't smell mint, but she almost would have sworn she could *taste* mint through the flesh of her arm.

"Let it go into the leaves," Tony repeated.

Chapter 21

EVERYONE SEES A TABLE

It was two a.m. on the clock in Tony's trailer. Saturday night. Or should she call it Sunday morning? It felt strange to be away from the ritual fire now, after all that time. Natalie had had so little sleep. It would be nearly an hour's drive back to her place in Salt Lake. She had clients to see Monday morning. She would need a long nap this afternoon.

She sipped a cup of tea Tony had made for her. It would make her feel better, he said. It tasted like grass clippings. She inhaled the steam. It made her think of her father, mowing the lawn. She didn't know what was in it, but it did make her feel better.

The pain in her arm and all the anger she'd felt toward Tony were gone. He'd burned the leaves she'd held to her arm in the ritual fire, and all that emotion and pain seemed to go up in smoke with it. Once again she was glad that she'd come and brought Matthew, and she was grateful to Tony, as difficult as parts of it might have been. She was amazed at the efforts he'd taken.

Now, Matthew was sitting on Tony's bed, looking stunned. Natalie smiled. Poor baby. Tony was rummaging through some boxes next to his little stove in the front end of his trailer. He came back with two smudge sticks and some herbs wrapped in a double sheet of newspaper and sat on the bed next to Matthew.

"You help him remember this, okay?" he said to Natalie.

Natalie nodded. She hoped she'd be able to remember everything herself. Up until now, she'd been existing in the moment, but now she was tired and spacey and easily distracted.

He put the smudge sticks into Matthew's hand. They looked like fat gray cigars of bundled herbs and sticks bound up with crisscrossed colored threads. "I want you to take one of these and light it back in your hotel room. Just light the end until it's burning good, and then let the flame go out. It'll burn down slowly making lots of smoke. You've seen these things before?"

Matthew nodded. His eyes looked like deep wells, his pupils widely dilated. That's what had made him appear stunned, but Natalie could see now he was at an intense level of concentration.

"Good," Tony said. "You go through your hotel room in a counterclockwise direction, smoking all the corners, all the areas of the room. Open up your closets and smoke everything in there, always going in a counter-clockwise direction. The same with all your drawers. Your suitcases. Whatever. Smoke everything while asking the angels to rid your space of any damaging ghosts or spirits."

"The angels?" Matthew said. "You believe in angels?"

"If I use the names of Guaraní spirits, what's that going to mean to you?" Tony said. "It don't make no difference what vocabulary you use, so long as you approach the spirits with an absolute sincerity of heart."

The word *angels* chimed in Natalie's mind. She looked at the two men and saw them suddenly as a pair of angels. How wonderful they both were! She felt a kinship to them that seemed centuries old. A wave of love for them swept through her. A wave of love for the world. She felt a radiance within her. She remembered her flashes of hatred for Tony as some strange aberration.

"Then I want you to box up them journals of your suicide friend that you told me about and smudge that box real good," Tony told Matthew. "Put any other artifacts of hers you got in that carton, too. Smudge it real good with the box top open, then tape it up good, and smudge the outside of the box again. Then you put it someplace away from where you're living."

"I have a storage closet in the basement of my building," Natalie offered.

"That's good," Tony said. "But you smudge it again when you put it down in there. Set it on the floor all by itself. And then you sprinkle a circle of ashes all the way around it to keep any spirits from going in or out of it until we can deal with it. Okay?"

Matthew and Natalie both nodded.

"After you get that carton out of your room, you smudge the place again with the second stick I'm giving you. That's sage and sweetgrass bundled together there. That's what you need for this work. Then you pluck three hairs from the top of your head and burn them on the end of the smudge stick. That'll keep the ghosts from being able to plant thoughts in your mind anymore. Okay?"

Matthew nodded again.

"And after you're all done with that, sprinkle a line of ashes in front of your door and along your windows to keep the ghosts from being able to return to your place. We'll get you a bag of ashes from the ritual fire. And when the maid vacuums it up, you just lay down some more. Don't worry, it'll keep working until you can renew it. And it doesn't have to be a great big pile, neither. It's a focus of intent. Like a physical prayer. Okay?"

Matthew nodded.

Tony turned to Natalie. "You feel like anything is interfering with your thoughts, your spirit, you do the same stuff. Especially the hair. It's important to protect yourselves now, because there are things in this world that don't want healing to take place. If that wasn't true the world wouldn't be in the mess it's in."

"Why do you think ghosts might be following us?" Matthew said.

"Sacrificing the chicken was part of a divination, as well as thanksgiving to the spirits," Tony said. "Some of them spirits did a little detective work for me. Something been following your friend Anna for a long time. Even before that, this something had been traveling through her family. It's been leaving a trail of death. It turns out your Anna was a real strong person. That's the only reason she survived as long as she did. But I think she picked up more of these bad spirits just before she died. Maybe in the past year? Something. I don't know how long. But these spirits see the old one that been following Anna all these years and they jump in. Let's have a party on Anna, they say. Let's eat her belly until she die. That's the way these kind of spirits operate. So, I'm afraid there's more of this around that had a connection with Anna. It didn't all follow her to the grave. And some of that jumped off on you right around the time of her death. Maybe when you came in for her funeral it happened. Maybe in your grief, you took on some of her despair. And with it came this alien thing. It started to eat your belly and that started up your cancer.

178 • RICHARD ENGLING

"The good thing is that you vomited up the thing you swallowed with Anna's death. The bad news is you got the weakness of your cancer on you. You could swallow up more of it again. 'Cause it ain't just one thing. It ain't just one ghost. It's like a swarm of mosquitoes. From a distance it looks like one thing, moving together. But you get close and it's a whole bunch of thing.

"This is why you need to protect yourself. In the divination, I seen her writing some of the ghost's story in her journals. So it's a good bet that part of the ghost is hanging around those journals." Tony could see Matthew wanted to respond to what he was saying. He held up a finger.

"I don't want you telling me about it now. You probably know a lot of answers already and didn't even know you knew them. But first, you got to get your strength back. We'll talk later. And if we can dig up some family history on Anna, that will be a big help. Because we want to free her soul from all this. And maybe we can rid the world of some of this pain that's been following you all."

"Thanks, Tony," Natalie said.

He smiled back at her. "This is what we're here for," he said. "Take care of yourselves. Take your share of the joy that surrounds you. This is part of the deliciousness of life." He pointed at the newspaper bundle of herbs on the bed next to Matthew.

"And don't forget to make that tea and drink it regular, like I told you," he said.

"Now that I'm doing this," Matthew asked, "what about my doctor? Should I keep doing what he's telling me to do?"

"Let's take a look at your drugs." He held out his hand and Matthew dug out his seven-slot pill case marked with the days of the week. Tony shook it and the pills rattled inside.

"A nice little maraca," he joked. He opened one of the compartments and poured the pills into his hand. "I can put these on the table over here in the kitchen and see if they want to fight with the herbs. But otherwise you keep doing everything that makes sense to you," Tony said. "Use everything that's available to you. Spirit medicine. Western medicine. That's what we call 'walking on both feet.'" He laughed. "And that's a good thing." He took the pills and a handful of Matthew's herbs to the table.

Tony looked out the kitchen window up at the sky. "We did this under this full moon. You come back to see me under the next full moon," he said, arranging the pills and herbs together on the table. "And you bring along that carton of your suicide friend's stuff. We'll figure out what to do with all that then. Rest for two weeks, keep your mind off of this stuff, and after that, see what you can find out about Anna's family history. In the meantime, you think about what your life is supposed to be."

◆　◆　◆

Matthew took a shower at Natalie's apartment that night. His skin felt gritty from smoke and ash and sweat and his long ordeal at Tony's. As he let the water spray onto his head, he suddenly saw a horrifying face in his mind's eye. The face startled him so much, he stepped suddenly back in the shower and nearly lost his balance. After that, he was afraid to close his eyes again.

He had the strange feeling that this was the face of the homunculus he vomited. Or the ghost that had created it.

But it was off him now. Out of him. He wasn't about to let that thing back in.

He'd been through so much that night. He was too tired. Too battered in his soul. He felt grateful Natalie had invited him to stay over, so he wouldn't have to be alone.

He came out of the bathroom wrapped in Natalie's terry-cloth robe, only slightly tight on him as Natalie liked such garments overlarge on herself. He found her in the dining room wearing flannel pajamas, sipping chamomile tea on a stool at a peninsula counter that separated the dining room from the kitchen.

Natalie lifted the teapot. "Want some?" she said.

"I'd rather a brandy."

Natalie stood, opened the cabinet above the counter, and pulled out a bottle of scotch. "This is the only hard liquor I've got," she said. "Aside from some ancient crème de menthe."

"The scotch, please," Matthew said.

Natalie pointed through into the kitchen. "Glasses above the sink," she said.

Matthew retrieved a water glass and a former jelly jar from the cabinet. The kitchen was small, but it looked efficient. The sink stood in the center of a horseshoe of cabinets. The stove was on the left. To the right was an opening above the counter and below the cabinets where you could look through into the little dining room.

"This is nice," he said. "Your guests can sit at the counter and have a drink and talk to you while you make dinner."

"For the little I entertain."

Matthew poured a glass of water, put some scotch into the jelly jar, and sat down at the stool next to her.

"You remember last night, I said I'd *seen* you," she said. "During the ritual."

"Yes," Matthew said. He felt himself wake up a little bit as she said this to him. He remembered his own vision of her: The two of them flying through space and combining into one being, a single person they had been in some lifetime of the past. All that had been so powerful. So filled with love. Could it possibly have been true for her, as well?

"When I was playing the drum," she said, "there came a point where I was so fatigued, I didn't know if I could keep my arm moving. The time between the beats seemed to quadruple. I tried to push my arm faster, to get back to the beat, but I looked around and saw that everything was moving four times more slowly than it had before. And that stunned me. I realized I had crossed over into some other kind of space. Nothing looked the same. I couldn't feel the pain in my arm anymore. Pretty soon I couldn't feel my arm at all. I wasn't aware of playing that drum. Something else was playing my arm. Most of the time, I kept my eyes closed. I was moving through some dark space. Moving and not moving. The darkness was velvet."

Natalie closed her eyes. "And then I was aware of you being in the darkness with me," she continued. "I felt you there, in the same space. I could feel your mind." She opened her eyes and looked into his. "Or your soul," she said. "The absolute you with all your experience and knowledge but without the baggage of your pain or disease. And I felt like we'd been together ever since gods had walked the earth." She picked up her cup and held it with both hands, feeling the warmth in her fingers. She took a sip, then looked down into the tea, remembering.

Matthew wanted to tell her his experience, but he held back. She took another sip of her tea and continued.

"After a while, it was just as though I was in a dream," she said. "I was no longer at the fireside. I was walking up a set of long wooden stairs up the outside of a house, to the second floor. I knew this was the house of my father. Not my flesh and blood father who lives in Nebraska. And not some archetypal father. He wasn't God. He was some specific father of mine, not exactly of this lifetime, or this world. And still, he *was* something like a god. Powerful and wise and otherworldly. Or maybe still, it was like he was human, but an incredible genius. A Buddha. A fully ascended master.

"I went into the house through the second story door, and the first room was a gallery. Your room was the next room. That was your bedroom or something. And I could feel you were in there. You were my brother, and I could sense you in there as clearly as if I could see you. And we shared this genius father, whom we seldom saw but was some nearly perfect being to us. I felt this great love for you, knowing that you were there. It was like a love that would have knocked me flat if I felt it here on earth. You know what I mean? Have you ever seen one those couples that are so in love that they are totally incapacitated?"

"Like Romeo and Juliet?" Matthew suggested.

"I'm thinking of people who probably couldn't get up the necessary coordination to kill themselves. It's like they cannot function in the world. Gravity is too much for them. But in that dreamscape that level of feeling was possible without being crippling. We could love like that and not be crushed. We could be separate or together and still feel that love—and still feel other things, too."

"Yes," Matthew said. "Extreme love and joy without dependence."

"Right," Natalie said. "I began looking at the paintings that hung on the walls. It was a big collection, hanging on all four walls of the room. Each of the paintings contained images and words. Sentences. Phrases. The combinations were so brilliant! I thought: *If only I can remember this, my work will be* made!"

"You wanted to reproduce them?"

"Oh, my God, yes," Natalie exclaimed. "I wanted to bring them out to the world. Listen: You came out of the other room, and we walked around the studio together. We'd look at a painting, and it was as if we suddenly understood the meaning of the world! And we'd look at each other, and in the joy I felt and the joy I could see on your face, I saw that we'd understood the same thing. It was as if in the presence of these paintings, we were in the presence of our father again. And we were so grateful. Such a gigantic spirit! Such an overwhelming intellect! It was like we were so grateful to have come from him and so much wanted to be reunited with him. But the paintings were so fabulous, we didn't feel the sense of loss of being away from him. Just this overwhelming joy and enrichment. Because with each of the paintings we looked at, we understood more. Our own souls became larger— like this was some amazing food. Or—no—looking at each painting was like absorbing an entire lifetime of knowledge."

"Were you able to remember them? After the ritual?" Matthew said.

She smiled and shook her head ruefully. "Not a thing," she said. "All I can remember is that they contained words and pictures and that they were brilliant." She sighed. "I'll never be able to match the brilliance of those paintings I saw."

Matthew touched her hand. "Maybe you will."

She gave him a resigned smile, and shrugged. "But you know, I'll never forget how happy I was looking at those paintings and being with you."

"Yes," he said.

"And you saw me, too, during the ritual?" she asked.

"Yes," Matthew said.

He told her his whole experience. The flying together. The lives they'd remembered sharing in other lifetimes. But most of all, the recognition that they were two fragments of one much larger being. That their experience would be part of the "conversation" of that being— part of its huge mind—when they rejoined it as integral parts.

"What I was hoping," Matthew said at the end of the story, "is that you might have remembered the same thing."

"I'm not sure that I haven't."

"What do you mean?" he said.

"In this world, when we look at a table, everyone sees a table. Maybe it's not like that in the other world. Maybe we had precisely the same experience, but we just saw it differently."

"I don't get you," Matthew said.

"Look," Natalie said. "We each were very aware of each other's presence—and of a profound love for one another—and we remembered having experience of each other that went way beyond this life-time. The image of our father that I had is not so different from your image of a larger being that we would return to at the end of our lifetimes."

"Well. I see what you mean, but it's not all *that* close," Matthew said.

"That's your novelist/screenwriter mind talking," Natalie told him. "If you were a painter or a poet, you might see through to this easier. As a novelist, you take a subject and make a long work out of it. Then you move onto a whole other thing. A poet or a painter will return to a subject again and again. Each time the treatment is a little different. But the subject remains the same. I think we may have experienced the *exact* same event. Our minds painted the subjects in different ways, in ways that made sense to each of us individually, but the same essentials still shine through.

"Think of all the different religions, Matthew," she continued. "Each began with a prophet or some set of prophets who had a vision of what is essentially the same mystical experience. As individual hu-mans, they each interpreted that vision in an individual way. But the *subject* beneath those interpretations remains the same: a vision of the world of God. A vision of the world of the spirits that surrounds us."

"But mine was about reincarnation," Matthew protested. "It was about being part of a larger mind—and about returning to that after death. Yours seemed to be more about wisdom and painting."

"I don't think so," Natalie said, stifling an unwelcome yawn. "I think, essentially, both visions were about being connected. Us being connected to each other and to some larger thing. Okay, now—you are a man con-cerned with his death—and so you get your version of the vision. And I am a woman who loves painting—and so I get mine. Right?"

Matthew considered it for a long moment. "You may be right," he said.

"Of course I'm right." She smiled and hugged him once, then stretched and got up from the stool. "Come along, my brother, let's to bed."

◆　◆　◆

It had been seven years since Matthew had been in a bed-room of Natalie's, and she had been in a different apartment back then. But of the spaces in her apartment he'd seen, this felt the most familiar. She still slept in a big futon on the floor, and it still looked like an oversized rodent's nest of scrambled sheets, pillows, and comforters of many colors. The idea of spending time arranging her bed neatly when she would only mess it up again the following night struck Natalie as a frivolous waste of time. Matthew remembered her telling him that she regarded the swirling shapes of colors of the messy bed as a self-creating abstract art. She even had a collection of photographs of her bed she'd taken when she'd found its messiness particularly pleasing. One of those photos included the sleeping Matthew with one of his bare legs sticking out.

Natalie lit four votive candles, two on her dresser and two on a low table along the wall where she often meditated. She selected candles in glass cups, so they would not set the apartment afire while she and Matthew slept. The low table was scattered with a dozen candles of various shapes and sizes, and art works and images from various religions. It was Natalie's little altar. Above it hung a dreamcatcher and a yarn eye of god and antelope antlers hung with scarves.

There were two of Natalie's paintings on the walls. These were new. However, like the ones Matthew remembered from years before, they were both nudes. One showed a nude mother breast-feeding a naked child. The second showed a man in the act of masturbating as seen from outside of a house through not thoroughly closed blinds.

This painting caught Matthew for a moment. Natalie often showed "caught from the outside" scenes. And somehow these did not feel quite voyeuristic. Nor quite alienated. What was it exactly, the mood of these paintings?

Her work always reminded Matthew how much of Natalie was beneath the surface. There was so much of her that he did not now, nor might ever, understand.

"When we return to the mind of the father, after this lifetime, I'm finally going to *get* these pictures," Matthew said, indicating the man.

Natalie turned off the lights and crawled into bed in the soft glow of the candles. "What's to get?" she said.

"That's precisely what I want to find out," he said.

He crawled into bed, making his way through the tangle of blankets, and put his hand on her cheek. He looked into her eyes and felt his heart melt.

"I'm so glad you came to get me," he said.

"I am, too," she said. "Even if you are a faithless pain in the ass."

She leaned toward him and they kissed, a gentle kiss on the mouth. Matthew felt the stirrings of arousal. How long had it been since that had happened?

They looked into one another's eyes again and smiled.

"It's a good thing we're both exhausted," Natalie said. "I don't even want to think about any meaning to that kiss."

"Good night," he said. He felt happy about his momentary erection, even as it faded away.

What would happen with Natalie, he wondered. Could they possibly become lovers again? At least he felt some promise that he would be able. Not like in the past, before cancer, of course, but at least something.

For a moment, he wondered if he'd be able to sleep. There was so very much to think about, and Natalie's room was delightful in the candlelit twilight.

He looked at Natalie's face, lying on the pillow. She was so beautiful, it nearly broke his heart to look at her. His lovely sister. His lover. His wife. What all could they have been to one another over the centuries?

He'd never been sure about life after death—not since he'd lost the religious faith he'd had as a child. But now he felt utterly convinced of reincarnation. It was a far cry from the Catholicism he'd grown up with.

He came to Salt Lake hoping, illogically, to learn something about the afterlife from Anna. But his experience at Tony's gave him his first comfort about facing death. At some very deep level, he believed both his and Natalie's experiences were authentic.

He looked at Natalie's face again and watched her breathing, falling asleep, until he was sure she was soundly asleep. He was so tired himself, it did tricks with his eyes in the candlelight. He saw her face changing, from one face to the next. A man. Another woman. Another. The face of a boy.

Who were these? Though he did not know them, they seemed remarkably familiar. Could they have been faces that Natalie had occupied in other lifetimes? Other identities in which he had known her?

He watched her for a while longer, then the exhaustion overtook him, and he passed into a deep and uninterrupted sleep.

CHAPTER 22

AT THIS POINT ALREADY

MATTHEW AWOKE IN THE tangle of blankets to the aroma of frying bacon and brewing coffee and the distant sound of a radio playing in the kitchen.

What a joy to wake in this messy bed with the late morning sun shining in on all Natalie's belongings! All her candles. Her jewelry. Snapshots of friends attached to the corners of her dresser mirror. Belts and strings of beads hanging from a peg by the closet. Clothing and shoes abandoned on the floor. And all her bedroom scents, hiding beneath the invading breakfast aromas: her favorite lotions, soaps, perfumes, incense, the personal scent of her body.

This bedroom was like a beloved foreign country. A place of the heart from which he'd been exiled too long. How good to be here again!

It all gave him such a feeling of comfort that he didn't notice the back pain that was his morning companion until he tried to rise from the futon.

"Oh, God," he said aloud. He crawled over to where he'd left Natalie's bathrobe the night before, put it on, and hunted down his pill case. Then he set out toward the smell of the coffee.

"So this is you in the morning?" Natalie said as he came into the room, a wave of sudden sympathy transforming her face.

"I've got a couple of maintenance items to do," he said, easing himself onto one of the stools on the dining room side of the peninsula countertop. "Then it gets a little better."

"What do you need?" she said. "I'm making us some breakfast."

"How about a mug of half milk and half coffee for starters?" he said. "I need to let some hot water pummel my back. Then I'll be a little more human."

"Sure thing," she said.

Matthew washed down his handful of Sunday pills with the full mug of the lukewarm milky coffee and hobbled off to the bathroom, looking forward to the moment when his analgesics would kick in.

As the near-scalding water began to melt some of the knots in his back, Matthew thought about the imperative Tony had given him on parting the night before: "Think about what your life is supposed to be," he'd said.

One thing of which he was certain: he was not supposed to be living as isolated as he had been since his marriage had failed the second time. He wondered how it would have been if he'd stayed faithful to Natalie instead of going back to Patty. Perhaps if they'd stayed together, Natalie would have agreed to come on location with him for the next film. Perhaps she would have discovered she loved it.

Well, there was nothing to be done about that now. Certainly there were reasons why all that had happened. He couldn't quite subscribe to the idea that everything happened the way it was "supposed" to happen, in some cosmic Pollyannaish sense. But the fact that he was here in Natalie's shower and she was out in her kitchen cooking him breakfast gave him a surprise loft of joy. This was the best development that had come into his life in quite some time.

♦ ♦ ♦

"Three days in the same clothes," Matthew said when he walked into the kitchen. "Next time you offer to take me to meet someone, I'm going to pack a bag."

Natalie laughed. "So you smell like the ritual fire," Natalie said. "That's not such a bad thing." A large lock of her long, morning-messy black hair fell into her face, and she pushed it behind her ear.

"I'm afraid what I actually smell like is the ritual armpit. But it's kind of you to lie so charmingly."

She smiled an acknowledgement and lifted the coffeepot. "Would you like another milky coffee?" she said.

"Yes, please," he said. "It's the only way my stomach will take it. And if I don't have the caffeine, the drugs will put me in dreamland."

Matthew sat down at the counter, and she put his refilled mug in front of him.

"How are you after all that at Tony's?" she said.

"I was trying to get it straight in my mind," he said. "I seem to remember being poisoned by a spirit spider and passing out, then vomiting up an inflammable man, and having an epileptic fit, all in less than thirty-six hours. The amazing thing is that I actually feel better for it."

"I wasn't expecting quite such an epic experience, either," she said. "But I wouldn't have missed it for the world."

"You know, I had the sense that we had known Tony many times before this lifetime. It's like something Colin told me. He had this whole theory of people being reincarnated in groups."

"So you think Tony is in our group?"

"And that's part of the reason why we were allowed to know his shaman name."

"Tony White Spider Cappelli. I love the sound of that." Natalie pulled two plates out of the oven and set them on the counter. "Be careful of the plate," she said. "It's hot."

"Wow," Matthew said. He admired the breakfast she'd made them: poached eggs, bacon, fried tomatoes, toast. She set strawberry jam, butter, and orange juice on the counter, then came around to the other side of the counter and sat next to him. "This is so nice of you," he said.

"It's nice to share a Sunday morning breakfast." She gave him a one-arm hug around the back, and then took a sip of her coffee.

Matthew felt the warmth of her affection. Then a wave of sorrow and regret washed over him. He felt tears welling up in his eyes. "We've wasted so much time," he said. "*I've* wasted so much time."

"Everything has had its reasons, Matthew."

"But not necessarily good ones," he said.

"Eat," she said, pointing her fork at him. "It isn't often that I cook a breakfast like this. If you are going to sour it by being maudlin, I'm going to kick you out in the street."

"Sorry," he said. "This really is wonderful."

"And look," she said. "The strawberry jam is from France. Anna used to love that stuff."

Matthew picked up the jar and smiled. "*Confiture de fraises.* She did love this. A chunk of baguette spread with that wonderful French butter and *confiture de fraises.* I don't know how many times I had that with tea in Anna's little room in Paris."

"So enjoy it."

Matthew spread his toast with the jam and took a bite of his egg. It was delicious.

"After breakfast I'll help you pack up Anna's journals and smudge your hotel room," she said. "I think it's better you have company for that."

"Thanks," he said. He felt a tear come to his eye again. He felt so grateful to her. And to Tony. It was ridiculous how emotional he was today. Just anything might plunge him into tears. Even the texture and crispness of his bacon. Had he ever had bacon that had struck him as being so perfectly prepared?

He felt so full of emotion, he knew if he tried to talk about anything, he'd break down in tears. And so he listened to Natalie talking about the first time she'd met Tony, and he listened to the piano concerto that was playing on the radio, and he ate his breakfast.

When breakfast was over, and Natalie had cleared away the plates, Matthew took her hand. "Before we do anything else," he said, struggling to speak over the emotion that constricted his throat, "I want to tell you: I don't want us to go out of each other's lives. I don't want to lose you again."

Natalie looked uncomfortable, and she looked away. Matthew let go of her hand.

"What's the matter?" he said.

"Oh, God. How are we at this point already?" she said.

"Nothing is gradual for me anymore," he said. "I don't have time for gradual." Matthew felt the tremulousness clear from his heart. He felt the presence of that fierce companion of his soul: his mortality.

"I suppose not," Natalie said. "But gradual is the way I live. My clients only get well gradually. My life only changes gradually. Usually. Only ideas come and go quickly." She pulled her long black hair into a ponytail behind her head, then flipped it up and clipped it to the back of her head with a large tortoiseshell barrette. With her hair swept away, Matthew saw the emotional strength in the angles of her face: the high gypsy cheekbones, her sharp, slightly hooked Spanish nose, the honest rich brown of her eyes. It was a beautiful, noble, passionate face, and he loved and admired it, for it reflected her soul. But he felt the dread of her slipping away from him again.

"I was hurt when you went back to Patty," she said. "Although we hadn't got there yet, I sensed how deeply I would be able to love you. And now, after what we've experienced at Tony's, I understand more of why I felt that. Because after you left me, I felt like I'd been stupid. How could I have believed in this incredible love if you could leave me like that?"

"Oh, but wait . . . "

Natalie held her finger to Matthew's lips to stop him from interrupting her. "I felt disappointed when you left, not because I couldn't live without you, but because of the loss of possibilities. I really sensed that we wouldn't have to censor ourselves, to hide parts of ourselves, to please each other. That we could take delight in all the weird facets of each other's personalities. I have been in a couple of really deep love affairs in my life." She shook her head, clarifying. "Not affairs, I mean, but really deep relationships. But I'd never felt my whole self welcomed by anyone who'd ever loved me. And I was beginning to think that that was too much to hope for. But when we met, I felt that hope revive."

She got up and poured them each some more coffee and poured milk in it as she continued to talk. Matthew watched the sad, thoughtful gracefulness with which she moved, and he felt wistful in turn.

"I'm not sure what the visions we had of each other at Tony's meant. I'm not ready to jump back into being lovers with you again. And I don't know if I ever will."

Matthew sat for a long time, considering this. Natalie got up and cleared off their dishes.

"Let's go to your place," she said at last. "We've got work to do."

It was a relief to them both when they arrived at his hotel and were able to throw themselves into the ritual smudging of his room. Matthew offered to accompany her back to her building to put the carton of Anna's journals in her storage closet, but she refused.

He was just as glad she did.

CHAPTER 23

THE LABYRINTH OF STONE

"Is it foolish," she wondered, "to love a man who would kill you?" She sat on the curb and looked up for a moment at the peaks to the east of the city. Her black hair frizzed slightly in the humidity. Having drunk the moisture in the air, it expanded to a greater thickness before gathering into the heavy barrette at the nape of her neck. "Or what if he was the one to finally drive you to kill yourself," she mused, looking curiously serene. The girl with the apple cheeks.

Apples in her cheeks.

The girl.

Once upon a time there was girl who swallowed her sister in her dreams and then could not come awake. A Russian among Mormons. An artist among healers.

Oh, how she'd wanted to vomit.

But the man. She thought of the man. His shoulders drawn up like a raptor's wings. An eagle. Or a vulture. A necromancer.

"The magic. The magic." She whispered it to herself. "The magic." She wanted that part so very much. To look through the darkness to the other side. To feel the spirits around her.

Surround her.

And it went on. Words and more words.

Matthew opened his eyes slowly. He was careful not to move. Bright light shown from around the edges of the heavy drapes. It was morning. He closed his eyes cautiously.

He knew from the days when he'd cultivated his dreams that if he moved too abruptly on awakening, he could lose large sections. Dreams had to be carried gently to wakefulness or they would break and fall out piecemeal from the basket of memory. He would not even think about what the dream meant—though it was tempting. There was the troubling presence of *the man.*

Colin? Probably.

But there was more underneath. The less obvious.

He did not want to lose this dream. He could not remember ever having a dream like it before, a dream that was entirely words, without vision, without action, without any sense of himself participating—except as an attentive listener.

A dream entirely of words.

But wait. Wasn't this precisely what Tony had warned him about?

The dream had been a voice reciting. But whose voice?

The story was in Anna's style. It sounded like the long novel she had been writing when they were living in Paris, fifteen years ago.

So was this dream an invasion of the mind? Was it the voice of a suicide ghost speaking to him?

He'd done everything Tony had told him to protect himself. The room still smelled of burnt sweetgrass and sage. He and Natalie had each plucked three hairs from the crowns of their heads and burned them on the smudge sticks. They'd smudged the room. Packed up Anna's journals.

He recalled the voice from the dream. Was it Anna? The rhythms were hers.

To feel the spirits around her.
Surround her.

He heard those words again in his mind. It was so much like Anna: the transformation of sound and meaning

. . . the spirits around her. Surround her.

He heard her voice from his memory: *Once upon a time . . .* It was a motif she'd returned to again and again in *The Labyrinth of Stone,* the novel she was to rewrite for over a decade. She called it her "poor, beloved masterpiece" and had never been able to publish it. She'd not been able to publish any of her three novels, though her short fiction had begun to win awards before her death.

He heard her voice again, coming up from the long past: *Once upon a time there was a woman who lived in the sound of the waves. Each day she walked down the steep cobblestones of her village. The voices in the market as she passed did not vibrate within her ears. Only the sound of the waves.*

He heard her clearly. The rhythm of it. Her voice touched as dexterously and lyrically on the rhythm of the words as fingertips might touch on the piano keys for a nocturne by Chopin.

He remembered the words distinctly, though it had been fifteen years before. They were not the words of his dream, but the words she had read at one of the weekly open readings at *La Pensée Sauvage* or the Shakespeare and Company bookstores in the Latin Quarter:

And like the waves, she lived without future or past. Like the waves, she always returned. Once, perhaps twice per day, she broke upon the beach. She washed down the steep cobblestones of her village from her ancient house of stone. She stood looking out over the waves without hope. Without thought. Without hunger.

And then one day the man came . . .

Matthew did not want to mix the two, the dream and the memory of Anna's novel. He pushed the memory away and eased himself out of bed. He wrote the words of the dream as clearly as he could remember, careful to keep his mind quiet, so as not to lose any details.

He concentrated so fully on his task that he did not notice until after he had finished the writing that he did not feel quite so physically miserable as he usually did upon awakening. That would be Tony's doing. His healing was beginning to work.

But what was Matthew to think of this voice in the dream? Tony had put Anna's ghost in some place of stasis, where she could think and wait until they performed the ceremony for her on the following full moon.

He reread the story he'd transcribed. It was remarkably long for something recalled from a dream. He'd filled three pages with longhand. Was it, in fact, from Anna? Was it her dead soul speaking to him? Or was it a dangerous suicide ghost?

In truth, he did not think of Anna's ghost as dangerous. But he understood what Tony had meant. *It wasn't the pure soul of his dear friend Anna.* It was an infected spirit. Suicide ghosts attempt to infect the living with despair to reduce their own torment. They carry contagion. This was why suicides tended to run in families. Suicide ghosts were parasites that carried the contagion like the fleas on rats carried the bubonic plague.

And now Anna was dead and Colin had AIDS and he had cancer. To free Anna's soul, he had to help Tony find that source.

He thought of the voice in his dream. Could it lead him to the source of Anna's infection? Was it something that had happened in Paris when she'd begun *The Labyrinth of Stone*?

He thought about Anna's writing in those days, and he thought about his own. In Paris, Kolelo had taught him to listen to the *voices*. The voices were holy. Kolelo never mentioned that there might be dangerous voices from parasitic, suicide ghosts.

He saw her face again, in his mind. Her cheeks with their impossible rosiness. (One of his friends told him he didn't like all the rouge Anna wore—but if one looked closely, one could see the light tracings of capillaries and veins beneath the translucent skin. She never wore makeup). He saw her lips pronouncing the words. Her hands holding the typescript. The shelves of books behind her.

Yes, this was the small reading room at *La Pensée Sauvage*. One of Paris' two bookstores with large English-language collections. And there was Anna, reading in that fairy-tale voice, her black hair frizzed slightly and gathered into the heavy barrette at the nape of her neck. The girl with the apple cheeks.

Apples in her cheeks.

He remembered those readings with pleasure. He and Anna and their other university friend Rebecca had become regulars by then. They attended both readings every week: Mondays at *La Pensée Sauvage*, Thursdays at Shakespeare and Company. They were to become frequent readers. Anna and he with their fiction, Rebecca with her poetry. Matthew sat back in his chair, remembering with fondness those months when they'd lived in Paris. He remembered how Rebecca would turn her soulful, owl-eyes up from the page as she read, catch someone's gaze, and hold it as she finished a line. Whenever she did that to him, he got the chills.

Matthew looked down at the notebook where he'd transcribed the story from his dream. He walked to the window and looked out at the morning sun rising over the mountains to the east.

He remembered Kolelo's words again. "There are times when your voices will speak. It is your job to listen."

Kolelo had taught him to listen to the voices. Tony had taught him to suspect them. But Kolelo had not been wrong. Many of the voices that had spoken to Matthew were holy. How could you tell the difference between the holy and the damned?

The story dream came into his mind once again. There was something it was telling him. But where was *it* coming from? Who was telling the story in this dream? Was this voice holy, or was it damned? Was it connected somehow with a demon Anna might have collected in Paris?

The girl with apples in her cheeks.

The girl.

Once upon a time there was a girl . . .

He saw the scene again in his memory: the small reading room at *La Pensée Sauvage*. There was Anna, reading in that fairy-tale voice, her black hair frizzed slightly and gathered into the heavy barrette at the nape of her neck. The girl with the apple cheeks.

He saw her face again, in his mind. Her cheeks with their impossible rosiness. He saw her lips pronouncing the words.

Once upon a time there was a woman who lived in the sound of the waves. Each day she walked down the steep cobblestones of her village. The voices in the market as she passed did not vibrate within her ears. Only the sound of the waves.

And like the waves she lived without future or past. Like the waves, she always returned. Once, perhaps twice per day, she broke upon the beach. She washed down the steep cobblestones of her village from her ancient house of stone. She stood looking out over the waves without hope. Without thought. Without hunger.

And then one day the man came . . .

That's the way it always was in Anna's work.

And then one day the man came . . .

It was the same in her journals. There were journals as far back as junior high school. Always with the obsession with boys and men. Who did she love? Who would love her? Who was attractive? Who was impossible? For whom did she thirst?

Obsessive and desperate.

And then there was the man of Matthew's story-dream:

But the man. She thought of the man. His shoulders drawn up like a raptor's wings. An eagle. Or a vulture.

He could not think of that line without seeing Colin's face. Colin was not the image of a necromancer. His ringlets of tightly curled, bright red-orange hair and his multitude of freckles belied that. Only his gauntness and the depths of his eyes suggested a sorcerer.

Matthew remembered Anna's voice from his delirium visions of the day Natalie had come to see him. In his delirium, Anna told him about Esther, about how close she had been with her twin all these years. Anna wanted Matthew to know that her sister loved Colin, even if none of her friends trusted him. Esther understood the attraction. Of course, Matthew knew Esther had died before her fifth birthday.

In his delirium, Matthew had seen their weird sex, he'd seen their happy, smiling faces. All Anna's sincerity about spiritual exploration. What was that?

There were sections in Anna's journals in which she wrote about her sexual explorations with Colin. He could not help but be uncomfortable in reading these passages.

Love and sex were part of the deliciousness of life, as Tony would say. But when does appetite become gluttony? When does pleasure pass over into perversion?

Matthew had the sudden mental image of the beautiful Metta Lindquist at the window of her room in Paris, looking out at the city scene in front of her hotel. He remembered the hours he spent with her. He remembered how he had luxuriated in the opportunity of loving her: taking his time to explore every moment of her flesh, to bathe her in warm water, to lick her round belly, to find out how her toes tasted, and how her earlobes smelled.

Metta Lindquist had offered him a great banquet, and he had eaten of it fully and gratefully. His only regret now was that he had not partaken of her largesse even more. She was the bounty of life, and the memory of her made him hungry.

Metta was the purest sensualist he had ever known. Matthew had met her for the first time at a university cafeteria at the south end of Paris. They were passing themselves off as university students to get in on the subsidized lunches, and a mutual acquaintance introduced them. Metta invited him back to her room. She was staying in a cheap hotel near the university. When they'd run out of things to talk about, Matthew found himself looking into her pretty turquoise eyes and began to feel shy. She was lovely, but they hardly knew one another, and he could think of no smooth line with which to take her into his arms. Matthew excused himself to leave, but Metta took his hand to draw him near and kissed him on the mouth.

Metta was a great voluptuary. She was twenty-two years old, on vacation from her home in Norway. She had long, straight, blond hair and fleshy red lips. She was sexily plump, with pale, lightly freckled flesh and a wonderful, throaty laugh. She'd taught herself English by reading pornographic novels. Only the pleasure of this reading could push her past her natural laziness.

Metta was an accomplished kisser. As they kissed, she dragged her tongue slowly across his lower lip, then his upper. And when they were undressed, Metta showed him the immense erotic possibilities of a simple basin of warm water and a soft washcloth. "It makes you taste good," she whispered, as she unwrapped the warm washcloth from around his penis and slid her mouth over it.

Heavenly.

And, indeed, when he returned the favor to her, he found her warm, washed vagina tasted as delicious as a fresh oyster.

What Matthew would have given to have his youth back! His testosterone. His potency. His own smooth and lovely flesh that Metta had so apparently enjoyed, and to have that opportunity, that time with her again! To have that moment back and to fully savor their youthful beauty. An attractive young couple walking the boulevards of Paris. (The image of Natalie rose before his mind's eye. *Well, that was a whole other problem,* he thought).

He remembered walking the Boulevard St. Michel with Metta one evening. He'd invited her to the reading that evening and they were walking toward Shakespeare and Company. She stopped at the window of a patisserie and stood admiring the array of little pastries.

"Look how beautiful are these little cakes. They are exquisite, yes? When I wish to give myself pleasure," she said, "I buy six of these, or twelve, and eat them all. One after another. This is a beautiful experience." She laughed. "In ten years, I shall be as fat as a pig," she said with apparent enthusiasm.

Matthew had taken her to the reading and to the café afterward, and he noticed the other men looking at her. Desiring her. It gave him an enjoyable smugness.

Why had he not taken the time to enjoy this more? To make love to her more? To walk the streets of Paris with this gorgeous creature and see the eyes of other men desiring her, and to take the pleasure of knowing that only he, for that moment in time, had access to her soft, pale flesh?

Ah, but Paris had been many pleasures. He was engrossed in the world of his novel, in the life of the mind, in the association with other writers. He was engaged with his voices. For him, at that time, it was the love affair that took precedence above all others. The voices satisfied the soul in way that reduced the need for other pleasures. If that were true, perhaps it was no accident that Anna had killed herself during a long dry spell in her work. Had she been abandoned by her voices?

The girl with apples in her cheeks.

"The magic. The magic." She whispered it to herself. *"The magic."*

She wanted that part so very much. To look through the darkness to the other side. To feel the spirits around her.

Surround her.

What would Kolelo have said?

Matthew remembered when Kolelo had told him to listen to his voices. Inspired, Matthew got down to work on his novel and then was amused to discover his little sports car had been stolen. A few days later he invited Kolelo to a café for a glass of wine in thanks for his advice.

"I am happy for you," Kolelo said. They raised their glasses and clicked rims before drinking. "Perhaps now that you are hearing them, you will even begin to discern their personalities."

"Personalities?"

Kolelo looked at his quizzical face for a long moment, and then laughed heartily and pointed his finger at Matthew. "You think the voices come from some part of your own brain, don't you?" he said. He shook his head and laughed some more. "You think I was telling you to listen more carefully when you talk to yourself?"

"I didn't think you were saying *that*," Matthew protested.

"Perhaps yes, perhaps no," Kolelo said, "but you didn't believe I was saying *exactly* what I meant, either." He shrugged. "Well, you would have been a most unusual American if you had." Kolelo raised his eyebrows and frowned. "Then again, the French are worse. That block-head Descartes with his *cogito ergo sum*."

Now Matthew laughed. "Descartes is a blockhead?"

"Of course," Kolelo said. "He put mathematics at the heart of all reasoning. He 'proved' the existence of God by steps of logic." Kolelo shook his head sadly. "Up through the middle ages it was understood that the individual's consciousness was a mélange of voices. A great portion of what *modern* Europeans perceive as their own thoughts, the medievals heard as the voices. They heard them as spirits of the earth, the voices of angels, the voices of devils and saints—perhaps even God himself muttered the occasional word."

"So you think that the voices that would help us with our fiction, with our poetry, are individual beings?" Matthew said.

"It is not a matter of thinking." He held up his glass of wine. "Like with this: You do not stop and think: 'This is wine.' It is a *sense*. You see the color. You raise the glass and smell its aroma. You taste its flavor on your tongue. You don't need logic to *conclude* this substance must be wine."

"And this is the way it is for people in Cameroon with the voices? They discern individual voices in their minds and know what they are?"

"Well," Kolelo shrugged. "Certainly for the Bantus of my grand-father's generation. The contagion of materialism and Christianity drives out the old values. Against my grandfather's wishes, my father sent me to be educated by the Jesuits when I was twelve. From there I went to the University in Douala and then studied here at the Sorbonne. Now I know more about European art and philosophy than I know about my own people."

"Then how do you know the voices?" Matthew asked.

"I came back to my village to visit my grandfather. I was telling him about Paris and the great cathedrals and museums—all things he had never and would never see. Then he held his hand to my face, and he said with great concern, 'Mbella, how long has your stomach been hurting you?' This stopped me cold. I had not told anyone about my stomach. I was too proud to admit that I had had a stomachache for over a year.

"You see, in my time at the Sorbonne, I had become so accustomed to ignoring the voices of the spirits, I had stopped hearing them al-together. From the point of view of the spirits, I had become some-

200 • RICHARD ENGLING

thing like a stupid cow, and so the parasitic ones felt free to feast on my belly—and that was what caused my pain. I cannot tell you all my grandfather did to rid me of them because that is a sacred confidence. But I will tell you this: He trained my ear to hear the voices. He wanted this both for my health and because I had begun to write stories and poems. He said that it was as bad for a storyteller to be deaf in this way as it would be for a painter to be blind.

"He said to me: 'First, Mbella, hear the small voices that cannot fool or escape you.' And he took me to a clearing to listen to the grasses and insects. He sat with me and instructed me in how to slow and quiet my mind and then to align it with the rhythm of the thing I wanted to hear." Kolelo laughed. "I heard him talking to the other old men one night, as they were drinking the homemade beer of the village. 'Paris has crippled the mind of my grandson,' he said. 'I don't know if he will ever hear again.' Until then, I had been doing what he asked, but it had not struck me as serious. I imagined my doctor in Paris would find the cure for the gnawing in my belly. I had my own intelligence to write stories and poetry. But when I heard the sorrow in his voice, I suddenly understood that I was not indulging the desires of my grandfather. He was sacrificing his time for me! I was crippled, and only my grandfather could restore me to wholeness.

"The day after I heard my grandfather talking to the other old men, I tried all the harder. This, of course, was a disaster!" Kolelo bent his head back and laughed his deep hearty laugh. "My grandfather saw this and finally lost his patience. He grabbed me by the ears and held my face close to his as he talked to me. So close that the tips of our noses practically touched. 'You are my grandson, Mbella,' he said to me. 'You know what I can do, do you not?' 'Yes, grandfather,' I said, for everyone knew my grandfather was a powerful man. Once, one of my cousins had been raped. My uncle took his weeping raped daughter to my grandfather as soon as she staggered home from the assault. Grandfather found one of the man's pubic hairs clinging to his granddaughter's body. He took that one pubic hair and used it to create a spell. The rapist did not live in our village, but in a village fifteen miles away. Within a week his testicles ballooned up. Sores broke out all over his body. It took a full month for him to die in the most painful way. So I knew my grandfather's dreadful power. But he could also bless. He was a generous man. His garden fed many neighbors when the drought times came. Grandfather's spells caused our lands to produce like no one else's.

"'My blood runs in your veins, Mbella,' he said to me, with his terrible eyes, just inches from mine. 'Most men lose the wisdom of their village as they gain the wisdom of the Europeans,' he said. 'For most men, these two wisdoms are too much for one mind to contain. But it is not too much for you, Mbella, because my blood runs in your veins.' He let go of my ears, took his knife, and quickly tapped the tip of it to the center of his forehead. A single bright drop of blood welled up there. He touched his fingertip to the blood and held it out in front of my face. I opened my mouth. He put the drop of blood onto my tongue.

"'This is simple, Mbella,' he said. 'Stop trying. Look at the grass. See its vibration. Feel its vibration. Join with it. And hear the voice of the grass.'

"I tasted the saltiness of my grandfather's blood on my tongue. At that moment, Matthew, I could feel the full power of that brilliant man. I had been dazzled by the learnedness of my professors at the Sorbonne, but now I understood that my grandfather was one of the geniuses of his culture. His depth of learning and accomplishment was the equivalent of a half dozen PhDs. And his blood ran through my veins.

"Once again I sat in the meditation that he had taught me. But now I sat with the full expectation that I would hear. I was not aware of how much time it was taking me to succeed in this task, for I was no longer aware of the passing of time nor of the desire for success.

"It had rained early that morning. I heard the grass speak. It was saying, over and over, 'I am water.'" Kolelo smiled a beneficent smile at the simplicity of this. "'I am water,'" he repeated. "It was filled with joy! It could think of nothing else because it was in a state of ecstasy, a state of oneness with the water coming up its roots into the green fuse, as Dylan Thomas would say. I told my grandfather what I heard the grass say, and we laughed and laughed. My grandfather said: 'You see, Mbella, the grass is like you in its moments of great joy.'"

"So how do you know that you weren't just imagining what the grass might say?" Matthew said.

"Because it was a *sense*, Matthew. If I was imagining what the grass might say, that would have been a thought. A sense has a much different feel in the mind." He considered it for a moment. "A sense is astringent and sharp, like the aroma of juniper berries. Do you know juniper berries? That is what gives gin its distinctive flavor. A sense is sharp like that. A thought is more...liquid and warm," Kolelo said, grasping for an image, "like a thick sauce or a soup."

"Senses are like gin and thoughts are like sauce? And that is how you know the grass was truly talking?"

Kolelo pointed at Matthew and gave him a slow grin. "You think you can ridicule my images, Matthew, but you are only ridiculing out of ignorance. You are like the ignoramus laughing at the astronaut: 'Rocks on the moon,' he says, 'what nonsense! We know perfectly well that the moon is made of green cheese.'"

"I'm not trying to ridicule," Matthew said. "I just don't understand gin and sauce as senses and thinking."

Kolelo held his crafty smile, looking into Matthew's eyes, then he looked thoughtfully up at the ceiling. "These are subjective images, Matthew. Think again of juniper berries, the aroma of gin, or the taste of mint, the green smell of evergreen needles. All of these things are penetrating. Like sense. Sense comes from the outside and penetrates the mind. Thoughts rise from within the mind, with warmth and liquidity." He sipped his wine and considered it further. "Sense has the ability to surprise to a much greater degree than thought—naturally, since thought arises from the context of the mind itself, whereas sense can bring in totally new information." He sat up sharply in his chair and leaned in toward Matthew, lowering his voice and speaking intensely. "I was so very much surprised to hear what the grass was saying, Matthew. It was such an incredible surprise that I laughed. 'I am water!' You know, this statement was not an *image* for the grass. This was a joyful declaration of belief. 'I *am* water.' Not 'I am grass filled with water.' I *am* water—the wonderful flowing element of all life. This—to hear this—surprised me to my bones."

♦   ♦   ♦

After the conversation, surprise became the key to discerning the presence of the voices for Matthew. As Kolelo's grandfather had worked with him, now Kolelo worked with Matthew, passing along the techniques for hearing the voices.

Matthew, however, never was able to sense personalities in the voices, or even to hear them speaking sentences to him. To him, they felt like revelations, only barely discernable from his own thoughts. They came to him with the surprising turns of plot, the surprising elements of character, the surprising solutions to the problems he faced in writing his early works. They were the eccentricities that brought his fiction to life.

Hearing the voices was a joy. An inspiration. And sometimes a frustration. Sometimes what he heard forced him to rethink and rework many pages that he had thought were done and complete and good.

Thinking about Kolelo and Paris made Matthew feel lonely. He got up from the chair in his hotel room where he'd been thinking and remembering and looked out the window at the mountains above Salt Lake.

He thought of Anna again. What had happened to her in Paris?

Matthew suddenly remembered something. When Anna arrived in Paris, she got a part-time job doing household chores for an elderly woman in one of the suburbs south of the city. Part of her pay was free rent in the old woman's *chambre de bonne* on the top floor of the building. Then Anna got a second part-time job, typing for a doctor who lived near *Place Denfert-Rochereau* in the city. He also had a vacant *chambre de bonne*, which he was willing to let Anna use. What Matthew suddenly remembered was that the doctor was reluctant to let her have the room because another young woman had killed herself there. The doctor was afraid if Anna stayed there, it would make her depressed.

Matthew remembered when Anna took him there for the first time. The room was small, with a tiny window letting in a paltry, gray light. The only furnishing was a bamboo pallet, low to the ground, for sleeping. The walls were a soiled slate color. Scraps of paper littered the dirty floor. But worst of all was a creepy, suicide *feel* of the room. As though the haunting presence of the dead woman's desperate last act still hung in the air.

"Oh, Anna, you can't stay here," he told her. "This is so depressing, you'll be slitting your wrist within a month."

"Just wait until you see what I do with it," she said. "You'll see."

To give her credit, she did transform the room. She painted it a cheerful peach color. She covered the bare bulb hanging from the ceiling with one of those big, round Chinese paper lanterns. She constructed and decorated low shelves from the ubiquitous fruit and vegetable crates. Her camping mattress and sleeping bag fit the bamboo pallet perfectly. And the doctor found her a small desk and chair, just big enough for her typewriter and notes.

He remembered the first time she'd invited him back to the room. She'd made dinner for the two of them. She sautéed fillets of chicken breast on her little *Camping Gaz* stove and put them on their plates with a dollop of mustard. She served the main course with wine, baguette and butter, sautéed green beans, and those wonderful French beets. The beets came wrapped in coarse paper, already prepared from the market. You just had to peel off the outer layer and eat. These beets were nothing like the ones he'd had in America. These were like sweet onions. You could peel layer after layer of juicy beet until you got down to the core. The wonderful red juice would stain your fingers, and seeing your purple fingertips the next day would remind you how succulent and alive those beets had tasted.

Anna and Matthew sat on the mattress with their legs crossed and their plates on their laps, eating like they were camping out, indoors. Yet Matthew remembered the event as having a certain elegance. Anna took such a delight in cooking their dinner and having Matthew to her new "home." The little room that had looked so depressing was truly unrecognizable.

But there was something else . . .

Matthew had a peculiar sensation, like something physical connecting him with that long ago memory. He smelled a trace of smoke in the air. He looked out in the hallway of the hotel and then in his bathroom.

No evidence of smoke.

This scent was in his mind's nose. It was the smoke of Tony's ritual fire.

Matthew sat in the large easy chair and closed his eyes.

Something stretched back to the long-ago memory. Anna in her room at *Denfert-Rochereau.*

Matthew allowed himself to drift into a trance. The aroma of the ritual fire grew stronger until he could see it once again: the fire in its circle of rock. Tony's hide lay on the ground with its array of objects atop. Matthew saw himself sitting on the ground. Copal smoke twirled into his nostrils changing the aroma. It was sharp, like a sense, as Kolelo would say. Like gin. Like true voices. Like surprise.

He heard the explosion, elongated, muffled, expanded in time. He saw the ghost, its atoms heading out into space, that moment of destruction frozen. The flames held still. Time stopped.

Matthew drew closer to the ghost in its moment of annihilation. Something stretched away from it. Long tendrils of energy. Bungee cords of the spirit. From the moment of the ghost's annihilation, they stretched back through time and space.

Matthew followed the chords, careful not to touch them. He sensed a destination, somewhere back along the ghost's path, and he acquiesced to it.

He traveled at tremendous speed, like an electron firing through a transatlantic length of fiber-optic cable. He doubted, suddenly, the wisdom of acquiescing to the destination. But just as suddenly, he was there.

It was Anna's room, of course. Her *chambre de bonne* in *Denfert-Rochereau*. He drifted above the scene frozen in time. He and Anna sat on the floor, about to eat their dinner. Their glasses were raised, locked in the moment of toast. The chord passed into the belly of the suicide ghost. Or demon, really, would have been a better name. For it was not the lost spirit of the girl who had killed herself in this room. It was the demon that had helped push her to it. It looked like one of the gargoyles atop Notre Dame.

All three were smiling, frozen in time: The Anna and the Matthew, raising their wineglasses at the beginning of an enjoyable meal. And the demon, too, smiled a happy smile, sitting with its arms around Anna from the back, embracing her as it gnawed at the lower left corner of her skull.

Matthew felt frightened and sick. He leaned back toward the present and found himself shooting along the demon's chord through time and space. He stopped above himself once again. His frozen self was alone on a couch, sitting in another moment of the past.

He was sitting alone, but there were many people.

It was Anna's wake. And there was Anna, above, tormented by her demons, as Matthew had sensed at the time. He was sending a prayer in her aid. And that was the moment in which the *Denfert-Rochereau* demon had transferred itself to him. Had it gnawed on his skull, too?

Matthew took a look around the room. All of the frozen people there looked gray. Even Natalie and Patty looked gray. But not Anna's mother. She had a peculiar, painful glow.

♦   ♦   ♦

Matthew opened his eyes. He felt as though he'd passed out for a moment. He remembered everything of his journey, but he did not remember coming back from the wake. Suddenly, he'd simply been back.

His head felt foggy. Matthew got up from his chair by the hotel room window and stretched. The morning sun had risen high in the sky, and the day had grown more beautiful. Suddenly his room reminded him of being in a tomb. It was time to get out.

It was time for a trip back to Chicago.

CHAPTER 24

SURROUNDED BY DEMONS

"ESTHER AND ANNA WERE different, right from the start. Right from the moment when they were born," Mrs. Toyevsky said. She looked out the front window of her Chicago bungalow and shook her head. Her blond-dyed curls shimmered in the light from the stained-glass window behind her, above the sofa, giving her hair an eerie glow. Then she smiled at Matthew as though she'd forgotten where she was for a moment, and she refilled their cups with black coffee, pouring it right to the top. She had expressed her amazement at how much milk Matthew wanted in his first cup. Now, of course, she didn't remember. This was not creeping senility. This was one of the things that had driven Anna crazy. Her mother had frequent lapses of attention when it came to other people.

"Were they identical?" Matthew asked. He leaned forward in the wingback chair and took a cookie from the coffee table.

"They were," Mrs. Toyevsky said, her Eastern European *th* coming out like a *z*, making her sound a little like Dr. Ruth, the TV sex doctor, to Matthew. She was roughly the same compact size and shape as Dr. Ruth, as well. "People always talk about how similar identical twins are supposed to be. Even twins separated at birth will grow up to be quite similar, with preferences even for similar foods." Mrs. Toyevsky laughed. "I saw a funny thing on television once about twins. There was a set of twins put up for adoption. Different mothers raised them. And they interviewed the mothers when the children were maybe four years old, I think. The first mother said, 'Oh, she's impossible with the food. She won't eat anything unless it's got cinnamon in it.' Then they interviewed the mother of the second twin. She said, 'She's terrific. She'll eat anything. All I have to do is sprinkle a little cinnamon on it.'" Mrs. Toyevsky shrugged theatrically and laughed.

Matthew laughed, too. "The second twin lucked out."

"Yes." Mrs. Toyevsky smiled and nodded for a moment, then shook her head. "But not Esther and Anna. Esther was delivered first. The nurses told me that she calmed down very fast. She stopped crying and lay there, moving her arms around, looking around at the light coming to her eyes. She was fascinated by the world. But when Anna was born, a few minutes later, she cried and cried and cried. Inconsolable. And that is the way they were. Esther was a calm, normal child. A deep thinker, she seemed to me. And Anna was the fearful child. She was like . . . someone was after her."

"She certainly grew up to be a deep thinker," Matthew said.

"Oh, yes, she was always this, too," Mrs. Toyevsky admitted. "They were identical twins in every way than this: Esther was at peace in the world, and Anna was not. I don't know why." Mrs. Toyevsky gave a deep sigh. "It is a horrible thing to say, I know, but if Esther had been the one to survive childhood, I would still have a daughter. With Esther, I believe, my daughter would have buried me, instead of me having to bury my daughter. I have had to bury *both* of my daughters."

Mrs. Toyevsky looked out the window again and sipped at her coffee. Matthew felt uneasy. There was so much he needed to ask her, but how to do it gracefully?

"Anna always seemed haunted by her sister's death," Matthew said. "I remember in Paris, she talked about writing Esther's story. She said it was very hard for you to talk about Esther's death. That you would never tell her the details she needed to write the story."

Mrs. Toyevsky looked at him quizzically. "There was not much of a story to tell about Esther's death," she said. "Sam and I felt horribly guilty. Terrible regret. You know, people were not so fast to go to the doctor in those days."

"Go to the doctor?"

"Yes, you know, we were using the baby aspirin and the Vicks VapoRub, and giving her the steam, but her fever would not go down."

"I don't understand," Matthew said. "Anna told me Esther had been murdered."

Mrs. Toyevsky looked offended. "We should have got the doctor sooner," she said. "But I would not call that murder. I took care of her day and night. But we thought it was just a chest cold. We did not know the child had pneumonia."

"Esther wasn't kidnapped?" Matthew said. "She wasn't abducted?"

Mrs. Toyevsky gave Matthew a long, strange look, then she laughed suddenly. "You are talking about Anna's Aunt Esther!" she said. She took a deep breath, and the sorrow returned to her face. "Yes, I remember Anna questioning me about her. But really. That sordid business." She shook her head. "My father suffered so."

"And Anna's twin was not abducted?"

"You got it mixed up, Matthew. My daughter Esther died in the Cook County Hospital when the girls were four years old. They could not save her from the pneumonia. We were devastated. It was my sister Esther who was murdered. And my father . . . They might as well have killed him, too. Esther died before the girls were born. But we never burdened Anna about either of the deaths. She was already such a fearful child, as I told you, from the moment she was born. So we didn't talk to her about death when she was a child. We never even took her to the hospital when Esther was sick, because we knew it would have been too much for her."

Matthew took a tiny sip of his black coffee. Could Anna have been mixed up? Had they "burdened" her with so little information that she thought the murder of her Aunt Esther had happened to her twin sister?

"Could you tell me about your sister's death?" he said.

Anna's mother looked at him with suspicion. "Frankly, Matthew, this is not something I want to think about."

Well, that's it, he thought. He'd have to lay the cards on the table.

"Do you remember Anna's friend Natalie, in Salt Lake?" he said.

"The pretty, black-haired girl?" Mrs. Toyevsky said. "The one who looks like a gypsy?"

"That's right. Natalie took me to an Indian medicine man near Salt Lake."

Mrs. Toyevsky began shaking her head. "Be careful, Matthew. These so-called healers are mostly charlatans."

"Well, what I didn't tell you about my cancer is that the doctors say it's incurable."

"Oh, Matthew, I am so sorry," she said.

"This man is quite remarkable. I'm already feeling better than I did."

"Well, this is good," she said, hesitantly.

"The doctors can't help me now."

"Doctors," she said, shaking her head dismissively. The doctors hadn't saved her daughter Esther. Nor had they saved Anna.

"This medicine man uses herbs the way our doctors use medicines. But he also travels into the spirit world."

"And you believe in all this traveling to the spirit world, Matthew?"

"If you had seen what I've seen with this man, you would believe, too." he said. "It's not so very different from what we believe as Jews and Christians. We believe in God and the devil."

"*This* Jew is not so sure."

"Let me tell you something. When we were all in Salt Lake for Anna's memorial service, I was sitting on the couch by myself."

"You were a good friend to her, Matthew."

"But then I got this horrible feeling, and I sensed—I could see in my mind's eye—Anna surrounded by demons. I tried to help her."

Mrs. Toyevsky grew very still. She felt a little light-headed, and her face began to go pale. "Believing in demons is the way to madness," she said.

"Maybe. But the shaman in Utah believes in the demons, too. He's going to perform a ceremony to free Anna's soul, and he wants to know where they came from. He thought perhaps they had come through the family. Maybe these demons had something to do with Esther's death."

"With my Esther's pneumonia?"

"More likely your sister's murder."

Mrs. Toyevsky got up and looked out the front window of her bungalow. She put her hand on the glass and leaned her hip against the tall steam radiator beside her. She let her head drop forward until her forehead rested on the coolness of the glass. She'd never talked about this. She'd never talked about this with anyone. Not even she and Sam discussed it. But it had never gone away.

She pulled herself back up and looked at the stained-glass window above the sofa. She'd always loved its clean, geometric shapes. She'd been so happy when she and Sam bought the house. These brick Chicago bungalows were so fashionable back then. And people liked them again now: the ones in which the old woodwork had not been painted over, nor the built-in hutches torn out. She'd felt so safe when they moved in here. But that had been an illusion. They had never been safe. Anna knew it from the moment she was born.

"My father talked about demons," she admitted. "My father thought he *saw* demons. The Nazis bent his mind." She looked down and shook her head and then looked at Matthew. "My family was well-to-do in Russia. My father traveled very often, buying and selling gold and silver, jewelry and precious stones. Esther was twelve years older than me. She was almost like a second mother to me. There were just the two of us. Two daughters and my parents. And so my father decided to teach Esther the family business. She learned the books. She accompanied him on his travels. My mother didn't like this. She said they should look to Esther's husband for this, once Esther was married. But my father did not listen. He was a headstrong man. No one could ever tell him what to do. And so on a business trip to Switzerland, he traveled through German-occupied territory, despite the warnings. He and Esther together.

"We were told they both were killed. My mother sold everything and got the two of us to America. My father actually survived the camp, however. The allies rescued him. He was one of those skin-and-bones prisoners you see in the photographs, dressed in rags. Finally, we were reunited, here in Chicago. But my father's mind was bent.

"The Nazis made him watch what they did to Esther. He never talked about it, but I heard him scream in his nightmares. And he would have his episodes. He would throw me in the closet and nail the door shut on me, because he thought they were coming. He could see demons in the air. Sometimes he would fire his pistol down the hallway of the apartment building. It was a miracle he never killed anyone. And he would shout. From what I heard him shout, I could piece together what they had done to Esther.

"Sometimes, when he was lucid, my mother would have her griefs. She would weep and turn her blame on him, saying, 'You had to teach her the business. Nobody teaches their daughters the business.'"

Mrs. Toyevsky turned back to Matthew and looked him in the eye. "But this thing you said. It made me remember something that happened just before my father died. I hadn't thought about this since, because he did so many things. His mind was so bent.

"When he came to see the twins in the hospital, shortly after the girls were born, he picked up Anna and looked into her eyes. He got this great look of joy on his face. 'Esther,' he says to her. 'You have come back to me.' And I said to him, 'No, Papa, the other twin is the one we named for Esther.' But he would always make this mistake, calling Anna Esther. And then his episodes got worse again. He was always seeing the demons around Anna. He got his hands on another gun, and he ran out one day, chasing the demons all the way into the street, firing his gun. The police shot him down dead. You couldn't blame them. He could have killed someone, firing wildly at something no one else could see. He could have killed anyone."

Chapter 25

CLAUSTROPHOBIA

All the way back to Utah in the plane, Matthew felt something calling him. From the airport, he did not return to his room at the Inn at Temple Square. Instead, he began driving toward the canyons.

In the weeks since his experience with Tony in the desert, indoors had felt like shelter to him. Comfort. Protection. But now he recognized it was also a barrier. There were things he would never understand by remaining indoors. It was as though he suddenly sensed some kind of radio waves that he had to get outdoors to receive.

In Paris, Kolelo had taught him techniques for opening to the voices outdoors in the *Jardin du Luxembourg*, the large park on the grounds of the *Palais du Luxembourg* in the Latin Quarter. Sometimes when he wanted to feel at home in a spiritual place, he would imagine himself back in there. He would remember entering the park by the west gate from *Boulevard St. Michel*. Inside the tall, wrought iron fence, the *Jardin* was a world apart: the long walkways bordered by flower gardens and statues, the people congregated on the metal chairs scattered throughout the park, the expanses of grass and trees, the children sailing boats in the reflecting pond and the old men playing chess. He sighed thinking about it. How he would love to go back there. To sit in the grass with Kolelo and learn again about the hearing of voices.

He suspected now that new voices were attempting to come to him. Voices that were opening to him as a result of his work with Tony—and perhaps, too, as a result of what he'd learned from Anna's mother. He had to go to them.

At first he thought he would head south—the direction toward Tony's. But Matthew felt drawn to drive up into one of the high canyons to the east of the city. He followed his inclination and drove for a half hour, up into the rocks, enjoying the sunlight. Then, after slowing for a sharp turn, he saw a gravel road to the right and turned into it on impulse. His rental car struggled to climb the sharp hill it took, its tires gripping and then slipping, kicking gravel behind as he ascended.

At the top of the rise, Matthew pulled into a clearing. He got out and looked around with a feeling of expectancy tingling at the back of his neck. He walked over the top of the rise, feeling the dry desert earth beneath his feet. He followed the road a while, then turned off to walk down into an arroyo, the ground crumbling under his feet as he crossed over the edge of the gully. Something here struck him as familiar. He felt as though there was something here he needed to find.

The eroded gully took a turn to the left, and he followed it, noticing what the carving of water had done to the rock and the earth. There was no water here now. Everything was dry. A tumbleweed blew over the ridge above his head. He followed the channel down deeper where there still wasn't any water, just the deep gully left by erosion. A channel cut in from the left after the bend.

Suddenly he remembered this place. Matthew sat abruptly on the ground, feeling faint. He remembered Anna had been standing in the center of that channel. He remembered how startled he'd been to see her.

"Nobody knows anything," she'd said.

It took a moment to remember it had been a dream.

He'd had that dream twice since he'd arrived in Salt Lake. Once when he first arrived and then again the day Natalie had come and had taken him to Tony.

He remembered the second time even more clearly. The dream started the same, but it went on longer. He remembered feeling tired and sick. It was hot in the desert of that dream. Intolerably hot. He questioned Anna, but a male voice answered. He saw only the bottom half of the man: His large snakeskin boots. Dusty black jeans. A large silver and turquoise ring on one of the fingers. A big clump of feathers, like the torn-off wing of a large bird, hung from a piece of rawhide on his belt.

It had been Tony! How was it that he never remembered the dream all through the weekend with Tony? Tony wore the same snakeskin boots. The same jewelry. And how could he not have remembered that bird wing once he'd seen Tony use it to direct the flow of smoke and to flick away spirits?

Matthew got up off the desert ground and brushed the dust off his pants. The dizziness of his initial shock of recognition had cleared. Now his puzzlement took over. Why had he dreamed of this place? Why had he seen Anna here? And Tony? And what had brought him here today, driving on impulse?

He began walking again, following the eroded channel higher into the hill. After the dry crust of the first arroyo, this felt like walking on stale cake. The gully grew shallower as he climbed higher. Ahead he saw a magnificent juniper, thirty or forty feet tall, in full bloom. It had more juniper berries on it than he'd ever seen on a single tree.

People used various species of juniper back in Chicago as lawn shrubs. Matthew's parents had large juniper bushes across the front of the house he'd grown up in. But they had never grown above four feet high. And his principal memory of them was of the sharp clusters of needles they dropped that stuck in his flesh when running barefoot in the yard.

But here was a magnificent juniper tree in its native habitat, huge with spiky arms curving up into the air giving it a silhouette like a huge maple leaf, its gray-green branches intense against the brilliant blue of the desert sky.

This was a tree so alive Matthew could practically hear it hum as he approached. He stroked one of the fresh branches upward with his open hand. The new needles felt soft, like firm grass against his skin. Farther in along the branches and down on the ground he saw the hard, brown, old needles that had dried to sharp points and that—he knew from experience—would itch if they penetrated the skin. The needles were succulent and pleasant in their youth, but unforgiving in age and death.

Matthew plucked some of the juniper berries from the branch. They were a little bigger than black peppercorns—almost as large as small blueberries—but colored deep green and textured with a scaly surface. He squeezed hard to crush one of the firm berries between his fingers and raised it to his nose. It smelled quintessentially green. It opened Matthew's sinuses with an astringent aroma like menthol or mint. It brought to his mind the characteristic flavor of gin. This was the sharp, penetrating scent that Kolelo had compared to the sensation of hearing authentic voices. Matthew gathered a handful of berries and sat beneath the branches, like Buddha beneath the bo tree. He recalled Anna once again, standing in the dust, telling him: "Nobody knows anything." He recalled Tony saying: "Learn to ask the right questions." In his mind's eyes, he saw faces slowly cascade, from one to the next: from Anna to Tony to Natalie to his ex-wife Patty to AIDS-infected Colin to Kolelo to Metta Lindquist to Anna to Natalie again. He remembered something Lawrence Durrell had written in *The Alexandria Quartet*: "There are three things you can do with a woman. You can love her. You can serve her. Or you can turn her into literature."

He thought about Natalie. Sometimes she was like the desert lizard: quick to retreat, solitary, incommunicative. In order to hear her words, you had to wait in silence. Often you thought she wasn't going to say anything at all. You needed the patience to wait through the silence until she was ready. And then she would open up. Then she would tell you everything.

She frustrated her friends who tried to reach her by the phone because even when she was at home, she would seldom pick up. She refused to have an answering machine because then she felt she'd be obliged to return calls she didn't want to return.

Communicating with Natalie was like listening for the voices. Not only did you have to ask the right questions, you had to have the patience to wait for the answers.

The voices, he thought.

The voices.

If he had listened to the voices faithfully all his life as Kolelo had instructed him, would he now be a healthy man, with many years ahead of him? Children surrounding him? Grandchildren to come?

He plucked a few more berries from the juniper branch above his head where he sat.

He knew it didn't work that way. If he had followed a sainthood of letters, being faithful always to the voices, that would not have guaranteed a smooth life. No sainthood did.

But saints, we were supposed to believe, were best prepared for death. They would be the great success stories of the afterlife. Theirs was to be an eternity of bliss. And a difficult lifetime was just a blink of an eye in comparison to eternity.

Matthew grew impatient. He felt the sharp pebbles in the dry earth digging into his buttocks and the undersides of his thighs. He felt the desert air drying the insides of his sinuses and imagined suddenly his dead body drying in the grave. He breathed a heavy sigh and looked up into the branches overhead. This was no bo tree, and he was no Buddha.

Maybe it didn't make a damned bit of difference what he did with the rest of his life. Not any more than the actions of an ant in an ant-hill mattered. Maybe we were all just random specks of life that came and went like the sparks flying out of a campfire, glowing and then going out. We came, we lived, we were gone, and once we'd faded from memory, nothing remained. Nothing at all.

Matthew took a deep breath. He smelled the deep, penetrating greenness of the juniper. He raised to his nose the crushed berries that he still carried in his hand and inhaled the aroma. He heard a comforting male voice, deep inside his mind. "Take a hike," it said.

Take a hike.

He smiled.

He could do that.

He pushed himself to a standing position, stretching to release the stiffness in his bones.

Take a hike. Maybe that was the meaning of life. Take a hike. When it's done, lie down and die. Simple.

So which way? He smelled the aroma of the juniper again more strongly and turned to face the tree. He looked down at the deep green berries in his hand, put them in his pocket and reached up to gather some more. Which way would he go?

Through the tree, he thought.

Was that a thought? Or was it a voice?

He smiled and ducked his head and walked under the low branches of the tree, dried needles crunching under his feet. As he passed directly under the tree, the aroma grew momentarily intense. Stronger even than when he lifted the crushed berries directly to his nose. He stopped for a moment, bent over as he was, and waited there, crouched nearly double, with his eyes closed, and simply inhaled. He inhaled deeply, with his eyes closed, and felt a quiet joy coming into his soul through the deep chambers of his lungs.

This moment . . . he thought.

And then the words stopped. He simply felt himself there, floating in that quiet joy, in the presence of the tree, in the presence of his mentor Kolelo who'd told him so many years ago about the aroma of juniper. He felt himself standing over the deep living juniper roots that dug into the dry earth, next to its strong trunk, beneath its branches reaching up and out. He stood crouched there and felt the companionship of everything he knew, and for a moment he was in life, absolutely in it in a way that demanded nothing else.

He took another deep breath, opened his eyes, and then pushed on, still crouching, out the other side of the tree.

The light looked different to him now. Bluer. He looked up at the same blue sky, still cloudless, still the same and not the same, and he walked on up the hill, not perplexed by the change but in the afterglow of the moment he'd had. He breathed in the dry air deeply and felt its dryness cure something in him—cure like leather is cured or certain meats or cheeses. Cure like wines or brandies in the cask.

He took the hill in long strides, pulling deep draughts of the air into his lungs with pleasure. He could feel the gentle sting of the juniper scent down his throat into his lungs, and it felt as exhilarating as the snap of frigid air after the first deep snow of the year back in his native Chicago. It was rejuvenating! When had he last walked with such energy? It was as though his precancer stamina were coming back. Did he have Tony to thank for that? Tony and his herbs?

He felt his faithful hiking boots hugging his feet as he climbed the slope, crunching over hard dry earth and pebbles. Sharp stones scraped against rock beneath his feet, but the tough boot soles kept his traction. He remembered camping trips when he was in his twenties, camping alone in the Rocky Mountains, traveling across the country to California, wearing these boots.

But that was odd. Hadn't he lost these boots years ago? Or no, hadn't they been ruined when he left them too close to a campfire, trying to dry them after his canoe capsized during a trip through the Boundary Waters?

Matthew didn't have time to think this through before he reached the summit of the hill. He looked down into a bowl-shaped declivity. A little path lay clearly before him, running down to the mouth of a cave at the bottom of the little valley.

There was something about this valley that reminded him of the valley in which Tony had set up his trailer and temporary homestead. Something about its unexpected nature: how it was so totally hidden and unexpected until you were actually upon it.

Matthew looked back the way he'd come. There was the massive juniper tree on the lower slope behind him, the rocky slope up which he had climbed, but there was no path he'd followed. There were no paths at all behind him, save what was created by the gullies of erosion. He looked forward into the valley again.

How odd: such a clear footpath. And here, at the top of the ridge where he stood, he noticed a dark marking in the rock almost directly under his feet. He crouched down to look at it more closely. It looked like an animal's head: Pointed ears. Long snout. A coyote. It was looking back in the direction from which Matthew had come. The corner of its mouth turned up slightly with the suggestion of a smile.

Matthew stood and descended the path. The little valley was so perfectly round and bowl-shaped, Matthew had the impression he was walking into the cup of a chalice rather than into any landscape created by nature. It was a crater, he suddenly realized, like on the surface of the moon. Perhaps it had been created by the crash of a meteorite.

The air grew more and more still the deeper he walked into the crater. It was warmer in the crater, and the scent of juniper grew strong once again, almost as strong as it had been when he crouched beneath the tree. How could that be? There was only scrub vegetation here. No junipers.

Had a breeze carried the scent into the bowl where it remained, undisturbed again by wind?

He continued down to the bottom of the crater and looked into the mouth of the cave he'd spotted from above.

Curious.

He went inside.

The channel of the cave was tall enough that he could walk nearly fully upright. The walls were remarkably smooth, like a channel dug by an enormous worm.

He had to walk slowly and brace his hands against the walls, for the channel went sharply down into the rock. There was a little loose stone on the ground, and he worried about losing his footing and falling on the steep slope because the passage became dark very quickly. Fear rose in him, and he was about to turn back when he saw a suggestion of light ahead. Perhaps the channel emerged out the side of a slope in a canyon wall ahead?

The passage leveled off, and the diffuse light grew stronger. He could walk with greater confidence again. Then he saw the source of the light: an alley cutting off to the left from the main channel. He turned in and found himself in a large room. Kolelo sat at a small table near the window.

"Ah, Matthew, it is good to see you," he said. "Come. Sit."

Matthew felt a perplexing mix of joy and confusion sweep through him. He sat at the café table across from Kolelo. "You look just the same," Matthew said.

"One does not age here," Kolelo said. "I am glad you have been thinking of me." He raised a glass. Matthew picked up the glass in front of him and raised it to click rims with Kolelo. He tasted the liquid inside. It was gin, with a twist of lime, astringent and clear.

"How are your beautiful friends?" Kolelo said.

"I haven't seen them," Matthew said, feeling the surprise of sudden sorrow. Of course Anna was dead, but Rebecca was not. How many years had it been since he'd called her? God knows if he'd even be able to find her anymore. And the others he'd been friends with in Paris. People he rarely thought of anymore. His friends at Shakespeare and Company. The writers he'd come to know at the readings.

"This is a shame," Kolelo said. "Those people were your riches. You were a wealthy man in Paris, Matthew. I saw this in you."

Matthew felt a moment's impulse to tell Kolelo of his successes and fame, but the impulse vanished almost instantly. He felt the enormous waste there was in his life, and it made him sad. "I worked very hard, Mbella," he said, calling Kolelo by his given name for the first time in his life.

"Yes," Kolelo said. "We talked about work all those many years ago. You took that to heart. But no human was ever meant to be so single-minded as you, Matthew. Work is not enough. There must be friends. Lovers. Children. Otherwise, what do you leave the world?"

Matthew shook his head. "My first novel is back in print," he said. "Well, my *only* novel as it's turned out. And then there are the films. I have loved doing my work. It's been exciting."

"This is good. If the work is honest."

If the work is honest. Matthew felt worried. All those compromises. He thought of the things about his films that had disappointed him. Was there time to write one great novel before he died?

"You confuse impressiveness with greatness," another voice said.

Matthew turned to look. Tony crouched by a fire at the rear of the cave. "This is not just you," Tony said. "This is your whole culture. You forget how to live your life every day. You adore celebrity. You want to outlive Shakespeare. But a great soul must husband his garden. A great soul gives praise and thanks to the spirits. The great soul enriches what part of the world it is his to enrich."

Matthew got up to go to him, but Tony was gone. Only his fire remained, burning in the corner of the cave. He turned back to the café table. Kolelo smiled at him.

"How does one prepare for death, Mbella?" Matthew asked.

"You were always a great dreamer, Matthew," Kolelo said. "For you, this is the key. Make yourself aware in your dreams. When you realize you are asleep, look at your hands. Then you will be able to do magic by pointing at things. Make them rise into the air. Fly where you want to, like Superman, in your dreams. Just point your fingers where you want to go. Feel the power and use it. Do this, and you will be training your spirit muscles for when you no longer have a body."

"I have had lucid dreams," Matthew said. "But I've never been able to have them at will."

"Tell yourself, before you go to sleep every night: 'When I see my hands, I will remember I am dreaming.' Train yourself, and you will die with confidence."

Matthew smiled at his friend. He looked back again at Tony's fire, but now the fire was gone. In its place was a narrow channel leading to another chamber of the cave. Light emerged from the channel, and far inside he thought he could hear someone moaning. He turned back to the café table. Kolelo was not there. Nor the table.

Matthew knelt by the opening of the channel and looked inside. This was much different from the rest of the cave. Everything else had been unnaturally smooth and rounded. This channel was sharp and rocky and narrow. Small stalactites and stalagmites jutted from above and below like pointy rock teeth. He heard the low moan again, more clearly.

He knelt on the floor of the cave and began to crawl into the channel, which was much too low to allow walking upright. He wished he had the gear that serious spelunkers wore for cave exploring. Especially the kneepads and gloves.

The channel looked to be only about ten feet long, but he felt a moment of panic when he got halfway there. The realization that he could not turn around if he wanted to go back crushed him with claustrophobia. Could he crawl out backwards if necessary? He wouldn't be able to see where he was setting down his knees. Even being able to see, going forward, he was bruising them—and the heels of his hands—repeatedly. What if he wasn't able to turn around when he got to the lit chamber? What if this channel collapsed? No one had a clue where he was. His car couldn't be seen from the road. He'd be trapped here until he died.

He heard the moan again, and his curiosity got him past his panic. Maybe someone needed help.

As he got closer, the light from the chamber shone on his hands in front of him as he crawled. The light was warm. Pastel.

He saw a wood floor in front of him. It surprised him so much that he raised his head abruptly to see more and bumped it on a sharp rock above. He rubbed the crown of his head hard to disperse the sharp, itching pain, and then looked up gingerly.

A wood floor. Flat, peach-painted walls. Low fruit and vegetable crate shelves. A big, round Chinese lantern hanging from the ceiling. And there was Anna, sitting atop her bamboo pallet, legs crossed, eyes closed, back erect, hands resting atop her knees. She was in her characteristic pose for meditation, as she had done twenty minutes, twice per day, for the whole of her adult life.

Was this where Tony had sent her to wait and think? Her room in Paris, transported to the depths of a cave in Utah?

Matthew crawled into the room and sat on the floor in front of her. "Anna?" he said.

He repeated her name several times before she slowly opened her eyes. "Anna?"

"You know better than to interrupt," she said. She slowly closed her eyes again.

Well, that was certainly Anna—though in life she would more likely have reacted with irritation, even out of the peace of her meditation. She did not tolerate the interruption of her routines.

Matthew looked at his watch. The hands were not moving. Of course not. There was no time here. The twenty minutes would never end.

"Anna," he said again. "Could you open your eyes?"

Her eyes slowly opened like the eyes of an owl. She looked at him with a queer, blank alertness. Her eyes were wide and receptive, but her face was totally emotion-free.

"Anna," he said. "How did you get here?"

She tilted her head slightly, like a dog does when it listens. "This is my room," she said, still without a trace of emotion. "I am meditating."

"Do you remember anything?" he said. "Do you remember that you killed yourself?"

She looked at him and tilted her head some more. "Did I?"

"You and Colin went to Owl Creek Canyon. You argued, and he left you there. You took a bus back to town. Do you remember any of this?"

"I'm not sure," she said.

"You ran the hose from your exhaust into the back window of the car," he said. "You took a drug to help you sleep, and then you wrote a last entry in your journal while you waited to die. Do you remember that?"

She sat still for a long time, and Matthew began to worry that she would never move or speak again. It occurred to him that he was interrupting the stasis Tony had put her in, and that it might be a bad thing for himself and her both. But he couldn't bring himself to give up.

"The exhaust," she said finally. "I remember the exhaust. It hurt my throat. And it made my mind so dull." She looked at him blankly for a long time again. "Is that why I am so dull now?"

"Oh, Anna . . ." he said. It was so pitiful, he suddenly wanted to cry. The grief choked up the back of his throat. Was this why suicide was taboo? Could you brain-damage your spirit for the afterlife? Or was this dullness part of Tony's spell that held her here?

"I remember. I did plan to kill myself," she said, looking down at her hands, "but I don't think I did it." She looked directly at him again. "Am I dead?"

"Yes," he said.

She looked around the room, her head turning evenly, like an owl's. Then she looked back at him. "It's not what I expected."

"No," he said.

She looked at him with narrowed eyes. "Are *you* dead?"

"No," he said.

"Oh," she said. This seemed to make her lose interest in him. Her eyes slowly closed, and her hands rested again on her knees, in her typical meditation position.

"I came looking for you," he said. "I might die soon, too. I came looking because I was afraid. I thought maybe there was something you could tell me. About what it's like."

"What help could I be?" she said slowly, her eyes still closed.

"Actually, I found help," he said. "Now I want to help you."

Her eyes opened again, owl-like, and she looked at him. "I'm okay," she said. Her expression was so totally emotionless that it chilled him.

"Why did you do it?" he asked her, feeling so horribly disappointed. "Why did you have to kill yourself?"

"They killed me, Matthew," she said. "Those men. They did horrible things to me, and they made my father watch."

What was this now? he wondered. Was he talking to Anna? Or was this her Aunt Esther, and she just looked like Anna?

He rubbed his hands along his thighs in discomfort and felt the small mound of juniper berries in his right pocket. He pulled out a handful and began to crush them, one by one, between his thumb and forefinger. He laid them on the floor between Anna and him. The room slowly began to fill with the astringent aroma of juniper. It made him feel more alert. It was this place, he suddenly realized. It had been making him grow increasingly dull. Like Anna.

She reached down for a demitasse of *café noir* from the floor and took a sip.

Where the hell had that come from?

She took another sip of the coffee and sat looking into its darkness for a long time. Now Matthew could see the possibility of emotion in her eyes. She did not look so much like a zombie. He waited.

She set the little cup back in its saucer and looked directly at him. She was farther away! The room was bigger.

He saw the intelligence in her eyes. That hadn't been there before. Now the room was wider, and he was farther away.

He saw her face change. She went from Anna to Aunt Esther. Matthew recognized her from the photo Mrs. Toyevsky had shown him. And then someone else. And then a man. And a woman. And another. These were her lives, Matthew realized, going back in history. Anna's grandfather had been right. His murdered daughter Esther had been reborn as his granddaughter. The demons from that haunted life followed her into this one. Anna had never been abused as a child. She was remembering her torture and murder from her last life. Her mind transformed them into childhood abuse so they would make sense in this lifetime. But the memories were more than she could stand. The demons saw to that.

Anna completed the cycle back to her own face. Matthew felt heartbroken. How did his poor, dear friend ever have a chance? He wanted to hold her, to help her.

He knelt there in the room and prayed that her soul be freed. He called on the spirits of Jesus and Mary and the guardian angels and the White Spider to help her. He called for her demons to be swept away.

All of a sudden he saw the swirling faces of the spirits and deities. He saw the horrible faces of the ghosts and demons, now filled with terror. His invocation had worked! But now he had to finish the prayer or, like the sorcerer's apprentice, he would remain surrounded by this horrific numinous storm. He had to direct all this swirl away, to a safe place. Where were the demons to go?

At the bottom of his vision, he saw something round. Something hard. Something porous. A grinding stone. He saw a small grinding stone lying on the floor of a canyon. It was the lower canyon at Owl Creek, where Colin abandoned Anna the day before she died. This was the grinding stone she had held on that other day long before, when she and Colin had camped together in the canyon. On that day, the spirits of the lower canyon infested her. That's what happened when she collapsed and Colin heard her cry out in the unearthly voice, and then carried her to the upper canyon. The demons that followed her from her life as Esther were joined by more ghosts and demons from Owl Creek Canyon, and they all followed her from then on, parasites and whisperers, until the day of her death.

The rage rose up in Matthew. He stood on his feet to his full height and raised his arms, imploring to the holy spirits that had answered his call. "Send them there!" he shouted. "Bury them in the stone!"

The swirling numina pulled into a tight circle, and cries of damnation shook the cavern. Matthew stepped back, the force of his rage tempered now by his terror. The swirl focused into the shape of a tornado, with its spike tip down on the grinding stone. The shrieks of agony grew louder, and yet louder, as the demons were driven and compressed into the porous spaces within the fist-sized rock. The overwhelming shrieking cacophony of their pain and fury rattled the joints of Matthew's body. It forced from his mind any hope of a clear thought until the screams were coming from his own throat, as well, and he feared against his own damnation that he would be sucked into the stone with them.

He fell to the ground and clung to the sharp rocks of the cave, his skin tearing, his nails breaking as he held himself back from the unbearable suction of the tornado, swirling ever faster, pushing itself ever deeper, into the porous rock of the small grinding stone.

And then, at last, it was over. Matthew lay on the floor of Anna's little room in Paris. His body trembled, and he felt cold.

So cold.

He pulled himself up to a sitting position. The room was larger now. Much, much larger than the tiny room his friend had had in Paris. He wiped the drops of blood and sweat from his hands onto his pants, and hugged himself tightly, trying to stop his trembling.

Anna sat, far across the room, sipping her demitasse of coffee, as though nothing had happened. She was not aware of what Matthew had just seen, just done.

Matthew saw a large white spider crawl up to the top of the wall and crawl through the ceiling, out of sight. He broke into sobs of fear and relief and horror at what he'd just witnessed.

"You can't see it from life," Anna said, after a long silence. "Death is big. It's not one place."

Matthew looked up at her. She looked so calm now. So much herself. And yet it wasn't like her. She was free of her body. She was free.

"There are many ways," she continued. "They're like paths in the forest. What you follow in life determines where you enter death."

He knew suddenly that this was the last time he'd see her while he was alive. The last time he would hear her voice. From his terror, he now felt blessed, and he wanted, above all, to understand what she was saying.

"But what makes a path?" he said. "How do you know what path leads where?"

The room expanded again. She was far away now, far across a cavernous expanse.

"You know."

You know? Is that what she said? She was so far away. Across Mammoth Cave. He stood up. "How do you know?" he shouted. "How do you know where you're going? Wait!"

She said something at first that he could not hear. But he could see she was still speaking. He held himself very still and listened with all of his might, not allowing himself to breathe. He heard a last phrase. He could see her lips moving, across that great distance. Only her lips and that tiny, tiny remnant of sound crossing the Great Divide. He put the sound and the lips together, the shape of the words she was saying: "Follow your path," she said. "Find your companions. And live."

And then she was gone.

CHAPTER 26

THE SNAKE

THE FIRE WAS WIDE, low, and smoky. Tony had set the fire rocks in a wider circle at the beginning of the ceremony. He'd built the fire out wide and kept feeding it with small chunks and branches of shattered wood and brush.

He'd begun dancing and praying at dusk, dressed in a beautiful handmade costume of white doeskin. The tunic was embroidered and beaded and inlaid with porcupine quills. The pants were fringed down the sides with feathers. Tony's hair was braided and tied with leather strips and feathers, and he'd painted his face. In the light of the fire, he looked terrifying.

Now it was dark. Tony stopped dancing and knelt, holding his face close to the ground, speaking something low, directly into the earth. The other three kept up the beat they'd carried since the beginning of the ritual. Natalie sat to the east of the fire, playing the same drum she'd played during the nights of Matthew's healing ceremony. Matthew sat to the south of the fire scraping the back of a guiro with a sharpened bone that reminded him of a letter opener. The guiro was hardwood and looked like a hollow fish with dozens of ridges across its back. It made an enormous "zipper" sound as Matthew scraped down the ridges.

To the west of the fire, Colin sat, shaking a maraca to the beat.

Behind them each, some artifact of Anna's waited.

The wide column of smoke rose directly into a sky in which stars were becoming visible. The moon had risen over the mountains to the east as a large orange ball and climbed into a smaller ivory sphere, high in the sky. Tony rose and fed the fire from one of three separate stacks of wood. The flames grew hotter and less smoky. As he fed the flames, he resumed singing. Then, as the new wood continued to catch fire and grow hotter, he took the abalone shell from among his tools, layered some copal over the hot coals in it, and brushed the rich, astringent smoke over the three with his ceremonial bird's wing, beginning in the east with Natalie.

When he'd finished anointing them with smoke, he told Matthew and Colin to continue the rhythm, and he took the drumstick from Natalie's hand. "Now is the time," he said to her.

Tony began singing again, loudly now, and dancing with large gestures around the outside of the circle. Natalie turned and picked up the stack of clothing from behind her and stood holding them before the fire. Tony completed three revolutions around the outside of the circle and stopped beside Natalie again, carrying a bag of herbs that he'd taken from among his tools atop the panther skin. Then he nodded to Natalie and began singing all the more loudly. Colin and Matthew played their instruments louder, as well.

Natalie took the socks from atop the stack in her arms and dropped them into the center of the fire, as Tony had instructed her before they began the ceremony. Tony tossed a handful of herbs atop them as they began to melt and burn in the hot fire. He nodded to her again, and Natalie gently lay the jeans into the fire.

As she handled them, Natalie thought she could smell exhaust fumes on the clothes and had to direct her thoughts away from the suicide back to the release they were all here to attain for Anna.

Because Colin had handled some of the arrangements immediately after Anna's death, before her parents got into town, he'd been the one who selected the clothes her body wore to her cremation. He'd been given (at his request) the clothing she'd been wearing when she died. And so, in the days before this ceremony, when Natalie told him they needed artifacts that might tie Anna to her death, he was pleased that he'd saved the clothing, though he was reluctant to give it up.

After Natalie had put the last article into the fire and Tony had layered it with herbs, he anointed her again with copal smoke and moved on to anoint Matthew once again. Tony nodded, and Matthew brought the carton around in front of him. Tony put some large fresh branches of desert sage on the fire, and the flames lowered and turned smoky. He tossed more herbs into the fire. Matthew pulled the final journal from the carton and held it over the smoke, as Tony had instructed him. He held the journal open, by the covers, so the smoke could curl in among the individual pages.

He did this with each of the individual journals, fluttering the pages to bathe them in the smoke, moving from the last of the journals through to the earliest, in counter-chronological order. He put the cleansed journals back in a stack on the ground next to the carton. When he lifted the last of the journals to be cleansed, a sheet of paper fell out from among the pages and dropped to the fire.

"Let it go," Tony breathed.

A corner of the sheet sprang alight. The rising heat of the fire carried the page aloft, and it rose burning into the sky. The page rose higher and higher, until its small flame crossed high in the sky across the face of the moon and disappeared.

Matthew watched it fly and go out, and he breathed a deep sigh when it was gone. He felt lighter now, and the ache in his arm from playing the guiro had lessened. He stacked the smoke-cleansed journals back in the carton and put the carton in its new place next to Tony's hide. Then he picked up the guiro again and played it with renewed energy. He felt the sound of Natalie's drum percuss against his chest. He felt the sizzle of Colin's maracas in the back of his neck and the zip of the guiro tingle in his eardrums. He was glad to be here and to be doing this thing for Anna.

Before they started the ceremony, Tony had looked worried when Matthew told him about his experience in the cave. Then he laughed and said: "Well, you might've made it a little more difficult, this freeing of the soul of your friend Anna. But then again, maybe you made it easier. We'll find out. And we'll do whatever it takes. 'Cause that's the kind of machos we are. Right?" And he slapped Matthew on the shoulder and went off to make his preparations.

So far, the ceremony felt good to Matthew. Natalie had done the burning of the clothes well. The journals were cleansed. Tony was standing in front of Colin, looking at him, and Colin continued to play the shakers. Matthew began to feel troubled. Time slowed. Pulling the scraper across the ribs of the guiro suddenly felt like an effort against gravity. The ribs looked like a mountain range.

Matthew looked back at the two men again. He saw the resistance around Colin's body like a radiating darkness. He looked at Tony and felt a queer fear curl into his gullet.

This was not Tony. This creature was taller than Tony. More powerful. Deadly even. Somewhere in the putting on of costume, the dancing, the singing, the fire building, the anointing with smoke, he had put off that which was Tony. The Tony-ness of him was gone, replaced by his totemic spirit, White Spider.

"Fight this," White Spider said to Colin.

Colin continued to play the shaker, though now he had lost the beat. Matthew keyed into what Natalie was doing on the drum. He played all the more insistently, locking in with her, feeling the absolute importance of holding the heartbeat of the ritual, which was now in danger.

Colin stopped playing and looked uncertainly at the creature he still saw as Tony. "I should not have brought the hose," he said. The dark fog around him intensified. His voice sounded drunk. "I'm not really...done with it," he said.

Oh God, Matthew thought, feeling the terror before it happened.

White Spider lunged. Matthew saw his two fangs cut through the breast of Colin's leather jacket and through his flannel shirt beneath. He saw the curved fangs penetrate the skin of Colin's chest. The fangs deftly punctured the flesh, dodged between the ribs, and sprayed the Spider's venom into Colin's lungs.

Colin jerked as if he'd received an electrical shock and then froze stiff as a department store manikin. White Spider began wrapping him in silk from the spinnerets in his abdomen at amazing speed. At the same time, he turned his head toward Matthew.

"He will live," White Spider said. It was Tony's face the voice came from, though it sounded inside Matthew's head, and his lips did not move. Tony's painted face was there, but his eyes were the segmented eyes of a spider. "You must do his job now without hesitation."

Matthew realized that somehow he had continued to play the guiro despite his shock. In fact, White Spider's attack had gone so quickly, only a few strokes of the scraper had passed. Matthew focused on the rhythm. This was White Spider's space. For better or worse, he had to carry through the ritual, for he could sense the danger to them all. Danger even to White Spider if they failed to complete the ritual with integrity.

Tony/White Spider danced the circle again, singing loudly to re-connect with the power and protection of the guardian spirits. He circled Colin many times, anointing him with smoke and building a protective circle around him to isolate him from the ritual and from any influence of the spirits, good or bad, around them.

Matthew avoided looking at Colin, for he could see the glowing strands of silk binding him in place, like a mummy sitting absurdly on the ground. He could see the red swellings on his chest glowing through the shirt and jacket, as though the clothing had become trans-parent in those spots. He could see how little oxygen Colin was able to breathe. The man was in a coma.

When Tony/White Spider completed his circuits, a calm descended over the area around the fire. He knelt in front of Matthew with his large sheath knife drawn. A stack of some kind of herb sat on the flat of the blade. He took a twig from the fire, held it to the herb to ignite it, and held the blade beneath Matthew's nose. Matthew inhaled through his nostrils, thinking the smoke smelled like marijuana. It looked more like sage. He inhaled anyway, again and again, as Tony/White Spider relit the stack and held it out for him. Then he did the same for Natalie and the same for himself.

Tony took another drum from atop his hide on the ground and began striking it with his "jawbone of the ass." When he and Natalie and Matthew were locked in with the beat, he nodded to Matthew and indicated the hose on the ground behind Colin.

Matthew set down the guiro and rose. He stood over the hose and felt a tremor of fear. For a moment he wished Tony would do this part, but he knew Tony could not. It had to be one of them. He looked up and saw Tony looking back at him with penetrating human eyes. His face was frightening in the firelight, but it gave Matthew strength. Matthew could taste the smoke from Tony's knife in his nose again, and he drew in a deep breath. He felt himself grow fortified. He'd felt this before, when Tony first gave him the smoke, but he hadn't recog-nized what it was. The surface of his body—or not his body—his what? His soul? The surface of his *spirit*, which was larger than his body, had become harder on the outside, as though he'd grown an exoskeleton, like a spider. It protected him from the influences around him.

Matthew picked up the hose. It was a short coil, maybe ten feet long, cut just long enough to carry exhaust from the tail pipe in through the back window of a car. One end still had the garden hose connection. The other end was the blunt plastic where Anna had cut it. This was the end that had come in through the window and fed her the poison. No one had told Matthew this, but he knew it as well as if he had seen Anna getting the car ready to kill her. The end with the metal fitting had gone into the tail pipe. The cut end came in through the window. The space around the hose, at both ends, she stuffed with rags.

Matthew held the hose over the fire as Tony/White Spider added herbs to the flames. He was following the instructions he'd heard Tony give Colin. Matthew felt the hose twitch in his hands as the smoke wrapped around it. He felt afraid for a moment. Tony caught his eye, and Matthew smelled the smoke from the knife again. He inhaled deeply and felt his shell harden. Then he realized he only had to imagine the smoke and it would be there. He inhaled it again and again, growing his exoskeleton ever harder.

When Tony completed the first phase of his singing, Matthew knelt and held the cut end into the fire. The hose twitched hard and suddenly Matthew was holding a snake's head into the flames. He nearly dropped it in shock, but he felt an overpowering blast of smoke up his nose, and it helped him recover. He held the snake more tightly.

The snake turned its head back toward him, twisting its body hard, trying to break Matthew's grasp. It turned its head sideways, back, and down, trying to reach Matthew's wrist to plunge its poison fangs into his skin, but Matthew was holding its neck too close to the base of its head for the snake to turn far enough. It whipped Matthew's thighs and stomach with its tail, stinging him intensely with the whipping, but Matthew would not let go. He plunged its head deeper into the flames, singeing the hair off his hands and burning his knuckles. The skin beneath the snake's hideous green eyes blistered, and the snake bucked harder. Matthew nearly lost his balance backward, but he held onto the snake. He braced himself again and pushed the snake's head back into the fire. The tip of its tongue spat out, blackened, and curled. A horrible gasp came from the snake's mouth—a gasp unlike anything Matthew could have imagined a snake making—and it frightened him, but he held the snake's face into the fire until its eyes boiled from the inside and ruptured, and its skin blistered and blackened all around. Its bucking against his hands weakened and faltered. He burned the snake's head until its mouth was cauterized closed.

The snake hung limp then in his hands, and Tony/White Spider took it from him. He carried it to the hole they had dug earlier, in the daylight, and Tony put it inside. He took the dried skull of an animal from among his objects, filled it with ashes from the ritual fire, and sprinkled them over the snake. Natalie and Matthew did the same. Then Tony took the shovel and began to bury it. As the first dirt hit it, Matthew saw it again as it had been before: a length of garden hose, now with one end melted shut.

When he finished, Tony walked over to the two of them and laid a hand on each of their forearms. "I must go to her, to complete the cycle," he said. "I want you both to play again. Matthew, use the frame drum I used before." He looked at Natalie. "You will also tend the fire. Keep it the same. Add wood and brush when you have to. Keep it the same." Natalie nodded. Then he looked at Matthew. "Hold the same beat as before," he said, "but if the spirit moves it, follow."

"I understand," Matthew said.

Tony pinched several chunks of copal onto the coals in the abalone shell and fanned them with his bird's wing until they were glowing. Clouds of copal smoke arose from the shell, and he bathed himself in it, praying to the spirits for their aid.

He moved to the beat of the drum, dancing around the fire, remembering the spirits that had helped him over the years. He gave thanks and called the spirits to him. He remembered his teachers and called blessings down upon them. He remembered his family and his friends. He remembered his serpentine journey of initiation into the shamanic life of the Guaraní. He remembered the ancestors who'd made the survival of his people possible. He remembered the spirits who'd helped them and opposed them. And he gave thanks to all. From his pouch he took a handful of ground roots that had been blessed in another ceremony, put the gift of his breath upon it, and lay it into the fire for the spirits to eat.

Tony went to the hide on which his ritual objects lay and selected a cloth pouch he'd prepared the day before. The pouch was a simple piece of cotton fabric filled with tobacco and herbs, copal and dried root. He'd tied up corners of the cloth into a pouch with colored threads. From his bag he took a bottle he'd received from one of the local elders. He opened the bottle and soaked the pouch with the strong cactus liquor it contained. He poured a few ounces into a small glazed ceramic chalice and knelt at the edge of the fire ring.

Tony prayed to Grandfather Fire, to the White Spider and the Spider Woman, asking their aid for the gift of vision. He set the liquor-soaked prayer ball into the edge of the ritual fire, and it burst alight. He lifted the chalice of liquor, put his breath on it, gave thanks to the spirit of the cactus and the desert, and poured the whole chalice into his mouth. The liquor burned his mouth when it went in. It stung the pituitary ducts beneath his tongue. It burned his throat as it went down and burned his stomach when it arrived. It seared his sinuses, buzzed his eardrums, and ignited a ball of fire in his skull.

Tony resisted the enormous urge to cry out, for he knew to cry out would dispel the spirit in the liquor from his body. He would lose the ally he needed in this quest. Instead of inspirited, he would end up simply drunk.

He rested one hand on the ground to keep his balance and stared at the flame rising from the prayer ball in the edge of the fire. As he stared, the heat from that large mouthful of fiery liquid spread through his body. The liquor radiated out from his stomach, from his throat, from his mouth, from his sinuses, into his head, into his muscles, into his organs, into his spirit, and now he was not kneeling in front of a simple fire on the desert floor. He was sitting in the sweat lodge with Grandfather Fire, having a drink together. He felt the high honor of Grandfather Fire sitting down with him, and he thanked Grandfather Fire, bowing low to him and kissing his hand. Grandfather Fire nodded to him, gracious and a little formal, for he was an ancient Grandfather, but with genuine affection for this sincere grandson.

Tony looked into the eye of Grandfather Fire. Inside them he saw the gift of vision waiting. Anything in the universe could be seen inside those eyes: past, present, future, in the physical world or the spirit world. Tony knew not to seek what was not his to see. To use this gift for his personal gain would be to lose himself. He flowed into the Grandfather's eyes, abandoning his physical self. He traveled bodiless into the vision world, propelled by his prayers toward the soul of Anna Toyevsky.

Now he could see her. She was in a larger space than the one in which he'd left her, but she was not yet free. On the other side of the boundaries of this space were the ghosts and demons that had pursued and tormented her. The barriers that protected her were good. That part of his spell still held. And the rituals they had already performed had loosened the bonds that held her to her death and to the sorrows of her life. That too was good.

Tony followed back the line of her life. He saw her suicide. He saw the occasions on which she had passed through a sinkhole of hungry ghosts. He sensed where the sinkhole was: in the canyons to the south. He saw when the snake had followed her out of there. He saw the demons that had been with her since birth, and before. And he saw her tortured death as Esther in her previous life.

She had been free before that. The demons had entered Esther's life with the Nazi torturers. He saw, too, the very brief time Esther had spent in the other world before being born into this life as Anna. He had witnessed this before, in others who had suffered similarly.

In the usual course of events, a soul spends considerable time in the other world before being reborn. It needs this time to consider the memories of its life and to allow those memories to be absorbed by the larger spirits, who eat these memories as their food. When a soul dies pursued by demons, as Esther's soul had done, it cannot progress in the spirit world. It cannot feed the larger spirits. And so the soul is born again in hopes of freeing itself. Its memories from the previous life, however, are close to the surface, and can cause great and inexplicable torment to the new person.

There were many of these hastily recycled souls walking the earth now. Souls damaged by evil deaths in the Nazi Holocaust, in the killing fields of Cambodia, in Pinochet's Chilean torture chambers, and elsewhere. Tony had heard of one young woman in Europe who had recognized the Nazi officer who had killed her in her previous life. She'd been able to find evidence and have the old man successfully prosecuted. That had gone a long way toward freeing her soul, Tony was sure.

Anna's only hope had been to rid herself of the demons in this incarnation. Instead, she'd unwittingly collected more.

Tony prayed to the larger spirits to which Anna longed to be connected. He mustered every bit of eloquence, for the spirits loved eloquence and beauty. They loved intricate ritual and beautiful handmade clothes. You had to dress up for them and court them and speak poetry to them. Only then could you catch their attention and curry their favor.

He described to them the delicious meal of memories that was trapped in this poor soul of the late Anna. Two lifetimes worth of memories—births, emotions, love, disasters, pain, deaths, sensations, hatreds—the savory and the spicy, the smooth, the soothing, the inspiring, the intoxicating—all of which they were missing because of the parasites surrounding this soul. They need only brush these bugs away to taste the fruits of two incredible lifetimes of this sensitive and intelligent soul, an artist among humans, a beloved daughter, a cherished friend, awaiting reunion with them if only they would take the moment to exorcise these demons.

He described to them the tender lovemaking he saw in this life, the ferocious arguments, the torments and joys. He sang to them of her depth of learning, her love of music, and her deep confusions and fears. As he described this life, he felt the large spirits turn toward her in curiosity. The parasite demons had kept her soul hidden from them. Look at this delicious thing they had missed!

The parasites huddling around the borders began to explode into dust. The spirits inhaled the dust like the smoke from good cigars. Others were eaten like hors d'oeuvres, and others fled. Tony wept with joy as the boundaries collapsed, and the ecstatic Anna was reunited with her true parent spirits.

CHAPTER 27

BIG, WET MOUTH

COLIN LOOKED OVER IN the direction of Natalie and Matthew. They were out of earshot, but their presence was still a distraction to Colin. Tony would have preferred to speak to him in his trailer, where Colin wouldn't be so distracted, but Tony did not want to spend half the night getting the remnants of Colin's gray fog out of his trailer afterwards.

"And?" Tony prompted him.

Colin looked back at Tony as though he'd forgotten what he'd been talking about. The parasites would hide Colin from himself just as they'd hidden Anna's soul from the large spirits. The fog was so thick around Colin, Tony could see him only in outlines, but for the eyes. Colin's eyes glowed red, like some creature that lived deep under the earth. His every move and gesture was furtive. The fog around him smelled like a blend of sweat and burnt electrical wiring.

"I'd used the hose a number of times as a focal point when I meditated," Colin said.

"Why would you do that?" Tony said.

"No. Anna is still very much around," Colin said. "She's done a number of important things for me since she died. And I suddenly realized I was not finished with that. That's why I didn't want it destroyed. The hose has helped me be in touch with her."

"Not her," Tony corrected. "The thing that ate her."

"No." Colin shook his head emphatically, looking down at the ground. "Being with her was the most profound spiritual teaching of my life," he said, not looking up. "You are wrong about Anna."

"We aren't talking about Anna," Tony said. He blew a great plume of cigar smoke up to the right and another to the left. The little parasitic spirits that were attracted to Colin were as thick as mosquitoes. Tony's mouth was getting hot from all the cigar smoke he was blowing. Colin flinched every time Tony flicked one of these mosquito spirits away with his feathers. "I saw what was in that hose," Tony said. "What you felt when you meditated wasn't Anna. It was a big, fat old snake taking one bite after another out of your life."

"That's bullshit," Colin said.

"How you been feeling lately?" Tony asked.

"Don't pretend you've *divined* something about me. I'm sure Natalie told you I'm HIV-positive. But I'm not afraid of moving on. I'll finish the things I'm supposed to finish before this lifetime is out. I can feel that. And Anna is a part of that."

"Do you know much about snakes?" Tony asked.

Colin looked at him for a long moment. Tony could see him trying to figure the angles of the question. For Tony, this was like being back in the village. Some people loved him. Some people hated him. A lot of people feared him—and even more mistrusted him. But when they needed a *pajarillo* to fly to the spirits, he was the man.

"I know something about snakes," Colin said at last. "I've been to the rain forest. That's been one of the positive things about being sick. I've got disability, so I don't have to work. I do traveling that I've never had time to do before—like going to the rain forest. So I do know about being in a place where any moment something like a deadly snake can get you. I never felt so alive as when I was in the rain forest."

"So you like that feeling," Tony said, "that any moment something might kill you?"

"Don't twist what I'm saying," Colin said.

"Let me tell you something about snakes. If you've got a minute," Tony said.

Colin looked confused. "Yeah. I've got a minute." He looked up at Tony. "I've got a minute," he repeated.

Tony sat on the ground across from him. He didn't actually have much hope he could reach Colin. Colin looked as though he'd made his choice and was sold on it. If he were in a Guaraní village, Colin might have had some friends who'd build a lodge for him and tie him up and put him in there while the spirits were battled. It would take an effort by the whole village. It wouldn't guarantee success, but it would give him a better chance.

If Tony had talked to him before the ceremony more, he might have seen how things were with Colin. He would have done the ceremony for both Anna and Colin. But Tony had had his own preparations to make, and he'd missed it.

"There's a kind of snake that lives in the country around my village that looks just like the snake that was in that hose," Tony said. "One of the men of my village stepped on this snake one day, and it bit him on the calf, and he was brought to me. We were able to keep him alive. He survived the bite. And he had a most interesting dream while he was gone from us, before we could bring him back." Tony rose from his spot and got the abalone shell. He used his large sheath knife to shovel new coals from the fire into it and then pinched on a piece of copal. The smoke rose up and pushed back some of the gray fog that hung around Colin. Colin's eyes cleared ever so slightly as the smoke rose and he inhaled it. This was not going to do anything big for him, Tony knew. Maybe he'd be more receptive. Tony'd actually lit the copal more for himself. Colin's gray fog was beginning to give him a headache.

"The snake bite was painful, of course," Tony said. "Especially at first: the penetration of the fangs. Then the muscles locking up as the venom began to spread through the blood. You know." Tony took a twig from the fire and used it to relight his cigar. He blew its smoke all around them. Colin pulled out a package of cigars, put one in his mouth, and Tony held the burning twig for him to light it. Colin was about to put the cigar pack back in his pocket, when he looked suddenly confused.

"I forgot," he said. "I brought these as a gift for you." He extended the pack toward Tony.

Tony nodded, and Colin set the pack aside the abalone shell. Tony took one out, said a quick prayer on behalf of Colin, and crumbled the cigar atop the coals and copal in the shell. The smoke billowed up, and Colin smiled a little. He sat nodding his head.

"What was the dream?" Colin said.

"The man dreamed he was walking through the jungle when he stepped on a poisonous snake and it bit him," Tony said. "It was painful at first, but then it started to feel good. It started to feel real good. The snake opened up its big, wet mouth and started to swallow up his foot. And that felt real good, too. It was like his foot was his pecker, and the snake was a woman who knew how to give real good mouth sex. It felt good as his foot disappeared into the snake's mouth. And then his ankle. And then his calf. And his knee. He was kind of disappointed when we pulled him out of the dream and back into the world of pain.

"You see, nature is merciful sometimes. She knows the snake got to eat to live, but maybe she can make the snake venom so it don't feel so horrible to die that way, with a snake eating you. That snake was too small to eat a man, but no doubt it has a similar effect on a rat, when it's time for the rat to get eaten."

"And no doubt there's a moral of this story for me," Colin said, blowing cigar smoke down at his feet.

"This world looks a lot like the other world. If the jungle snake has venom that seduces its victims into death, you can bet it got that from the spirit snake. So I got one question for you: Do you want to lie there and let the spirit snake eat you because it feels like it's sucking your pecker, or do you want to get loose and maybe have a chance to live on this delicious earth for a while longer—even though that is going to drag you through some pain?"

"That's a bullshit story," Colin said. He got up and walked toward Natalie and Matthew, leaving Tony at the fireside.

CHAPTER 28

THE VISION OF WOVOKA

"Y<small>OU CAN BE GLAD</small>," Tony said. "Her soul is free. But that suicide wasn't the worst of her problems. Whole bunch of hungry ghosts followed her in from her last life. She was just too weighted down."

Matthew sat on the cot that ran the width of Tony's trailer opposite the kitchen end. "That wasn't her fault," he said.

Tony smiled and cocked his head. "Here you are a sophisticated man, a famous moviemaker, and you still think the spirit world operates according to the rules you learned from the catechism? The spirit world, just like the physical world, is not fair. But luckily, you and Anna and Natalie and your friends, all of you were good and resourceful."

"So you think Anna did all right? Despite killing herself?"

"Look at what happened. It took her just one lifetime to free herself of a horrible catastrophe. Look at how she made you and Natalie and probably a lot of other people love her so strong. Look at how she got your fate tied in with hers. Maybe she was doing just the right thing to end her life. What were the chances that you and me and Natalie would have come together on the Utah desert to pray for her soul if she hadn't been such a spectacular fireball of pain?"

"You think she planned that?"

"Absolutely not," Tony said. "And if she had, it surely would have failed. What saved her soul was the way she loved her friends. And the way they loved her back. In spite of all of her spectacular mistakes, not *because* of them. That love in her lifetime saved her, even though she was already dead."

Tony winked at him. "You'll see her again. You and Natalie, too. I think you got some relatives in common on the other side." He got up and pulled bags of herbs from a cabinet and put them on the counter in his little kitchen. He measured out piles of herbs by the handful. "By the way, it's looking good for you, too, Matthew. You look better. Maybe you're going to live to be an old man, after all," he said, turning to appraise Matthew once again, and then going back to making piles of herbs and wrapping them in newspaper. "I think we are making progress."

"I could get rid of my cancer?"

"I don't know for sure," Tony said. He tied the newspaper bundles with a string and put the package in Matthew's lap. He pulled one of the vinyl-covered chairs away from the tiny table. He sat in front of Matthew.

"You see, I don't know if this cancer is the death you are suppose to have. The best thing is to get back on the path of sweetness, where you are living life in the best way possible. There's no doubt that there's something you're supposed to do before you die. I think the spirits *want* you to do that thing before you meet the death that is properly yours. We might not have added one minute to the length of life that you have left to lead. But if you can step back onto the path of sweetness, then you can lead the rest of your life with beauty. That's the best thing I can ask the spirits to do for you."

"And you think they're behind that now?" Matthew said.

"I do. We cleared away the parasite ghosts and low-class spirits that was swarming around you. You got to keep at it with the herbs and the prayers, like I taught you. And come back to see me again in a month, and we'll do something again around the fire. Give you a *booster* cere-mony," Tony said, grinning.

"And what about Colin?" Matthew said.

Tony looked down at the floor and shrugged. "I should've met with this Colin before we had this ceremony. I broke the bonds between Anna's spirit and him, but I can't free him of what he won't let go." He took a deep breath. "When I looked at Anna's life, I saw the sinkhole of hungry ghosts at that Owl Creek Canyon you and Natalie talked about. I'll have to go out there with some local people, some medicine people, to clear that away. When that's gone, maybe Colin can be stronger, too. Otherwise, the big snake is going to eat him up."

"Snake?" Matthew said.

"Yeah." Tony looked weary. "Just be careful around Colin. Don't take on his demons. That's not for you to do."

"You said a snake?" Matthew said. "I saw the hose change into a snake when I was burning the end."

"You saw that, did you?" Tony said. He laughed a little and shook his head.

"It tried to bite me."

"It's a damned good thing you didn't let it."

"So, you're saying that wasn't a hallucination? That I was seeing something real?"

"You got the gift of sight. If you was a twelve-year-old Guaraní boy, I'd be talking to your parents about making you my apprentice shaman." Tony's face turned thoughtful, and he brought out a cigar, lit it, and blew smoke in three directions.

"Maybe this is why the spirits is interested in you," Tony suggested. "Maybe you supposed to become a shaman and start bringing this knowledge and healing to your people."

Matthew opened his mouth, then closed it again. He hadn't been expecting anything like this.

"I been thinking about why I am back in this place of my ancestors," Tony said. "About why the life I had with the Guaraní was destroyed. I been remembering the stories of the Ghost Dance my mother told me when I was a child. My mother was a Paiute, and the Ghost Dance religion was brought to the people by the great Paiute prophet Wovoka. He foretold the end of white expansion, the restoration of Indian lands and ways of life, and the resurrection of dead ancestors. He led his people in five-day-long dances. He gave his braves 'ghost shirts' that would protect them from bullets. But many of them were massacred at Wounded Knee wearing these shirts, and Wovoka was disgraced. Still, I always thought he'd had a true vision. Somehow he had misinterpreted its meaning."

Tony leaned forward and pointed the end of his cigar at Matthew. "You see, I don't think Wovoka's vision was about who gets the land. I think it's about the 'enemy' going away. If you remember that this vision was a gift of the spirits, you got to ponder who is the enemy from the spirits' point of view. To them, the enemy is the ones who disrupt the people's connection with the spirits. In the end, I don't believe the spirits care if the people in the right connection with them is full-blooded Indians, or half-breeds, or people who ain't got a drop of Indian blood in their veins. I thought about this a lot, you see, because this is something I lived with my whole life. My great grandfather was an Italian Catholic priest, and I grew up among the Navaho with a half-breed father and a Paiute mother. And then I was a chief and a shaman among the Guaraní in the Amazon without a drop of Guaraní blood in my veins. So I think maybe it don't matter who your blood ancestors is. To live on the path of sweetness, mainly you need to feed and praise the spirits. And when the people of the Americas start to do that, then the 'enemy' goes away. And that is how the vision of Wovoka will come to pass."

"And you think if I become a shaman for my people, I can help bring that to pass?" Matthew said.

"Maybe."

"I've always felt that my calling is that of a storyteller."

"Storyteller is one of the things the shaman is," Tony said. "We are carriers of the healing stories."

"And that's going to save the world?" Matthew said.

Tony looked at him and laughed. "This is the thing with you gringos. If you can't save the whole world all at once, you throw up your hands and don't do a goddamned thing. The world ain't made for one guy to jump up and save it. The world is so messed up precisely because that gives everybody a chance to pitch in."

Tony sat looking at him for a long moment and then realized he'd been hearing an intermittent clicking. Tony got up and looked out the window of the trailer. Outside Colin stood throwing stones at the trunk of a tree. Natalie lay on the ground, looking at the stars.

"I am going to show you some ways to protect yourself," Tony said. "Your friend Colin has got the spirit fascination, but he don't know what he's doing. And you need to be careful, too." Tony pointed a finger at him. "Don't be calling up the spirit of White Spider again. You got to be initiated into his mysteries before that. You got lucky that time in the cave. But your gift of vision can be a danger to you, too," he added.

CHAPTER 29

QUEEN OF HEAVEN

MATTHEW TOUCHED THE FLAME to the wick and watched it take hold and melt a circle into the center of the candle's surface. He lit a second candle and a third, praying his intentions.

This was a ritual he had loved as a child, but he had not practiced it in decades. He stood at a side altar in a deep alcove to the left of the main altar—it was deep enough, in fact, that the alcove felt private. Against the deepest wall was an altar with a statue of Mary, Queen of Heaven, standing atop the globe with the serpent crushed beneath her feet. When he'd found the shrine and saw the statue and the snake, it'd made the hairs on the back of his neck stand up. Of all the many guises of Mary this church could have chosen, what were the chances it would have been this one? The serpent looked exactly like the one whose head he'd burned in Tony's ritual fire.

He extinguished the stick he'd used to light the three votive candles and knelt down at a red-velvet–covered kneeler before the shrine.

He felt more comfortable doing this than the rituals Tony had taught him. They were foreign to him. They made him hear that deep male voice sounding in the back of his head: "*Thou shalt have no false gods before me.*"

It had been decades since he believed there could be one true faith— or that any one religion had a corner on the divine truth. To Matthew's way of thinking, either all religions were right, or they were all wrong. Either there was a divine truth or there wasn't. And if there was, all any religion could do was offer an interpretation of that truth.

He came to realize he felt uncomfortable with Tony's rituals because he was doing them in isolation from any other religious practices he'd exercised in his life. What Matthew needed to do was to find the deep waters that connected Tony's system with the one that he'd practiced when he was a child. But it wasn't until he saw the serpent's head that the realization crashed upon him.

For two thousand years, the Mother of God had been crushing the serpent that had claimed Anna's life. He'd seen that serpent in iconography his whole life. He never dreamed that one day he'd be holding it in his hands, forcing its face into a fire.

However one invoked the divine, the battle never ended. Everyone had to work and pray. And Matthew suspected the quality of one's intentions mattered more than whether one prayed by a fireside or in a church pew.

He looked at the candles burning in the votive rack. They had a simple, familiar beauty. The rack was old and made of black wrought iron, like the one he remembered from his parish church as a child. It had rows of red glass cups that held muffin-shaped candles the size of golf balls. The rows of candles were raised, each one higher than the one in front of it, like rows of bleachers. The wrought iron of the stand was decorated with gothic crosses and swirls of metal. An offerings box to collect quarters to pay for the candles was built into the rack's frame.

Flames glowed from about half the red cups. Matthew looked at the three he'd lit. They formed a triangle in the upper left corner of the rack, the section closest to the statue of Mary.

He focused on the top one and prayed to the Queen of Heaven. With this candle, he prayed that his fate be brought in line with the divine will. He prayed that it would please God to heal his disease. He prayed that he would be allowed to walk the path of sweetness, and that he could live to bring his fullest contribution to the world.

With the second candle, he gave thanks for the beauty that surrounded him. He prayed for the work and vision of Tony and the others like him. He prayed that the "enemy" would be transformed, as in Tony's version of the Ghost Dance, and that all people would come to give gratitude to the spirits that lived in the earth and in its creatures, and to care for the physical world around them.

With the third candle, he prayed for the fates of his friends. He prayed for the soul of Anna. He prayed for the health and fate of

Colin. He prayed for the happiness of his ex-wife Patty. And he prayed for Natalie and himself.

As he prayed, he pictured the dual soul he shared with Natalie. He remembered the bliss of their union. Then the image of Metta Lindquist standing at the window of her room came to him, with the rooftops and chimneys of Paris stretching out beyond her. Usually he remembered her erotic prowess, but now he saw the sweetness of her face and the kindness of her soul. He recalled the feelings he had had for her—and the joy and pleasure they'd had together. It was just a brief love affair, but he saw the goodness of it.

And suddenly he had such a yearning to be with Natalie. To love her. To make love with her. Despite the barriers between them, he wanted to be with her, even if it were only for a short time. Even if she would *never* come on a film set with him. He would accept whatever they could share without conditions.

In his mind's eye, he saw Natalie at her easel, painting outdoors. He'd gone with her to one of the canyons, years ago. That moment came back to him now in complete detail: He could smell the fresh air and trees and grasses mixed with the smell of the oil paints she used. He saw the intense concentration in her beautiful eyes, the deftness of her long fingers as she wielded the brush. He saw her great competence in translating her vision to the canvas. He saw the richness of her soul in this thing she loved to do.

The emotion filled his heart as he knelt before the shrine of the Queen of Heaven. He felt the love spread through him until it filled his whole body and radiated all around him. He longed to be reunited with her as in his vision of the spirit world. He felt an incredible home-sickness for her, an inconsolable longing that was filled with sweetness. His lips trembled, and tears ran down his cheeks.

How good it was to be in a church at this moment! The consecrated space embraced and nurtured him. He looked up into the face of the divine Mary and blessed her for allowing him to feel so much life.

CHAPTER 30

THE VOYEUR-NATALIE

Natalie stood at her heavy studio easel. She put her hands on its hardwood frame and felt its solidity. She brushed her fingers over the spots and lumps of dry paint on it. She touched the cords that ran through its pulley to the marine winch on its base. She'd had to save a long time to buy this easel. It had a high double H-frame mast that allowed her to use canvases up to eight feet high and twelve feet across. She could hoist tall canvases high enough that she was able to paint the bottom section without lying on the floor.

Good tools gave her a feeling of well-being. Of strength. She took the same pleasure in them that a marathon runner would take in the hard tautness of his muscles.

She walked over to the worktable in front of the large display window that looked out onto the street. Natalie's studio was on the second floor of an old commercial building in a weathered part of town. The first floors of the buildings around her housed hardware, discount, and carpeting warehouse stores. Directly below her was a used bookstore. A hand-lettered sign in the window advertised: "Secondhand Books. Reheated Coffee."

Her studio had formerly housed some kind of offices. It was perfect for her. Its high ceilings allowed her to do the occasional big canvases, and the southern exposure brought in great quantities of light.

It was her secret. She'd never told anyone its location. She'd never installed a phone. It was her private retreat.

She was here now because she'd had a dream last night, and she'd woken up wanting to paint it. She'd held back the urgency of that desire as she'd taken her shower and eaten breakfast. She needed to come to the canvas ready. She wouldn't allow herself to rush to the studio with a take-out donut and coffee. A painting like this had to be stalked. She had to let the dream work in the back of her brain, without thinking about it too much.

She opened a drawer in the worktable and pulled out a box full of acrylics. Usually she worked in either oils or watercolors, but for this painting she wanted the acrylics. She wanted the feeling of working with colored creams that oil gave her, but she wanted the shinier surfaces of acrylic—and she wanted to be forced to work briskly. Acrylics dried faster than oil, and she wouldn't be able to ponder her way through the work, or the paints would dry on her pallet and brushes.

It was the stag in the forest, and she was the huntress. Once she started, she would have to be swift and sure, or it would escape.

She took out a package of brushes and selected from among them, giving herself three sizes to work with, and took out broad and narrow pallet knives, as well.

Natalie went to the south wall of her studio where she kept a selection of ready canvases. She stretched and sealed the canvases herself, not only because it saved money, but also because she liked doing it. She liked having a variety of sizes available so that, on days like these, when she wanted to start a work still in the trance of an idea, she could simply select one and begin.

She stopped and looked at her array of materials: Leaning in the corner was a bolt of linen canvas, rolled up on a seven-foot-long cardboard tube. Stacked along the wall was the lumber, stretcher strips, and crossbars she used to build frames. In front of the lumber lay the tools, the canvas pliers, the hammer and saws, the scissors and knives for cutting the canvas, the cans of sizing and primer, and the L-shaped construction bracket that helped her make her frames perfectly square.

And then there were the canvases, a few as small as a sheet of paper. There were a half dozen or so that ranged in size from one foot by two foot up to four foot by five foot.

The sight of all these materials pleased her. She stood by the bolt of fabric leaning in the corner and looked at the stacked canvases. She ran her hand idly over the bolt as she considered which of them she'd take. The feel of the untreated fabric caught her attention. She looked at its familiar grain and ran her hand down it, then rubbed her cheek against it and smelled it.

She thought of her dream.

She would want to show the exterior and the interior. Would she show the whole house? Or just a section of the outer wall with the window?

Without answering these questions, she knew which of the canvases she wanted: The big one. The four by five. If she'd had a larger one ready, she would have taken that. But she could always do a larger version later, if she wanted.

She leaned the canvas forward, slid it away from the wall, and grabbed it in back by the crossbar to carry it over to the easel. She raised the double mast on the easel to fit the large canvas in, then tightened down the top trays on the canvas frame and hoisted it to the height she wanted, so that the center of the canvas was about even with her chest. She gave the canvas a little shake to make sure it was secure, then she went back to her worktable.

As she laid out the tubes of acrylics onto the tabletop next to her pallet, Natalie allowed herself to remember the dream. Until now, she had not let herself ponder it, for she feared she might spook it before she had the chance to capture it on canvas. She took a moment to lie down on the daybed along the north wall of the studio and close her eyes. She reenvisaged the scene of the dream. Then she got back up, took her outlining pencil, sharpened it with a matte knife, and stood in front of the canvas.

Like so many of her dreams, this one began with her walking on a residential street. She stopped in front of a house with lit windows and stood there with a feeling of overwhelming déjà vu. She walked across the grass under a towering old tree in the front lawn and passed through the rectangles of yellow light on the grass from the windows. From this point the dream diverged from similar dreams she had had before. Inside she saw a woman painting and a man reading a book. She moved closer and saw that the woman was herself.

She stood in the flower bed and looked in through the glass. Inside she saw herself standing at an easel, working at a canvas, a brush in one hand, a pallet in the other. It was a large living room that gave directly onto a dining room with a beautiful old built-in hutch. The dream-Natalie and her easel stood on a paint-spattered tarp that protected a dark wood floor. Candles burned on the mantle above the fireplace. The man curled in a large overstuffed chair was Matthew. He was reading a thick book, a glass of red wine by his side. It was a gracious old house, and the two of them looked content, and interested, and engaged with their lives.

Natalie felt the dream tug at her. An extended daydream of herself in that world invited her, but she would not enter it. She took the pencil to the canvas and began to lightly sketch the outlines of the scene. Ordinarily, she would have done this preliminary sketch on paper, but today she was drawn directly to the canvas. It was like a magnetic pull, and she trusted it.

As soon as she approached the canvas, she knew she wanted the window to be as large as possible to allow a detailed look at the inside of the house. The spatial relationships came clear to her as she sketched. The voyeur-Natalie would be on the far right hand of the painting, peering in through the side of the window. Natalie the painter and her easel would be on the left side of the living room. Matthew in his chair on the right. The closer of the two candles on the mantle was at one o'clock above Matthew's head.

Natalie felt the dynamics of the angles from the candle above Matthew to the line from Matthew's eyes to his book to Natalie-the-voyeur's head outside the window to the painter-Natalie's brush. Those were the dynamics.

She sketched in the elements. This painting would keep the eye moving. It would have a feeling of suspense, of expectation, despite the peaceful subject matter within the frame of the window. The voyeur-Natalie changed all that, of course, both by her presence and by her angle in the composition. The voyeur's eyes and the painter's brush disrupted the peace.

Natalie stepped back from the canvas and squinted. Slowly the images came into focus. She saw the colors she would use, and the shapes. She could feel the brushstrokes as latent electric charges at her fingertips.

Natalie put on some music and began loading her pallet with colors. She took a three-quarter–inch flat brush and began painting in the frame of the window in fast long strokes—strokes very similar to those she might have used if she were a house painter, painting the frame of the window itself. When the frame was in—all those parts of it that would not be covered by something in front of it—she took a smaller brush and began painting in the shadows and highlights of the frame. The last highlights would wait until the first layers had dried.

She quickly moved into a state of flow with her work. She moved from element to element, laying down the first layers of color, painting in the large surfaces, working from brush to brush, color to color, mixing, painting, cleaning brushes and returning to the canvas—and never losing focus. It was this she loved about painting most of all: that state of intense concentration, when all that existed was the work, the brush in the hand, the smell of the paints, the shapes and images emerging from the canvas. And then, suddenly, the recognition that hours had passed and so much wonderful work had been done. And the sleepy, hungry, drained satisfaction that followed.

She was glad she'd selected the acrylics! She was moving through this painting at incredible speed, and the fast-drying acrylics allowed her to get back to sections and paint highlights over them in a dry state that still would have been wet in oil. That allowed the highlights to have sharper edges, and allowed her to layer them on more quickly than if she had been working over a wet, malleable surface.

She painted in this way for four-and-a-half hours straight. Then she stopped and stepped back from the canvas. A great deal of it was done. The three figures—the two Natalies and Matthew—were nearly complete. Most of the furniture was done, or practically done. The window, the house exterior, the edges of a juniper bush on the left side of the window were done. Details remained to fill in. There was an area rug on the floor. She had nearly painted it with a pattern of snakes swallowing their own tails, but then she'd hesitated and decided to wait, worried that it might not be right. It might draw too much attention to itself.

And the painting within the painting. She felt herself pushed toward having the painter-Natalie paint the same picture she was painting, which meant that the painting within the painting would include at least one more, and possibly two, smaller versions of itself within itself. But of that idea, too, she was not sure, and she wanted to sleep on it before filling it in.

Her mind was peaceful—almost blank—as she cleaned her brushes. This had been a very good session. She put away her tools and materials for the day and then stood at one of the large windows, looking out at the afternoon.

CHAPTER 31

BLESSINGS

MATTHEW TOOK A LONG walk through the streets of Salt Lake. He was feeling physically better than he had in a long time. He reached back and gratefully felt the transdermal patch attached to his skin, on the small of his back, just to the left of his spine. He'd been to a local pain clinic, and they had done their jobs well. Matthew wished down a blessing on the doctor and nurse he'd met there. But his well-being went beyond this masking of his pain. He felt the progression of his disease had come to a halt—or at least to a very welcome pause.

There was time for him now. He didn't know how much, but he no longer felt imminent doom. Whatever amount of time he'd been given, he would use it in a new way. He'd received blessings, and now he understood it was within his power to bless the world back again. That, above all else, was what he wanted to do.

Matthew stopped in a small diner and had a sandwich. Ideas for a new story had been coming to him, and he sat and made notes for some time. He had a wonderful feeling about this new work. His voices were speaking to him truly, and truly he would tell this story.

When he'd finished his notes, he got up and walked on again. He noticed a used bookstore across the street and stopped, thinking he would go in. He looked up at a woman standing at one of the large windows on the second floor, above the bookstore.

It was Natalie.

He'd tried calling her at home, earlier in the day, after he'd left the church, but she hadn't answered. And now there she was. Matthew looked up and down the street. What was this place? Certainly this wouldn't be where she worked. Today was Sunday.

He looked up at her again and saw that now she had seen him, too. She looked down at him quizzically, with her head cocked to one side.

Matthew crossed the street and went through a door to a long set of stairs.

♦   ♦   ♦

When Natalie saw Matthew on the street outside her studio, she suddenly wondered if perhaps she were still dreaming, if the whole act of painting of her dream was a dream within a dream, just as she had put a painting within the painting. But she turned and looked at her painting-in-progress and caught the smell of her acrylics in the air, and she knew that she was surely awake. She looked back down at Matthew standing on the sidewalk across the street. Now he was looking up at her. How could he have come to this place? No one knew about it. No one could have directed him here.

When he crossed the street and headed for the entrance to her building, Natalie turned and looked at the painting again. Suddenly the content of her work hit her. She had not allowed herself to think about the meaning of the dream, so intent she had been about capturing it in paint. But now she could think of nothing else. What did this mean? Was she supposed to be with Matthew?

But Matthew had hurt her. Matthew had gone back to his perfect Hollywood blond cover-girl wife. He couldn't be trusted.

She looked back at the painting.

But there they were. And they looked so . . . right. She did want to step into that scene. It was Matthew who had been with her when she'd seen the dream paintings of their mystical father. She remembered back to their lovemaking, years ago, in her messy bed: their smooth, young beautiful bodies.

And then Matthew came through the door. The painting! She wanted to rush to the painting and cover it with a sheet.

As soon as he saw her eyes, he turned to see what was making her so agitated, and saw it. He stood and stared at it.

Natalie felt as though he were staring at her naked. She felt embarrassed, and annoyed, and aroused, oddly, all at the same time. She felt betrayed that he had found her like this with the painting before she'd even had a chance to consider what it meant.

But some other part of her felt glad she'd been exposed. She heard it like some far distant voice in her head: *There!* it said. *Now you'll have to face your heart.*

But all these emotions were swept aside when Matthew turned back to her and she saw the stunned look on his face.

"This is my apartment," he said incredulously. "This is my apartment in Chicago. I mean..." He fell silent for a moment and walked closer to the painting. "Yes," he said. "Well, you couldn't actually be standing outside the window looking in because my apartment is the top floor of a three flat. But otherwise, that's it." He looked at her in awe and realized how very much he wanted to take her back with him to his apartment. Over the years he'd spent more time away from it than in it, but he'd never given it up. He preferred his house in Malibu, but sometimes he had to return "home" to where he'd grown up. It was his retreat when California became too crazy for him.

How sweet it would be to go there again now, with Natalie. Natalie who'd managed somehow to paint it without ever having seen it or heard it described.

He looked back at the painting and laughed. "I always thought this living room would be a good place to paint. I mean.... The windows are big across the front and they face south, so it gets lots of light. There's a great view of the skyline of the Loop from here. It's a nice angle. Northwest of the downtown area."

He looked from her to the painting and back to her again.

He realized he was babbling (talking about the view!), but he could see in her face that she was as torn open as he. They'd come to this incredible decisive moment.

He remembered the three candles burning in the church. They would still be burning now, and he felt them carrying the blessings of the Queen of Heaven to him, and it gave him strength. He looked at the painting one last time and then back to her.

"Don't stay outside the window, Natalie," he said. "Come inside, with me."

And now he had that same incredible feeling of nakedness that she had had, with his heart open and trembling to her. "Let me come back to you," he said.

And then they were in one another's arms.

At first they simply hugged one another, clinging tightly against all those years they had missed, clinging against anything that might tear them apart, against the threat of Matthew's death, against their own past hurts.

But then the stronger urge overwhelmed their fears, and they longed only to be united. They pressed their lips together, and ran their hands up and down one another's backs and arms and faces. Natalie pushed her fingers into Matthew's hair as she kissed him hard. It was a feeling so naked and so filled with desire that she felt as though she were being unzipped straight up from the base of her abdomen, up across her stomach, her breastbone, right up to her throat. She clung to him with her arms around his neck, her fingers knotted into his hair, holding tight to him as this unbelievable sensation of opening rose up through her body and her sex began to tingle. Her whole body, her whole soul opened and she longed to pull Matthew inside of her, to have him climb inside her. To be intermingled absolutely with him.

As he kissed her, as he held her, Matthew felt his flesh come alive. He felt so hypersensitive, it was as though his nerves tingled out into space and could feel that which he didn't touch, but was merely near him. He could feel Natalie's body glowing against him. He could feel her skin, the muscles inside it, the bones beneath that, and the tender organs at her center. He could feel her against him as though they were already naked. He could feel the moist heat and magnetism from between her legs, drawing him toward her. He could feel her flesh pulled in tight to itself all the way around and clinging to him in the tension of desire. He felt her belly to his, her nipples to his chest, every bit of their bodies vibrating with longing.

A great cavity opened around his heart. A cavity that could only be filled by her. Desire swept through his body, making his skin tingle everywhere, and he knew he would be able to make love with her. His body would not fail them.

The emotion overwhelmed him, and he began to weep with gratefulness, as though he were finally home from a long and painful exile. He loved Natalie, and her love for him was unmistakable.

She touched his wet face and drew back to look at him.

"What is it?" she said.

He looked at her, and her beauty broke his heart. Her warm lips. Her lovely eyes. He could see the soul inside her eyes. The soul he had known forever.

THE AFTERLIFE TRILOGY
SHE PLAYS IN DARKNESS
BY FERN CHERTKOW

"EXQUISITELY BEAUTIFUL AND HAUNTING"
—Tony Ardizzone

SHE PLAYS IN DARKNESS

a novel in *The Afterlife Trilogy*
by Fern Chertkow

Inseparable twins Cynthia and Rosemary agree to spend a year apart. But the petty distractions of office work and relationships take Cynthia's attention away from the artwork she loves to create. She suffers without Rosemary, who seems to be doing better on her own, but after they share a somewhat uncomfortable reunion, circumstances conspire to leave Cynthia abandoned completely.

The Afterlife Trilogy takes a unique journey through love, suicide, and the afterlife. Together, Fern Chertkow's novel *She Plays in Darkness* and Richard Engling's novel *Visions of Anna* and stage play *Anna in the Afterlife* provide a kaleidoscopic view of Chertkow as both author and muse.

She Plays in Darkness *is an exquisitely beautiful and haunting novel filled with such fully developed characters that readers will not soon forget them. This is a book to cherish, to re-read, the kind of novel that avoids sentimentality so fiercely that readers will give copies to their friends and tell them, "Read this, this is a how a woman's life truly is."*—Tony Ardizzone, author of *The Whale Chaser*

Haunting and lyrical, the late Fern Chertkow's highly original novel strikes a deep note of mystery that resounds throughout The Afterlife Trilogy. *Like the best music, the effect of* She Plays in Darkness *lingers in a wake of silence.*
—Elizabeth Cunningham, author of *The Maeve Chronicles*

www.petheatre.com/trilogy.html

CPSIA information can be obtained at www.ICGtesting.com
Printed in the USA
LVOW12s2102260914

406080LV00005B/9/P

9 780977 661022